THIS BLADE OF OURS

THIS BLADE OF OURS

SHALINI ABEYSEKARA

NEW YORK

UNION
SQUARE
& CO.
NEW YORK

This book is a work of fiction. Names, characters, places, and incidents are the product of the author's imagination or are used fictitiously. Any resemblance to actual events, locales, or persons, living or dead, is coincidental.

Cover design by Patrick Sullivan
Cover images by Alamy: Oleg Marchak (beetles) and Shutterstock.com: kipgodi (statue), Vladimir Korostyshevskiy (blade), Imhaf maulana (border)
Maps by Cartographybird Maps

Union Square & Co.
Hachette Book Group
1290 Avenue of the Americas, New York, NY 10104
unionsquareandco.com
@unionsqandco

First Edition: June 2026

Union Square & Co. is an imprint of Grand Central Publishing, a division of Hachette Book Group, Inc. The Union Square & Co. name and logo are registered trademarks of Hachette Book Group, Inc.

Library of Congress Control Number is available upon request.

ISBNs: 978-1-4549-6595-4 (paperback), 978-1-4549-6596-1 (ebook)

Printed in Canada

MRQ-L

10 9 8 7 6 5 4 3 2 1

To the disillusioned, hopeful souls fighting to exist within freefalling nations, may we be their reckoning

CONTENTS

CONTENT WARNING

This romantasy runs quite dark and contains events that may be difficult to read. Please do make every decision you need to keep yourself safe, even if that means stopping here. I remain so very grateful for your interest in *This Blade of Ours*.

This book contains the following: alcoholism; bigotry; coercion; explicit consensual sex; depression; drug usage; gore; graphic death; graphic violence; hallucinations; insect plagues; kidnapping; lifechanging injuries; mass execution; misgendering; murder; mutilation; nightmares about traumatic events; nonbinaryphobia; panic attacks; parental abuse; physical abuse; prejudice; PTSD; rape (off-page, side character); religious violence; sexism; strong language; suicidality; threat of rape (allusion, side character); and torture.

PRIMUS ROAD
WESTERN FARMLANDS
METALS GUILD
WEST GATE
TETRARCH KADRA
THE HALL OF RECORDS
STONES GUILD
THE ORCHARD
THE CAPITAL CITY OF
EDESSA
TO SOUTHERN WILDLANDS

TO NORTHERN SHORES
NORTH GATE
TETRARCH HARTON
CLAY GUILD
THE GREAT LIBRARY OF EDESSA
THE ACADEMIAE
WEAVERS GUILD
GRAINS GUILD HORREUM
TETRARCH AELIUS
CITADEL ROAD
THE CITADEL
GRAND ELSARIAN TEMPLE
THE EIGHT TOWERS
THE AEQUITAS
DORYPHOROS ROAD
EASTERN FARMLANDS
TETRARCH CASSANDANE
SOUTH GATE

C A I L L T E
THE
OCCIDENS
SEA
THE RUGGED LANDS OF
UR DINYÉ
MAPPED
IN THE PRESENT AGE
TO SOUTHERN WATERS

ARSAMEA
SAL FLUMEN
THE CHABORAS RIVER
KOMIS
TEMPLE
XĀRŌMAND DESERT
EDESSA
KAYCAKH MOUNTAINS
ERRIGAL

PROLOGUE
HER

"Beware you would-be, God-Summoners! Take heed, all you who would call the Elsar to our plane! For when the infinite touches the finite, the latter does not emerge unscathed. A scar forms at the point of the meeting. And from it, what blood will spill? Who else will part the seams of our world as a sword does flesh and enter?

Aim not for the lofty. Restrict yourselves to prayer and relinquish the selfishness of seeking out a personal boon. Let us worship as a hand does by the hearth. Plunge not into the fire!"

—excerpt from *The Teachings of Inquisitor Caminus of Ur Dinyé*

The collapse of a country was a quiet affair.

Few historians would agree. They preferred to point to crushing defeats in battle, assassinations, or civil unrest to explain the peaks and troughs of political chaos. Yet, those were merely the symptoms of a rotting land's disintegration. Its cause would have snuck in earlier, quiet enough that no academic would entirely pin it down and capable enough to reach gnarled fingers through history to throttle the present.

Countries died in silence. As Ur Dinyé would today. Its current iteration, at least.

Her lips lifted in a smile. Squinting against the wind hurling orange sand across the Xārōmand Desert, she urged her mare toward one of the imposing mountains ahead. Thousands of miles long, the Kaycakh Range's jagged terra-cotta peaks formed a land border separating Ur

Dinyé's inhospitable Xārōmand from the neighboring land of Errigal—with whom they'd been at war centuries prior.

But these rocky giants had seen more than history. They had once held the future.

A millennium ago, in the heart of one of these mountains had existed a temple of such renown that only Ur Dinyé's monarchs had been permitted to know its location. Within its cavernous halls, devotees of Lord Time had meditated upon the past and present and been blessed with brief glimpses into potential futures. The Seers' prophecies had steered Ur Dinyé from devastation for centuries, until they'd been massacred by a king who had taken umbrage at what would become the Head Seer's final prophecy.

Oh, the powerful and their fear. She cast a bitter look in the direction of Ur Dinyé's capital of Edessa, thousands of miles to the south. She wouldn't be freezing her ass off in the fucking Xārōmand if it weren't for them.

Temperatures dipped lower under the slow wash of night. Above, Praefa and Silun surveyed her nightly routine of the past three months. Time and time again, she halted before the sheer face of a mountain and listened. The desert graced her with a wail of wind and spit sand across her cheeks.

Another night without hope. It had ceased to cut. For ninety nights, she'd ridden through half the Kaycakh Range in search of the Lost Temple's entrance. The records she'd dug up from the Scourgemaster's time had spoken to the temple's rediscovery some five and a half centuries back but had neglected to mention the location after the unexplained deaths of those scholars and treasure-seekers who'd ventured within.

No matter. It was the nature of history to be lost and found again.

She steered her mare toward another peak. Her mare balked, whinnying in fear as they neared the base. Sand gave way to barren soil littered with chunks of limestone. No sooner had her lips shaped a frown than she felt it, soft as gossamer. A hum of otherness like the scrape of jaws over skin. Magic. Hunger.

Hatred.

The reins slipped from her trembling hands, elation heating her blood. *It's here.* Dismounting, she tethered her recalcitrant mare to one of the boulders fencing the mountain like teeth. Nothing in the rock face ahead indicated the presence of a door, yet the desert's fearful thrum under her feet spoke otherwise. A warning. A proclamation of recognition.

"*We know your blood,*" the wind seemed to hiss. "*It has spilled here before.*"

"*Go.*" Sand curled around her ankles when she continued up the incline. "*You are not wanted.*"

Cursed land. Soiled with the innocent blood of thousands of Seers and sundered by even uglier secrets the Lost Temple had witnessed. The laws of the mortal world applied loosely here.

Her smile broadened. *At last.*

The mountain's base vied with the Aequitas for breadth, rough slopes worn by Time's chisel. At one corner, a pile of rubble listed precariously to the left, shielding what must once have been an entrance. *A cave-in or a barricade?* she wondered. The elongated finger bones extending in silent plea from a gap in the rock could speak to either. She steeled her spine against a shudder. *It doesn't matter.*

She placed her shaky palms against the cool, stone face and felt an answering ripple within. *Now for the price of entry.* Withdrawing a dagger, she pricked each fingertip, barely noticing the pain. So great was her excitement that she barely winced. Five crimson streams rolled down her hand to dribble onto parched soil. Red faded to terra-cotta. The earth drank deep.

The wind halted.

Quiet. It was so very quiet now.

A hammering began in her chest, exultation and fear warping in a dangerous weave. She drew on the rock with bleeding fingers. A straight line, then a curved one, then several more. *Zuvrai,* the Urdish rune for "Time." Mortal concept and immortal god. A rune so dangerously taxing that to draw it was to risk all the time that the user had left. The same rune Seers would have drawn to enter the Lost Temple millennia ago. Her chest squeezed with every pass of her fingers over the rock face, breaths dwindling and labored. *Zuvrai* was a Tenth-Tier rune, demanding a torrential, inherently unsustainable flow of power from its user. She was no Seer. She didn't have long.

Faster.

Magic was a peculiar thing. An inner well of power shaped by ancestry and tied to blood, accessible only by drawing the right patterns in one's life force. Runes were the language of the gods, the Elsarian priests said, and their first gift to humans to allow them a taste of the divine. It was also their first test, a sieve to separate the greedy and power-drunk from those good and faithful who would pass the gates into the Bright Realms where the High Elsar resided.

When all was said and done, where would she be placed? Monster or martyr?

A choked laugh tore from her. Had she access to her own epitaph, she would have written it now before history did it for her: *Judge me or justify me, you know I was necessary.*

Red flooded her vision as she drew the final set of *zuvrai*'s lines, arteries bursting in her eyes like swollen streams. Blood laced her tongue when she swallowed. Her fingers drew the last stroke and paused midair. *Gods help me.*

The rune flashed gold. Soul-deep agony arced through her with the ferocity of a lightning bolt as *zuvrai* came to life, unspooling her time. Unspooling *her*. Invisible hands clawed at her lungs, wringing, *twisting*. Her screams were quickly swallowed by the now-cacophonous desert, alive with a thousand jeers. Every pulse of her heart was a clap of thunder. Falling to her knees, she clutched her head and gasped for air.

The ghosts laughed. "*You were warned.*"

"No," she croaked. Teeth clenched, she slowed her panicked breaths. "I won't die here."

Slapping a palm against the rock face, she dragged herself up, gaze fixed on the now-glowing rune drawn into the mountain. Scarlet wove into the gold lines, warning that she would soon be drained of power and life. *Fifteen minutes? No. Ten.*

"You know me," she hissed to her listeners, heart thudding so hard that she feared it would stall any moment. "You know my kin and my kind. You will *yield*," she snarled.

The ground shuddered. *Yes. YES.*

"Let. Me. In!" she screamed.

A chunk of the mountain's craggy face crashed down with an earthquake's force. She lost her footing and tumbled down the incline, cowering from the spray of rock and sand. Coughing, she raised her head when the rumbling ceased. *By the Saints and Wretched.*

The chunk had reduced the rubble blocking the entrance to dust. The Xārōmand quieted when she staggered back up to that pitch-black mouth. A torch flared in an ancient sconce by it. Then another, and another, leading her in. She shuddered. *Welcome or trap, it doesn't matter.* She was going where even the dead couldn't touch her.

Pain clawed through her chest, hooking in and ripping down. Blood gurgled in her throat. *Eight minutes.* She ignored the broken corpses piled around the entrance, red tears snaking past her jaw from her own bleeding eyes.

She ran into the temple.

Firelight hissed to life in her wake, drawing golden fingers down frescoed corridors of battles past, fates avoided, futures won, gods appeased, murdered Seers—*Elsar save me. The bones!* Hollow eye sockets regarded her flight with mockery, their jaws unhinged in laughter.

"*Will you make it in time?*" they asked. "*Can you control what even we couldn't?*"

I will, she vowed. The Seers had glimpsed the land's future but been sequestered from its workings. She knew the people of Ur Dinyé. *I can control them.*

Libraries. Lecture rooms. Worship halls. Marble columns and limestone walls. The gilt had been chipped off, gaping holes left where statues and prayer tablets must once have stood. How many treasure-seekers and scholars had the dead punished for it?

Three minutes. She had never known such pain even when–*Faster.* She rounded a corner, kicked down the banquet hall's rotting doors, then froze.

There. A mighty oval courtyard hollowed into the center of the mountain. It opened to the sky, milky moonlight accompanying braziers that roared awake at her entrance. Avoiding the mess of collapsed columns, she ran to the shattered altar at the center, split down the middle by an unnaturally large handprint.

There had once been a god here. Chained for centuries by magi and Seers alike and twisted into an abomination that had been trapped in a man's body so that Ur Dinyé could win its wars. But that had been during the time of the Scourgemaster, a time of monsters, prophecies, and men with honor. This was a new age. And yet, it needed a monster too.

She knew this to be debridement not death, but the arbiters of history took such umbrage to change. They needed their compartmentalizations of time and firm delineations of how the dust had settled. To stop it from happening again, they would argue, but knowledge of the past had never stopped its repetition.

Blood did.

Two minutes.

Dagger. She sliced both palms open. *Safsher*, she drew the Urdish rune for "Sword" atop the altar. *Tuhig* for "Void." *Zefis* for "Weave." Sweat slid down her temples, stung her eyes. Her strained gasps were a preliminary death rattle as the agony in her chest pulled tight.

"*Soon.*" Something caressed her neck. A fingertip? The past clawing for blood. She flinched. "*You will join us soon.*"

Faster. She bit straight through her lip and drew. *Khon, frazam, layk, sayag.* Blood, End, Unity, Shadow, and finally, Sleep. *Nibas.*

And she was out of time.

Thick iron welled at the back of her throat. She choked. Blood sprayed from her lips to coat the altar, smudging her desperate runes. *SHIT.*

She collapsed. The temple screamed in glee, a thousand voices grasping through death and time to claim her for their own. Blood seeped up from the courtyard's tile, reaching inky fingers for her. A new ghost. A new scream. She tried standing but her limbs no longer worked.

It can't be for nothing! She silently pleaded with herself as the blood neared. *Stand up! Stand–*

Blue-green flames roared from the altar and spread to fence her from the dead. Dazed, she watched the fire climb toward the sky and coalesce into a wall. The voices vanished.

She's here.

She had Summoned a god.

Her fingers moved quickly across the tile, drawing *zuvrai* once more. The magic unspooling from her stoppered. Pain fled like a ghost. Exultation brought her to her feet right as the goddess entered the mortal plane.

By all that's holy. She fell back on her knees. Like all Naaduir, Faragathe had been human before her elevation to the minor pantheon for her service to Lord Time of the all-powerful Elsar. It no longer showed.

Starlight wove through black hair that trailed long past the goddess's ankles to float midair. Midnight-blue ribbons of sky slid over her twenty-foot body like an ever-shifting gown. Four eyes, sans iris and pupil, blinked on each bare shoulder and across her clavicles. Two more apiece slitted open on both high cheekbones, and the human two stared down at her. Eighteen eyes, holding an esophageal darkness.

One dark, blue-green foot touched the ground. Faragathe tilted her head, curved horns gleaming bone white. "You call me to cursed land." For a melodious voice, it cut like a blade.

So, this is power. "I had little choice," she said bitterly. "I'm not so powerful a magus to Summon you otherwise. But those damned Elsarian priests were right after all. A Summoning does leave a mark of incursion on the mortal plane."

"So, you pulled me through." Faragathe's eyes narrowed as she took in the courtyard. "Great evil was done here. A god Summoned. Brutalized."

"I don't seek to do the same to you! I swear–" She screamed when the goddess hoisted her with a flick of her finger, inches from her unearthly blue-green face.

Faragathe waved a taloned hand, spinning her dangling body in a slow circle. "A mortal's oath means as little as their life." She grinned, baring sharp teeth. "You couldn't hurt me if you tried. Now, what do you *want*?"

For the first time, she wondered if she had made a mistake. *What if she doesn't care?* The goddess's many eyes were utterly blank. She had never seen anything so devoid of humanity.

"I ceased being human millennia ago," Faragathe sniffed daintily, reading her thoughts. "Why? Do you seek to offer your body as a vessel? Keep it. I take no pleasure in walking this plane."

"Because of what they did to you." She trembled when the goddess stilled but kept speaking. "Faragathe, Devotee of Time." She took a deep breath. "The Heretic Priestess."

The goddess's eyes flashed. "You *dare*–"

"I've risked everything to come here tonight for this, for *you!*" she screamed. "I spent years of my worthless, mortal life digging through ancient texts for how to Summon *you*. The woman whose prophecies everyone ignored because Time granted them through dreams instead of the out-of-context flashes of the future accepted as canon by the Elsarian Order. The priestess who was mutilated and burned alive for saying what the Order didn't like hearing. One of history's most brilliant minds, ultimately proven right and *still* all but written out of the Codices and every other religious text."

Faragathe's smile was tight. "A choice that the Order has since learned to regret. Fear is bred in the unconscious, in the nameless things that walk between death, sleep, and waking. Unlike some of the other Naaduir and even a few Elsar, my power doesn't depend on human belief. Everyone inevitably comes to me."

"I know. That's why I wanted to offer you–" She jerked when the goddess planted her on her palm and leaned in. The words died in her throat.

She had been wrong. It wasn't just starlight glistening in Faragathe's hair but bone and tar. The eyes on her shoulders were voids into worlds with terrors beyond comprehension. Darkness crowded the courtyard, extinguishing the braziers, and within it seemed to be a universe with the goddess as its epicenter, amid others of horrific, larger—*all those eyes*—

She realized she was screaming when Faragathe laughed.

"Well, mortal? What can you possibly offer *me*?"

Mind. Where was her mind?

"Recognition," she gurgled, a portion of her mind irrevocably altered. Her gaze shied from the goddess. "There was a time after your death when people heeded you. Now, they're viewed as mad. Remind them of you once more. Shroud this land and bind it to you. Make the priests of the Elsarian Order return your name to the Codices. We have a capital, Edessa. A cesspit of the pretentiously religious, corrupt, and greedy. Destroy them, and history will never forget you again."

"How quaint. So, this is about vengeance."

"You see my mind." She knelt on the goddess's palm. "It's about more than just that."

Eighteen black, empty orbs swiveled toward her and watched. Faragathe's brow pinched. "Yes," she murmured. "A great deal more."

A blur of wind and limestone and she found herself deposited on the ground.

"The Naaduir don't grant wishes, mortal." Faragathe sounded contemplative. "We accept what appeals to us and reject the rest."

Her heart sank. "Please, at least—"

"We never made the same promises to humans that the Elsar did. We reached this state of minor godhood because we served them and not you. You have Summoned me, and your request was heard. There is no debt."

A tear ran down her nose to drop on her bloodied palms. "I understand."

Blue-green filled her vision. A finger the size of her arm tipped her chin.

"But in this, I will hear you."

Her head shot up. To her horror, she realized that she was sobbing. "You will?"

"Violence may be the sinew of authority, mortal. But power, *true power*, lies in the shadows." Faragathe trailed a hand over the ruins they stood in, the remainder of a place that had once shaped the nation. "Let them see it," she said to the night sky. "Let it drive them mad. I will stand behind you."

Blood rushed in her ears, warmth spilling through hollows that life had carved in her chest and left to fester. *So, this is joy.* She bowed low. "My goddess," her voice cracked, "from this day forth, I bind myself to you and only you."

For the first time, something almost sad flickered in Faragathe's many eyes. "Very well, mortal. To ancient history."

She squeezed her still-bleeding palms. The blood spattered on the ground in a silent vow. "To ancient history."

1
ORDER

"Of the Dark Elsar, there remains none so beguiling as Lady Ruin. Her smile holds the fulfillment of every desire. But as you close the distance, a trapdoor springs beneath your feet, and you are forever lost to the Dark Reaches.

People of Edessa, hasn't she found us here? Unease foments in our city, and we know the source. Eight months ago, Head Tetrarch Aelius met his end at the hands of a northern girl. Despite his flaws, he should have been properly tried in a court of law. Instead, he was gutted in public like an animal. The girl and the madman she serves pronounced themselves judge, jury, and executioner and use the supposed Summoning of Lord Death to legitimize their dark deeds.

Now, omens plague our lands. Riots and plague in the crude north. A woman in crimson—Ruin's preferred color—saunters about as Head Tetrarch. The madman is Magus Supreme, which also anoints him as Headmaster to the Academiae to oversee the education of our children!

Ruin has taken this land by coup. But there is hope. The Elsar ask us to resist evil. We rid ourselves of one woman who tried to govern us. We must do so again. Demand an Inquisitorial Hearing to bring these acolytes of Ruin to justice.

If they can lay claim to violence, so can we."

—excerpt from a Cleric's sermon in Aelius's Quarter

Eighteenth day of the Month of Frost, eight months after the Great Unraveling

Most days, all Sarai saw was blood.

Its iron-rich tang trailed her from Edessan courtrooms to discreet bits of vigilantism to her dreams, where she, on occasion, still relived a night that had altered the course of her life. Then, eight months ago, had come a reckoning that had changed her future.

Today, the crowd bayed for blood too. This time, it was hers.

The Amphitheatrum Aequitas fenced her on all sides, stage and prison. Snowcapped white marble and intricate arches quaked with the tread of eager feet. A midwinter gust ruffled the tendrils escaping from her braid as spectators from Edessa and the most devout parts of Ur Dinyé jostled each other across the five tiers of seating in the land's largest courthouse, angling for a better view. She hadn't seen a more heavily attended trial than the Great Unraveling–the public's term for her Summoning of Death and killing Aelius eight months ago. Of course, that was why she was here today.

Even if they refused to call it a trial.

"Silence!" A stentorian voice sliced through the crowd's chatter. "This Inquisitorial Hearing is convened."

Hearing. Sarai grit her teeth. *Gods, the words they use to obfuscate a thing's purpose.*

A host of men emerged from the Petitors' Entrance to the Aequitas, sporting beige and blue robes and an irritated mien at the subtle insult. Cassandane had politely but firmly refused them entrance through the main doors, though she couldn't deny the Inquisitors access to the Tetrarchy's seats.

The priests of the Elsarian Order, Ur Dinyé's dominant religion, parted like a wave at the dais. Four Inquisitors took the Tetrarchy's seats, dark blue–edged robes spilling against the marble like the waters of the Meridies Ocean. Master Cleric Linus and his Clerics fanned out their lighter robes and arrayed themselves on the steps. The same ramrod-straight backs, the same sneer on all twenty faces.

She stilled when an Inquisitor openly raked her over with gray eyes. An odd, white veil shrouded the lower half of his face from philtrum to jaw, leaving his nose and gaze bare, but there was no mistaking his amusement. Her half-frozen hands curled into fists.

"Petitor Sarai of Arsamea," Inquisitor Blasius, who had called for silence, surveyed her from behind his beard with the aplomb of a man who'd caught a rat in a trap. "*Tibi gratias ago* for coming."

Not that I had a havïd choice. "I'm happy to make the time."

Jeers rose from the white and silver banners waving from the eastern flank of the Aequitas. Aelius's acolytes were out in full force to witness the verbal bloodsport they had demanded.

"Yes, there's the matter of time." Inquisitor Verentia cocked a dark eyebrow, her thin lips pursed. It wasn't lost on Sarai that the only woman to have ascended the ranks of the Elsarian Order had taken the seat usually occupied by Cassandane. "Eight months for an Inquisitorial Hearing. An unprecedented delay."

"Edessa had only two Tetrarchs until the Month of Seeding. My caseload was equally without precedent."

"Remind me again, why we were missing two Tetrarchs?" Satisfaction radiated off Verentia when Sarai exhaled. "You threw the capital and the *land* into chaos. You can't claim victimhood after the fact.

Sarai swallowed past the knot in her throat when the crowd roared their agreement. Why did this hurt? She was no stranger to dislike. The sour folk of Arsamea had made her youth a living hell. Aelius and Tullus had broken her body and left her seething at the wrong man for four years. Her dearest friend had delivered her into their hands. And the debacle with the scuta even before then certainly hadn't endeared her to the public.

Yet, there was a new virulence to the past eight months. People had been content to support her and Kadra when they had been seen as running counter to Aelius's established government. Now, Kadra was the established government. Every time he burned someone alive, justice began looking a lot like tyranny.

"Let's begin." Blasius stood, lifting both hands to the sky in an echo of Aelius's statue towering over the Aequitas, still smiling benignly skyward. "Today, we, the Inquisitors for the High Elsar, call to Truth, to Wisdom, to crack open the heart before us such that we may discern—"

That's my havïd heart you're talking about. Her fists went white-knuckled as he invoked all six gods of the pantheon of the High Elsar—Wrath had been relegated to the ambiguous Elsar again. Anger and exhaustion warred for purchase in her gut.

In the weeks after the Unraveling, she had dared envision her future: long years of righting wrongs with the man she loved. But her eyes had been too hopeful. Governance was a game of likability. She had lost before she'd had a chance to begin.

It had begun innocuously enough.

Outrage had swept Ur Dinyé after the reveal that Aelius's fulgur scuta, or lightning shields, were in fact lightning rods designed to prey on the devout while dispossessing them of their land when the inevitable bolt struck during stormfall and razed their homes to brick and ash. The Metals Guild had borne most of the public's scorn, but the Elsarian Order and the over-religious had seen their share of mockery. And that had been her first mistake—assuming that groups that had fallen from the height of power would accept defeat. Assuming that they would be too busy licking their wounds for immediate retaliation.

First had come their ousting of Aelius's replacement Tetrarch. Like Harion, Marzia had allied with the Guilds to fund her campaign and bought herself a victorious election, but Sarai had felt sorry for her when she'd fled the capital three weeks later after Aelius's Quarter had impeached her for incompetence. Then, throngs of hecklers had begun appearing at her trials with Kadra.

Marzia had been practice. She was next.

Protests, false accusations of Aelius's martyrdom and of her and Kadra having committed a coup—she hadn't expected any of it to stick. But repeating a lie long enough and loud enough gave it credence. Over months, a fringe belief had become a competing truth—an easy thing in the insular capital of Edessa, the proud jewel of Ur Dinyé's south. Because as much as she sought to do right by its people, they preferred a scapegoat for their woes.

Aelius's devotees had known that the Tetrarchy wouldn't prosecute her. So, in a devastating blow, they had allied with the Elsarian Order to spread venom. She had finally understood it then. The Unraveling had affected too much across the land: politics, religion, and the rule of law. Too many had lost power because of her. Now, they would reclaim it by discrediting her.

"All will be well," Gaius had insisted yesterday when she'd shown as much interest in her amphora of wine as Anek did in men. "You've nothing to hide."

"That's just it!" She had slapped the hapless table with mounting hurt. "I shouldn't have to prove a thing! Thousands *saw* me Summon Death."

"You can show people the truth, Petitor Sarai. But you can't make them believe it."

"Then what good is showing it to them?"

Gaius had wisely said nothing.

A dull roar rumbled through the audience. Inhaling sharply, she searched for who had spiked the commotion. Her gaze caught on the front row. A wave of relief nearly sent her to her knees. *They came.*

Garbed in her customary bronze-edged crimson robes, Head Tetrarch Cassandane entered the court's most opulent seating box—traditionally used by Petitors. Her stunning features pulled into the same strained smile that had graced it since the Unraveling. The country hadn't reacted well to its first female Head Tetrarch. No doubt the minutiae of her expressions would be picked apart by the crowd.

Anek followed Cassandane, fiery curls loosely contained at their nape. Sarai's throat tightened at the wink they shot her. Short black hair slicked to his skull, Harion sauntered in with a haughty sniff. *Here to see who wins and ally with them no doubt.*

And then, *him.*

Magus Supreme Drenevan bu Kadra, her very heart, strode into the box with predatory elegance. The morning sun ran adoring fingers over his silhouette, limning a face that was a monument to ruthlessness and a map of severity.

Few would call him handsome. High cheekbones framed a hard nose that had likely been broken in youth and a jaw like a blade. The stern line of his lips rarely knew genuine amusement, and the weight of his position had etched grim grooves around them too early. Yet, the potent brew of cunning and power that clung to him had every breath stilling in fearful awe. Under his grip, the gilded viewing seat became a throne. He was its black-robed god and the Aequitas an unworthy people. Quiet settled over the crowd when the piercing gaze that most of the country found terrifying settled on her.

Heat pricked at her eyes when he inclined his head, a smile curving his mouth. The quietest of salutes. Torn between laughter and tears, she raised her chin in silent, amused question. *So, this is "quietly observing"?*

The responding gleam in his eyes insisted that he saw it that way.

She touched a hand to his crest pin at her throat in silent gratitude and watched his eyes soften. Her spine ceased its painful stiffness. The crowd's interested murmurs told her that it wasn't lost on them that the Tetrarchy had chosen to arrive after the priests. They may as well have put up banners saying they intended to have the last word.

"You don't have to come," she had grimly informed Kadra weeks ago, once the realization that she was facing an Inquisitorial Hearing had settled in. "In fact, you probably shouldn't."

On the other side of the desk in his tablinum, he'd raised an eyebrow.

"They'll argue that your presence skewed the Hearing or that you put the fear of Death into the Inquisitors so they'd go gently with me. Everyone only sees me as an extension of you. That's—" *why I need to prove that I can handle this on my own*. She exhaled heavily. "Kadra, I need to beat them."

Black fabric trailed over the edge of his desk as he'd rounded it to gaze down at her with quiet gravity. "Inquisitors of the Elsarian Order do not see fairness as a strength."

Her stomach had sunk somewhere in the vicinity of her ankles. Master Cleric Linus was the Order's highest religious official in Edessa, but the Inquisitors oversaw the Order's reach across all thirteen lands, a powerful cabal within an already secretive organization. No one even knew how many there were across the world. "You think they'll overreach."

He'd nodded, absently circling the rim of his wineglass with a finger. "It isn't unheard of for Petitors to enter the Order. The Inquisitors will bring one."

So, I'll be Examined too. Her words tested for truth or lie like a defendant's. Her hands, tremulous on the best of days, had jolted at the thought. She'd quickly moved them to her lap, but the slight crease in his brow said he'd caught the movement.

"Won't you let me come?" The whimsical note in his voice had shredded her arguments more effectively than reason could have. "I'll quietly observe. No more."

She gaped at the wistful look on his face. On a man who looked like the epitome of Wrath most days, the effect was shattering. And godsdammit, his robe was slipping off his left shoulder.

"Well..." she cleared her throat when the robe slid down further and bared a muscled deltoid, "perhaps it wouldn't be so bad if you were there."

"The capital would talk if I didn't show," he agreed, leaning in.

"And you'd only be sitting there."

"An excellent idea." He'd tilted her chin up, a hungry glint in those black eyes. "Now, Petitor Sarai, it's past noon. What do you say to retiring?"

Still vaguely dazed, she'd let him draw her into his arms.

In the present, Sarai bit back a smile as it struck her that she'd been tricked.

Blasius seemed to be biting back something too, though it was likely less complimentary. "May our pleas bear fruit in the Bright Realms," he finished the prayer through gritted teeth.

"As the Elsar will it," Sarai mouthed the crowd's chorus as everyone took their seats.

And then, it was only her, facing twenty priests and four Inquisitors intent on evisceration. She hid her trembling fingers behind her back.

Verentia steepled her hands. "Petitor Sarai of Arsamea, why did you agree to this Hearing?"

To once again offer transparency to people who prefer conspiracy. "To speak the truth."

The nod one of the Clerics seated on the steps gave Verentia told her that Kadra had been right. They'd brought along a former Petitor. Her chest tightened at the insult. *Zosta*, the rune for "Examination," glowed on the priest's armilla, the rune-engraved bracelet allowing magic-users quick access to power without having to draw the runes in blood.

"*Certo*, you appreciate that an Inquisitorial Hearing is an extraordinary remedy," Verentia tapped the arms of Cassandane's seat to underscore the point. "Used only when the truth of a theological matter is so contested that we, who've studied and know the Elsar best, must provide clarity. We have been called to do so for the day now referred to as the Great Unraveling that occurred eight months ago here. Do you concur?"

Don't lose your temper. "I agree that we're here to discuss the Unraveling. However, if the events therein are being contested, it is by those who didn't see them. The truth was clear to everyone who was there."

"Truth cannot be decided only by those who experience it."

Of all the havïd nonsense. Anger cleaved the restraints on her tongue. "It *must*, or it slips into hindsight and hearsay."

Some in the crowd whistled. Her eyes narrowed at the glower that twisted Blasius's face. *An easy target.*

"I see why the people of Edessa demanded this Hearing. Your belligerence in the face of the accusations against you is astounding."

Belligerent. Bitter. Arsamea had thrown those words at her for eighteen years. "Those accusations are verifiably false, Inquisitor."

That brought on a cacophony of protests from Aelius's devotees. The priests smirked through the furor while the rest of the audience waited, torn between believing her and the allure of a scapegoat for their troubles. And it was the latter that hurt most.

How had so little changed after all she had done? She hadn't expected fanfare but dared hope for peace. Instead, she drank daily of the bitter brew doled out to women in politics, required to pantomime serenity every day while the land tried to crucify her. If Harion had killed Aelius, would he have faced the same scrutiny?

Verentia spread her hands in mock sympathy. "Unfortunately, the populace disagrees."

Sarai willed the blood pounding in her ears to slow. "Disagreeing with the truth doesn't change it. Former Head Tetrarch Aelius was a supremely cruel, religious hypocrite and mass murderer." She paused to let his worshippers bellow their outrage. "But I've since learned that he was quite generous with his ill-gotten gains. He earmarked a large portion of nationally collected taxes for his Quarter's benefit. It seems that his people see reverting back to equality as ignominy." Fury honed her voice to a knife's point. "I have read all the petitions made against me. Thousands insisted that I was siphoning funds intended for Aelius's Quarter. Unfortunately, it is their Quarter that has been siphoning funds intended for the nation."

That injustice finally brought the quiet majority of the onlookers to their feet. She knew that if she turned, she'd find a smile playing on Kadra's lips at her having turned the audience against each other.

"Silence!" Verentia snapped, gritting her teeth when the crowd ignored her. "I said—"

"By Wisdom," the veiled Inquisitor's voice broke in. Sarai cast around for his name. Silvus, the newest man to enter the Order's fold. "How very easy it is to get you all fighting."

The audience stopped cold in the same breath that she did. Silvus's gray eyes raked her, sans lechery yet infinitely more disturbing for how much they seemed to see. She held his gaze, granting neither of them any quarter. His cheeks rose, the veil over his mouth shrouding what could be a grin.

"Petitors Veritas," he murmured. "Seekers of Truth. The title of your job has shortened over the years, but you and I aren't so different. We provide the thirteen lands with clarity. You examine trees. I see the forest."

She stiffened at his meaning. The Order had chapters throughout the world. Eyes and ears that fed Inquisitors information and kept people staring skyward, contemplating a glorious afterlife rather than societal pains. Meanwhile, the Tetrarchy received limited news from outside Edessa's walls and relied entirely on Praetors and Tribunes to send them their locales' grievances.

Silvus blithely planted his chin in his hand and smiled. "Governments aren't institutions that inspire much devotion."

No, philosophies do. Like the Order. "Are you bragging, Inquisitor?"

His brows rose. "I only thought to note that you and your lover have legitimized the use of political violence. A dangerous precedent. Now, it can be used against you."

Air burned out of her lungs in a bitter exhale, fogging the frigid air. *Lover.* The designation wouldn't make a man lose credibility but the whistles and jeers that accompanied Silvus's pronouncement was proof that she had. He'd eroded the cautious trust she had built with the audience in mere seconds.

"The Elsarian Order demonizes violence when it's often the only way for oppressed peoples to throw off their yoke," she bit out. "Would you rather that we'd left Aelius's scuta to set Edessa aflame?"

"If your rule requires violence to enforce it, then is it legitimate?"

"I didn't kill Aelius to enforce anyone's rule, but to see justice done." She struggled to keep her voice calm when the spectators' epithets grew louder. "Perhaps the Order spends too much time watching forests to see it, but sometimes, the only way to justice *is* blood. Because the law, as largely shaped by religious determinations of morality, has failed people."

That earned her a chorus of contemplative murmurs, but Silvus's gray gaze lit with laughter. "Then, I hope you never fail the people. It would be a pity to see you impaled on your own blade."

Unease pricked at her nape. "I–"

"We've heard enough of your rationale." Verentia held up a hand. "Relate that day's events."

Her lips parted to repeat the same sequence she had given before curious crowds and diplomats for months in an effort at transparency. It had changed nothing. The fatigue she'd been reining in throughout the deluge of work since the Unraveling swamped her. The Elsarian Order were vultures, waiting for her collapse.

You wish it had been you. It was in their clenched jaws, slitted eyes. *The most important moment for the Elsarian religion in decades, and one of your own wasn't behind it.* Sliding her frigid fingers into her pockets for warmth, she ended her recitation.

"Quite a tale." Verentia's frenetic tapping on Cassandane's seat resumed. "How well-versed are you in the Codices?"

"I haven't read much beyond the Gospels of Wisdom."

"Have you pledged yourself to any god?"

Sarai tensed at the Inquisitor's thoughtful mien. *What are you planning?* "I haven't."

"Have you encountered one of the Elsar before?"

The audience was rapt, quiet. "I saw Lord Death some five years ago when I nearly died at Tetrarchs Aelius and Tullus's hands," she reminded them. Judging by the yowling from Aelius's worshippers, they thought he should have finished the job.

"Unlearned and unpledged, yet you've seen one of the most elusive of the Elsar *twice*." Verentia ceased her tapping. "Why do you think Lord Death appeared to *you* and not one of his many faithful?"

Sarai watched her warily. "Because I was able to Summon him."

"So, you're a Twelfth-Tier magus then?" Verentia's teeth gleamed. Her trap sprung shut.

Shit. Sarai flinched.

Among the challenges posed by her lack of formal education was her limited understanding of the complexities of magic. Her lessons with Magus Telmar had taught her that it wasn't so simple as an inner wellspring of power that was unlocked upon use of a rune.

A magic-user, or magus's, body had twelve inner Thresholds–spigots of varying strength. Crossing the First provided a trickle of power, sustainable for over a day by most. Runes like *zosta* that she used for Examination, required opening of the Fourth Threshold and could drain her in fifteen hours. But crossing the Twelfth unleashed a torrent that bled the user of magic and killed them in minutes–magic and life force being intertwined. Almost no one had the control to seal the Twelfth Threshold after crossing it. But the rare, *rare*, unfathomably powerful user who could access and leash that deluge of power at will were known as Twelfth-Tier magi. Like Aelius. And Kadra.

Not her.

A smile crawled across Blasius's face at her silence. "You are aware, *certo*, that Summoning runes are largely Twelfth-Tier Runes and require the user to cross the Twelfth Threshold?"

"I am."

"Then, you should have no difficulty with my question," Verentia said smoothly. "Are you a Twelfth-Tier magus?"

Exhaustion and anger buzzed in her skull. "In that moment, I was."

Blasius's gaze glittered with triumph. "That isn't how magic works."

"It's how *desperation* works," she bit out.

"Why were you so *desperate*, Petitor Sarai?" Spittle flecked his beard when he hissed the word. "Was it because the Magus Supreme's death stripped you of the power he'd cloaked you with?"

The Aequitas fell dangerously quiet. Rage balled in her chest, pulsing with a violent heartbeat of its own. Because there were a thousand things that had forced her into this Hearing. That she was uneducated. That she was a northern woman. That she was a salaried government official beholden to a people intent on tearing their own land to shreds in bigotry's name.

And that there was no better way to get to Kadra than through her.

"Absolutely not." Her voice rang clear.

Blasius's eyes slitted when the Order's Petitor-turned-Cleric confirmed that she wasn't lying. "Then what made you so *desperate*?"

Her breath puffed out in a smoky sigh swallowed by the wind. These hypocrites wouldn't understand love if it slapped them. Turning, she glanced at the man who held her heart.

A muscle worked in Kadra's jaw. He had told her that she didn't have to do this, to cut herself open before a crowd once again. But to be a politician was to either outmaneuver people or be deposed by them. She wasn't a Twelfth-Tier magus or a Tetrarch, but she could do this much. For him, for peace. Her smile was a quiet promise. Kadra's gaze altered and sharpened as he sat up in his seat. She turned around.

"There is nothing that I wouldn't do for Magus Supreme Kadra. No Threshold I wouldn't cross for his sake." She spoke faster when Verentia's gloating smile parted. "Exactly as you all feel about the High Elsar, I imagine."

The crowd's stifled laughter altered to stunned murmurs. The final Inquisitor who'd been silent until now looked staggered.

"The two aren't remotely comparable. You speak of *sentiment*. What we hold is–"

"Wisdom and Wrath, do the Inquisitors for the gods hold no *sentiment* toward them?" Sarai pressed a hand to her lips in feigned shock. "What is devotion without love? What keeps you tethered to your posts? Fear?"

A hush swept the Aequitas. Verentia shot the suddenly wordless Inquisitor a glare. "The *target* of that sentiment is different. One is human, and the other so divine that–"

"And yet, I Summoned the divine because of a human," Sarai mused. "How strange that your divine sentiment has Summoned no one."

One by one, the Elsarian Order turned a becoming shade of puce. Looking inches from an aneurysm, Blasius shot to his feet. "For all we know, it was Ruin you Summoned not Death!"

Finally. They'd reached the pinnacle of the accusations against her. "And what have I done to merit that *outrageous* accusation?" She knew she'd erred the second her voice rang out across the Aequitas. Too harsh, too loud.

Verentia's measured chuckle made stark contrast. "We're well aware that you have a temper, Petitor Sarai, but try not to embarrass yourself. You're the subject of a Hearing. Rein it in."

Her blood boiled. At the corner of her eye, she saw Kadra's features harden with lethal promise. It seemed to be costing him everything to keep his word to her not to interfere.

Blasius took advantage of her brittle silence. "The facts are that you continue to hide your disfigurement, proof itself of an unnatural survival—"

The audience gasped when Sarai touched a bloodied fingertip to her armilla. She hadn't needed to prick it with the pin slotted into the white gold bracelet. Her nails had already drawn blood from her clenched palms.

Crimson sank into *nihumb*, the rune for "Concealment," which flared silver. The weak illusion over her skin faded, scars unfurling like vines. Hundreds of eyes fastened on her and slid away in disgust. She hated their morbid curiosity. She might even hate them.

Stalking toward the slew of priests on the dais to the Tetrarchy's seats, she presented herself for their perusal with a raised eyebrow. "Well?"

Verentia seemed lost for words. Fascination briefly lit and vanished from Silvus's gaze before it turned impassive.

"Inquisitors, yours is a tiresome reaction. I'm no priest with too much time for leisure, but a Petitor to a Tetrarch. I conceal my scars to save the minutes of gawking each petitioner would otherwise eat up during my workday." Heat throbbed behind her eyes, making the tilt of her chin feel short of the strength she wanted to exude. "Twice now, Lord Death has allowed me to live. A good portion of Edessa saw him at the Unraveling. Any accusations that I Summoned Ruin are *baseless*."

Blasius slammed a fist against the arms of his seat. "How are we to prove that? The memory is walled off, can't be Materialized by a Petitor! We dug and dug, but–"

"Enough!" Verentia roared with sudden panic.

Sarai's jaw dropped as Blasius's meaning registered. "You've dug?" she repeated. "You Probed people who were at the Unraveling to see if I was lying?" She turned to the Petitor-turned-Cleric sitting on the steps, who avoided her gaze. "Searching people's memories is a *punishment*, reserved for those on trial or on their deathbed before it!"

Blasius waved a hand. "They were handsomely compensated."

Verentia flinched when the crowd erupted, roaring from all five-tiers.

Sarai dug a hand into her tangled braid, still reeling. *Wrath's teeth, they just fucked themselves over.* Ur Dinyé wasn't pleased with her infractions, but they wouldn't abide the Order's either. She wanted to revel in how thoroughly the Order had compromised their case, but she couldn't find any glee.

"This is madness." She walked away from the dais, too weary to look at them. "I haven't read all eighty-three volumes of the Codices, but I can imagine why the Elsar prevent Probing and Materialization of memories involving them and why they don't appear during a second Summoning by the same person. Else they'd be called to heel over and over to grant wishes for some Twelfth-Tier with a swollen head and dreams of conquest. Or the rare moments when they interact with us would be Materialized and exploited as tools of oppression, and they *would* be, wouldn't they, Inquisitors?"

"*We* are not on trial!" Blasius seemed to have given up on professionalism. "There are omens that the gods are angry with *you*–"

"By all means, let's talk about these omens! Do you mean the riots in the north due to Guild greed? The whispers of a beetle plague ravaging northern cities? I'm neither a Guildswoman nor a proper healer, Inquisitor, so please do tell me how I am to blame for these woes and what I've gained. Because if there's anyone who has ever benefited from waxing rhapsodic about *omens*, it has only ever been the Elsarian Order."

She had never heard the Aequitas so quiet. A vein throbbed in Blasius's temple. *A push, and he'll go over.* She readied to lance him and end this, when Verentia cleared her throat.

"The land hasn't seen such upheaval since the fall of the monarchy. The Tetrarchy is spread thin. The Order must ensure that you aren't following false gods into the future."

Sarai slanted a withering glance at Blasius. "And you still didn't see anything wrong with Aelius."

He tipped over. "To proscribe violence is to become an *animal*!" Ignoring Verentia's attempts to grab him, Blasius strode down the dais to brandish a finger in her face. "Your duty was to arraign him!"

"While he was trying to purge the Aequitas? If you Probed those witnesses, you saw his actions before Death's arrival. You *know* his guilt," she roared, facing the amassed crowd to indict them for their role in this insanity.

"The gods had a purpose for him that *you* cut short! Who are you to determine his guilt?"

"I'm a godsdamned *Petitor*!" The world throbbed around her. "It's my job!"

"You never trained for it, you fucking mountain bitch! You staged a coup with *him*." He jabbed the finger she was dying to break off in Kadra's direction and froze at the raging malevolence in his eyes. "You're nothing without him…" The insult came out as a croak.

"Gods, every accusation is always a confession with you lot! *You're* nothing without this tale of being favored by the Elsar. That's why you descended here, because I succeeded in meeting one when you didn't. As for those who wrote to you, who want my head," she glared at the ivory and silver banners draping the tiers, "you've been so coddled by the privilege of existing in the wealthiest Quarter in the capital of Ur Dinyé that you can't stomach anyone else receiving the same benefits you do!"

At their taunts, she shoved up her sleeve and pressed more blood from her nail-scratched palms into *tasum*, the rune for the Fourth Threshold, then *zosta*. A stable stream of power unfurled from her chest like a lock had clicked open. Blasius's speech took on the faint echo that meant that she was Examining him for truth.

"Go on. Deny it then!" She gestured. "Say that you're here because of my actions and not your greed."

Verentia had frozen to her seat as the Hearing disintegrated around her, fingers uselessly tapping the seat. "We're only here," she tried again, "to settle the truth of what happened."

A discordant note rang through Sarai. *Lie.* "Then, settle it." Her voice hardened. "If you're so certain, then toss me in a dungeon and formalize Aelius as a Saint. Elsar knows he wanted that badly enough. Let's see what *omens* the Elsar'll rain down on you for proclaiming a megalomaniac as a minor god."

The spectators' roar told her she'd finally won most of them over. Aelius's group's jeers had a desperation to them now. Blasius seemed to finally realize that he'd blundered badly. He looked to a near-catatonic Verentia on the dais and a blatantly amused Silvus. His face darkened.

"This is why you need the gods," he snarled at the Aequitas. "This animalistic, moblike idiocy will be your ruin!"

Verentia sunk her head into her hands when the crowd began tossing produce at the dais. A tomato splattered on a Cleric's face. *Ruin's teeth, that would've been for me had I lost.*

She faced Blasius and dropped her voice. "People don't like to be told what to believe, Inquisitor. They like to think that they reached that conclusion on their own."

"Don't lecture me, mountain bitch–" He froze, gray eyes widening with dawning realization.

She smiled pleasantly. "Why do you think I agreed to this?" Leaving him to blanch, she turned to Verentia. "Well? What truth have you found today?"

The Inquisitor heaved a sigh. "It happened as you said it did, Petitor Sarai." Her eyes shone with bitterness and a grudging respect. "This Hearing is concluded."

Aelius's people rose in a wobbly wall of white and silver, swearing up and down that every one of the Inquisitors had been bought while the rest of the audience viewed them with the mocking amusement reserved for those who had no chance at intelligence. Silvus spared her a veiled smile before the Elsarian Order numbly rose and followed a raging Blasius out of the Aequitas to peals of laughter.

She felt nothing as they maneuvered around her. Neither victory nor relief. Only cold, hard certainty that this wouldn't be the last time she would have to play this game and find a new way to win.

Verentia was the last to leave the dais. With one last wistful glance at Cassandane's seat, she strode down and paused by Sarai. "Silvus wasn't wrong. Law and order fell by your hand." There was no venom in the words, only resignation. Perhaps this had been as much pantomime for her as for Sarai. "You must contend with the consequences—everyone now knows that they can do the same."

I know. And I don't know how to fight them all. The fatigue she'd long held back sank bone-deep, endurance and magic stretched thin. She took a shaky step toward the seating box the Tetrarchy waited in and found herself swarmed by new well-wishers and admirers. *For how long? Until the next crisis has you turning on me again?*

"Never doubted you for a second." A woman pumped her hand furiously. Sarai fought a flinch when a man attempted to do the same.

"—the *extent* of the coin Aelius's Quarter must have received over the years!"

"The roads in Cassandane's could use some work."

"I—" she sagged when the volley of questions continued. *Ruin's teeth.*

Hands gripped her shoulders and drew her back against a warm chest. “That’ll be a matter for Head Tetrarch Cassandane,” a beautiful, dulcet voice pronounced. Kadra’s thumbs found the back of her neck and drew a long, tender stroke down. She nearly melted, her heart squeezing hard with love and exhaustion.

A hand pulled her from Kadra’s grasp. He let go, gaze as hot as a knife on her cheek. *Rest*, those black eyes ordered, *I’ll contain them.*

Faintly heartsick, she allowed Anek to drag her toward the Petitor’s Entrance, feeling rather like the world had liquefied into an ocean. It tipped when they wrangled her onto her mare, Caelum.

“I haven’t spent any time with him in weeks,” she mumbled.

“Wrath and Ruin, I don’t need that picture in my head. And that’s with my having read every volume of *The Alternate Histories of the Sidran Tower Girl.*” Anek patted Sarai’s shoulder when she groaned. “Nicely played. I wondered why you agreed to this, but it was a masterstroke.”

She slumped into Caelum’s mane. “You think it worked?”

“Oh, yes.” Anek’s incisive gaze swept the crowd. “Cease thinking and rest. You’ve had quite an ordeal.”

They sent the mare off with a slap on the rump. By the time she reached Aoran Tower, she was practically insensate. But Verentia’s pronouncement haunted her when she unlocked the gate into Kadra’s home, when she nearly drowned in the bath while falling asleep as she sloughed off travel dust, and when she finally trudged upstairs to his bed and collapsed into a sea of black and gold sheets.

Law and order fell by your hand. Everyone now knows that they can do the same.

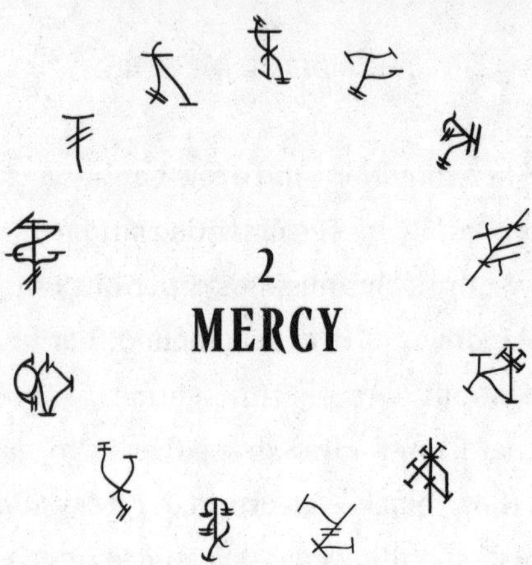

2
MERCY

"When the land burns, history will ask why. It'll wonder how we missed the signs that flare rune-bright in hindsight. It'll sigh that we fell like the malleable, ambivalent creatures the Elsar know us to be, without any cognizance that war's bitter tide rose from a spring of our making.

Beneath Ur Dinyé's placid surface after the monarchy's fall, roil a thousand currents that any enterprising student of history can steer into war.

The powerful, secretive Elsarian Order seeking to impose religious governance. The Guilds' long-held monopoly of northern resources against the economic reform posited by Tetrarchy. The elite wealthy against us all. Stormfall crowning our skies.

A historian's task then rises above an arbiter of fact to an observer of pain. To examine these conflicts for betterment, detriment, or stagnation. Learn how they've been woven into each other. Find their weavers and those threads that, if strengthened in one fight, can ruin another.

Watch for symptoms of war. If the public is vigilant, then the public cannot be fooled."

—excerpt from a lecture by Magus Telmar

Winter mornings drained Edessa of color, painting the citadel that housed the Academiae with charcoal and silver and draping the Tower Gates in gossamer shadows. For once, the city seemed as it was: an insular spiderweb of secrets that dictated life in Ur Dinyé. Home, and yet a battlefield.

Frost limned Sarai's cloak and trailed the length of her braid. The first rays of sun broke over the Academiae's presently bauble-laced tree boughs, its artfully trimmed gardens hidden by a crisp carpet of snow. Just off the cobblestone path, a group of tall, blond, water magi from the distant land of Usten sat in bewilderingly thin leather tunics and trousers, murmuring in melodic accents as they shaped ice into a frozen flight of birds. The Academiae spared no expense for its winter graduation, and despite Kadra's opinions to the contrary, Cassandane insisted that everything proceed as it always had.

"We've much to prove." The Head Tetrarch had looked haggard at their last meeting before the Hearing, crimson robes echoing the strained blood vessels in her eyes. "We can't give the public any reason to believe that we'll upend their lives more than we already have. People don't care that you did it to protect them, Sarai. They only remember that it made them feel scared."

The irony. Kadra's deviation from established law had ruined Edessa's tyrants. Now came the bitter task of holding on to power via the same system that had been proven not to work, all because folk liked the idea of change more than they liked its implementation. The people she sought to protect had become those she had to outmaneuver.

Ahead, an ornate metal steeple pierced the bruised dawn sky like a sword thrust through flame. The Academaie's marble student chapel rang with a lusty chorus of song and prayer for glorious careers, coin a plenty, and a blessed beginning to a new era in the graduates' lives.

The cavern of dead dreams she barely visited these days let out a sad thrum. If the Fall hadn't happened five years ago, she would have been among those gleeful graduates last winter, linking arms with friends, reminiscing of sneaking back into their dormitories after a night in the city. She would be...young. The thought was as foreign to her as the Elsarian chapel was to Usten's water magi, who were casting flabbergasted glances at the uproarious singing.

She silently added her voice to the mix. After all, the gods were real, even if she found them in other places. Her soft exhale drew a shroud over a past that had not been, and she walked on toward what was.

She nearly ran into an agromagus after two steps.

"Petitor Sarai, I wrote to you last week and have heard nothing." The violet-robed man's chest swelled at this ignominy. "Bad enough that the north is rioting, but now, word abounds of this beetle plague they've got. Should we be concerned?"

Not this again. She sighed. "I know as much as you do. The coalition of northern Praetors have not shared the type of beetle causing the damage or the extent of the injury to their cities, so my lack of response was no insult. I cannot share what I don't have."

The agromagus puffed his chest out further, bringing his crest pin of a desert ironwood—Ur Dinyé's national tree—to prominence. "Northerners visit Edessa daily," he spat as though the poorer half of the land were beetles themselves. "Having them inspected prior to entry is fine and well, but what if the vigiles miss something? The south holds most of Ur Dinyé's viable farmland! We risk *famine.* As a northerner, you may not understand—"

"I do," she said with more ice than the eavesdropping magi from Usten were sculpting with. "As I have repeatedly told your colleagues, the coalition of northern Praetors has informed us that these beetles swarm cities. Unlike the north, the south lacks mountainous terrain to veil a swarm's arrival. The magi patrolling our city walls will raze them long before they're a threat."

The agromagus looked mollified. "They'll burn to a crisp?"

She pinched the bridge of her nose. "Yes."

"Nevertheless, ask the Magus Supreme to consider a ban on northerners. I await your reply."

He was off before she could snap that *this* northerner had no intention of writing back.

"I," she muttered to no one, "am not Kadra's errand girl."

"Keep telling yourself that." A heavy hand came down on her shoulders. Harion snorted when she flinched and darted away. "How *does* our Magus Supreme handle this jumping?" His brows rose. "Does he restrain you during a fuck? That'd be excellent material for a new volume of *The Alternate Histories of the Sidran Tower Girl.*"

Usten's magi had given up all pretense at work and were blatantly staring now. An intricate sculpture of a desert ironwood bled water behind them.

Had she been in better spirits, she would have given voice to the epithets burgeoning on her tongue, perhaps ribbed him for the bruise-like colors he had chosen upon becoming Tetrarch—sapphire blue and emerald green—or perhaps she wouldn't have reacted at all to the jibes of a man who, for as long as she'd known him, sought self-aggrandization at everyone else's expense. But now, scarcely a day after the Hearing, she just felt raw. Looked at and judged so much that parts of her had been scraped off.

"What the fuck do you want?" A hiss like a dagger through air.

Harion's brows rose, sly levity winking out in his eyes. "Touchy. Inform Kadra to calm down with his inspections of Guild wagons leaving Edessa. The new Grains Guildmaster is highly displeased with this interference into how he runs his business."

Anger bristled up her spine. "This would be the same Grains Guild that insists that their crop yielded poorly this year and that they can't meet their obligations under the Distribution Act? The one that's *directly* led to the northern riots?"

Harion adjusted the button at the notch of his throat with a shrug. "The truth is vastly overrated, mountain girl. Quell the riots the old-fashioned way and spill some northern blood. You and Kadra are slim on allies, and going after the Guilds won't do you any favors."

It wouldn't. But blame for the riots could be laid at the feet of all fifty-eight Guilds. Once hailed as bastions for the working class where they could earn some shred of power during Ur Dinyé's monarchical era, the south's Guilds had evolved from independent mercantile coalitions to powerful institutions, largely unbeholden to the law in the name of good business. The only leash that kept them from bleeding every Urd dry was the Distribution Act—a centuries-old contract between north and south stipulating that resources mined, harvested, or collected in both regions must be shared with the other as per the Act's percentages. Percentages dictated by the Guilds, of course.

Despite their wealth of ore, limestone, and clay, the north had little viable farmland. And the snobbish south had refused to barter food for metal without the Guilds as intermediaries. Thus had come a trade bargain worthy of Ruin herself. The coalition of northern Praetors hadn't stood a chance during the "negotiation" of the Distribution Act. Only the Guilds had the coin for investing in mining operations and the numbers to ensure nationwide supply of gathered resources. Or to destroy any northern business that attempted to compete with them. The choice had been to bleed or bow, and the north had folded forward. Centuries later, the results remained catastrophic. Northern locales had no claim to their resources, and their peoples were little more than the Guilds' indentured labor.

"The Tetrarchy legislates crime and social governance. It has no oar in the free market," Ioratius, the newly appointed Grains Guildmaster, had reminded Sarai when she'd raised the subject weeks ago. Iron-gray beard trimmed neatly, he wore a genial smile like a sword and had emptied a pouch of aurei on the table between them like a shield. "Your visit is an unjustifiable incursion into Guild business."

"Not if Magus Supreme Kadra is receiving petitions on the matter." She ignored the bribe. "Every northern locale is entitled to an allotment of grain under the Distribution Act. You can't halt wagons on the basis that your yield was poor."

He tossed a gold coin in the air and caught it. "We must care for our own first."

"Last I examined, the north is still part of Ur Dinyé and barely has the farmland to grow a few ears of wheat." Her nails had dented the seat of his plush armchair. "It's half ice and half desert."

Ioratius had merely raised a brow and offered her a bound copy of the Distribution Act. "Point it out. Show me what the consequences are for putting Edessa first and halting wagons elsewhere."

She had nearly bitten through her tongue trying not to snap that they both knew that the Act only slapped a paltry fine on the offending Guild equivalent to two weeks of profit.

A grin had crawled over Ioratius's austere features at her silence. "It seems that the Tetrarchy has a quarrel with the Distribution Act not the Grains Guild," he'd said, smoothly. "Please inform your Tetrarch that he may amend the Act if he finds it lacking. The Guilds will, of course, respond accordingly and reject any government overreach."

Her teeth ground together at the memory of departing the Grains Guild compound only to spot sacks of grain perched atop the unyoked wagons outside the horrea—outbuildings that were part granary and distribution warehouse. *An artificial shortage so he can inflate prices.*

"Harion, I know that Guild votes got you elected, but they aren't just stealing resources from the north. Your hometown, Dídtan, received only fifty-two percent of its grain allocation last month."

"And?"

She stared. "Your people are starving."

The smirk slipped from his mouth and, for a rare moment, she saw him as he was: twenty years old, with an inferiority complex the size of the Occidens Sea, dwarfed only by his hunger for power. And yet, there was feeling there, smothered under both. Because like the north and like her, Harion had learned early on that the only paths left to the powerless were to bleed or to bow, and he had folded forward.

"Is that how you justify it?" His voice was low gravel. "Someone's dead or dying, so you break every one of our laws to put things right. Don't you see the precedent you set? If a Petitor defies the framework of this land, then why shouldn't everyone else? If a man kills a passerby for coin so he can afford to take his sick wife to a healer, will that cease to be *homicidium* because she was *dying*, Sarai?"

The use of her name alone robbed her of speech for a few seconds. "That's a disingenuous hypothetical, and you know it. That man would have killed an innocent. The Guilds are anything but."

He laughed incredulously. "One of the many things Aelius had right was that people are fools. Look around. No one cares about innocence or guilt. People only want their needs met, and thanks to you and our resident madman, they now believe that they can spill blood to do so. And if you say that they can't, they'll ask why *only* you and Kadra have that power."

"I *know*, godsdammit," she grit out, bitterness weaving through the hollow spaces in her ribs. "So, your solution is to let the north and poorer southern towns starve?"

A smirk slid back on his face, derision swallowing the fierce glint that had hinted at humanity. "Hierarchy is all that keeps us in order. Make the Magus Supreme cease pressuring the Guilds. Let them feel like they're in control again. They're so amenable when well-fed."

While half the land goes hungry. "I'm *not* Kadra's errand girl."

"But you're nothing else either. And you're without allies." He drew away in a swirl of blue and green, breath fogging from parted lips as though he were smoking a roll of blazeleaf. "Don't be stubborn. We both want what's best for the country."

"But I won't make the country pay for what I want."

He spoke over his shoulder. "Then, you'll pay for what the country wants."

The morning breeze stung her half-frozen cheeks. Yards away, the water magi's ice sculpture had melted to resemble a gnarled, frozen hand as the group split their gazes between her and Harion's departing figure, evidently waiting for her to deliver a rejoinder.

But he's right. Months of belittlement before yesterday's Hearing had driven that truth in so deep she wondered that she wasn't bleeding. It was one thing to rid the land of evil politicians. But how did one reckon with the bigoted, swathes of the population who'd allowed them to amass power and sought to carry on Aelius's mantle? There were too many to kill or imprison, and both decisions would make martyrs of them like it had with Aelius. But leaving them alone forced those rebuilding the country to contend with their divisive cruelty.

No good answers. She offered her audience a weak grin. "Please tell me that Usten's politics are simpler."

The leather-clad magi broke into guffaws, awkwardness dissipating like hoarfrost. "We are a land of glaciers with a monarchy," a statuesque woman explained in accented common tongue, rolling her *r*'s like the warble of glass over marble. "You will only find simplicity in ice, and even that requires"—she gestured at their melting sculpture with wry mirth—"maintenance."

Smile broadening, Sarai conversed with the group through their resurrection of the desert ironwood and as they engraved the sculpture's base with runes for it to last through the night's graduation ceremony. When students poured from the chapel like spilt grain to gape at seeing water magi in action, she made her farewells and slipped into the now-barren hall of the gods.

No Cleric waited in the narthex to startle at her visit. She knelt before the steps marking the start of the chancel and loosed a sigh that sapped her strength.

Sixteen gods examined her from the altar, the light filtering in through the chapel's high windows lending their painted eyes an uncanny brilliance. The ten-foot-high fresco spanned the altar's width. Six High—the Elsarian Order had once again relegated Wrath's status to Ambiguous—seven Dark, and three Ambiguous gods faced off against each other baring weapons—and in Wrath's case, fangs—with otherworldly enmity.

Sarai hid a laugh at the artist's depiction of Death as an old man wielding a scythe. "Well, they certainly got you wrong." Her lips trembled, the strain of the past few months yearning to free itself in a flood. She bowed until her head met the cool stone steps and didn't allow a single tear past.

Political turmoil was a foolish thing to resent. She had power now. Gone were the days where she'd had to watch the world go mad and been left with little recourse. But she fought every day for every inch of public approval. The knowledge that other battles lay ahead tasted more like poison than hope.

Was I wrong? Would the land be in such turmoil if I'd taken Aelius to trial and watched him wriggle his way out?

Perhaps this was futile. The gods hadn't spoken to her since the Unraveling. They might never do so again. But she couldn't stop talking to them now that she knew they were listening.

I shouldn't be lonely, should I? She stared at Lady Wisdom's luminous features, at the goddess holding her sword aloft with utter surety that her path was the right one. Sarai couldn't relate anymore. Nothing felt certain in Edessa. Her every step seemed to be on shaky ground, and the fight felt empty. *I shouldn't complain. You've given me more than I dared imagine.* She let out a brittle scoff against the porphyry steps up the chancel. *Temperance's heel, I sound like a child. It isn't as though I'm the only one who's overwhelmed.*

Kadra had always worked himself to the bone, but he'd begun pushing himself to inhuman heights after the Unraveling. The three Tetrarchs shared Aelius's Quarter's responsibilities while the country chose a successor, so she barely saw him outside of adjudication. He was either swamped at his vigile station or curbing stormfall, in addition to his new duties as the Headmaster to the Academiae. He hadn't been home in a week, and she doubted she'd get a moment with him at the graduation tonight when the nation wanted his ear.

She railed against the ache building behind her nose and eyes. "He has more to do than see to me," she whispered against the steps. "I shouldn't impose."

The chapel's quiet enveloped her, undemanding and all-seeing. As stalwart as the Tetrarch who ruled her heart. Stern and intensely guarded in public, Kadra shed that formality within Aoran Tower, and she had bloomed in the warmth of a man as deeply tender as he was judicially vicious. Yet, he wasn't without his secrets. Buried within the ice and lightning that comprised him was a barrier so impenetrable that she had stopped short when she'd first come up against it.

"When were you born?" she'd asked on the night of her nineteenth birthday, the eighteenth day of the Month of Harvest. His vigiles had just thrown her a raucous celebration–her very first–and she'd been effervescent.

Something undefinable had crossed his face before he'd distracted her with a rough kiss that had quickly turned into more. He'd never answered.

Her lashes battered against the steps as she sucked in a steadying breath, recalling the deft way he'd avoided other queries over the past several months. *This shouldn't sting.* His secrets were his own, and she had no right to demand them when she knew, down to her soul, that he would never betray her. But that didn't stop her from wondering, *fearing* his reasons for keeping them from her. Especially, now that he was–

"The Codices also call Lady Truth the goddess of despair." A voice pronounced at her shoulder.

She started so badly she nearly broke her nose on the steps. Scrambling upright, she fixed the newcomer with a hard stare.

A familiar man in ocean-blue robes smiled–at least, what she could see of his face did. Inquisitor Silvus's customary veil began below his nose and ran under his wavy mass of black hair to knot at his nape. "Forgive me, I didn't mean to interrupt."

Discomfited, she thrust her hands in her pockets. "What brings an Inquisitor to the Academiae?"

"I conducted today's service." He walked up the chancel and closed the volume of the Codices on the pulpit. "It's customary for us to impart wisdom to the graduates."

She could only imagine what sort of wisdom he'd been imparting. Cassandane's exhausted face came to mind. Strain had made a new woman of the Head Tetrarch after months of protests that she wasn't fit to lead the country on account of her sex. An easily reinforced opinion when the dominant religion's greatest villain was female and canonically had a penchant for red robes.

Her hands fisted. "Interesting. Good day, Inquisitor—"

"Lady Truth often gets short shrift compared to Lady Wisdom." Silvus gestured at the altar, singling out a goddess with tear tracks permanently etched on her face. Her mouth widened in a scream at her twin brother, Lord Deceit, who was frozen in the act of reaching for her—whether to hurt or aid, Sarai couldn't say. "Wisdom provides the more interesting gifts. Creativity. Intelligence. Truth has only ever been, well, a sword without hilt. Cuts the wielder and the victim."

This was no longer about the Elsar. "Truth is my only task."

"And yet, it is Wisdom and not Truth who is the patron goddess of Petitors."

Her eyes narrowed. "You're here to impart the Order's wisdom to the graduates not to me."

"You could've been a graduate had the Magus Supreme spared you a thought that night five years ago." Gray eyes met her furious ones. He winced. "All I mean to say is that this chapel has no easy answers. No matter how you wield the truth, people will bleed. The gods know it too, or Lady Truth wouldn't weep. I hope you don't blame yourself."

Oh. Relief swelled in her chest, unexpected in its arrival and its source. She tempered it with wariness. "You sought my head at the Hearing only yesterday."

"I was doing my job. Like I said, you and I aren't so different. We serve difficult masters, don't we?" He ruefully indicated the altar. "I don't know if I'd prefer serving a fickle public to serving the gods. Though seeing Blasius humbled was a delight. Never agreed with his methods, but he's been an Inquisitor for longer." His faint twang turned *methods* into *maythuds.*

She blinked. "You're from the north?"

"Ah." His features went carefully blank as he dug a finger behind his clerical collar. "Keen ear."

"I picked up the capital's accent during the assessors' visits to Arsamea," she admitted. "Vowels were my tell too, but I was young and"—*Cisuré helped*—"malleable."

"All that to fit into a city that doesn't want you."

The air in her lungs turned scalding. Winded, she stared at him. "What do you want?"

"Why would you think—"

"You either stopped me from leaving to impart a religious lesson or a verbal beatdown, and I like to think that Inquisitors have more important things to do than either, so what. Do. You Want?"

His face tautened. "Take a message to the Magus Supreme."

"I am *not* Kadra's errand girl—"

"You are. As I said, the truth cuts." Gone was his wry, gracious manner. This man was jagged stone. "Yesterday, if you'd lost, the Order would have forced an exorcism on you, saying you were possessed by Ruin."

She was suddenly terrifyingly aware that the chapel had only one exit. The length of the nave to the doors seemed to double in distance behind her. She held his stare, thanking every one of the Elsar that she had activated *beshaz,* a healer's rune that could both mend and rend muscle, before she had left home.

"Blasius must be devastated that he failed." She withdrew her hands from her pockets, readying to snap his ligaments the second he attacked.

His pupils blew wider. "Are you aware of what an exorcism entails? You. Splayed out and chained to the floor in a room so far beneath the

Grand Elsarian Temple that no one will hear you scream. Circled by Clerics who'll take your every plea as proof of madness–"

"And you'd love to put me there, is that it?" Fury pushed her fear aside along with the mental image he described. "*That's* what you want me to tell Kadra?–"

"Tell him that he has ruined your life," Silvus bit out. "I hear the whisperings of this nation faster than the Tetrarchy. In the past eight months, members of congregations have confessed to me of hatred, revenge, and disgust. They *liked* things the way they were. You have enemies in places you've never heard of, because you trusted a man singularly unworthy of faith." Vehemence flushed his face and turned his eyes molten silver, spittle wetting the veil shielding his mouth.

What the fuck? She took an unsteady step back. "What does the Order care when you were about to *exorcise* me?"

His hard stare tilted over to frustrated bewilderment. "Petitor Sarai," he spoke slowly. "*I* am not your enemy. I don't want to be. The only person to blame for all of this is the Magus Supreme. You're nineteen and too honest for your own good. He knew better."

I may as well be arguing with Cisuré. Her chest twinged. "So, the Order thinks I'm Ruin's puppet, and you think I'm his. Thank you for that sterling assessment of my character. Meanwhile, you're the one at the pinnacle of a group that has more earthly influence than Ruin and Kadra, and who has used it to ensure that everything in this country stays *exactly* the same." She whirled on her heel, tensing for a breath in case Silvus stalked after her, but he remained at the pulpit.

"When everything comes crashing down, you'll wish that you had denounced Kadra," he called after her, sounding oddly resigned. "You're at the nation's mercy."

She let the doors out of the narthex slam shut. *The nation has no mercy.*

Yet another hard-won truth that had sliced to the bone.

* * *

There had been a time, early into her start as a Petitor when she had believed that power would allay her insecurities. In reality, it had worsened them.

True power, the sort that left people untouchable, was inextricably linked to the extent of violence they could mete out. Consequently, Kadra, as a Twelfth-Tier magus, was equally revered and feared. She, a Seventh-Tier with about as much skill at swordplay as Harion at flirtation, was prey. *What would it be like to be so powerful that everyone fears me?* A cruel thought. And yet–

"You aren't focusing, barmaid," Telmar chided, pulling her from the reverie.

His office no longer resembled the cramped abode she'd visited days before the Unraveling to beg for help. Gone were the crates of *ibez* and dust plumes crowning his books. Now, the mahogany-paneled space felt homey. Despite the corpse at the center of the room.

Telmar tapped his foot on the oiled, leather mat atop which the body rested. His once-splotchy features had turned pleasantly round-cheeked after he'd given up the bottle. She initially hadn't wanted to take private lessons with him out of fear of being perceived as elitist, but he had pointed out that having her in a class with hundreds watching her performance wasn't conducive to learning. Despite primarily being a lightning magus and swordsman, an enthusiasm for learning had made him a font of knowledge, albeit a rather strict teacher.

"There's no need to be gentle when he's already dead," he reminded her.

Kneeling beside the dead man, Sarai huffed out a breath, trying to blow away a sweaty tendril stuck to her forehead. "But I won't be fighting a corpse. The people who want my head are the same who'll cry about excessive retaliatory measures if I deck them."

"Then, end them in one blow like you did Aelius."

She gave him an unamused stare. "I was just on trial for that yesterday."

"Use a smaller sword."

Shaking her head, she gripped the corpse's shoulder and analyzed his circulatory system, noting where best to slice to bring down an assailant. *Beshaz*, the most rudimentary rune used by healers, allowed visual and magical access to a body to heal simple ills or cause simple damage. Without Kadra holding her perpetually quivering fingers still, she could only perform the latter.

"Good," Telmar concluded when she finished listing all the vessels she could slice as well as the ones beyond *beshaz*'s reach. "Remember, cut first and think later."

She exhaled, groggy from the amount of magic she'd used. "There has to be a better way of protecting myself than studying corpses and swordsmanship. Has no one ever permanently increased their power from Seventh-Tier to, say, Tenth-Tier?" she tried hopefully.

Telmar gave her a speaking look. "There've been all manner of powders and potions that've purported to do that since time immemorial, but there's always been side effects. Our magic's linked to our life force. Draw on it too heavily, and you risk death. Just like you did when Summoning Death."

Gods, what I would give to be that powerful every day.

Spotting the slump of her shoulder, Telmar tutted. "Keep your head high. There isn't a government alive without enemies. And you're a savvy one, barmaid. I'm a genius to have seen your potential in Arsamea, even while drunk to the gills."

She shot him an exasperated look and halted at the pity in his eyes.

"That Hearing must have been hard."

"I was hoping I was subtle."

"About the fact that you offered yourself up as a target? I'd say Edessa realizes that now."

She suddenly cared nothing for studying anatomy. Rising, she washed her hands in the sink by his shelves and leaned against it. "I was distracted by the onslaught of cases at first," she admitted quietly, "so I missed the shift in public opinion. Everything hit at once. First, the objections to Cassandane as Head Tetrarch. Then, *Harion* gets elected, Marzia's elected and impeached, the riots in the north and, now, a hitherto-unheard-of beetle plague that Kadra's still trying to gather more information on. Allegations of a coup were the last thing we needed."

"You saw a chance when they focused on you." Telmar looked thoughtful. "Distract them while Cassandane and Kadra rebuilt and steadied the government."

That wasn't the entire truth of it, but she nodded. "People like nice, tidy targets." *It just hurts that they chose me at all.* She refused to allow the ache building behind her eyes to grow. "Little seems to change. I perform in public every day, and some asshole with no knowledge of law, economics, or human decency raves that I'm a northern bitch who got the job by spreading my legs. Then, all I've done gets dismissed. At this point, I'm a liability to Kadra. This morning, I was accosted by *three* people, who all wanted something different, and all expected me to ferry word to him. I feel like I'm pulled in a thousand directions!"

Telmar opened the door to his study and indicated for the vigile outside to return the corpse to the morgue. "Well, if you want my two denarii, politics is public theater, and you're an excellent actress. It's one thing to wrest power from the ruling government. It's another to maintain it. You've borne a lot of ill-will, but you damaged the Order's credibility. That's something."

"More like I've made another enemy. Do you know they'd planned an *exorcism* if I'd lost?"

It was a testament to how horrifying one must be that Telmar flinched. Little surprised him. "*Havïd*, they're more upset than I thought."

She thought back to Silvus's insistence that she would never be safe. "Who do you think would win in a contest of information? The Order or the Tetrarchy?"

"The Order," Telmar said bluntly. "We're a large nation. News takes at least a month to travel by wagon from one corner to another. Unless you can find a Bridger, but they're rare here." At her quizzical look, he explained, "Bridgers are magi of the land of Kashyal to the south, whom we conquered before the fall of our monarchy. We've since relinquished it, but…"

"Relations are poor?" she guessed.

He nodded. "Only a few Bridgers around here, and they cost a small fortune. The Tetrarchy uses one's services at times, but she's usually sent on diplomatic matters. We even have a few specific Bridging points within Edessa and outside the city walls. The rest of the capital's warded off to prevent unwanted entry by enemies or a foreign army."

"Do you think the Order has a Bridger? Wait, no." She expelled a defeated breath when Telmar opened his mouth. "Of course they do. Their coffers are at least four times deeper than the Treasury."

"I've heard that they've *two* of them," he supplied helpfully. "The Tetrarchy's only one government. The Order's beliefs span all thirteen lands."

"Thank you, I feel so much better knowing that they're all-powerful." She slapped the sink's rim in frustration. "*Gods*, I feel like I'm going mad. Do we let these religious fearmongers spew their drivel, pollute minds, and build toward another uprising in twenty years? Or do we fine the lot of them and have them yell about freedom of speech?"

Telmar raised an eyebrow. "I'll tell you something that's never helped a government. Wallowing. You've endured much, you'll have to endure more, and your training isn't going to complete itself."

"You're a right spot of sunshine," she said wryly. "Ever considered becoming a Cleric?"

"I'm sure the gods are grateful not to have me."

Afternoon veered into evening as Telmar steered her through magical history and practical application.

Each of the thirteen lands had an element of nature that its people could wield offensively and defensively, though the nature of that symbiosis remained elusive. Whether Ur Dinyé's storms had begotten its people's control over lightning or vice versa remained a matter of theological and archeological debate, but there was no denying the pervasive, evolving connection, like there was with Usten and ice. Unions of magi from different nations resulted in intriguing powers, such as her own, or the odd Illusionist—a magic that had originated in the neighboring land of Errigal—but Ur Dinyé's magical hegemony remained lightning magi. Even most Guildsmen who manned supply wagons to the north were at least a Fifth- or Sixth-Tier.

She'd also discovered that she'd been quite inefficient with her use of power. Not having learned about Thresholds, she'd brute-forced her magic. Rather like kicking down doors instead of unlocking them, Telmar had remarked at her first lesson. Magic was a meditative process. One rune to release the Threshold matching the Tier of the rune she intended to use, then came the rune itself.

Nihumb, the rune for "Concealment" that she used to hide the full-body scarring she'd sustained from the Fall, was a Second-Tier illusion rune, requiring a steady trickle of power. She'd been feeding it a deluge and constantly draining herself of magic by the end of a workday. Limiting herself to only release the Second Threshold felt incredibly strange.

Her brow furrowed as she made her scars disappear once more. "It's easier but quieter."

"Because you aren't wasting magic." Telmar touched a bloodied finger to two runes on his armilla and spun a tiny sphere of lightning over his palm, weaving the delicate strands until the little ball pulsed fiercely but didn't explode outward. "Control is a magus's strongest weapon. Take your Magus Supreme. He's the strongest in the land, *certo*, but he's also a master at control. If it ever comes down to two contenders for the position, the one with greater mastery of their Thresholds always gets it."

Good. A powerful man without control was a danger to everyone.

"Speaking of which," Telmar eyed her speculatively, "how's he holding up after his trip to the afterlife?"

She froze, her control slipping enough for scars to crawl back over her hands. She shoved them in her pockets. *Distract him.* "He's alive and well as you can well see! Just buried in parchment what with having to be Tetrarch, Magus Supreme, and consequently…" She winced. "Headmaster."

Every Magus Supreme held the position of Headmaster to pass on their knowledge to the next generation of magi. Unfortunately, most noble families whose scions attended the school weren't fond of Kadra.

Telmar blew out a breath in commiseration. "I hear parents are complaining that his behavior is unseemly for an educator."

"They didn't mind when it was Aelius."

He offered a tepid shrug and switched tacks. "Nevertheless, you can't put me off that easily! Has the Magus Supreme said *nothing* of the afterlife? There's no record of anyone returning from the dead in Ur Dinyé. I wouldn't be surprised if the Order fixates on him now that they failed to get you. Can you imagine if he was *Godstouched*?"

Her heart plummeted like a stone, tongue freezing to the roof of her mouth.

Mistaking her stillness for confusion, Telmar went on, "Sometimes the Elsar take a shine to those they encounter, you know? Offer them all kinds of gifts in return for service or whatever else gods want of humans. Always a caveat, though. Take Wrath: According to the Codices, he offers men great power, which usually drives them mad."

She forced out a laugh. "I'd rather take the ability to mass persuade enemies."

Telmar snapped his fingers. "Coercion. A magic from the land of Ilohe."

"It's real?"

"Rare and dangerous for obvious reasons. There have been campaigns in Ilohe to eradicate all those with the magic. No one wants to be sapped of free will."

"Still, to kill them for existing?"

"That's life." He didn't sound too upset. "The Elsar are fair. Almost every magic has an equal and opposite in some land. Ice in Usten, and then, fire in Oriti, for example. A Coercer might be your opposite. Both magics have the same root–sound. Only difference is that you read people through their words, and a Coercer controls them through words. Could turn you into a puppet in a heartbeat."

"Wisdom's breath, don't speak one into existence. The land is in enough trouble."

"You'll have to deal with all sorts, barmaid." Telmar's tone had the taste of sympathy. "Magi who warp ice, shadow, and even themselves. Many lands use True Illusionists of Urd and Errigalese parentage. They can alter their faces in a heartbeat and mimic everything down to the placement of your scars. Your Magus Supreme was careful for a reason. Now, he could die at the hand of someone with your face." He took in her stricken look, and another sliver of compassion chipped at his customary indifference. "This is your life now."

"I know." The void in her yawned wider. She tracked the sun's slow progression outside the office's narrow window. In a few hours, the graduation would begin.

Telmar cleared his throat. "But rest assured, I'd be quite concerned about anyone who could take you on, Summoner of Death."

The words prompted a startling heave of her stomach, fear snaking around her limbs until she went stock-still. Another voice reached through the past to whisper in her ear.

I'll see you soon, Death-Summoner.

Winded, she rubbed her breastbone. *Who said that?* And why had it terrified her so much?

Bidding farewell to Telmar, she left his office in Safsher Hall and took the closest path to Aoran Tower. Snow crunched between her boots and cobblestone. Most southerners found the Month of Frost unbearably cold, but winter was an old friend to her after years in Arsamea.

She yawned, massaging her temples when spikes of pain cut into them. *Wisdom and Ruin, not this again.* Never mind the Order–at this rate, a constant lack of sleep would do her in first. She rested her throbbing head against a passing ice sculpture for relief. *I should've asked Telmar about this.*

It had begun with an odd gap around her visit to the Stones Guild some months ago. A moment she'd forgotten but whose absence she could sense. One that remained oddly painful to recall. There had been a few more gaps since, during her walks home.

Sweet Lady Wisdom, don't tell me I'm going mad. She scrunched her eyes shut, trying to reach for the memory. A shaft of pain speared her, snatches of sound and sunlight blurring behind her eyes. *Albanus offering a bribe. A window looking out into the Stones Guild's inner courtyard. And—*

A third arrow of pain lanced so deep behind her eyes that she gasped. *Wrath's teeth!* She abandoned the pursuit. A warm bath should fix everything. The memories couldn't be anything important; she'd lost no more than a few minutes. Perhaps she'd dozed off while walking.

Close to Aoran Tower, she felt for the key around her neck that would take her through Kadra's wards when a warning prickle raised the hair on the back of her neck. A second and she felt it again, a quiet exhale where there should have been none.

Shit. She spun, readying to attack, and stilled at the man in gray-green robes behind her.

"How," he said ruefully, "can you always tell?"

"Who the hells are—" She froze at the sudden, horrified realization that she *knew*. "*You.*"

"Good evening, Death-Summoner. I must say, I didn't expect you to handle the Hearing so well, but I respect it enormously." He grinned. "Even if it has delayed my plans."

Find Kadra. Fear was a vise around her head, squeezing tight as the missing pieces of her memory reoriented into an uglier whole. "I won't do it," she whispered when he issued the same command he must have uttered last time and the time before. Stars burned behind her eyelids when he spoke louder, frustration edging into his voice. She didn't move.

A muscle twitched below his eye. "Your will won't hold forever. I want to have mercy on you, Death-Summoner. Help me do that."

She had no chance at hurting him. She had to get out of reach before he–*just move, godsdammit!* She whirled around, muscles coiled to run, when he spoke again.

Then, the thought slipped away.

Sarai stared at the deserted path leading from Aoran Tower and wondered why she'd turned around. Her heart thudded like she'd run a marathon, sweat trickling from her hairline. She touched it with mild confusion. *Gods, the things stress does.* She parted the gate and quickly locked it behind her, only staring briefly at the odd shadow on the other side.

It almost looked like a person.

Shaking her head, she readied for the convivium.

3
THERE IS NO WAR

He had never cared for winter.

Kadra drained his third wine bottle of the night and set it atop his overladen desk. Heat burned a path down his throat before the alcohol sank lower to soothe the ruined nerves of his spine. Enough to tide him through the next few hours.

Beyond the window of his office within the Academiae, Praefa and Silun crawled across a cloudless sky, throwing the courtyard below into sharp relief. In an hour, it would ring with applause as five hundred students graduated. At present, it hosted a game of fear, extravagance, and pedigree. A hunt where everyone believed themselves a predator.

Snow gilded the school into resplendence, embellishing the ice sculptures lining the cobblestone paths. Spheres of lightning illuminated colonnades bedecked with banners and baubles and noble families bedecked with more. Throngs split and interwove, rife with social-climbers eager to impress each other in a ceaseless circle of envy and hunger. A replica of his own graduation, nine years ago. Cassandane had gotten her wish. Nothing had changed.

The peel of an orange parted under his hands, the scent brisk and invigorating. He popped a segment in his mouth with a faint smile. A small pleasure. Oranges had been a rarity in his youth.

Steps vibrated up the staircase before the door to his office crashed open, dislodging a volume of the Distribution Act from a shelf and sending it into the roaring fireplace. No loss.

"Godsdammit, are you *eating*?"

He spared a glance over his shoulder. Cassandane had abandoned her much-malingered crimson robes for a bronze gown. One of several concessions she had made since becoming Head Tetrarch.

She rounded his desk to plant herself between him and the window. "You've a half hour before your speech! Even Sarai is out there, mingling, *trying*, while you're watching us from on high!"

"My presence will not aid you." It would upend the carefully delineated social lines along that courtyard. Enemy would align with enemy. Middle-class matrons would ingratiate themselves with noble families by cursing him. The last time he'd shown at a convivium to ensure Sarai's safety had been equally eventful.

"Nevertheless, we must show everyone that *nothing* has changed." She pulled the curtains shut with more force than needed. "We can't alienate the upper classes in the name of reform when we need their backing. Tonight, we prove that the Tetrarchy has no intention of rocking the boat. This is how we hold on to power, and *this* is how we move forward. In increments. Change can come once we're established."

She would be highly displeased with his plans then. He smiled humorlessly. "Apathy in the midst of war, Cassandane?"

"There is *no war* in Ur Dinyé!" It was more plea than pronouncement. "None that we can acknowledge. We're on crumbling ground, Kadra. One wrong move, and all will be rubble."

His lips curved at the familiarity of that excuse. Many a *iudex* had warned against interpreting the law too liberally when he had entered the profession at fifteen. Progress, they had insisted, had to be a slow crawl lest the upper class notice and throw the weight of their power behind stymieing it. People would die during this incremental justice, grave wrongs would be rewarded, but the land would see a brighter future if lawmakers and judges went quiet and slow with progress. A philosophy of delayed gratification undoubtedly inspired by the Elsarian Order's notions of morality. Drivel.

He tilted his head at the pile of parchment on his desk. “The coalition of northern Praetors has answered.”

Frustration leeched from Cassandane’s face, replaced by the same fear he kept seeing in Sarai. Her fingers stilled around the scroll he handed her before she set it down. “I can’t.” She swallowed. “Not tonight.”

“Hmm.” Another concession then.

“Godsdammit, don’t you judge me, Kadra!” Fury splintered her voice into jagged marble. “For the next three hours, I must smile and wave and project enough strength to prove that I am worthy of being Head Tetrarch, while bowing before every Guild to prove that I’m also a *mere* woman who knows her place. Do *not* ask me to do that while holding whatever dreadful news the north has sent us in the back of my head.” She sought the fireplace, staring at the still-burning volume of the Distribution Act with grim resignation. “It *is* dreadful news, yes?”

“Yes.” He was alive to her troubles. “You aren’t without allies. You have my blade, and Sarai–”

“I’m deeply grateful that she threw herself forward to protect us, but I cannot live as you both do.” Her jaw pulled so tight that she seemed poised to gnaw off her tongue. “Have you even seen her lately? Don’t you notice the exhaustion and fear in her posture when anyone approaches her? She’s *nineteen*. She should be *young*. Dancing, failing, loving the wrong men, so she can look back and wonder what she was thinking and laugh at the life she led. Instead, she carries the weight of a country and the fear that she might have broken it. She can *never* put a toe wrong because the public will tear her to shreds.” Cassandane gripped the fireplace mantel like she wanted to break it. “You’re unrepentant about what you do and what you want, but others pay the price.”

Three bottles of wine, and they still didn’t numb him as the barb struck. The chasm in his chest tore wider. “Do you think,” he fisted the neck of a bottle, “that I don’t know that?”

Cassandane risked a glance and nearly tripped into the fireplace when his eyes tore into her. “Then hold back. A fearful nation is a dangerous one.

Get the Guilds on our side tonight." She warily glanced at his clenched grip and cursed. "Kadra, are you fucking *drunk*?"

His damaged spine burned as he rose. Three bottles hadn't been enough after all. "The Academiae's previous Headmaster threw people off Sidran Tower. Its reputation will survive me."

He barely noticed her furious departure, still consumed by what she'd uttered. The same truth that kept him at his vigile station for days at a time. That had driven him to ally with Aelius's enemies and write to Praetors and Tribunes in towns with powerful economic reach. Because he had planned his death but had nearly taken Sarai with him. He had forced her into a bitter world, shackled her politically to the very man who had ignored her as she bled to death. And she'd inherited his enemies.

Cassandane was wrong. *Dancing, failing, loving the wrong men.* Sarai had already done one of those things.

He was outside before the sonorous water clock by the courtyard struck ten. Wine poured freely from a fountain of ice, spilling onto beige cobblestones. Students in the Academiae's dark-gray robes bustled around a banquet table with enough to feed a small village—roasted slabs of beef, herb-stuffed fish, steaming pies, with myriad soups and roasted root vegetables. Bards sawed and plucked at their instruments. A cozy sight were it not for the frenzied whispers at his arrival.

Wind wrested a needle from a nearby pine and wove it into a bitter gust that pushed at him, seeking weakness and finding none. He was too familiar with the cold for it to trouble him, born into ice but destined for lightning, the years in between little more than a cloud of blazeleaf smoke and blood. The ever-present strain of the ruined nerves in his spine had been his only companion throughout. There were nights when those memories didn't resurface. He'd known many of them after Sarai. Tonight wasn't one of them.

Throngs splintered at his approach, slinking forward with the same feverish intensity he had witnessed in childhood. Proximity to power was a drug as strong as wine. These people had drunk deep. They offered flinty eyes and primal fear, along with false cheer in their voices as they greeted them. Obsequious grins belied their sly hatred. Some families wore a jeweler's entire stock; some snuck a few portions of the roast into beeswax cloth for another day's meal.

Then, there were the *other* beings. The whispers at the back of his mind and the spills of crimson bubbling from the courtyard's tile. Skeletal figures watching with overlarge eyes from behind the distant conifers. An oil-slick miasma distorting the air above segments of the crowd. Invisible to all but him, and proof of a truth that he couldn't tell Sarai when she was so burdened. That he hadn't returned entirely unchanged from the dead.

"My daughter's a Petitor too." A noblewoman thrust a graduate in front of him. "She'll be one after tonight. Top of her class before she left because of that unfortunate situation with Petitors...losing their lives. Very generous of you to allow everyone to return to complete their studies. She's *eighteen*."

Why this was significant escaped him. "Congratulations," he addressed the air above the girl's head and moved past, but the mother blocked his path.

"I beg your pardon, Magus Supreme, but she's a Tenth-Tier." The woman summoned an ingratiating but determined smile. "Properly trained. *Certo*, you must wish for a more powerful Petitor to help with your caseload. We're all aware that the current one is only a Seventh-Tier and a bit...broken," she said with a high laugh that echoed across a suddenly silent courtyard.

Gold winked at the edge of his vision as a figure carefully set down her wineglass.

Fuck.

Anguish bloomed like a bloodstain in Sarai's eyes before she smoothed her features into a blank canvas. That winded him even before he took in the vision she made. Black fabric embroidered liberally with golden vines and flowers wound around her torso in a bodice that bared the gentle upper swell of her breasts and clung to her waist before proceeding to a floor-length gown. A shawl of some gauzy fabric with all the substance of gossamer shielded her shoulders along with black gloves that crested above her elbows. To hide her hand tremors, he realized.

She carries the weight of a country and the fear that she might have broken it. Cassandane's barb sank deeper when Sarai caught his eye and managed the same reassuring smile she'd worn for months. Saying that she wasn't hurting. That he hadn't robbed her of the life she should have had.

Anger and self-hatred licked at him when the woman kept talking.

"There's nothing saying that you must wait until next year's Robing to take on a new girl—" She froze when his eyes bored into hers. A weak puff of air fled her throat.

"A tragedy to be loud and wrong." The ice in his voice sent a ripple through the crowd. Steps away, Cassandane stiffened. "Crawl up the social ladder if you must, but be circumspect about your target. I *have* a Petitor. She is entirely whole." He caught Sarai's gaze, and his heart eased at the glow suffusing her golden eyes.

Hushed laughter circled the red-faced noblewoman. Grains Guildmaster Ioratius separated him from Sarai while vociferously complaining about the northern riots. He struck down his proposed solutions—all variations on the same theme: violent retaliation against the rioters—and continued through the crowd. Nothing had changed. The same dance, the same game, the same system that knelt to power.

A vise gripped his head upon his next breath.

You could end it, murmured a voice that sounded like guilt and a desolation more ancient than his. He was no stranger to its intrusion over the last few months. *Burn them all to the ground and safeguard her.*

She wouldn't appreciate the cost, he replied dryly. *I'm more partial to building than burning these days.*

A quiet laugh scraped across his senses. *This city and its inhabitants thrive off the suffering of the rest of the country. They want blood not bridges. If you don't appease them, it'll be yours that spills. Relinquish the present and take back your past. Power waits for you in the shadows. Reach out, and you'll see everything.*

He gave that the same consideration that he did every offer of infinite glory. None.

Upon his next step, the unearthly tension in his head tightened and grew thorns. Pain lanced through his eyes. His vision grew dark, forcing him to a halt.

This won't convince me. Kadra's jaw tautened when the pressure worsened. He reached for his armilla when a different, familiar voice spoke at his shoulder.

"Magus Supreme."

The assault on his mind ceased. Blood rushed back into his beleaguered skull. Exhaling, Kadra turned to consider the half-veiled newcomer with faint menace. "Inquisitor Silvus."

"We finally meet." Silvus's muffled voice held an odd note of elation. "I've been following your career for some time."

Kadra's lips curved. "A pity, I can't say the same."

Silvus chuckled. "Well, I did hope to surprise you. I hope you don't mind the unpleasantness with your lover yesterday. She did hold up rather well after all."

Wintry rage lapped at Kadra at the way the man referred to Sarai. "If only the Order could say the same."

"Be that as it may, the Order didn't expose her to ridicule in the first place Magus Supreme. She put out one fire as you did tonight, but there'll be more." Silvus sucked air in through his teeth. "What a bitter life. To watch over your shoulder forever and work for a country that sees you as either a usurper or a whore." He met Kadra's incandescent eyes with amused calm. "She cannot fight forever."

"She won't have to."

"Yes, *certo*, the might of men. Let me tell you a story. You may have heard it before. Five and a half centuries past, before the monarchy fell, it was served by five powerful Clans. Each with their virtues and vices, *certo*, but none as feared as Clan Kader."

The echoes of wine on Kadra's tongue suddenly tasted sour. "Ancient history, Silvus?"

Gray eyes laughed, something slithering in the striations of his irises. "You'd like to think so, wouldn't you? But allow me to finish. Now, only Clan Kader and Clan Am Semni survived the monarchy's ruin by retreating north, where they were able to still find some deference. There, they set down roots in the mountains."

There was a hint of blazeleaf in the air, tart and bitter. A student smoking inferior product. Kadra's spine throbbed. The past seethed at the periphery of his mind.

"Clan Kader rebuilt itself into the north's preeminent drug producers, then the land's most powerful crime syndicate. The northern city of Komis was the center of their underworld and the forested Drust Mountains held their warehouses for blazeleaf farming, drug production, flesh-trade, and any other unholy deed they could perform. They loomed over Komis like vultures, immutable." He tipped his head back with a hard, incredulous laugh. "No one dared question the occasional corpses thrown in ditches."

The pressure in Kadra's veins surged dangerously. "Edessa has seen the same."

Silvus shrugged. "I suppose so. *Violentia nervus potestas* or 'violence is the sinew of authority' was the Clan's motto, and they performed it with relish. Clanlord Clevsin ruled with an iron fist, the women he used as broodmares were rapidly sent to the afterlife, and children, they say, were evil incarnate. Only a few survived to adulthood, often offing each other in shows of ability to their Clanlord."

Kadra's back was aflame.

"As a child, I was foolish enough to pity the Kader boys. What sort of life was it," Silvus wondered quietly, "to be locked in a vast property and forced to prove your worth by the amount of pain you could dish out and take?"

It took everything for Kadra to feign impassivity. "And?"

"Well, those questions didn't last long. Eleven years ago, on a cloudless night, a fire suddenly gutted most of Clan Kader's manor in the Drust Mountains. No one could claim to know the cause though some argued that a bolt of lightning, wide as a boulder, struck the manor. And the Clan and its scions were never seen again." Silvus sighed. "An empire fractured."

Memory dug teeth into him. Kadra raised a brow. "Illuminating."

"Funny, your *Petitor* didn't care for the story either." Silvus chuckled. "But you see, might is a frail thing. If a power that outlasted the monarchy can crumble in a night, then might won't save her."

The tension in Kadra's jaw threatened to shatter his molars. Taking a wineglass from a passing server, he swirled it, searching for the oily sheen of poison as the liquid hugged the sides before taking a sip. "There is more to power than might. Clan Kader learned that too late. I am not the same."

A bitterness that approached hatred passed over Silvus's half-hidden face. "I suppose we'll see how true that is."

Fabric rustled at his shoulder. Cassandane cleared her throat. "Magus Supreme, it's time."

Tempering his surging adrenaline, Kadra moved past Silvus. The audience broke into applause as he took to the limestone dais that students would cross as they graduated.

Sarai hadn't gotten the chance.

That last glass of wine seemed to have finally numbed him. Words sprouted from his lips as he read Cassandane's carefully prepared speech, omitting the more ingratiating points to her thunderous scowl. He passed nervous students their scrolls with his congratulations while a drunk Harion nearly toppled into the wine fountain. Once it ended, he surveyed the cheering with cool equanimity. It was time.

When Cassandane motioned him down from the dais, he spoke.

"Tonight, we gather from near and far to celebrate the five hundred who leave the Academiae's halls."

Riotous applause greeted his pronouncement. From a corner of the courtyard, Sarai gave him a quizzical look. Cassandane's brows knitted. "*What are you doing?*" she mouthed.

"We salute that they shed their old haunts for new. We praise that they have been acknowledged by our most renowned school and found worthy to proceed toward what will largely be lives of prestige. In short," his voice hardened, "you came here to celebrate *change*."

The cheering faltered. Panic made bruises of Cassandane's dark eyes. She began shouldering through the crowd to reach him. He was sorry it had come to this. Yet, she didn't see what he did.

"Strange." He let his gaze sweep the crowd and watched it quiver. "For I have heard that many among you do not like *change*. You wish to teach your progeny the same bigotry that you were taught. You seek to maintain the same conflicts you grew up with in a balanced state of imbalance. You cultivate a new generation of enemies and scapegoats, so that when they fight back and war blooms you can blame history and roar that you have *never* been at fault. And your coffers bloat all the while."

Cassandane's frenzied steps halted. She stared as though he had stabbed her.

"What the fuck do you think you're doing," Clay Guildmaster Septimus snapped from the agitated crowd. "How dare you commandeer tonight for your personal–"

"A land that refuses to change is a land doomed to rot." His voice engulfed the courtyard. "Yet, these students have been taught that to be radical is to ask for death, that progress is a few orders signed into force by a Tetrarch right before they die so they can't be repealed, and that keeping the peace at the cost of justice is democracy. The upper classes and Guilds," he cast a sardonic glance at Septimus, "have made self-fulfilling prophecies of these lessons to the extent that they killed *me*."

A hush fell over the audience. They parted when he swept down the dais.

"And I, too, learned a lesson. No longer will I leave progress to my last breath. I won't ask our oppressed to *wait.* So, on this night that celebrates stepping into the future, understand that the land is going to change." His lips curved as frenzied muttering built around him. "And it will start with this, here, at the scene of *my* crime." His throat thickened when he found Sarai's gaze. She had gone perfectly still, golden eyes blown wide in the moonlight. Beside her, Anek pressed a hand to their lips.

"From this day, the Academiae will cease charging for entrance exams and will welcome students of all backgrounds. Prospective entrants will receive three tries to pass and a full scholarship if they succeed. The coin will come from *my* coffers, and this school will be richer for their presence. As for our graduates," he cast a glance at the wordless group, "who undoubtedly wish to return me to the afterlife for running roughshod over their night, accept my heartiest felicitations and a gift of five hundred aurei each to smooth your journey forward." He spread his hands with a glacial smile. "Goodnight."

The courtyard erupted, setting the cobblestone thrumming. Eyes darted from him to Sarai. Uproarious applause and wild whistles from the graduates, racing to his vigiles with open hands for their gold, yelling to him that this was the best night of their lives. Cassandane tottered, white as a sheet. Guildsmasters and nobles swarmed him to screech about him destroying the Academiae's prestige. But he only had eyes for the woman watching him with a love of which he would never be worthy.

I love you. He had put her through so much, and this had been an announcement of war. Yet, Cassandane was wrong, because Sarai saw the battlelines too. She fought because the world had abandoned her, *he* had abandoned her, and she would leave no one.

He wouldn't betray her ideals. No matter how badly he hungered to keep her safe.

Tilting his head toward Gaius, he smiled when she caught his meaning and raced over to the vigile who passed her the note he'd written hours earlier.

Grains Guildmaster Ioratius has a secret horreum. A nighttime stroll, my Petitor?

She scanned it and broke into a wide grin, cheeks pinkening, eyes bright. And in that moment, he had never felt closer to peace, so there, under the veil of night and surrounded by detractors, he tried to imagine that there was no war in Ur Dinyé, that there was nothing he'd hidden from Sarai, and that the façade of his life would never crumble.

If only that were true.

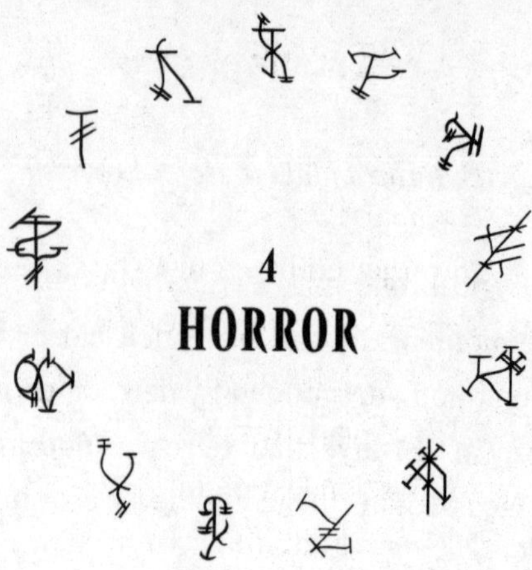

4
HORROR

It boded ill for a land when its officials had to resort to vigilantism to see justice done.

Sarai dismounted on a lone stretch of road in Aelius's Quarter, squinting at the gated compound ahead. Midnight draped Edessa in an indulgent quiet. A brisk wind ferried smoke from the hearths of nearby farms and the crisp scent of crushed pine needles. Despite being close to the edge of the capital, the road was well-paved cobblestone not a dirt ribbon. Aelius's taxes at work. *No wonder his people vaunt him as a Saint after such excellent treatment.*

Snow crunched under her boots as she steered her mare into the tree line. A familiar black stallion tethered to a pine whickered upon sighting her. Anchoring her mount to Kadra's, she squinted at a hilltop ahead, to the left of where the road sloped up.

Ten aurei says he'll be surveying the horreum from there.

Excitement lent her steps a spring. How many weeks had it been since they'd last had a moment alone? She'd thank the Grains Guild for giving them a few hours together if the *havïd* assholes weren't artificially manufacturing a grain shortage.

Conifers creaked as she walked up the hill. The compound on the other side came into view. Enormous and two-stories high, the main building was raised on pillars to keep grain away from the damp when stormfall inevitably came. Ramps slanted up to the main doors, the grounds circled by the high wooden gates that she'd glimpsed from the road. Unremarkable to passersby but unmistakable when viewed from above—the Grains Guild's secret horreum, a warehouse and granary.

Though it did seem rather empty. A few spires of smoke coiled above dying braziers, and the score of unyoked wagons on the grounds were as barren as they were. She wouldn't begrudge an easy victory. Vigilantism was dangerous these days, especially in Aelius's Quarter. And after Kadra's announcement at the graduation last night.

Gods, he was magnificent. Radiating ice and power. Entirely in control of the chaos, having anticipated every argument down to buying the graduates' approval.

"Ruin's breath, that was entirely mad. Yet, I've never felt more hopeful about the state of the country," Anek had murmured dazedly afterward. *"Still don't see the appeal, but he's devoted to you."*

The worries that had plagued her at the chapel dissipated like spun sugar. She suppressed a giddy laugh, then stilled at the dark figure standing at the top of the hill. Her pulse quickened.

Robed in his customary black with a baldric running crosswise over his shoulders, Kadra's profile was unmistakable. A god of the night surveying his prey. Breath left her, replaced by what the wind carried of him—oranges, parchment, smoked wine, and something crisp, uniquely him, that set her aflame. What a strange thing to yearn for someone when he was steps away. To want to dangle her feet over the edge of the abyss and ask for it to swallow her.

The moons lovingly lit him when he turned. "Sarai."

Gods, his voice was so beautiful. She'd missed feeling it clamp around her heart. "I can never take you by surprise."

The cruel slash of his mouth curved in a smile that always made her heart stutter. He held out a palm, and the world quieted, coalesced into a single, powerful truth when she took it. *Home.*

Tipping her chin, he searched her eyes, warmth heating his gaze. "I wouldn't say that. You threw yourself to the wolves at the Hearing."

Longing thudded through her limbs as she wove her fingers with his. “I couldn’t feed them anyone else.”

A low sigh brushed her cheek. “I didn’t realize it until you began.”

“Look at that, I’ve surprised the mighty Kadra.” She squeezed his hand. “You did too.”

“I try not to be entirely predictable.” He slipped a hand around the back of her neck, a thumb making a hungry foray across her cheek. All at once, she was wordless. Lightning-struck, and so hyperaware that she could feel every whorl on his fingers.

“Thank you for last night.” The words felt wholly inadequate. “This’ll change so much! Though I fear for your coffers.”

“I’m wealthy,” he said with wry amusement. “But, my Sarai, for the sake of my much-weakened sanity, warn me the next time you plan on eviscerating a religious institution?”

“You and Cassandane have been holding the country together by your teeth.” *I felt like a burden.* “I couldn’t impose.”

“You’re never an imposition.” She flushed when he brought her wrist to his mouth to press a kiss over her veins. A rare public display of affection from a man who was extremely circumspect about whom he allowed to see him without his mask of cool formality.

“Understood?”

“Yes.” She smiled, knowing he saw the same weariness in her that she did in him. But rest would have to come later. She tilted her head toward the horreum. “I met with Guildmaster Ioratius weeks earlier, and he swore up and down that this year’s yield of grain was abysmal. How did you find this?”

“Gaius did.” Kadra followed her gaze. “It’s a trap.”

“What?”

“Nothing has stirred beyond that fence in the last half hour.” He contemplated the unmanned wooden gates into the horreum. “Our arrival was anticipated.”

"I knew it was too much to hope that we caught them off-guard," she sighed. "By the Saints and Wretched, all this grain piled here while the north begs–" She paused at the grim set of Kadra's features.

The callused hand curled around hers thrummed with tension, the divot in his brow deepening the longer he examined the compound. Apprehension bubbled in her chest when his eyes altered, an unearthly cold brewing within. *There's that look again.* As though he had penetrated deep into corners that she couldn't see and found something almost…frightening.

"Kadra?" she whispered, and he blinked–as close to a jolt as one would ever get from him–turning to her with unflinching intensity. She wet her lips. "What is it?"

He shook his head with a faint smile, another avoidance of the same question. "Be careful, yes?"

"Always." Pulling out the pin in her armilla, she pricked her thumb and pressed the blood into *beshaz* to tear a few ligaments in the event of battle.

He strode down the hill to the wooden gates and raised a hand. She waited for lighting to collapse the wood to ash as he usually did during their bouts of vigilantism. But his hand dropped. The same eerie expression tightened his face before he brought both palms to the gates and pushed.

They swung open.

Her breath fogged out in a rush. *Something's wrong.* Trap or otherwise, the Guild would never leave the place unlocked. Catching Kadra's gaze, she tilted her head left. He nodded and veered right.

One step, another. Nothing stirred within the dark arches of the horreum's three entrances. The quiet that draped the grounds didn't belong to winter, devoid of its windy whistles and creaky boughs. Only a half-dead brazier sputtered at their invasion.

Where is everyone? The hairs on the back of her neck rose to full mast when no Guildspeople ran out, weapons aloft.

Did something drive them away?

"Empty?" she mouthed to Kadra, who gave the barest shake of his head, indicating the footprints in the snowy dirt, cased in half-frozen puddles from a bout of stormfall hours earlier.

All leading in. None going out.

Realization lanced through her along with a bolt of fear. If no one had left and no one was outside, then that only left... *within.*

Kadra's features grew harder. Ice threaded through his eyes as they entered the granary. With the flick of a finger, he lit the oil lamps in one sconce then another, unveiling a labyrinth of brick storerooms, piled high with sacks of maize, wheat, barley, even rice—near impossible to grow in Ur Dinyé's cracked soil. Yet, underneath the earthy scents lay something sour, cloying.

Dread gripped her tighter with their every echoing step and the lack of challenge that met them. Ahead, the hallway forked in two, the paths forming a pair of dark eyes daring them to approach.

Kadra's steps slowed. Her heart stuck in her throat at the stillness that came over his taut features, his pupils blooming large as he stared at the left path.

What do you see? she wanted to plead. *Do you say nothing because I can't help?*

"I'll take this one," she whispered instead.

He had barely begun to turn to her with mild surprise when she grabbed the closest oil lamp and strode into the dark, her heart beating out of her chest. Another step, three more, and her head whipped up at a familiar stench threading the air.

Blood.

She ran. Gooseflesh swept her skin as she sped through room after room, uncaring that she was dripping lamp oil in her haste because something had happened here. And it had been far worse than a nation's worth of stolen grain.

Turning into a hallway, she recoiled. The oil lamp slipped from her shaking hands to fragment on the tile, fire licking at the spilled oil and spreading in a pool. Bile crawled up her throat at what it illuminated.

Blood undulated on the floor in thick ripples, only a tiled step stopping it from flooding the horreum. Within that red sea stood contorted bodies in the Grains Guild's livery, piled against each other like rats who'd been petrified in the act of fleeing a ship.

She had seen Death's work before, but this had been no gentle going into the afterlife. Jaws agape, eyes bulging, the Guildspeople lay frozen in a horrible rictus of pain. They formed a blockade in the hallway, outstretched limbs still desperately clawing for salvation from gods that had taken them anyway. Gray already mottled their skin.

What monstrous act was this?

Fire burned beside her, casting garish shadows over the dead. The dark invited her closer. She felt her feet rise over the step holding back the blood. Crimson swallowed her boots and lapped ankle-high. She could hear her breaths, ragged and fast. Yet, she walked as though caught in a dream not of her making.

The dead can hurt no one. You've met Death. He isn't one to bother engendering such fear.

So, why was she shaking?

A woman lay face down at the front of the human pile, the back of her skull bashed in by the Guildsman behind her. Clumps of brain matter curdled in the liquid at her feet.

Shit. Sarai closed her eyes, forcing back memories of another night, her ruined skull, when a watery gurgle came from below. Fingers seized her ankle. A scream tore from her as she sprung back until she realized what was gripping her.

The woman with the broken skull was alive.

Blood cascaded down the Guildswoman's face when she raised it. Sarai's nails cut into her palms, twitching to the terrified drum of her heart. *Don't panic. You were once in this position too.* Mercifully, the woman's face was intact. Dark hair, dark eyes. She clawed up to Sarai's knee, gripping it with such strength that Sarai had no hope of crouching.

"You–" The Guildswoman choked on a thick blood clot and spat it out. Her voice was a ragged gurgle. "*You.*"

Was this how I looked five years ago? Sarai swallowed and reached for calm. "Let me help you sit up–" She froze, eyes trailing to where the woman's back should have been. She'd been bludgeoned in half, her exposed spine the only bridge between her torso and legs.

The woman followed her gaze and shrieked, part desperation, part resignation.

Sarai's eyes burned. "There may be hope yet. I'll ride for a healer. Wait–"

"I am out of time, *Petitor*," the woman spat, propping her torso on her elbows. "You can't save me when you brought this upon us."

"What do politics matter when you're at Death's door? Let me help!"

Laughter wracked her bifurcated frame, bubbling out of her with more blood. "Help?" She bared her teeth. "Didn't *you* bring this on us, northerner? Our hourglass runs low. A reckoning has followed in your wake. The gods have spoken and call for our end. The sky itself will *laugh*."

I don't understand. Fear traced cold fingers down Sarai's spine. "I swear on all the Elsar I know nothing of this. What happened here?"

"Vengeance." A guttural note underlay the word. "You have proven your point, *Petitor*."

"Please believe me, I've done *none* of this–" Sarai halted when the woman's dark irises grew and grew until they swallowed her sclera. *Almost like Kadra's.* Terror choked her, burgeoning until her inhales came thick and labored. "What do you see?" she whispered.

"That life is a shared nightmare. And you can always wake up."

The Guildswoman smiled beatifically, staring at something unfathomably distant. "Have you ever seen so many…eyes?" She heaved a rattling breath and fell face-first into the blood.

She didn't move again.

A dull buzzing filled Sarai's ears. She felt herself stagger, turn, and run out of the pool of blood, inhaling deeply in a bid to calm her pulse. But the sight, the *smell*. Just like it had been back at Sidran Tower. Her chest constricted to the point of pain, every heartbeat battering against her ribs. Darkness seeped across her vision.

And then, she couldn't breathe at all.

Blood swamped her lungs. It trickled from her throat to flood the empty socket of one eye and spread questing fingers from her shattered body. A man spoke above her, his mellifluous voice a caress to her dying senses. She knew him, and yet she didn't. But her heart bled further when he walked away while her mouth gurgled a plea.

"Come back!" she screamed, wondering why her voice worked. "PLEASE!"

His boots were so far–

Footsteps thundered to a halt. "Sarai, look at me," ordered the same beautiful voice in glacial tones, tearing through terror and memory. Hands gripped her shoulders when she didn't respond. "Breathe." A hoarse note this time. She complied. "That's it. Again."

Sound blurred as she struggled to get her bearings, sucking in desperate lungfuls of air. The agony in her chest eased with every gasp. Reality returned slowly.

"You're safe." Kadra released a low breath when she sagged against him. His arms banded around her like steel. "I have you."

She realized that she was whispering pleas into his chest and nearly bit her tongue in half in her haste to trap it between her teeth. *Shit. I was doing so well for months.* She knew what she'd find even before she raised her face to the quiet self-hatred lining his too-severe features.

Her heart ached. She had forgiven him, but he would never forgive himself. "I'm–"

His finger against her lips gently forestalled the words. "You have nothing to apologize for." With a flick of his wrist, he contained the fire from her oil spill and regarded her gravely. "Come outside."

She squeezed his hands. "I'm well." Forcing herself to face the macabre sight, she flinched anew. "Ruin's blood, what happened here? They look like they were fleeing something, froze mid-scream, and bled out. Yet, they've no weapons but that rock." She indicated the limestone chunk that had broken the Guildswoman's head. "And the bodies are…"

"Pristine." Releasing her, Kadra stalked into the bloodbath, uncaring of it soaking into the hem of his robes. "No offensive or defensive wounds." He pulled down some of their collars and examined their wrists. "No ligature marks or visible attempts at suicide."

Then how did they die? She stared at the blood lapping at his boots, then took a deep breath and walked over the tiled step holding back the waves. Kadra's gaze followed her, sharp and tinged with concern, as she approached the newly-dead Guildswoman. *I don't even know her name.*

"She was alive when I got here. I–" She drew a ragged breath and steeled herself. Kadra would never ask this of her, but they both knew it was necessary. Forensic information degraded by the second. By the time a Lugen arrived, it could be too late. "I'll take a look."

He tracked the frenetic trembling of her fingers. Guilt mingled with quiet pride on his face before he moved behind her and gently steadied them over the woman's skin. Closing her eyes, she let her magic feel its way into the body's fraying workings. A second sight of its own.

She came up empty.

To reach into a corpse was to enter an abandoned domus on quicksand. Decomposition threaded through the walls and furniture, and to touch anything was to risk its collapse. She could only observe the slow spoil and attempt to piece together how it had happened. Telmar's lessons had prepared her well.

Thighs, feet, arms. No damage. Odd welts on her shoulders. *A rash?* Nothing in the liver or stomach that indicated poison, but traces of what could be a drug. *Blood in the throat too.* She examined the esophagus. *A lot of blood. Hemorrhage?* She glanced up at the brain stem. *Perhaps a brain bleed.*

Shifting her gaze higher, she examined the brain and froze. *What in havïd?* She rapidly drew down, past the woman's ribcage and to her heart. Chills pricked up Sarai's neck, burgeoning into terror the longer she stared at the shredded organ.

Opening her eyes, she relinquished the body in a rush. "Her brain and heart–" She swallowed. "They're pulverized. Like she had a hundred heart attacks in a minute or her mind fell apart and her body followed suit. There are a few welts on her shoulders and indications that she consumed some sort of drug, but I don't have the ability to look deeper. *Gods!* You know what people will make of this. Especially, the Order." She couldn't keep the tremor from her voice. "Kadra, she said it was my fault. That a reckoning followed in my wake."

"It isn't." Low and hard, his voice cut through her fear. He considered the woman's frozen mask of terror before drawing her eyelids shut. A crust of white powder lay over them, visible even through the blood on her face.

Whitesleep. Clan Kader's most dangerous creation, if she had her history right. Aroamea had been too remote to see any drug-trafficking, so she'd been kept innocent of the numerous ways people induced joy or oblivion. Ten months in Edessa had left her much wiser.

Blazeleaf was ubiquitous and legal, albeit controlled by the Tetrarchy's dispensaries. Ibez had been banned for sheer potency. But whitesleep, an addictive analgesic rubbed on the eyelids, had aided as many as it had harmed. One of Clan Kader's last known inventions prior to their mysterious end, it had capitalized on the fact that there were pains that even healers couldn't pinpoint the cause of, diseases that could only be slowed and not cured. Whitesleep, when diluted, allowed most users to lead largely normal lives. It was the pure version of the drug that was highly addictive. Once hooked, there was no getting anyone off that euphoria. Their bodies couldn't survive it.

She tested the theory. "A pure batch that disintegrated their brains and made them hemorrhage through every orifice?"

"Potentially." Perturbation flickered across Kadra's features.

Because it doesn't explain why they all died screaming. Terror wound around her. *This is something new.*

"And it *had* to be Aelius's Quarter too—" She halted at the cold sweeping across Kadra's gaze the longer he examined the tableau. Taking his arm, she spoke louder. "I'll stay here. You're the faster rider. Off you go to Cassandane's."

Turning to her, he arched an eyebrow. Something amused and tender broke through the ice in his eyes when she frowned back. "Very well." Inclining his head, he swept off in a cloud of black.

She stepped out of the blood and slumped against the wall once his footsteps faded. That was the thing with Kadra. He never second-guessed her decisions. If she said that she would wait with a slew of corpses, he'd believe her capable of it. The trouble was that she was doing it for *him*.

Death had returned Kadra as whole and hearty as she had wished. Yet, the god had made no promises that he wouldn't be haunted. She could fathom only one explanation for what she kept seeing in his eyes. She was no stranger to the piercing weight of that gaze, but this recent emptiness she kept sighting held something akin to madness.

Kadra had spoken little of what he'd seen in the afterlife, and she would no more push him to speak of that torment than he would ask her of the Fall. She could only wait until he was ready. Until then, leaving him with the dead felt wrong.

Hours passed in a slow bleed. Cassandane's vigile station was a four-hour ride from this lonely stretch of farmland, and Kadra had to notify his station and Harion's too. Needing to stretch her legs after the second hour, she wandered the horreum, finding rooms decked in Aelius's white and silver, including a miniature shrine to him as the Naaduir of Invention.

She snorted. If Aelius ended up elevated to the pantheon of minor gods for anything, it would be corruption.

She took to loading grain sacks onto the wagons outside as per the allotments to the north that she'd memorized from the Distribution Act. Dawn suffused the sky, as she finished. She rolled her shoulders and flinched at a stab of agony in her temples.

I'll see you soon, Death-Summoner, a garbled voice murmured. Both memory and challenge.

Gods, like I've the time to dig into this. Tugging at her braid in frustration, she stalked into the horreum's ice-room and rested there until her skull eased its throbbing. She was going to have to ask Anek to Materialize this bit of memory and put her at ease. *Likely just a threat by someone visiting the Stones Guild that day.* Wisdom only knew why her mind kept fixating on it.

Hooves clopped outside, accompanied by raised voices. She raced out to find Kadra, Cassandane, Anek, and a group of vigiles and Lugens tethering their steeds. The tang of blood had worsened over the hours, and the air reeked of death. Horses and vigiles alike eyed the horreum with mute fear.

Cassandane looked defeated. "I almost don't want to know," she muttered after a good minute of silence. "We put out one fire at the Hearing—*Tibi gratias ago* for that by the way, Sarai—and here comes another. I hear you found whitesleep on one of them?"

Sarai exchanged a glance with Kadra. "Yes, but it might not be the cause."

The hollows under Cassandane's eyes deepened. She tried for levity: "Well, how bad could it be?"

"Gods and Saints, preserve me!" A vigile ran out of the horreum, stark white. "Elsar, save us all!"

Cassandane contemplated the heavens for a moment. "Being a god," she finally said, "seems an enviable job. They don't have to answer. *I* do."

She strode up the steps and went in, muttering under her breath. Kadra followed, after a parting brush of his thumb over Sarai's wrist.

Wincing at the litany of shrieks that followed as vigiles and Lugens found the dead, she went to the wooden gates into the compound. An audience had already begun to form beyond, farmers pulled from their crops by the screams and hooves thundering down their normally placid stretch of road.

Her chest tightened. *This could undo everything.* All the goodwill she'd built after the Hearing could dissipate like smoke.

Shoving the gates shut, she rested against them and recalled how Kadra had uncharacteristically chosen not to burn them down. *He knew that they were open.* She let out a long breath. *There's no denying it, is there?* And he still wouldn't confide in her.

Violent retching startled her out of the reverie. Red curls almost touching the ground, Anek doubled over and vomited some more onto the mud. A host of echoes told her that other vigiles and even a few Lugens were doing the same.

"What," they gasped, heaving again, "in all the fucking hells," another heave, "is that?"

"I don't know," she said quietly.

Anek threw up their hands and the last of the contents of their stomach. Patting their back, Sarai led them to the ice-room where they sucked on ice chips until they felt well enough to speak.

"I'll agree that this is more than just whitesleep. The amount of blood—" They broke off with a shudder. "It's no natural death, but I know of no weapon that could do *that* to so many at once."

"The Guildswoman I spoke to said that a reckoning follows in my wake and the very sky would laugh."

Anek rebuffed both notions with a shake of their head. "Of course she'd try to blame you. I saw their little shrine. These people are largely Aelius's cultists. I wouldn't put it past them to follow him to the afterlife and pin this on you as a final middle-finger salute."

"If that's true, then there's a vile poetry to them faking their suicides as murders when their Saintly Tetrarch did the opposite." She leaned against the ice-room's frigid walls. "Did we handle them wrong? Should we be leaving them to their conspiracies and hatred when they could burgeon into homegrown insurrection groups in the future?" She shifted awkwardly when Anek cut her a startled look. "Look at where we are! They're dead, and we *still* have to fret over how they could upend the land."

"We can't very well round them up like pigs for slaughter. They've a right to freedom of movement and speech too. Even if they use it for shit like this," Anek added darkly.

Sarai slung a hand over their shoulder in commiseration. Anek had borne as many slings and arrows as Cassandane had since the Unraveling. Clerics had mocked their identity as a neutralis in sermons across the capital and lambasted them for aiding her during the Unraveling.

"How are you holding up?" She leaned against the frigid wall. "I heard someone leaked the location of your domus to a Cleric."

Anek scowled. "He woke me at three in the godsdamned morning by roaring outside my window that "amorphous gender is a mark of amorphous morality." I've never been so close to killing a man." They released a breath through their teeth. "Cassandane's offered to house me at her tower until I find a new domus."

Shit. Sarai pulled them into a one-armed hug, and they managed a laugh, muscular shoulders releasing their tension.

"It isn't all bad. Who knows? I might be able to pull off with her what you did with Kadra." They snickered at Sarai's dropped jaw. "Don't tell me you wouldn't! She's devastating."

"Alright, I'll concede that." Sarai squinted at Anek, trying to imagine them with Cassandane. Her smile faded at the deep lines that had threaded themselves under their eyes and across their temples. These Clerics spoke so easily of "marks of amorphous morality" without taking any responsibility for marks of indelible pain.

"We won at the Unraveling," she said quietly. "So, why are *we* the ones scrambling now? The Order harasses us without second thought. The Guilds disregard the Distribution Act while their profits bloom. The north riots and starves and suffers from a beetle plague, of all things, yet few here even see them as human. We ask the oppressed to live alongside their oppressors and prattle about 'mutual respect' when one side's beliefs are abhorrent. We try to meet them at the bargaining table for the sake of national unity, while they erode public faith in us. And people *still* fall for it!"

Anek chipped off a piece of ice with a wan smile. "Don't take it to heart. That's the nature of the game. We had no hope of being respected."

"Then why is Harion?" she wondered. "Can you imagine how easy it would be? Wasting less breath, less *time*. Not having to prove your worth along with doing your job. Not worrying that the smallest crisis could have the public turning on us to elect another Aelius!" She realized she'd said it all in one breath when Anek pressed an ice chip into her hand.

Their eyes held a world of sympathy. "You, my friend, care too much. Don't let the job become your life. This city will eat your heart if you let it."

I don't know how to stop. "It may have already eaten my mind. There's a memory from months back that I can't remember without my head feeling as though it'll burst. It involved someone calling me 'Death-Summoner' at the Stones Guild." She shrugged sheepishly at Anek's deadpan stare. "I know. I should have mentioned it sooner."

"I was outside the Stones Guild then too," they recalled. "It could be stress, unless you're Godstouched and about to horrify us with some eerie power gifted by one of the Elsar–" Anek stared when Sarai stumbled against an ice block and nearly fell. "I was only joking–oh godsdammit." They recoiled as a group of vigiles carrying a corpse barged into the ice-room and deposited it atop one of the coffinlike slabs piled around.

Kadra and Cassandane followed, sporting identically dour expressions. Stones Guild and Godstouched people forgotten, dread curdled Sarai's blood. *This can't be good.*

Cassandane's personal healer and Lugen, Destus, was the last to enter. A steely-eyed man in his mid-fifties, he stripped the corpse after quick examination of the extremities and shut the door to the ice-room. Lightning flared at a flick of Kadra's finger, latticing from wall to wall until the room gleamed.

"From this point onward, nothing we see here can leave this room. *Tetrarch* Harion will receive word once we solidify a theory, no sooner." Cassandane folded her arms, speaking through gritted teeth. "I have a feeling this may be at least partially his fault."

Taking a deep breath, Sarai turned to the body. Eyes bulging out of his head, the man continued to silently scream, rigor mortis having frozen his fear forever. The muscles of his arms had distended in death, purple-gray and splotchy. But what had her stop cold were the circular welts across his skin—pale in the center, with a raised, red, fleshy ring around them. Like a wax seal made of flesh, they dotted his chest, his back, even the soles of his feet.

Is it a pox or a—hold on. Realization struck her like a boot to the face. She could barely hear over the roar of blood in her ears. *By the Saints and the Wretched, don't tell me this is…*

Cassandane let loose a barrage of curses so foul that Anek looked mildly besotted. Their smile guttered when they squinted at the welts. "Well fuck."

"This," Cassandane pronounced in the hardest tone Sarai had heard from her, "isn't the first corpse I've seen like this in Aelius's Quarter. There were two others that fell to our errant Tetrarch Harion to investigate. I didn't expect matters to escalate this grotesquely, or I'd have taken the cases myself."

Water trailed down the slab of ice and splattered on the ground. She looked up at Kadra's taut features and sadly recalled the hours he'd spent frowning over the few reports he'd received from the coalition of northern Praetors, trying to make sense of the paucity of information therein. Their conclusions had been fourfold.

The six-legged cause traveled in swarms. They still hadn't identified the type. The condition wasn't airborne. But in the north where it had originated a few months back, it was deadly.

She said it: "The northern beetle plague has reached Edessa."

The hollow quiet that followed was only broken by the drip of water.

Then, Destus cleared his throat. "I'm afraid so," he said with all the gravity of a funeral proclamation.

Things seemed to move in a blur after that. Vigiles and gray-robed healers rushed into the ice-room and took the body. Kadra led her outside, lifted her onto her mare, and bid her to meet him at a marketplace in his Quarter for their daily public court sessions, weary eyes tracing her face before he re-entered the fray. She found herself on the road before her mind finally left that ice-room and what they'd learned therein.

Plague. Riots. Inquisitor Blasius's voice slithered into her head. *Omens.*

She wasn't one for superstition. The gods seemed more steadfast than people, and if Death was anything to go by, they communicated directly. Yet...the woman's words haunted her. *A reckoning has followed in your wake.*

Plague, riots. Omens?

A Guild-wagon-turned-hearse trundled past her, carrying a mountain of corpses.

"The irony," Anek muttered, riding beside her. "From ferrying sustenance to death."

"Hoarding sustenance," she said as the wagon veered past a crowd of accusing eyes. One by one, they slowly turned to her, saying nothing, yet she knew their minds as keenly as though they'd spoken them. *How do I prove that I've done nothing wrong if even I can't tell anymore?*

"It's a difficult matter, but you'll have answers soon," she said firmly to every barbed question thrown her way as she rode past. "Yes, Head Tetrarch Cassandane is aware. All will be well."

And as she rounded the curve that took her out of sight of the Grains Guild's horreum of death, she was painfully aware that Anek knew exactly when she'd been lying.

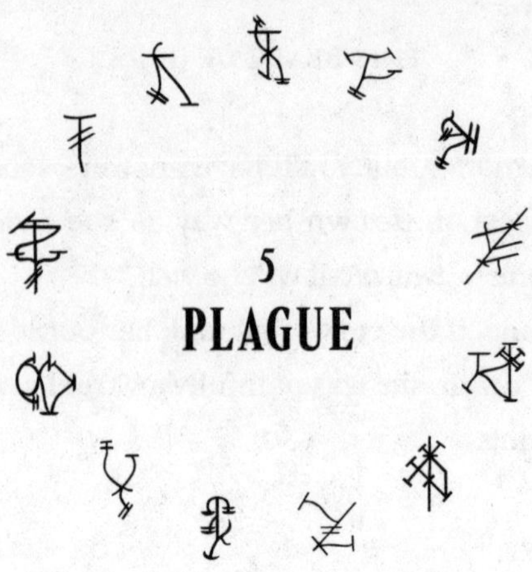

5
PLAGUE

"A tale of two countries. That's how most historians view our land. The starving north and the well-fed south squabbling over the allocation of resources as though there remains a question of entitlement. In case the mountain of research I have condensed into these pages for you wretched southerners doesn't make it clear, I'm saying that the north deserves as much as you have. I'm saying that while you sit in your domii and feast, the north withers. In your limited understanding of poverty, you dare believe that a poorly negotiated, centuries-old Act entitles you to our resources. I say you ask for civil war. The north may be politically weak, but we understand more of hardship than you lot ever will. We will rally around evil if it means remaining untouched by what you call good.

And when we come and dispossess you of all you took for granted, we will show you the same sympathy that you showed us."

—excerpt from *The* ~~Distribution~~ *Deprivation Act: Legal Robbery*, author unknown

Afternoon brought an odd banality to the day that sat ill with her after the horreum and its aftermath.

She'd endured an ear-splitting conversation with Grains Guildmaster Ioratius that had begun with her offering her condolences on the loss of over thirty of his Guildspeople and ended with them threatening to arraign each other on charges of theft—him for hoarding grain from the country, and her for pillaging it and sending it north—and reaching an impasse. But the rest of the day had been…pleasant. The cases were simple, the cold not too sharp, and the throng that engulfed the marketplace in which Kadra held court was blessedly quiet. The petitions spanning the length of the table they worked from had dwindled over the afternoon with nary a screech of "mountain bitch" or worse. It felt wholly ominous.

Tomorrow would be a different beast. Cassandane was already informing the vigiles at Edessa's four points of entry to examine all who entered the city for welts. *Word will spread, and another wave of anti-northern sentiment will flood the city. What a havïd mess.*

Telling herself to enjoy the quiet while it lasted, Sarai winced at the renewed cheer on the crowd's faces. How ironic that she'd sought to convince them only three days ago that the Elsar hadn't cursed the land and now was barely sure of it herself. How badly would this fragile peace shatter tomorrow?

"It was terrifying!" the plaintiff whose case she was supposed to be hearing suddenly cried. Sarai jumped. "I had no other choice!"

She glanced at the petition. *Guildsman of the Wine and Spirits Guild seeking restitution.* She started at the listed defendant, wondering if her eyes had it right. *The north?*

"The crowd swarmed my wagon—I mean, the *Guild* wagon—like gnats. I've never feared so greatly for my life. Naturally, I ran and left the wagon behind," the Guildsman finished.

Kadra smiled pleasantly. "Naturally."

"I shouldn't have to pay for the missing goods. *I* didn't ask the north to riot. Least it can do is compensate me for the value."

"'The north' isn't a valid defendant," Sarai said wearily. "Can you describe your attackers?"

"How would I know? These mountainfolk all look alike!"

Sarai frowned. His voice held the defiant thrum of a man who believed what he was saying, even if it wasn't necessarily how others would see it.

"What were you doing in that marketplace?" Kadra's arrowlike gaze pinned the Guildsman. "Guild wagons are to deliver their allotments under the Distribution Act directly to the locale's receiving warehouses or to establishments that purchased additional quantities."

Guilt snuck into the man's eyes and fled just as quickly. "Just stopped to examine some wares."

Just stopped to make a secret profit off marketgoers and deliver the remaining goods to the warehouse while shrugging about how the quantities came up short. She turned to Kadra and smiled at the exasperation in the stern line of his lips.

"*Furtum* is a crime." Kadra used the Corpus Juris Totus's term for theft. "The north has already compensated you well."

The man turned purple. "I am owed for an entire *wagon* lost. This doesn't compare to small profits here and there–"

"You've been a Guildsman for some twelve years," Kadra's voice took on the quiet timbre that meant danger. "Your skimming will have earned you enough to account for several wagons of supplies. Your case is dismissed."

Vigiles waved the man off when he attempted to argue further. Cries of "but my coin!" faded into the background.

She shook her head, sigh deepening upon unrolling their final case of the day. Assault, or *iniuria*, as per the ancient tongue used in the Corpus. Junia of Edessa was demanding compensation for apparently horrific injuries caused by one Lucanus. *This could get ugly.*

Surveying the crowd while Kadra called both parties to the chairs in the middle of the marketplace, she stared in confusion when a pair of silk-robed nobles stalked forth, looking equally put out with each other. Neither looked horrifically injured.

Kadra considered the duo. "What manner of assault brings you here?"

Junia rose with trembling lips. "I have been *disfigured*!" she wailed. "How am I supposed to go out in public like *this*?" Before Sarai could stop her, she flung off her birrus and robes in one swift movement, leaving her clad only in her undergarments.

Gaius's neck nearly snapped at the speed with which he looked away. Lascivious howls rose from the now-boisterous crowd while Sarai sighed into her palm. *Wisdom's teeth, it's winter.* "Please put your clothes back–" She caught sight of Junia's bare shoulders and jumped out of her seat. Ugly, familiar welts patterned her skin, arcing down her chest.

Dread dug into her throat like a blade when she found Kadra's grim eyes. "Robe yourself," he ordered Junia, who complied with a flinch. "How did this happen?"

"Well, *he*," Junia spat at Lucanus, who studiously ignored them all, "decided to take himself up north via Bridger. Gods only know why, there's nothing to do unless you fancy tradeswomen or miners, but he seems to have had an excellent time with both. *Then*, I saw him last week when he returned. I thought his welts were from whipping, because he's fond of–"

"Godsdamn you!" Lucanus jumped up at that. "How was I to know it was that northern plague?"

Whispers of alarm came from the crowd. They darted back from the two in a frantic wave.

The pit in Sarai's stomach widened. "When did you become aware that you had it?"

He rolled his eyes. "Few days ago, when a fucking larva popped out of my skin. Went straight to a healer and got myself purged."

"But the *scars* remain, asshole!" Junia snarled.

"What sort of beetle was it?" Sarai stood, circling around the table. "Can you think of where you were infected?"

"Elsar only know that. I wasn't entirely sober up there." The man had the gall to grin. "But I think they said something about boil beetles."

Sarai felt her jaw drop. *That makes no sense.* She had seen a few during her time as a snowgrape climber, but Arsamea had been too cold for the crimson, fingertip-sized pests with bright-yellow venom sacs to pose a problem. They nested within heavily forested areas and largely lived off *animal* flesh. Upon biting their targets, their venom loosened the top layers of skin so that they could tunnel in and gnaw at the meat underneath. But boil beetles had only ever been cattle killers at worst. Not *plagues.*

Tension seeped into the air when she met Kadra's eyes. Their audience stuffed their exposed hands in their pockets, swiftly shielding all visible skin with silent horror. The worst part was that she couldn't entirely tell them not to fear.

"Bad enough that the north creates a hue and cry over the Guilds every day, now they're spreading their diseases?" someone yelled.

"Oh gods, I've children! What if I infect them!"

Lucanus waved a dismissive hand. "Ruin's tits. Just see a healer."

"Not everyone can *afford* a healer, you rich fuck!"

"That's enough!" Pulling herself together, Sarai spoke brusquely. "According to reports from the north, you *will* feel if you've been infected. There's no mistaking the sensation of a beetle or larva burrowing into you. I doubt anyone here has felt that over the course of..." She trailed off as the crowd ignored her in favor of fleeing the marketplace, frantically patting themselves as they ran.

Wisdom save us, this is a disaster.

"Where," Kadra's voice cut through the furor with deadly precision, "did you encounter each other for the larvae to go from him to you without your notice?"

Junia froze, exchanging a rapid but unmistakable look of guilt with Lucanus.

"Others could have been infected at the same place," Sarai bit out. "If anyone is hurt as a result of your silence, *iniuria* won't be the only charges you face. Never mind a plague, your skin," she glanced coolly at Junia, "will look far worse after a month in the mines."

"A whitesleep den," Junia immediately blurted, then fidgeted in her seat when Lucanus glowered. "Look, it was just a bit of fun."

Whitesleep again. She thought back to the Guildswoman's crusted eyelids. *Is there a link?*

"Where." Kadra's voice brooked no refusal.

"Absolutely not!" Lucanus sputtered. "No one'll let us into one again if we rat out–"

"The people there could be–" *dead* "–gravely injured. Especially if they've had one too many rubs to realize that they were infected," Sarai said flatly. "Where is it?"

"The owners frequently change the den's location in case it leaks to vigiles," Junia mumbled. "But it's in Tetrarch Harion's Quarter."

Of course it is. Sarai looked into the terrified faces of the few still remaining in the marketplace and knew there was no hope of containing this fear with a tidy announcement tomorrow as Cassandane had hoped. The quiet hadn't so much as lasted three days.

Numb, she transcribed as Kadra delivered his judgment in favor of Junia–only insofar as making Lucanus pay for a healer. Fatigue worsened her hand tremors. Steadying her wrist with her left hand, she told herself that this was the last of it. She could return to Aoran Tower and perhaps even sleep before Edessa descended into paranoia once more.

A white-hot streak flashed above, sending her hand across the parchment in a splotch of ink. She stared at the steel-lined sky with consternation while Kadra's vigiles darted into motion, herding people away from the marketplace and into the vigile station, only a street away.

Rolling up the half-finished judgment, she glanced askance at Kadra when he didn't move. Foreboding coiled in her gut at the familiar ice solidifying in his black gaze even as a deafening clap of thunder made the ground throb beneath their feet.

What do you see? she wanted to plead. *Why won't you tell me?*

Instead, she followed Gaius and the much-dwindled group of spectators down the street and into the station, catching the first burst of rain before the skies sent down a deluge.

For all its wanton destruction, there was something dazzling about stormfall. In the lightning dancing between the clouds, in the hums and roars of thunder. In how it brought a city to absolute quiet and ordered it to catch its breath. Yet, the new strain on Kadra's face said that he saw too deeply into its workings now.

Feeling a headache coming, she strode down the hallway toward his office and collapsed into her chair, raising her head in surprise when Gaius followed her in.

"You received this." Gaius thumbed through one of the stacks of correspondence he brought Kadra daily and pulled out a ragged bit of vellum, rolled into a semblance of a scroll.

Well, shit. Only the coldest parts of the north wrote on vellum instead of parchment, so the ink would last the long journey south. She'd written several such letters to Cisuré what felt like an eternity ago.

Sarai didn't have to break the crude seal to know the sender. She quashed the urge to toss it out of the window. Chieftain Marus wasn't one to ask for help, especially from her. Her nerves flared with adrenaline as she unrolled the square. Her eyebrows rose. *Two lines.*

Arsamea is in need of aid. Do your duty.

Gaius fidgeted. "I take it you aren't fond of your hometown."

"No," she said slowly. "The only home I've found is here." *And I don't know how to protect it.*

Like his Tetrarch, Gaius didn't pry further. "You and the Magus Supreme look like you're on the edge of collapse." He peered past the office's floor-to-ceiling window to wince at the storm slickening the roads to shallow rivers. "I saw him adjust his back several times today. Has he injured it?"

She frowned. "Not that I know of, but on the gods, he hasn't so much as slept the past week."

"He'll turn the land into a fortress for you yet."

She swivelled to him in surprise.

He took the seat across her. "I've seen Magus Supreme Kadra run himself ragged for years. At first, I thought it was out of atonement for the crimes he had to overlook while amassing the power to climb up this city. But there's something heated about how he pushes himself now. Almost like desperation." Worry underpinned his voice. "Hours before the graduation, he said something about the life you should have had if it hadn't been for…" He cleared his throat.

She closed her eyes, twin waves of fondness and heartache squeezing her chest as she saw his persistent overwork in a new light. *A guilt complex the size of both moons.* "I haven't been able to convince him that he has no debt to repay."

"This may be more about your future than the past, Petitor Sarai. The Unraveling brought every thread of conflict in this land into prominence, and we've been walking a tightrope since." The vigile pondered Kadra's laden desk for a moment. "Do you believe in omens?"

Her hands curled into her palms. "I'm trying not to."

Gaius's genial features turned grave. "For months, the Elsarian Order pointed to the northern riots and beetle plague as your doing. They called you Ruin's handmaiden, plotting to deliver the land to her. But after you dispelled that at the Hearing, people are noting that there were Summonings in Ur Dinyé, many centuries before, without subsequent upheaval. What there hasn't been is someone—"

"Who returned from the dead," she finished. Fear bubbled in her chest. *How much faster will they turn on Kadra after they learn of the deaths at the horreum?* "What do you believe?"

"I have had the privilege of working for the Magus Supreme for nine great years. I have never seen him in greater danger. Politically and…" Gaius's expression fractured, and the breath caught in Sarai's throat.

He's guessed it too.

They sat in silence, confirming each other's knowledge by speaking nothing of it.

Gaius tracked her tense stare to the crackling hearth. "Omens or not, I believe the country's enemies remain quite mortal."

She rested her forehead against Kadra's desk. "Thank the gods for that. If they aren't in fact raining down omens, that is."

Problem after problem knotted in her head like the snowgrape vines she had once climbed. A clap of thunder set the windows aquiver reminding her of the way Cretus's tavern had shaken during an Arsamean snowgale. What was her hometown facing for Marus himself to have written to her? The beetle plague?

"I. Don't. Understand." She hit her head against the desk with each word, and Gaius shoved a stack of parchment under it before she could addle her brain further. "I've never heard of boil beetles infecting people let alone entire cities. Then, there's the rioting."

"Everything seems to stem from the north,' he said sadly.

She stilled. "Say that again."

He squinted in confusion as he did.

The vines in her head loosened into an ugly pattern. "*Northern* riots. A *northern* plague. The Guilds, the Order, and Aelius's puppets all have ties to actively dispossessing the north or fostering anti-northern sentiment—*Gaius*, you're brilliant! We've had our attention split between a thousand fires a day, but what if they stem from one inferno?" Her heart sank. "Something's been brewing up north."

"The odds are good, Petitor Sarai, but without a Bridger, it's at least a fifty-day journey there and back again." He sighed. "The Magus Supreme won't like it."

Neither do I. But it merited consideration. Wondering how she hadn't seen it sooner, she thanked Gaius and left the office, making for the frightened group of marketgoers huddled together and watching the storm. It was dangerous to have them so unanchored. Fear was a weapon, and the Order would wield it once they heard of the plague. She had to get ahead of them.

Sitting beside the group, she spoke quietly, "It may not feel like it, but we aren't at a loss. Everyone here fights for you daily. Help us by believing it."

She reassured them until hope returned to their eyes, then resumed her writing of the plague case's judgment. She finished as the storm dwindled to a close.

Rainwater pooled into Edessa's deep storm gutters. Petrichor scented the thick evening air, devoid of the smoke that indicated a burning home. The city was already cooling. Soon, all would be ice.

She took the long way back to Aoran Tower, avoiding busy streets that could get a deluge of questions thrown her way. Leading Caelum into the stables at the edge of Kadra's property, she unbuckled the mare's saddlery and brushed her down. *At least the rain's over with.*

A sharp clap of thunder was her only warning that she'd assumed too much too soon. Standing under the eaves, she glowered when a second bout of stormfall slammed down, wrenching out memories of the Fall. Of spiteful drops peppering her skin like arrows.

Don't think about it. She closed her eyes. *It'll pass.*

Long minutes slid by to rain's accompaniment. She was contemplating a run for it when the patter wetting her sleeves ceased. As she raised her head, her heart fluttered at the lattice of lightning doming above the stables to enclose her. Rain hissed harmlessly as it struck the shield. She turned to find Kadra leaning against the stables' doors, severe features relaxed in amusement.

"Trapped in the rain, Petitor?"

Warmth and longing uncurled in her gut. There was no one to see them, and *for once*, the world was standing still.

She moved, and his arms parted, sealed around hers even before she closed the distance. He pulled her tight against him, tension draining in a long exhale. Her breath drew in rain, citrus, and the sweat curving down the blade of his jaw. He had ridden hard to return home, to return to *her*, and it burned her resolve to ash.

"I miss you," she said fiercely. "Dearly. Deeply. I only ever see you in court or at the station." She pulled back with a raw exhale. "I'm not complaining, Kadra. You've better things to do than attend to me when the nation teeters on the edge of chaos. I never want to impose—"

He trapped her jaw in his hands, something pained flitting across his face. "What have I told you about not being an imposition?"

"You're spread thin. Gaius was just saying that your back seemed to be troubling you. I can't make demands on your time when the land's the priority."

"Have I made you feel like you aren't one?" There was a stark note to the question that had her clutching his arms.

"No!"

"Then, come to me," he ordered, drawing a thumb down her cheek. She leaned in, and his eyes gentled "Give me your burdens."

"Very well." She rose on her tiptoes to cup his face, loving how he leaned down to make up for the remaining inches. "I'm scared," she admitted, brushing her mouth over his jaw. "I've sorely missed you."

He cupped the back of her head, his other hand caressing her spine. "And?" he whispered against her lips.

"I've turned around at night, hoping you were home and that work hadn't kept you at the station. I've worried about whether you're sleeping, and how to help, and whether I'm helping." She took a jagged breath. "It's been weeks. If only I could hold you for longer than—"

His mouth covered hers with a harsh groan. Caging her against the stables' doors, he drank from her lips, drawing on the lower one and chasing the curve of her cheeks when she inhaled. Hunger streaked through her. She made a desperate sound that he devoured.

"I know, sweet Sarai," he murmured. "I've been aching too." For a man whose features rarely wore tenderness, his voice was awash with it. "You shouldn't bear the weight of the land's battles. You smile and tell me you're well, but I wonder when you'll regret this."

Her eyes flew up to his. Desire warred with grim acceptance in the black storm of his gaze. "Is that still what you see?" she whispered. "Someone who'll leave you?"

"You have every right to."

"And I won't. You needn't push yourself to exhaustion in atonement for the Fall. I would live through Sidran Tower a thousand times over just to end up here. I love you." She smiled tremulously. "Do try not to forget it."

The words always seemed to cut him at the knees. His arms shuddered around her. Sweeping her up, he rapidly covered the distance to Aoran Tower, pressing stubbled kisses to her neck.

"Wait! Is Cato—"

"Not home." He kicked open the door to the atrium and bent to her mouth.

She found his first. A soft breath, then her lips clung to his, parting, taking his tongue in and drawing away for air until she only knew the sheer joy of seeing his pupils expand, tasting the column of his corded neck between labored breaths.

Undoing the first few buttons of her tunic with one hand, he carried her into his study, then up the stairs to their chambers. He heaved a satisfied breath upon reaching the bed. She laughed at his haste, and his eyes went liquid.

"I missed you too." His thumb traced the corner of her mouth then made a slow foray past her lips.

Need bloomed in her core. "Show me."

His eyes darkened when she stepped back and discarded her tunic. Black and gold pooled by the bed before he blanketed her on it. Then, it was just the press of wet skin against skin. Pulses straining in yearning to draw even closer.

Hers was a feral devotion, all the more ravenous for the wait. She gloried at his harsh breaths when she rolled her hips into his as he disrobed with sleek efficiency. Nothing came close to the way he made her feel. Safe, protected, known. Cherished.

Removing her armilla, she undid the illusion over her skin. Kadra followed the progress of her reappearing scars with his mouth. A kiss behind her ear, a taste of her clavicle. A surge of affection squeezed her heart. She locked her legs around his waist and rolled them over. He obliged with a wicked grin, reaching for her when she nuzzled her way down his throat, past his chest. A hiss erupted through his clenched teeth when she licked over the damp head of his cock.

"*Weeks* without you." He knotted a hand in her hair. "How badly do you want me?"

She answered by taking the thick length of him deeper, relishing the way he spat her name when she reached his base.

"*Fuck.*" A harsh sound of pleasure ripped from him when she flattened her tongue, tasting salt and musk and him.

There he is. The undone god beneath the man of ice and seething control. This was the only time he ever lost control, and gods, she loved seeing him aflame. He stroked her cheek, giving her a second to breathe before shuttling into her throat. Lips stretched around his girth, she should have felt achingly vulnerable, but he looked the supplicant, jaw tight, hard grunts punctuating his thrusts, hands tightening on the back of her head.

"Beautiful." He ground out, caressing her flushed jaw. "Come here."

She hollowed her cheeks in playful refusal and watched a wild gleam heat his eyes. The next second, she found herself pulled off her prize and him heavy-lidded and hungry above her. His breath came fast as he traced his own path down her body, drawing her breasts into his mouth and nuzzling her navel, taking his time despite her impassioned pleas. Pressing her hips down, he trailed his fingers through her sensitive, slick core. A needy sound left her when he breached her with two fingers and curled them into her, and it seemed to turn him feral.

Holding her gaze with smoldering eyes, he hoisted her thighs over his shoulders and made a slow, deliberate foray into her with his tongue. Her back arched off the bed when he did it again, tasting her in unhurried strokes. He made love to her core, as relentless in bed as he was in life.

Pleasure blurred her vision and transported them to a fracture in time that was entirely their own. Her heels dug into his back as darts of lightning coiled through her. The gods, the Saints, the Wretched, she invoked them all, pleading, gripping the thick silk of his hair when the movements of his tongue sped, angling right where she needed it. She throbbed to the tune of her pulse and his fingers, and still craved more.

"Kadra, *please*!"

He licked a stripe up her core before spearing her with his fingers again. Lust painted him with a luminous flush, a rare teasing light in his gaze. "Need me that badly?"

"Badly," she hoarsely agreed.

Rising up her body, he caught her lower lip between his teeth. "Why's that, hmm?"

She twined her fingers with his. "Likely because I love you."

A hoarse breath sawed from him. He rested his forehead against hers. "Say that again."

"I love you," she whispered.

The severe planes of his face didn't alter, but his cavernous eyes glowed. "I'm yours." A rough mating with her mouth, then a guttural order. "Spread for me. "

Passion darkened his cheekbones when she did. One hand angled her thighs higher, the other palm-down by her head. She whimpered when the head of his cock slid against her in a long stroke. His resulting smile should have been illegal.

"Take me in." He reared above her, part desire, part darkness, and all power.

Dazed, she reached between them to press him against her entrance, holding his stormy gaze as he pushed in.

"That's it, sweet girl. Show me how much you missed me," he growled, shuddering when he buried himself to the hilt. Cupping her face, he watched her breath hitch at how full she was.

Sweat dripped down his jaw when he pulled out and slowly thrust back in, dipping his head to draw her breasts into his mouth. There were nights when he tormented her for hours with ruthless patience, seating her on his lap and rocking into her while teasing at where they were joined. She hooked the thigh he held higher over his hips and tried to curl deeper.

A low laugh rumbled through him, before he slammed back in. *Hard.* Her mouth opened on a scream of ecstasy, heat fracturing between the slap of their bodies as though he had summoned lightning. He drank her cries, curved a hand around her throat and pressed with breathtaking tenderness, tilting her chin down and demanding that she watch him plunge deep.

She couldn't think; her voice was raw, nerve endings afire. She tasted his earlobe, mouth, every part of him she could reach, wordless but for his name. His muscled shoulders bunched, hips hammering into her with agonized need. Sparks flared at the edge of her vision, magic escaping him as he lost himself.

Her body tightened around his with impending release, and he bit the curve of her neck with a raw moan, hauling her closer to take her more deeply. A fierce kiss, and his hand on her throat cut off her breath. She flew over the edge with a scream. Her body twisted, scattered, inundated with fierce wave upon wave of pleasure. A base, thick sound tore from him as he spasmed, thrusting in deep, desperate strokes as wet heat filled her.

"*Fuck*, take it all, Sarai." He rumbled a string of filthy praise, shuddering into her, rubbing his stubbled cheek against her hair. His heartbeat slammed against her skin. Boneless, she breathed to it, protesting when he withdrew to clean her.

A generous lover, he was quiet with his affection and had only said that he loved her once, after the Unraveling. Yet, she felt it in the brush of his lips against her temples and the arms that always banded around her in sleep.

"That," she pronounced, "was a first. I didn't think the extremely proper Magus Supreme Kadra ravished women before nightfall."

He raised an eyebrow drolly, looking more relaxed than he had in months. "I asked you to live with me after knowing you for a day. Propriety isn't one of my strengths."

She turned into his neck with a laugh. "Are you certain you aren't needed to manage the storm?"

"No, this is the last of it. Let's take a few hours."

"Do you think the country'll be standing when we wake?"

"There's a fair chance." He cradled her and loosed a gravelly sigh of contentment when she wrapped an arm around his waist.

She allowed the tension and fear of the past few months to slip through her fingers like nightmares. And when sleep found their entwined figures within Aoran Tower, they succumbed peacefully.

6
A BITTER DANCE

Eleven years ago, a month before escape

In truth, he did not understand why he had to kill the man.

Blood slid down the walls of the stone cell where Noceo had just forced one of their former workers to saw off his own wrist. The man screamed at the mangled stump, pleading for mercy.

It was a foolish crime to skim from Clan Kader's warehouse stock of blazeleaf rolls and attempt to distribute it on Komis's streets for cheaper prices than the Clan's. It was even more foolish to do so while bragging that Clanlord Clevsin was too much in his dotage to find out.

The man had likely expected that his fellow workers and the street rats to whom he'd sold would keep his secret. But solidarity among the captive and the impoverished was a pretty myth. Everyone stood equal before greed. The man had been turned in by both groups within a week.

Still Drenevan believed the loss of a hand sufficed, in addition to the offending tongue if Clevsin were so inclined. To splay his entrails over the warehouse seemed unnecessarily taxing.

Yet, here he was.

"Get him upstairs," Clevsin coolly ordered Noceo. "Make them all watch."

Inclining his head, Noceo directed his voice to Coerce the man, who lurched to his feet and sped down the short hallway toward the stairs that would take him from the holding pen underneath the Clan's blazeleaf warehouses to the aboveground production facility where leaves were cured, sorted, and rolled. His compatriots in the other cells were already dead. No one lasted long enough to stay there indefinitely.

Dalvia wrung her hands. "Clanlord, do you wish for me to tidy the cell?" She indicated the bloodstained walls with a trembling finger.

Drenevan exchanged a glance with Noceo. The girl kept giving herself away.

The grooves bordering Clevsin's lips pulled back in a chilling smile. "Trying to hide again, Clandaughter?"

She flinched. "No, Clanlord."

He tsked. "Such unbecoming behavior in a woman. Lying." His smile held a black victory. "You will present yourself afterward for punishment."

Dalvia's features crumbled for a hair's breadth before she bowed and tottered upstairs. Drenevan's back throbbed as he followed her unsteady gait. The oppressive damp down here was hell on his bones. By the way his brother was subtly rotating his wrists, his injuries were acting up too.

The scent of blazeleaf struck in a rush as he emerged on the landing. Theirs was the largest illegal warehouse in the country with over eight hundred workers, all forcibly confined to the compound, with no hope but to toil. He passed workers sorting blazeleaf by size, color, and quality into steel pans. Others cut and moistened the leaves in preparation for steaming to make them more pliable.

"An approximation of life," Clevsin had informed him while breaking his spine again last week for failing to bring in more workers. *"Someday, you will hold all power here, Drenevan. But it is not yet that day."*

It never would be if his plan with Noceo succeeded.

They walked past the steel threshing pans for a final sort of the leaves, then the re-drying ovens that set the leaves' moisture content close to the necessary twelve percent, and the cylindrical irons that pressed and rolled the cured product into wrappings of flavorless bemizan leaves for smoking.

The warehouse exit loomed ahead, wagon tracks gouged into the snow beyond the parted doors. A last glimpse of unattainable freedom. Drenevan's victim walked with stuttered desperation to the stage of his demise and halted at a word from Noceo. His brother turned to the crowd, forehead wrinkled in strain as he yelled at full Coercive strength.

"*Watch.*"

The workers halted in their tracks and turned as one toward the condemned man. Terror brewed behind their glazed eyes, forced to stay open. Noceo's mouth fell shut. Sweat trickled down his temples. He had reached his limit.

Drenevan unsheathed his knife before Clevsin could note the way his brother had sagged against a crate of product. It was always messier with knives, but a sword risked sending the man to Death too early. One of the first breaks in Drenevan's back had been for doing just that.

Moonlight slid down metal. And Drenevan got to work.

Crimson dotted, then sprayed the warehouse floor. Rivulets ran down his knife like a smile through red teeth. First the digits, then the tongue. He belonged to this bitter dance, most at home within that frozen second between a blade and its meeting place. He notched into the stomach, then lower. The long strings of the man's body and waste came from his gut in a slippery ribbon. His eyes rolled back in his head, going into traumatic shock. Death's arrival was imminent.

Ah. Drenevan hid a flinch. *Clevsin won't be happy.*

Pain burst across his back as he tried to make the kill pleasing. Shattering the man's sternum, he kicked the gaping torso over to the workers, hoping it would suffice. The screams, swoons, and loud retching told him it had. The hand Noceo had seemingly casually placed against a crate quivered. Dalvia looked away, paler than the snow blanketing the Drust Mountains.

Monster, their eyes said. *Monster.*

He found Clevsin's eyes and knew it still wasn't enough. Menace bled from his father in waves that rivaled the Chaboras River at high tide before he stalked off, and Drenevan knew it would be him receiving punishment before Dalvia. He wiped his knife on his robes. Crimson bled into gray-green.

Noceo eyed him warily before approaching. "He isn't pleased."

"I slashed the gut too soon."

His brother shivered. "You really don't feel anything afterward?"

"He shouldn't have had to die." Drenevan watched Dalvia hesitantly approach the wreckage of the man's body. Her retching rose above the sounds of the workers trying to go on with their day after another reminder of how disposable they were.

"Is that it?" his brother asked hesitantly. "You don't feel revolted or angry at having to do it?"

Drenevan wondered what purpose that would serve. Blood had never disgusted him, and anger was best saved for the day he'd have the power to act on it. He still had none. "Someday, afterward," he used the synonym that referred to their plan of escape, "I think I'll feel anger. Maybe a lot of it."

"Me too." Silence stretched comfortably between them. "What do you want, afterward?"

Drenevan thought about that a moment. "A drink, maybe." He had only recently traded the mild languor of blazeleaf for the deeper oblivion of alcohol.

Noceo let out a breath that could have been tinged with relief. He tilted his head to the exit. "Do you think Clevsin will let me out for an hour? I wouldn't mind seeing Parvine again."

His brother's infatuation with the Poxtan girl evidently hadn't dimmed. "He'll be distracted with me," Drenevan noted. His back tensed, knowing what it was about to face. "Ask him once he starts."

Something that could have been a flash of sympathy lit his brother's eyes before he left. Drenevan followed, their paths diverging at the house where his punishment waited.

What did he want? The question chafed at him through the shattering of a vertebra at Clevsin's hands and its careless half mending by a healer doing precisely as they were told. It pelted him through dinner where Dalvia spilled her soup all over herself, by trembling when their elbows touched. The answer wasn't love. It could be power, but even that rung partially false.

Hours later, curled on the floor of his room, teeth ground in pain, he thought he might have it.

It might be nice to be understood.

With that settled, he took a deep draw of his blazeleaf roll and drank some more filched wine.

Sleep came easy after that.

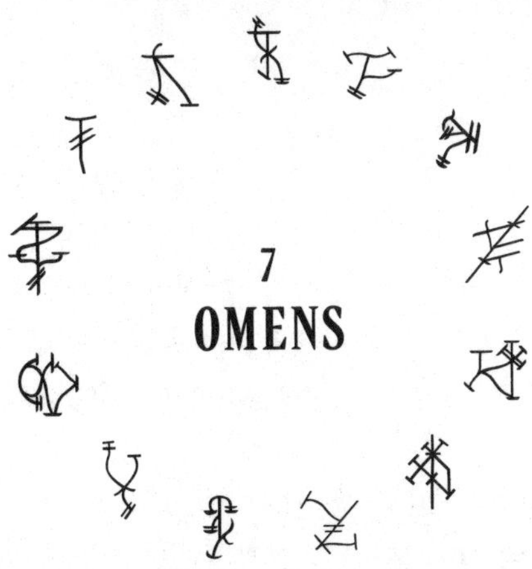

7
OMENS

Whose dream had that been? Whose life had she walked in for a few bitter hours?

Sarai opened her eyes to darkness and the echoes of a man being butchered on a warehouse floor. Names, faces, they eluded her now, yet the anguish behind her breastbone felt alive.

Rubbing her aching sternum, she sat up and stilled at the cool stone under her hands. *Tile?* Sconces flared one by one in a ring around the ballroom and she *knew*. These walls, the hit of this tile against her cheekbones, all of it indelible. Yet, panic was an echo, and her mind too sluggish to scream.

A burst of wind forced the unlatched balcony door open, knocking it into an object atop a tablecloth on the floor. It twitched with an agonized moan, and she knew even before she approached the figure, knew the dark stains spreading from her even before she bent toward the badly wounded girl on the ballroom at the top of Sidran Tower.

Her past self stared back, pulling breath through bleeding lips. A laceration split her face horizontally above her mouth, continuing behind her ears. *Tullus's work.* Her hair had been shorn by lightning, chunks stuck to her scalp. Brown eyes not gold. Too young to have known this.

Sarai's throat worked. "This isn't real," she whispered. "We aren't here anymore."

"We aren't?" A voice of gurgled blood.

"No, I promise—"

"But what if you're wrong?" Her younger self sat up in an eerie rush and pinned her with milky-white eyes. Her voice distorted to a raspy hiss, crimson slithering from her wounds. "What if we never left Sidran Tower? What if we've been dreaming and screaming all along?"

Panic struck Sarai like a knife when blood dripped from her younger self's mouth.

Shaking, she stumbled back when the girl reached for her, growing cold when she chased her with unearthly speed. Wind sent the balcony door open again, and Sarai darted through, slamming it behind her. She stilled when the door vanished, her hands closing on nothing.

This can't be real. Her chest tightened with panic when pinching herself did nothing. *Why am I here?*

She froze at a footstep behind her, turning in slow degrees and knowing what she would find even before white and silver robes entered the corner of her vision. A too-wide grin split his face like a scar.

"What a shame." Rot carved chunks from Aelius's cheeks. "A reckoning has followed in your wake. The gods have spoken and called for our end. The sky itself will laugh."

She tottered back when he advanced, but the balcony railing behind her felt all too solid, the wind all too eager to howl past her falling body.

What if we never left Sidran Tower? Another step. *What if we've been here all along?*

She screamed.

"*Sarai.* Look at me." Hands cupped her face. "Open your eyes. I have you."

Reality struck in a garbled rush. She woke to her frantic gasps, the last note of a scream still hanging in the air. Sitting up, she let out a ragged sound at finding Kadra's grim features above her.

"Breathe—" He broke off when she hugged him hard.

"Wisdom's teeth, I've never had a nightmare like that," she mumbled into his sweat-slick skin. "I'm sorry for startling you."

"You never need to apologize." Brow lined with worry, he held her while her pulse slowed its frantic drumbeat, reluctant to allow her out of bed until she insisted that she was well.

She related what she remembered of the dream while they bathed and tucked into the meal Cato had left atop Kadra's desk. "Sidran Tower was bad enough, but I felt like I saw someone else's dream before then." She pressed a mug of tea to her throbbing forehead. "Likely something borne of a long workday, but Elsar only know how I conjured up such explicit details of illegal blazeleaf production."

A muscle worked in Kadra's jaw. "Did what you see trouble you?"

Acid burned up her throat at the blurry memory of the boy's smooth knifework. And yet, that had been as much a performance as murder. She couldn't remember what he looked like, but she'd caught the resigned glance he'd given his father, and his silent acceptance of his siblings' fear. She'd seen the same loneliness in Kadra before they had become lovers.

His hard face was oddly closed when she raised her eyes. "I don't know if I was afraid of him or *for* him," she confessed. "He seemed so young, and it looked like he had little choice. But someone like that could turn monstrous, if the wrong cause got its claws in him." She thought of Aelius's defenders and the Inquisitors of the Elsarian Order. "Do you think people deserve the chance to change?"

Something utterly bleak swam in the frozen depths of Kadra's eyes. It was a long moment before he spoke. "They might not."

Both dreams didn't leave her mind throughout their descent from the Academiae's citadel and into Edessa. Her Tetrarch was equally, strangely somber, broad shoulders tensed under some new strain. They'd just entered his Quarter when he exhaled heavily.

"Sarai–" He broke off at a sharp scream down the road.

Feet drummed against cobblestone coupled with the staccato snap of doors being flung open. Dawn was still new to the horizon, bleary-eyed folk roused by the ruckus and emerging from their front doors with confusion. Riding toward the source of the sound, she stilled at the pandemonium flooding the streets.

Throngs jostled each other, running from an unknown evil. Others vomited onto the road, trembling fingers pressed to their temples.

"Magus Supreme Kadra!" one wailed upon spotting him. "The plague! It's here!"

She went cold, urging her mare into a gallop. Frightened faces blurred; the screaming rose in volume as they neared the marketplace in which she had adjudicated with Kadra only yesterday afternoon. Pale-faced and trembling, his vigiles had formed a wall around it, but there was no hiding what lay within.

Corpses. Limbs splayed, eyes crusted with whitesleep, mouths agape in variations of agony. Seated, clustered, as though awaiting Kadra's judgment, they were frozen dolls draped in crimson. And on every face, the same circular wax seal–like welts, and a seething wave of glistening creatures, gnawing endlessly into exposed flesh.

Time seemed to ebb slowly as the small lake of blood traversing through snow dripped onto the road, patterned with equally scarlet boil beetles. Every sound deepened, heightened.

A rough rustle of fabric as she and Kadra dismounted. Dull shrieks echoing upon their entry into the marketplace. Her hoarse exhale fogging out when his irises seemed to grow impossibly wider, turning his piercing eyes into something unrecognizable, *other*.

What do you see? Fear sank fangs into her bones, pulling her from the stupor. She stepped in front of him to break his line of sight and pretended not to notice his startled blink.

Bile butted the back of her throat when a larva squirmed out of a man's ear and fell into a clump of snow. Barely a day ago, she'd told the marketgoers here not to worry. She'd assured that godsdamned agromagus that all would be well. Now, here they were, overrun with beetles. *How?*

She dimly heard Gaius report that he had confirmed with the magi on the city walls that no one had seen a beetle swarm approach. That left only one other explanation: infectees, like Lucanus, had brought them into the city.

"We've a few survivors, but they're badly infected." He indicated a cluster at the back of the marketplace that she hadn't noticed amid the horror of the corpses. "They seem to have taken a few whitesleep rubs too many. Couldn't get much sense out of them."

Kadra's eerily blank gaze drifted over to consider the group.

"I'll go to them," she forced out before he spoke. If anyone noticed what she and Gaius already had, then the land would implode.

"There are beetles *everywhere*." Gaius's voice quaked. "Best to wait for a healer, or this could take you too."

"I'll be careful. They could die before a healer arrives, and we'll have no answers then." She worriedly sought Kadra's eyes and loosed a breath upon finding them back to their knife-sharp intensity.

A crease formed in his brow when she strode past him to the infected survivors. She felt the weight of his stare between her shoulder blades and wondered if she should have admitted that she knew of what kept distracting him or asked why he'd said nothing for eight months. But right now, it was a crisis too many.

Ignoring the blood-flecked ground and its miasma of rot, she knelt beside the snow-covered figures, rocking back and forth in the throes of visible agony.

"What happened here?" she whispered.

Only one woman turned to her. Sarai stilled, recognizing the plaintiff from the plague case. Welts patterned Junia's face, her eyes crusted with remnants of whitesleep powder. "Our hourglass runs low. A reckoning has followed in your wake." Her pupils engorged to swallow her irises. "The sky *laughs* at us all."

Sarai's hands quivered even worse at the familiar words. Dream-Aelius, the horreum's dying Guildswoman, and now Junia all saying the same thing. "What sort of reckoning?"

"*Alllllll* the lightning. And so many *eyes*." Vessels burst in Junia's own scleras.

"Gaius, she needs a healer!" Sarai yelled.

Across the marketplace, he spread his hands with a helpless look at the gray-cloaked group retching into the snow and looking in need of medical aid themselves.

"It was just a bit of whitesleep," Junia whispered in a burst of clarity. "Why did it come to this?" She dissolved into a fit of laughter.

Numb, Sarai tottered upright. Blue robes billowed at the corner of her eye, and her teeth clenched at the Cleric elbowing his way toward the tableau while proselytizing to an ever-growing audience about the need for an exorcism of a *certain* servant of Ruin.

Realization coalesced into quiet, bitter clarity. *Omens*. The Order would scream it now, and the public would believe it. A land that had been threatening to collapse under the weight of its infighting could do so tomorrow. And she didn't know if they were wrong.

Didn't you bring this on us, northerner? A reckoning has followed in your wake. The gods have spoken and call for our end. The sky itself will laugh.

Why were the afflicted all saying that this was her fault?

Anguish and doubt clawed at her gut. She barely registered Cassandane and Anek's arrival, or Harion vomiting over his robes and horse. She walked to the edge of the marketplace, seeing the hawk-eyed figure there too late to avoid her.

Plague, riots. Omens.

Inquisitor Verentia gave her a wary glance. "Petitor Sarai."

So, it's begun. "I am no servant of Ruin, Inquisitor."

The woman splayed a hand toward the death around them. "The gods say otherwise." She indicated someone in a gray-green uniform at her side. "Clanlady Dalvia Am Semni from Komis. She's been monitoring the spread of the boil beetle plague and just arrived by Bridger. Her Institute has been leading efforts to combat this."

Clan Am Semni. Along with Clan Kader, they were the last extant Clans from Ur Dinyé's monarchical days. She hadn't heard much of them unlike the powerful, infamous, and now-defunct Kaders.

"A pleasure. I'm sorry we've had to meet under these circumstances—" Sarai froze mid-recitation. The woman was *stunning.* A sheet of white-blond hair fell to her shoulders, contrasting sharply with her dark eyebrows and hair. Light seemed to weave through the strands and reflect around her. The effect was both ethereal and eerie.

Yards away, Anek's jaw hung by their knees as they darted fascinated glances at her in between nodding at Cassandane and Kadra, whose back faced them.

Sarai recovered, offering a smile that drooped at the edges. "Is there nothing in the north that can stop this?"

"One can't till a barren field for grain, Petitor Sarai." Dalvia's voice was surprisingly timorous. Her dark eyes met and fell from Sarai's like someone unused to being perceived and discomfited by it. "The capital has everything. So, I thought it might have hope too."

The gentle way she said it forced a ragged breath from Sarai. "The south is greedy with its hope, Clanlady. Don't let *them* cheat you out of a high price." She cast Verentia a sidelong glance and left, flinching only slightly when the Inquisitor called after her.

"One among us has indeed made an ill-fated bargain, and it isn't the Order!"

The now-raging Cleric clearly believed the same.

"Make no mistake this country faces a war from within. The ungodly have wrested power from the righteous." He furiously pointed at Kadra. "*We* innocents pay the price. Despite the Order attempts at conversion, the north has always mocked our devotion to the Elsar. Now, they've sent Pestilence herself to decimate us! A plague? No. This is *evil* work. Our brethren have been left madness-struck!" The Cleric swallowed and turned pained eyes onto the crowd.

If the gods ever toss him aside, the stage'll take him. Her nails dug into her clenched palms.

"We never saw such turmoil under Tetrarchs Aelius and Tullus. These usurpers have tried to convince us of their right to rule, but they cannot veil the divine truth. We have strayed from goodness. Only the High Elsar, in their infinite love, can save us," the Cleric insisted. "And all they ask is that we reject the Dark Elsar. That we destroy those who threaten the natural order and sow division, distraction, and debris in our great country. Our enemies will be our neighbors and countrymen, but if they can purge *two* Tetrarchs, we can purge them!"

She recoiled when cheers rang from the crowd and burgeoned into a battle cry. Her tongue froze to the roof to her mouth, ice water sluicing in her arteries as she beheld a country in freefall. This would spark civil war, and there was nothing she could do. She had no answers, no cure. Only the ugly certainty that the Cleric had one thing right.

This was no plague.

"Boil beetles alone don't explain this," a voice confirmed behind her.

Silvus seized her shoulder in a steadying grip when she started and slipped on a patch of ice. She twisted out of it, and his silver eyes followed the motion with mild curiosity.

"Do you travel in packs?" she asked tightly with a glance at Verentia and the warmongering Cleric.

Masked as usual, he tilted his head. "A bitter feeling, isn't it? Powerlessness."

"What would you know of powerlessness?" she bit out with more venom than she'd intended.

"You might be surprised."

She closed her eyes at the even way he said it. *Right. He's a northerner too.* Shame stifled her anger. "I'm sorry." She registered his start of surprise. "I shouldn't have jumped to conclusions. Ideological differences aside, it can't have been easy to climb up the Order."

"It wasn't." An air of bafflement laced his brief pause as though he'd surprised himself by admitting it. "Eleven years ago, I lost everything. I had no talent at lightning magic, and the Academiae had no place for me without coin. The Order was my best chance at power."

She watched the Cleric spew vitriol. "Has it been worth it?"

"It will be."

"Then, I hope the knowledge warms you at night when the land goes to shit." She made to stalk past Silvus, but he cut into her path. She halted a handspan away, glaring up at his strangely taut features.

"So, you resent my choices and not me," he mused.

"I don't know you well enough to resent."

"You don't know them, and you care about their deaths." Silvus considered the blood-soaked marketplace. "Why?"

She stared. "Who wouldn't?"

He dipped his head, eyes slitting in disbelief. "Do you see yourself as benevolent, Petitor Sarai? Any aspirations to Sainthood?"

Anger gathered in her throat. "Only to basic decency, though I suppose the Order wouldn't understand."

"Oh, I understand a savior complex when I see it," he murmured. "Childhood neglect, a hunger to fix chaos and a delusion that love is earned through sacrifice. The afflicted give endlessly, usually to their own detriment." He transferred his attention to the mob like she was no longer worthy of it. "Petitor Sarai, you're tragically boring."

Every arrow found its mark. Pierced through, she swallowed, swamped by a fury so all-encompassing that her vision swam crimson. "Do you have *nothing* better to do–"

"I don't. Who are you saving?" He languidly stepped forward, edging her boot with his. She stumbled back. "It isn't yourself–half the country despises you. It isn't the south, given the madness you've brought here, and it *certo* isn't the north, which you've scarcely glanced at since becoming Petitor."

"I didn't bring *anything* here! And I've corresponded with the coalition of northern Praetors—"

"Every month? Every two months?" His smile widened when she ground her teeth. "Without a Bridger, word takes much too long to travel across the country. You barely catch up to a northern locale's going-ons in one letter before you hear of a new crisis in the next. You have no understanding of what the north even faces now. *Who are you saving?*"

"*Everyone* I can!" she spat. "Can you say the same?"

"Why should I? You fought two Tetrarchs, a Guild, and the Order and got this in thanks." Silvus indicated the riotous crowd.

"People like you are *exactly* why Aelius thrived for so long."

Pale eyes traversed the length of her shaking frame and lit with what looked oddly like elation. "Others like him will rise. And you'll be just as powerless when they do. Unless..."

"Unless?" she echoed, rage evaporating into scorn. Her pulse slowed its slamming against her ribs. "Unless I ally with the Order? Now, *that's* boring, Inquisitor."

A frisson of fury on his veiled face. "We needn't be enemies. Abandon your Magus Supreme, or you won't survive what's coming."

Dread arced through her. "So, the Order plans on targeting Kadra." *If they find out that he's*—she shoved the thought away. "Thank you for the warning. He'll appreciate it."

Silvus's face gained a dangerous edge. "He's had such a stroke of luck, hasn't he?" The words formed a strangely dulcet hiss as though he was struggling to modulate his voice behind that veil. "He merely had to die for you to trust him implicitly. Did he fuck you hard enough into believing that you know him?"

Air fled her in a rush. She willed herself into blank composure. "I think I'd prefer that we be enemies, Inquisitor, seeing how you treat prospective allies."

"I thought truth was your only task," he reminded her of their argument in the Academiae's chapel. "Did you want it sugarcoated?"

A bite of pain in her palm told her that her nails had drawn blood. Without releasing his stare, she wiped it over *zosta* on her armilla and waited.

He wet his lips behind the veil. "You don't know him. You know nothing of his secrets."

True. She swallowed. "And you do?"

"You…" he prowled forward and paused when she didn't recoil this time, "might be surprised."

An unhappy suspicion coalesced into clarity. "What grudge do you have against him?"

"You've greater concerns than that." His shoulder-length black hair fluttered in the wind, half-pulled off his face with a few loose strands to soften his angular cheekbones. He looked around Kadra's age. "Boil beetles alone can't cause this widespread madness." He tilted his head to the raving survivors now being piled onto wagons. "I hear they were largely whitesleep users, but that won't aid you either. No drugmaker worth their salt aims to kill their clientele. And they're all spouting the same thing."

"I know." Faces boiled red around them. Voices followed the war cry led by the elated Cleric. She could almost feel her hands clinging to the edge of a cliff. She no longer had the strength for anger. "Did you or the Order cause any of this?"

He cut her a startled glance before pity smoothed his brow. "No."

True.

"But it is to our advantage." He departed from her line of sight to stand at her shoulder, surveying the chaos. "A crumbling country needs a scapegoat. Don't let them take you." He tsked at the people shoving at the vigiles guarding the site of the massacre as Kadra and Cassandane began torching every beetle in sight with lightning. "Offer up the Magus Supreme instead."

She let silence speak for her.

"I won't warn you again." His diction altered, northern accent coming to the forefront, and something almost hypnotic underlying the words. "I understand your powerlessness, but I won't excuse your stupidity. Use that saviour complex on yourself, Petitor Sarai. No one else will save you, and what's the world to do if even you won't?"

He swept past her and into the crowd. It was almost a relief. She had no rebuttal. She'd barely been able to keep track of the blows.

At least that is two suspects eliminated. He and the Order–to his knowledge, at least–weren't behind this string of deaths. Which left only one place with answers.

Across the blood-streaked marketplace, the Tetrarchy had vanished inside a makeshift tent. *Good.* What she needed to do had solidified over the last half hour. And it cut to the bone.

She approached Gaius. "How many vigiles do you trust to undertake a fifty-day journey?"

He caught her meaning and smiled sadly. "A few, Petitor Sarai. Shall I tell them to be ready?"

"Please do." Her throat drew tight. "If Kadra asks for me, tell him that there was something I needed from Aoran Tower," she managed a watery smile. "It isn't a lie, so he won't be able to tell."

Gaius bowed gravely. "Please be very careful, Petitor Sarai. Kadra just may raze the land should anything happen to you."

She turned before the tear clinging to her lashes could fall. Then, she headed to Aoran Tower to pack.

Cato was a genial man most days, iron-gray hair brushed back and deep smile lines on either side of his mouth, but he looked practically apoplectic silhouetted in the doorway to Kadra's bedroom.

"Wrath's blade, you can't believe the rumors that this is your fault?" He stormed in as she shoved a tunic into her satchel with too much force. "Don't let them drive you out of town! Fight back–" He caught sight of her face, and his eyes widened.

Her throat seemed to have swollen shut. "I *am* fighting," she croaked. "The Order's about to wreak havoc with this, Cato. Only the north has answers." *And I don't know what to do if it doesn't.* She pressed her lips together, knowing that she'd sob if she said it.

Cato leaned against the doorframe. "Drenevan won't like it."

"He's needed here." She secured her satchel and fought the burning behind her eyes. *Twenty-five days there. Twenty-five back. But I can't protect him from here.*

"Cato, you're an Illusionist, aren't you? A strong one?"

He nodded. Concern lined his kindly face.

"Watch over him. There's something greater than us at work here, and it might be targeting him." She slung her packed satchel across her body. "Please don't let him take any risks."

"Oh, my dear." He gathered her in for a hug, and she almost bawled at the fatherly way he patted her head. "He'll be alright. He's weathered a lot, our Drenevan."

But this is new, and it isn't the only battle he's fighting. Holding herself together, she hugged Cato back and left.

Mounting Caelum, she glanced back, gripping Kadra's key as the gate swung shut. One last glimpse at the black tower and its obsidian pillars. Her heart climbed up her throat and stuck her in an aching mass. Then, she rode to a marketplace of corpses.

8
NORTHWARD

Healers, vigiles, and loved ones patterned the snow-powdered ground with bloodstained steps in a dance of desperation and defeat.

Sarai strode quickly toward the makeshift tent the Tetrarchy had set up around a table in the marketplace. Scorched beetle corpses crunched under her feet. The surrounding mob spewed accusations and threats as she passed, but all that penetrated was the bitter knowledge that she had no right to offer anyone consolation. She had no answers, and Death had set her free twice and released Kadra from the afterlife's grasp. What right did she have to kneel among the grieving and tell them that she *understood*?

Some yards from the tent, Anek folded their arms while arguing with a cloaked woman. "I understand, but the Tetrarchy is presently preoccupied." Catching Sarai's eye, they wearily nodded in greeting.

"Temperance give me strength. I have information they need!" the woman snapped in a distinct northern accent, vowels elongated in comparison to Arsamea's softer ones.

A Komis accent, just like Clanlady Dalvia. Sarai thought back to the other woman's quiet desperation. "Is this about the plague?"

Anek's conversant shoved back the hood of her birrus with a frustrated grunt. Wary eyes stared back at her from a heart-shaped face framed by short, dark hair. She looked around the same age as them. Anek let out a garbled sound, eyes climbing up all six feet of her, then down again. Something that looked like worship slackened their jaw.

Sarai hid a laugh. *Cassandane has competition.*

"Petitor Sarai." She bowed. "I'm Méherre, a Bridger. Weeks ago, I was hired to Bridge some asshole noble named Lucanus to Edessa, who certainly didn't inform me that he was infected with the same plague that's decimated my city. I just heard that he's caused an outbreak. Let me *help*."

Recovering, Anek subtly angled their armilla to show Sarai *zosta*'s glint. They'd been Examining Méherre. "Bridger make excellent assassins," they muttered under their breath before turning to the woman. "Why do you want to help us when Edessa has been no friend to the north?"

"Is anyone?" Méherre threw up her hands. "Yes, I abhor the Tetrarchy's focus on the south and Edessa to the exclusion of *everything* else. But all of us could perish at this rate. My city, Komis, has been sealed to outsiders because of the beetle plague. None are allowed in save by the Praetor's order. Our time is running out. We need help!"

Our hourglass runs low. A reckoning has followed in your wake. Sarai flinched when Junia's words reared in her head.

Méherre glowered at their silence. "If you think that I'm trying to harm the Tetrarchy, let me swear here and now that I have no intention of hurting them or either of you. The north has little respect for you lot, but killing you does not serve my purposes."

Anek's defeated breath said that she was telling the truth. "We could use your aid," they admitted. "We're equally at a loss."

Méherre's expression fractured. "A *loss* is twenty thousand bodies atop a pyre outside city walls, Petitor Anek. Not a handful of privileged lives and people who scream of omens in every other breath."

Sarai went cold. *Twenty thousand dead in the north?* "We didn't know."

Méherre's sidelong glance said that she doubted that the Tetrarchy would have cared even if they had.

"A loss is a loss, regardless of number," Anek said pragmatically, unblocking the way to the tent. They squinted at Sarai. "Come to think of it, why are you dressed like that?"

"You'll see." Sarai sighed as they entered the tent, Méherre in tow.

All three Tetrarchs clustered around a map of Ur Dinyé, ink blots marking the spread of plague. An oil lamp burned at the center.

"There she is, our very own envoy of Ruin." Harion drawled. "Any reason you're killing us all?"

"Pure irritation. Watch out. You're next." Anek reared back with a sniff. "You've still got vomit on your robes by the way."

Kadra's gaze fell on Sarai and stilled. The ink pen in his hands fell to the ground. Silence settled over the cramped space as everyone within registered that she was dressed for travel.

"I'm going north," she said quietly to Méherre's start of surprise. "We've northern riots and a northern plague that's somehow made it past our city walls without any of the magi seeing a swarm. Edessa has enemies but no answers." She didn't have every thread comprising this knot, but those she held hissed of danger. "We need information before the Order wreaks havoc, and as a northerner, I have the best chance at investigating what's been happening there."

A divot formed between Cassandane's eyebrows. She'd abandoned her crimson robes as though sick of the colour and sported a simple gray dressing gown. "It's a long journey."

"Not anymore." Anek indicated Méherre and filled everyone in. "I've Examined her. She can be trusted."

Cassandane acknowledged the Bridger with a grateful nod. "Nevertheless, you could both be infected and then…" She gestured helplessly to the corpses that were still being removed from the marketplace.

Sarai drew the tent's fabric shut. "I don't think that's a result of plague." A boulder sank into her gut as she dared voice the theory that had brewed in her mind all morning. "It's murder."

Harion cast her an exasperated look. "Not everything is a fucking conspiracy. We've a godsdamned carpet of dead boil beetles outside. *Certo*, it's them."

"Beetles alone don't explain any of this! I was," she sighed, knowing that she was giving him more fodder for abuse, "a snowgrape harvester as a child. I've seen boil beetles in infected animals, and they looked *nothing* like what's outside. And there wasn't a single beetle at the Grains Guild's horreum, was there?" She exhaled when his mouth snapped shut. "I examined one of the bodies there, and the heart and brain were practically liquid. No parasite would kill its host so quickly. These are serial killings. We just don't know by whom or *how*."

"The whitesleep," Kadra reminded softly.

She had avoided looking at him all this while. Risking a glance, she felt the ache in her throat worsen at his taut temples and grim eyes, when he'd looked almost carefree last night.

"A potential mechanism," she croaked. "The victims so far seem to have been exposed to it–likely at the same den Junia spoke of. But that still doesn't explain why they're all raving about an upcoming reckoning." *And why they blamed me.*

Anek blanched. "Sarai, you need a retinue of magi if someone up north is behind this. This isn't the sort of power you face alone."

"That's just it," she said bleakly. "I won't be facing them. I think the perpetrator is *here*."

Cassandane slapped her forehead. "Two massacres in two days."

"The north could have been the culprit's initial hunting ground before they came here. It'll have answers or, at least, help us rule out theories. You're needed here–well, most of you," she amended with a dour look at Harion. *But I don't think Edessa will miss me.* "I'll slip out without fanfare. If I'm right and the killer's here, I don't want to alert them immediately."

Kadra remained dangerously still. With a wary glance in his direction, Cassandane leaned over the table. The hollows under her eyes had never been deeper. "It's a sound proposition. We have no choice. Head north and find everything you can. I'll fence off the city and declare it a plague hub as I believe Komis has implemented the same. No one will be allowed in or out–we'll contain this if nothing else."

Méherre cleared her throat. "If I may, your people will blame the north. This could cause civil war."

Cassandane surprisingly winked. "No, my position will be that the Grains Guild's lax transport practices brought the plague here when their supply wagons returned from the north." At Kadra's raised eyebrow, she offered a sheepish smile. "Powerful allies also make powerful scapegoats. They hoarded enough grain to feed half the country, and their horreum was our first bloodbath. The story'll stick."

Harion scowled. "I don't see the need for false accusations."

"*Certo.* I can always provide the truth–that you didn't investigate the first few fucked-up bodies in Aelius's Quarter, and now, we've a nationwide crisis," Anek said sweetly.

Turning ruddy, he stormed out of the tent, muttering something about not being omniscient.

"I'll go with her." Kadra's tone brooked no refusal.

Cassandane pressed her knuckles to her brow. "You know that isn't sound. The city will riot if you both run off, and we need to find the whitesleep den at the center of this plague case." She gave Méherre a once-over. "How good are you?"

Méherre didn't back down. "I've done three round-trips between Sal Flumen and Edessa before. In a day."

Cassandane whistled. "Then, you'll transport our Magus Supreme the moment Sarai hits upon a theory and needs assistance." She met Kadra's gaze and winced. "Wrath's blade, put those eyes away. I'm making a concession here."

A vein pulsed in his temples.

At the corner of her eye, Sarai caught Cassandane giving Anek an utterly unsubtle elbow in the ribs, before the two sidled outside, dragging Méherre with them. Then, it was her and him.

She fought to keep her voice stable. "I'll take my leave here. Better that no one knows I've left until—" He was before her in a breath.

"Did you not say," he said hoarsely, "that you would give me your burdens?"

Tears brimmed at her lashes. "Aren't I? I'm leaving you to a city gone mad." When he would have spoken, she gripped his forearms. "The survivors keep saying that this is my fault, but I think that the culprit is after *you*. Who would Aelius's acolytes and the Order have gone after if I hadn't offered myself as a target? You. These bloodbaths that hint at an unearthly end? You returned from the dead..." She trailed off when his hands fell to his sides, the aloof, cruel god she'd known at her Robing resurfacing in slow increments.

He's guessed it too.

Grim lines deepened on his face. "This shouldn't be your responsibility. Cassandane said that I gave you the weight of a country and the fear that you'd broken it. I ask you to endure too much, Sarai. Deny me."

"I have it on good authority that the Order wants your head! I barely stopped them at the Hearing, Kadra. We need something more tangible now than rhetoric. You shielded me from Aelius and his ilk. Let me do the same."

Perturbation darkened his gaze. He cupped her cheek. "Why did you really allow the Order to drag you to a Hearing?"

"I had to distract them. Because if they Examined or Probed me, they'd find nothing. But..."

"But?" The softest syllable.

If they Examined you... The knowledge she'd sat on for months slipped loose. "You're Godstouched."

He went stock-still. Fathomless eyes watched her for a long moment. "How long have you known?"

"I know you," she said simply. "I didn't want to force the truth from you, or—"

"Impose?"

"Yes."

He closed his eyes on a low sigh. Guilt and quiet pride softened his austere features. "My Sarai, you've borne so much."

That was the straw that broke her self-control. She hadn't shed a tear despite months of turmoil, but they rolled free now. Kadra's jaw clenched before he pulled her into his arms.

"The hell of it is that I thought I was protecting you by staying quiet," he murmured, holding her tight. "After your Fall, my purpose was vengeance. I burned everything down in its pursuit. Now, I seek to build. With you." He wiped her wet cheeks. "I don't know how."

"Let me learn with you when this is over." She took a deep breath. "Will you share your burdens with me then?"

With a bitten-off exclamation, he kissed her hard. "When this is over, I will give you *everything*," he swore against her mouth. "Stay safe for me."

When she left a short while later, it was without a backward glance. She knew what she'd find. Worry, yearning, and the man she wanted to protect.

The gates out of Kadra's Quarter parted open. Méherre and a small contingent of vigiles waited there with their mounts.

The Bridger closed her eyes. A fissure ran through the air before it split open, a town blurred by snow on the other side of the hole through space. Silver laced the portal's edges.

Méherre gave her a reassuring nod. Sarai steeled her spine.

One by one, they walked into the night.

9
REBIRTH AND REINVENTION

Twenty-eighth day of the Month of Frost, six days after Sarai's departure

There was no better graveyard than a sea of snow.

Between the chill and the thaw, a body lost too much in the way of integrity to easily glean its cause of death. Ice preserved even as it penetrated. The truth would slip away as water come spring.

Yet, even winter couldn't veil this death.

Kadra examined the frozen body outside the whitesleep den masquerading as a domus. The man's reddened eyes were one clue. The lack of external wounds said the rest. *Whitesleep overdose.* The man had been too deep in oblivion's throes to realize that Death had come. His city couldn't say the same.

It had taken six days to locate the den attended by Lucanus and Junia of Edessa's now-notorious plague case. During that time, eight hundred Edessans had fallen. Three hundred dead. Five hundred in a state that the Order called madness-struck, screaming of reckonings, eyes, and laughing skies to the despair of healers. All could trace a tenuous exposure to whitesleep.

The drug's ubiquitous use was no surprise to him. It had been made for pain, and Ur Dinyé had no shortage of that commodity. The Tetrarchy's decision to ban it shortly after it entered the streets eleven years ago, had furthered curiosity, then popularity, leading to a network of dealers and middlemen funneling it across the land. Inevitable.

Drug use wasn't a symptom of society's ills but an effect, and he, of all people, had no right to condemn it. Yet, *this* drug and this beetle in his city at a dangerous juncture was a fourfold coincidence too many.

Kadra didn't believe in coincidences any more than he did in omens.

Night hid the small army of vigiles stationed around the domus. A fresh smattering of snow masked Gaius's nervous tread.

"It's supposedly owned by a minor noble, but the Hall of Records lists him as long dead." He passed Kadra the purchase records for the domus. "If the beetle plague's spread began here, then the culprit's covered his tracks well."

"Nothing stays hidden for long in Edessa." Kadra considered the den's double-door entrance. "Our priority is the mechanism of spread."

If those inside the den were merely addicts, then the drug's correlation to the beetle plague was incidental. However, if what he found within that den resembled the countless, crimson-drenched scenes sweeping Edessa, then death and madness had spread via whitesleep. A trail that invariably led to Komis.

Tension tightened his jaw. It couldn't be *them*. The past was a closed book to him in most respects, but he'd kept an eye on Komis and its goings-ons. Successive Praetors had insisted that there had been no sign of them in eleven years. Yet, unease curled beside the agony radiating down his spine. The past was close tonight.

Gaius made an annotation to the deed on the presence of the corpse. "Is there any other rationale I should record for our breaking and entering, Magus Supreme?"

Kadra indicated the road-salt glinting off snow. At least a sack had been poured from the pillars framing the doors to the road.

Gaius snorted. "You'd think they would realize that it gives them away."

"Unlikely." Prolonged use of whitesleep dulled more than vision. Loss of smell set in after a year. Limited motor function crept up after a few more. A den-owner could flood the damned roads with salt, and their unseeing patrons would still be none the wiser as to how their feet stayed on the ground when they staggered out.

"To think that the drug outlived Clan Kader." Gaius rolled up the deed. "They must be screaming in their graves at the lost profit."

Kadra reasoned that whichever of the Ten Hells Clevsin was in undoubtedly had him on a worse rack of torment than that.

His vigiles circled the domus, reporting no guards and a boarded-up back door. There'd be a sentry behind the main doors then. *And a dealers' exit.* Examining the snowcapped foliage behind the domus, he spotted the bare stretches that spoke to an underground passage. They hadn't replanted the shrubs after filling in the ground above the tunnel.

"Head to the tunnel's exit," he ordered his vigiles. "I'll go inside."

"Should I accompany you?" Gaius looked sheepish at Kadra's raised brows. "This is a dangerous time. The plague claims more every day, and the Order say that you and Sarai brought Ruin here. Frightened mobs do frightening things, and you'd face blame if you defended yourself." Unspoken yet evident in his torn glances were the events at the Unraveling. *You've already died once*, his eyes said.

"I died on purpose, Gaius. A repeat performance isn't in the cards."

The other man looked uncertain but cleared his throat. "*Certo.* We'll have the dealers indicted right away."

Kadra sighed wryly as he left. *Ten hells, how I've fallen.* A year ago, none would have dared fear for his safety. The concern didn't rankle—he was only a man. Yet, his enemies needed the reminder that he wore the appellation loosely. Or Sarai would always be in danger.

He examined the den for a Warder's runes that would trigger traps upon an outsider attempting to gain entry. Finding none, he raised a hand, and a bolt of lightning spread branches over the front doors.

Smoke spiraled high, to the blissful ignorance of the users within but not to their ever-watchful suppliers. In minutes, surprised yells sounded down the road, announcing a scuffle between his vigiles and the drug dealers exiting the tunnel. His people would endeavor to secure them all, but some would vanish in the chaos and reemerge in a wine-soaked xann, hawking product to the mix within. Rebirth and reinvention were a dealer's true professions.

He was proof.

Inches from the conflagration he'd made of the doors, he could almost hear Sarai's voice. Brow furrowing, she would have searched his eyes, always confused at his stillness before entering a den.

"Does it trouble you?" she had asked one night. "Seeing people so hollowed out?"

His nod had been another brick of omission in his tower of illusion. Because it was always here, outside a den that he sensed the vibrations in his foundations, rippling like seconds on a water clock, warning him that the façade of his life was long overdue to crumble.

He pulled his gaze from the patch of cold where she should have been standing and raised a hand. Fire relinquished the door, hissing across salted snow until only smoke remained. He kicked down the charred wood and entered.

A blur of motion greeted him. He sidestepped as the sentry lurched onward, driven by the force of his momentum.

Slipping behind him, Kadra wrenched the blade from the man's hand and shoved it into the easy give of his gut, clamping a hand over his mouth as he slit it back and forth. The man's bloodshot eyes strained, muffled screams beating uselessly against Kadra's palm, intestines sucking at the dagger when Kadra pulled it out and stuck it into his neck. His eyes fell shut on a croak for mercy.

Kadra dropped the corpse, paying little attention to the bolt of fire that shot down his spine at the exertion. Metal clinked as the body slid down the wall and stained it red. The moonlight slitting through the entryway glanced off the cruelly-sharp brass studs in the man's gloves. *A sellsword or a bounty hunter.* The den's owner had thrown a great deal of aurei into its operation.

He spared a cursory glance at the slick gold now oozing from the man's mouth. Skeletal hands and tentacles with teeth wove from the liquid and carved at the eyes. Pulling his gaze away, he left the beings of worlds beyond his own to their machinations.

The door into the atrium parted under his hand. Beyond, a central courtyard opened to the night sky. The silent crowd mulling around it took no note of his entrance.

A wide fountain within the impluvium listlessly spurted flecked rainwater. Dark figures floated in the basin, irises milky white, leaking rot. Browned feather mattresses and stained pillows littered the courtyard, atop which figures curled like snails, twitching. Under the peristyle, blank-eyed nobles lounged on ornate divans.

There were no plague victims here. Only addicts.

A muscle bunched in his jaw. The softly-falling snow seemed to darken and take on the powdery guise of ash, drawing him to a night when both had rained from the sky. The past was too close tonight.

So many lives lost. The dangerous, bitter voice that kept attempting to crush his skull resurfaced. *You could restore balance.*

By? He ignored the shadowed courtyard's beckoning lull, its inhabitants fusing into ink blots against a greater dark.

Butchering all who gainsay you.

Tedious. I have little interest in tyranny. His vision was black now as though he stood in a dark room. He watched wisps of smoke bloom and coil around him, prodding at his skin to send bolts of agony radiating through him and promising pain if he dared move.

Democracy is predicated upon tyranny to all who aren't the majority. Isn't that what you've been rectifying for years with vigilantism?

Amusement curved his lips. *I don't believe the solution is to terrorize the majority as well.*

A familiar vise clamped around his head at the rejection. Paying no mind to his protesting nerves, he stepped forward, breaking through his smoky bindings and absorbing the resulting fire that streaked down his nerves. He was no stranger to pain.

An irritated snap of sound from the voice before Kadra's head quieted. Reality and the den's atrium returned in a slow bleed. He could only imagine how he looked to any whitesleep user rousing from their stupor. Too still, too quiet. This was what had given him away to Sarai.

Lighting every sconce in the atrium with a sweep of his hand, he considered the dazed sellsword they illuminated in a corner.

Recognition dawned on the man's face. "Fuck, they weren't wrong. You're alone," he whispered reverently, sliding out a pair of daggers. "I'm going to get so much aurei for this."

Not a sellsword. Kadra grimly took in the crest pin affixed to the man's tunic. *Bounty hunter.* He raised a hand, and the man mirrored the motion, pointing his blades at the sky where icy wind met the courtyard's warmer climate.

A familiar pressure sank into the atrium, air currents of different intensities and humidities clashing and sparking. Light flared, multiplied, until lightning sizzled along the hunter's blades, wrapping around them like twin tongues.

He leapt forward and released both right as Kadra lazily brought his hand down. A lightning bolt slammed the daggers to the ground, metal warping in white-hot protest. Thunder rattled the pillars.

The hunter stumbled back as Kadra advanced. "Wait—" He broke off as a cage of lightning enclosed him without a hair's breadth of mercy.

Kadra extended his palm. "Your pin."

Swallowing, the hunter tore it off and gingerly extended it through the fiery bars.

Bronze Grade. Newly-badged hunter. His unease returned at the sight of the four safshers—ancient Urd swords—engraved in a circle on the inch-wide crest. "How much were you offered?"

"Nine thousand aurei." The hunter's northern twang turned the *thousand* into a *taysand*. "The dealers promised that you'd show."

"When were you hired?"

"Two weeks ago when the den relocated here."

A week before he and Sarai had heard the plague case. A whitesleep den masked as an ordinary domus. Two hunters paid handsomely to watch for him. His enemy had anticipated his moves.

Eyes had begun following him from across the atrium as the battle interrupted the users' pleasant oblivion. His gaze narrowed on a familiar pair that looked just as irritated to see him.

Harion peeled himself off a divan and a naked, comatose woman to stagger forward. "So, you're behind the racket. Here to ruin the fun?"

Interesting. Kadra studied the younger man's bloodshot eyes and the sweat trickling from his hairline with faint humor. *Three rubs.*

"This place has nothing to do with the plague, alright? My vigiles are as busy as yours, trying to hunt down a..." Harion snapped his fingers in search of a word and gave up. "They'll find something."

Kadra considered the coincidence. Harion had ignored the first few victims in Aelius's Quarter. Now, he was here. If it was an act, it was a brilliant one. This man didn't have that capability.

Harion's sly grin faded at Kadra's silence. "I'm well enough to do my job, godsdammit. No one cares about a couple rubs when we've three hundred dead. People want answers. You can only blame the Grains Guild so much. Cassandane's lies aren't holding."

Kadra hid a smile. Six months as Tetrarch and Harion still couldn't conceal how new he was to power. His improved verbiage, crisp vowels, all of it mimicry of a position he knew he hadn't earned. So, he construed everything as an attack and rushed in, teeth bared so tellingly.

Kadra spared a glance for his companion, now stirring awake.

Following his gaze, Harion snickered. "That one's mine."

"Stones Guildmaster Albanus would disagree."

"Not much the fat oaf can do about it when his daughter's smitten. The courtship's nearly over. You can't blame me. It's a bad time to be a Tetrarch, and the Guilds have always weathered everything."

Kadra's lips quirked. "How many of her rubs have you paid for?"

"Enough to secure the marriage. Best coin I've spent."

"Her betrothed agrees."

Harion's chest swelled. "Little premature for titles, but yes. The announcement's coming soon."

Kadra grinned. Most people fell into two camps when they caught that rare occasion. They flinched. Or quailed. Harion was among the latter. "I refer to her engagement to Clay Guildmaster Septimus's son. The marriage is in two weeks." His smile broadened. "A Guild alliance."

The smugness slid off Harion's face. "You're lying."

"But you would know that."

The Petitor-turned-Tetrarch twisted his armilla around and paled at *zosta*'s glow. "She wouldn't," he said after a long look in her direction.

"She's drained her father of coin and patience, and unfortunately, Septimus's son has inherited the family tightfistedness with aurei." Kadra noted as the girl tottered to her feet, looking distinctly alarmed. "You must have seemed gods-sent, paying for everything."

"Fuck off!" Harion reddened. "She isn't sold off yet. If I secure her, then *I'll* have blood ties with the Guilds, and the Tetrarchy'll be under my fucking feet."

Kadra nodded. "If."

Leaving the sputtering man to his folly, he made for the atrium's only decor, a thick tapestry in the peristyle. Behind it, was a staircase to the den's bowels. Descending, the iron tang of blood hit him in seconds.

The cellar door stood ajar, a sanguine handprint on the handle sending trails to the ground. In their haste to flee, the dealers had turned on each other. The victors had thrown the bodies in a corner, the blood on the walls already frosting in the cellar's cold. Murder not plague.

A leftover candlestick cast a glow over the sacks by the bodies. The den's owner had been busy. At least a hundred thousand aurei in powder.

He slit a sack, snow-white chunks trickling out like wet sand. That had been part of the allure at first. Whitesleep didn't require the months of curing that blazeleaf did. Venom could be reduced to powder and concentrated in days, and there was no need for anything as conspicuous as ingestion or inhalation for effect. One rub on the eyelids for relaxation. Two for relief from aches and pains for a day. Three for euphoria. Five for respiratory distress.

Jaw tight, he dipped a knuckle in and inhaled. A familiar stench burned the back of his throat. Sweet, some users would profess. So sickly that they smelled it for hours after use. But this batch had a sour note that he knew well.

He eyed the wriggling bodies with yellow venom sacs emerging from within the sack with interest. A corner of his mouth curved in an empty smile. One answer and a renewed question. *Who?*

A familiar tread sounded on the stairs.

"Mind the blood," he called absently as Cato gingerly toed the door open and swallowed at the pile of corpses. "Our dealers added themselves more charges. The product's infected with beetle larvae."

"Wrath and Ruin, is that how the plague's been spreading?" Cato hurriedly stepped back when a larva landed on the floor. "What is *that* doing in whitesleep?"

A connection that had baffled even Sarai. And the same one that he had known since the horreum.

"Boil beetle venom is the main ingredient in whitesleep."

Cato's head whipped up from the sacks, jaw agape. "Is that how the plague's been spreading? *An ingredient* gone rabid?"

"Partly." An insensate user wouldn't notice a larva burrowing in. "But beetles and whitesleep alone can't explain the raving. This isn't our murder weapon."

"Something that causes immense blood loss and shared hallucinations? Sounds like a nightmare." Cato shuddered, examining a sack. "Can the healers still use any portion of this?"

"No." Diluted whitesleep was a powerful analgesic, so Kadra had made a practice of donating the spoils from den raids to healers across the country. But the larvae made that a risk. "Venom's already leaked in."

The people upstairs were in for hell once they sobered and found patches of their memory gone.

"I've never understood how you can tell." Cato sniffed the powder and coughed. "How'd you learn about whitesleep's ingredients?"

Eleven years ago. "An unwilling source."

"A useful one. Perhaps our scholars can create a safer version. Eleven years of that drug ruining people." He shook his head. "Didn't it hit the streets just after Othus found you?"

Kadra paused while lifting a sack. Pain burst in his spine. "Yes."

The older man's face creased in thought, still trying to put together the sparse pieces he'd been given back then, when his husband had suddenly brought home a northern boy and announced that he was adopting him. Othus had never been able to explain it beyond repeating the same answer, looking equally baffled at himself as he'd said it. *"I had a feeling. Seeing the boy on the streets, I knew that there was greatness in him and that I could bring it out."*

Even at death, he had never guessed at the lie that had been perpetuated on him.

Kadra's jaw tightened as he hefted another sack. The past was too damned close.

"Drenevan, as helpful as this find is, it doesn't take us far with the public when they've already been told to blame the Grains Guild," Cato wrung his hands. "We're no closer to identifying a culprit, let alone how they're doing this. Meanwhile, no one can enter or leave Edessa, and the Order's fomenting suspicion that you're Ruin's scion."

A more interesting appellation than the ones he generally got. "Sarai'll send for me when she finds something. In the meantime, patience remains to our advantage."

"I hope you're right. All those poor people screaming of laughing skies and eyes." Cato took the sacks from him with a shiver. "I'll get these on a wagon for disposal."

"There's a body upstairs too."

"And another in that lightning cage of yours. Gaius is handling them. He'd probably prefer if you dissipated the cage."

Kadra spared a thoughtful glance at the ceiling, now drumming with footsteps. "I seem to have acquired a mother hen."

"Try an entire coop. Sarai was firm in her instructions to watch over you. Your vigiles are taking no chances when half the city's turning against you." At his exasperated sigh, Cato clicked his tongue. "No one's forgetting the Unraveling in a hurry. You may be Magus Supreme, but you can't blame them for fearing that you'll die, when you already did."

Ten hells. "It was for *her* sake."

"Remind me how she feels about that again?" Cato kicked the cellar door open with a pointed look. It slammed shut.

Kadra blew out a breath. "I was fearsome once."

Heading upstairs, he frowned at the scorch mark where the hunter had stood in his lightning cage. A glance around the atrium revealed no sign of him in the queue of bleary-eyed whitesleep users being checked over by healers for removal of any larvae in them.

"Everything's taken care of." Gaius swept in cheerfully. "An Inquisitor heard of the den and dropped by to pray for their souls, but he's more irritation than hindrance."

"What of the hunter who was here?"

"The dead one? Burning outside."

The unease that had sought purchase in him for hours hooked deep. "He was dead?" Kadra repeated evenly.

"*Certo.* Didn't you dissipate the cage for that reason?"

"Describe him."

"A knife through his chest. Thought you were making an example, leaving him on his knees like that, half burnt." Worry flared in Gaius's eyes at Kadra's sudden stillness. "Was that not the case?"

He hasn't noticed. "I left him alive for questioning."

Gaius's face cleared. "Oh, he must have preferred death to that and offed himself."

“Hmm.” Kadra strode outside. A pyre sizzled by the domus, the two bounty hunters’ corpses stacked on top.

It could have been suicide. But he hadn’t dissipated the lightning cage, and the similarity was too dangerous to ignore. *A knife through his chest. On his knees. Half burnt.* For all his vigiles’ regard for his safety, they’d forgotten that he’d died in the same position. Their enemy had sought to remind him. And they had been here tonight to do so.

His mouth curved. *They’re coming out to play.* He ran through the listless faces he’d sighted in the den, searching for familiarity, for someone who wanted to oust him badly enough to murder innocents. *Where were you hiding?*

Gaius stared at the pyre morosely. “Things are getting bad.”

“They are.”

“Nine years, I’ve worked for you.” His gaze was steadfast. “I saw a young man who truly fought the world, when I only dreamt of doing so. I’ve never regretted it. We’ll get to the bottom of this.”

Kadra raised an eyebrow. “We may soon be on the receiving end of rotten produce.”

Gaius shrugged.

A smile tugged at Kadra’s mouth, fading only at the hiss of the pyre before them. Memory warped the rising smoke into a gray, iridescent river, circling around an infinite dock, no hint of land on the horizon. His first sight upon death. He’d been one of countless dazed souls on a dock, despairing at his end, ready to sell what was left of his soul so the woman he’d lost would survive the battle he had left her. And she’d not only won, but had taken him from Death.

Black yawned within the pyre, spiraling outward in a haze that defied sanity. Arms and teeth twisted from the void, clawing for the dead hunter. He twitched upright on the pyre, realizing that the afterlife had found him. His mouth widened in a silent scream. Teeth tore at his body.

At Gaius’s concerned look, Kadra ceased to watch. His right-hand man and Sarai had fiercely guarded his secret. *Godstouched.*

Resurrection had made a million pinpricks into the fabric of his reality. Other worlds bled in, altering what he knew and replacing it with a vast unease at how much he didn't. He'd glimpsed battlegrounds future and past, hands and teeth where there should have been none. But it was stormfall that had become deeply unsettling, the skies split by a large many-fingered hand of smoke, lightning arrowing down from it like punishment.

The gods were real, and he made do with that knowledge as he did with having known death—by not dwelling on it. He had no hope of piety or atonement. But perhaps, as Sarai insisted, the ten hells were for worse men. Even if he couldn't think of many.

Firelight glinted off bronze robes at the corner of his eye. He acknowledged Cassandane with a tilt of his head as she took in the pyre.

"Infected drugs," she said without preamble. "You and I both know that there's only one place where whitesleep's been manufactured since its inception."

Komis. A curl of disquiet tugged at him. It couldn't be *them.* They'd vanished in the aftermath of his destruction of the Clan. He had found no trace of their new lives or identities, and Komis's entrenched drug network had gleefully inherited the Clan's clientele. Yet, he couldn't ignore the possibility.

"We kept our focus on Aelius and Tullus for too long. Something grew in the north during our distraction."

Dread sank into Cassandane's face. "You think that whoever manufactured this batch of whitesleep *purposefully* infected it with beetles?"

"There's a chance." It would mean a visit to Komis to trace the manufacturer once Sarai called for him. Kadra's spine stiffened at the thought. Dismissing the resultant pain streaking down his back, he mounted his horse and steered it toward Aoran Tower.

Cassandane followed him west, looking drawn. "I wish I could say that I'd thought of the north, but our problems always felt greater."

That had always been the point of tension between both halves of Ur Dinyé. Consecutive iterations of the Tetrarchy had considered the sending of goods under the Distribution Act as the start and end of their obligations. So, the north had turned to more dangerous powers for protection.

"What do you make of Clan Kader?" Cassandane wondered. "They got the country hooked on whitesleep and vanished in the same week."

"The land's well rid of them."

"A mysterious end, though. Tetrarch Othus frequently went north eleven years ago, didn't he?" Cassandane looked faintly uncomfortable, as most did when bringing up his foster father. "I wonder if he crossed paths with them."

"He could have."

And he had. For all his flaws, Othus had understood that the north wasn't to be ignored. Only he had seen that the fault lines threading the country could someday create a chasm of no return. Which meant that his sharp, discerning Petitor could see it too. Would she still choose him after that?

"Temperance's heel, that's a foul look you're wearing." Cassandane whistled. "May Sarai call on you swiftly. Gods only know what she's found up there."

Blazeleaf smoke seemed to flood his lungs, the familiar burn like a phantom limb. For the span of a heartbeat, he almost saw *their* faces, reminding him of what she could find, of who he'd been.

I should have told her. He exhaled. When this was over, he would exhume the past from the Drust mountains to lay at her feet.

And pray to every one of the Elsar that she'd still choose him at the end.

The ruined nerves in Kadra's back pulsed with the jolt of his steed's hooves over cobblestone. Dismounting yards from his tower, he absently registered the fire spearing down his spine. The exertion with the bounty hunters hadn't helped, but four bottles would dull the pain. He had no illusions of it ever vanishing. It was the nature of old wounds to linger.

Steps away, the Academiae's statue of Wrath snarled at an unseen enemy. Crimson paint dotted his burnished armor and hung in droplets from his stained shield.

Kadra walked past it.

"Stop," ordered a voice like the roar of rocks tumbling down a mountain.

Kadra kept walking.

A thud. Armor clanked and dogged his steps, arrowing the sun's dwindling rays into his eyes. He unlocked Aoran Tower's gate and arched an eyebrow when no one pushed inside past him. A quiet evening then.

He locked the gate, turned, and found Wrath scowling at him.

Amber eyes pinned his, flame flickering within the irises. With an exasperated breath, the god abandoned his armor for blood-red robes that pooled around him in liquid threat. Long, black hair melded with the mass of fabric. Skulls and voids blinked from every hint of shadow.

Kadra tilted his head consideringly. "No."

Lord Wrath, among the most feared of the gods despite the Order consistently revoking and reinstating his status as one of the High Elsar, smirked. "Your city implodes. Your woman struggles in the north. Your people are being laid to waste. And you still dare refuse."

"Will you tell me who the culprit is if I agree to join you?"

Wrath pursed his lips. "No. Struggle belongs to humanity."

"And detachment to the gods," Kadra observed. "No."

An imperceptible shift took place in Wrath's frame, broadening the line of his shoulders, magnifying his eyes. Less an attempt at intimidation than a god unused to feigning human form. No mortal could comprehend the Elsar's true faces. The façade was for Kadra's benefit. This wasn't their first argument. He had the irritating sense that it wouldn't be their last.

"Few enter into the minor pantheon of the Naaduir in this age," Wrath said slowly in a voice like slate scraping against slate. "Millions profess to worship us, but few truly do. You mortals have formalized more Saints than exist in truth. Many of the vaunted names you pray to are vestiges of souls being impaled in some hell or another." He bared wide fangs in a grin. "Repeatedly."

"Yet, you still want me as one of the Wretched." Like the High Elsar and the Dark, the minor pantheon of the Naaduir contained both the Saints and their aptly-named, crueler compatriots. Kadra had under no illusions as to which one he was slated for. "Is there such a dearth of candidates that the gods no longer vet them?"

That seemed to amuse Wrath. "The gods have their ways of evaluation. You were already positioned for a seat once you died given your inspiring number of kills. Your service pleases me greatly."

Kadra leaned against the gates. "I've never thought of you."

A flicker of annoyance on the god's face. "Your choices find me. There are other Elsar those decisions have served, but the sum of your life has led my way. I have Touched you. There is no returning to the world you knew. You will always see and know more."

"Like the compatriot of yours who seems to have a penchant for crushing my skull?" Kadra asked dryly. "She offered me power too."

The god seemed to halt in his tracks for a second, before continuing. "She can never give you what I can. Accept. In life, you will have strength beyond any you've known. In death, you will be the god you choose."

"The same strength that has driven many men mad," Kadra noted with amusement. "No."

Blood dripped absently from Wrath's hands. Bone extended from his nail beds like talons.

"Your position fetters you," the god said darkly. "Tetrarch, Headmaster, Magus Supreme, they bind you to human notions of morality. Your constituents are equally your enemies and turn on you at the hint of crisis. They laud you for dispensing justice and shun you for how you enact it. Your land sees you as only fit for battle not rule." The liquid pool of his robes widened. Skeletal hands emerged from it, clawing at the air. "Your woman is scapegoated by the very land she risks life and limb to save. You work yourself to the bone, trying to turn this country into a fortress for her, and for what? A reckoning comes. And it will force your hand between love and country. You will need me then."

Reckoning. Wrath's use of the word didn't escape Kadra. "A shunned god seeking to rebuild his name," he said evenly as rage tightened the Elsar's face. "I know why you need me, but you've given me no reason to agree. My people are dying. Who is my enemy?"

A crease formed between Wrath's dark brows. He was quiet for a long, barbed moment. "There is someone here who shouldn't be."

"And I am not to know who."

"Some battles are necessary. While here, you are Godstouched and mortal. Only in death will you gain the privileges of godhood."

"Quite an exchange. Power that'll drive me mad when alive, and an eternal contract to work after death."

The god laughed, short and pitiless. "Death would bore you. Who are you if not a politician? You have no purpose in the quiet. You need the next war, the next enemy."

"I have both."

"You will lose against them without me." Wrath's grin exposed four rows of teeth this time. "I will return, mortal. When you are ready to beg."

Kadra inclined his head. "As you've just done."

Wrath's eyes kindled seconds before he vanished in a screech of warping metal.

Kadra paused and turned. He examined the tangled knot of iron that had once been the gate to Aoran Tower. The gods, he decided, were a headache.

Yet, Wrath had been more forthcoming than he might have realized.

There is someone here who shouldn't be.

That the culprit was in the city meant they were trapped by Cassandane's edict that none could enter or leave. They would be running out of places to hide. They'd already come out to engage him today. *They didn't want me to interrogate that hunter.*

The spill of blood always meant war and the start of a game. There were only six questions to ask each time: Who were the victims. Who or what did they know. What did they do. Where and when did they die. How. The more one killed, the harder it became to muddy the answers to those questions every time. There was no avoiding the creation of a pattern.

This one was a jagged thing of blood and bone. He saw it straining to coalesce. It had begun in the north, and the north held the key. Sarai would find it. As for him…his spine burned with every step into Aoran Tower. He uncorked four bottles of wine, sloshing the crimson liquid into a glass, and leaned against his desk with a cruel smile.

He would play the game.

10 HATRED

Seventh day of the Month of Breath, first month of the new year, fifteen days after Sarai's departure

Homecoming was a bittersweet thing.

Sarai couldn't call Arsamea her home any more than a blade could call an anvil "father." It had only borne her as she had formed. She had grown despite it, not of it.

And yet, this still felt like homecoming.

It had taken fifteen days to reach Arsamea from the port town of Sal Flumen. Bridgers could only open Bridges, also called portals, to places they had already visited, and Méherre had only ever been as far north as Sal Flumen. The resulting lengthy ride up the mountain had been a test of their mounts' endurance and the southern-born vigiles' tolerance for cold. She didn't know how the Academiae's assessors—especially a drunken Telmar—made the trek every year.

Sarai dismounted from Caelum and held the mare's reins as she trudged through the snow. The Month of Breath turned Arsamea into a sea of the softest white. It draped the stone houses, knee high at its lowest and piled as tall as she was on the sides of the village's lone street.

And she knew this too. How cold Cretus's shed would get in the winter. How much the men would drink and the hundreds of cups she would have to clean and polish every night. Her feet traced the path to Cretus's tavern with such ease that she feared for a moment that the last eleven months had been a dream. So much had changed. So much stayed the same.

Here, in Ur Dinyé's most remote village, time held still. The comings and goings of Tetrarchs, gods, and plagues meant nothing to the good folk here, so long as they got their grain, vegetables, and tallow and hoarded it while their less fortunate starved. That Marus had sent for her meant that something had thrown this gentle balance balance off kilter.

"Why does he call himself 'Chieftain'?" a half-frozen vigile called over the howling wind. "Thought we did away with those titles hundreds of years ago."

"Arsamea enjoys clinging to the past," she said dryly. "In more ways than one, if you see how they treat the womenfolk."

One of the women among the vigiles scowled. "Are you certain you don't want us to come with you?"

Sarai liked them all immensely, but something in her rebelled at the thought of them seeing the reality of her origins. "Thank you, but I'll manage." She softened the refusal with a smile. "These folk aren't a pleasant sort."

"I've always wondered if they really do smell of goat." Méherre trudged through a snowdrift with the natural ease of a northerner.

Sarai smiled despite her disquiet. The Bridger had largely kept to herself during the trek up the mountain, but had a welcome dry wit, wore no masks and couched nothing in fawning terms. It was hard not to like her.

The vigiles fenced the tavern while Sarai tied Caelum under its awning. Her hand tremors made a mess of the knot, but it didn't have to hold. She didn't trust this place enough to stay the night.

A blur of candlelight peered through the frozen windowpanes. Voices drifted past the door. They stopped when Sarai knocked. A familiar, heavyset man threw it open. Her gaze trailed up his white-flecked beard to his small eyes, glittering with dislike.

"You're here," Marus said after a moment.

"You asked," she reminded him.

The ugly look on his face said that he hadn't wanted to. The feeling was mutual. But she'd come north for every piece of the puzzle it could provide.

Her eyebrows rose at his silence. "Shall we continue this indoors?"

"By all means." He didn't move from the doorway, arms folded.

She pulled off her gloves, *beshaz* already active on her armilla in case this all went south. "I won't play your games, Marus. We can speak indoors or I return to Sal Flumen, and you suffer whatever had you writing to me in such a tizzy."

Red splotched his face. "You ruined my daughter's life. You have no right to anything, *patchwork* creature!" he snarled.

So much stayed the same. "Sal Flumen it is." She walked over to Caelum when a brawny paw gripped her shoulder and pulled her inside.

Fear struck her with breathtaking speed. Memories arrowed through of the numerous times he had done this where she had ended up with some form of damaged or broken limb.

She jerked away and rounded on him. "Touch me again, and I'll break that hand."

A nasty laugh from a corner of the tavern. "Can you really?"

Sarai coolly examined Ethra's pale, pinched features. The healer had been Marus's bit on the side the last time she'd seen her. "Yes. But can you heal him?"

Ignoring the woman's glower, she took in the tavern. The same sneering crowd assembled along the tables. Nothing had changed.

Wait. "Where's Cretus?"

Marus threw his bulk into a chair. "Dead."

"May his soul rest with the Elsar," she recited automatically. "What of?"

"Same thing that's taken many a good man here," another man growled. "Whitesleep. Someone's dosing us secretly."

Whitesleep again? She leaned against the counter with a frown, pondering a connection to Edessa's victims. "How did the dead look? Clustered together?" *Raving of laughing skies and a reckoning?*

Ethra gave her a withering look. "Blue skin and lips from respiratory depression. What else?"

No bloodbath. Just whitesleep overdoses then. But how had it made its way here? The cold kept Arsamea close to oblivion. Alcohol was their preferred drug for its illusion of heat.

"Only healers can legally prescribe whitesleep," she murmured.

By the looks several in the tavern gave Ethra, this topic had been well-explored.

"I'm *innocent*," the healer snapped. "This isn't a joke. We have eleven dead."

Well, shit. For a village as small as Arsamea that was a cull. "Who were the victims?"

"Our best trappers," Marus snarled. "How the fuck are we to hunt without our men?"

"Ask the women," Sarai said coolly to a round of snickering within the tavern.

The women dropped their eyes to their laps, wearing the bitter exhaustion of those who were tired of asking for respect. *Wrath and Ruin.* The north remained as immutable as the ice it was encased in.

She sighed. "You said someone was dosing you. Any suspects?"

"Plenty," a man said. "Fucking tunnel rats are behind this. Nothing they wouldn't do for coin."

"We got rid of them all, but it keeps happening." Ethra's face hardened. "Should never have allowed them to take root. They must still be hiding here somewhere, now that we've emptied the tunnels."

Hold on. Sarai went still. "Got rid of who?"

"Tunnel rats. Threw them all off the mountain road," the healer said with bored disdain. "Then, another one of us dies two days later. They're toying with us."

Off the mountain road. Her blood went cold upon recalling the abyss on the other side of the narrow path into Arsamea. Caelum had almost balked on the trip. "You murdered them?" she whispered.

Marus's fist struck the table. She hated that she had to hold back a flinch. "Still fending for your fucking kind while we starve and die. They're poisoning us. You'll find where they are." He snarled. "Least you can do after what you did to Cisuré."

"She chose her road." The hole Cisuré's betrayal had made in her had barely clotted. "Don't you *dare* pin that on me."

"Don't *I* dare?" He rose with the menace of a blackstripe bear. Past merged with present. This time, she failed to suppress a flinch when he approached with the same stride that had always promised pain. "I dare do a lot of things, patchwork creature. You're going to scour every inch of this village for the rats who did this, and you'll see that we're compensated for the loss of our hunters by making the Tetrarchy send up more supplies. If you're going to spread your legs for a madman, you earn us something and show gratitude for all we did–"

"All *you* did?" Fury slid a noose around her throat. "I've earned every ounce of my power. You–" She froze when the tavern burst into guffaws. Eyes roved over her black and gold cloak and lit up with glee.

"You have no power. We don't care about your big titles, *Petitor Sarai*." Marus laughed, stepping closer. She involuntarily shrank back and hit the counter. "Everything you have comes from the man you're fucking. You couldn't stop us from tossing you into the tunnels if you tried. Blood will out, tunnel rat. Yours belongs with your own."

He touched her, and she kept her word. Gripping his hand with her free one, she reached past skin into his tendons and flayed them open with controlled slivers of magic, just as Telmar had taught her. He released her with a roar, and she sprang for the door.

It flew open before she reached it. The Arsameans surrounding her reared back at the sight of six angry vigiles with their blades out. Behind them, Méherre looked strangely pale.

Breathing hard, Sarai faced the tavern. "You were saying?"

Marus sneered, Ethra bending over his ruined hand. "Run along, patchwork creature. You have no strength of your own."

A bitter feeling, isn't it? Powerlessness. She grit her teeth at the memory of Silvus's comment.

Walking through the vigiles' parted ranks, she went outside, making for the metal trapdoor that led to Arsamea's underground tunnels. Crusted with trodden snow, it looked like it hadn't been opened in days. And she knew. But she still tapped her foot over the door, her heart sinking with every second that passed without an answer.

Kadra's vigiles helped her wrest it open. She called into the pitch-black space, telling anyone within that she could help them. A couple of vigiles nervously accompanied her down the ladder, sparks of lightning serving as their sconces.

During childhood, she had thought the tunnels to be mazelike and endless. Now, she saw the claustrophobic space for what it was—a prison, a punishment for poverty. She took in the piles of filthy clothing, the long-dried trails of blood leading toward the ladder where people had been dragged up. There was no one here. There would be no one here until one of the vaunted families in that tavern fell on desperate times and had no other choice. Then, they would understand. Then, they would search for a mercy they had not given.

Anger burned up her throat to sting her eyes. *I should have returned sooner.* Climbing up, she shook her head at the other vigiles' inquiries.

"That's *homicidium.*" One glared at the crowd amassed outside the tavern. "We could arrest them all. Get them to Sal Flumen."

"I can bring your Magus Supreme," Méherre added, a turbulent ocean in her dark eyes. "There's enough reason to kill them all."

"Like the north wouldn't erupt into civil war if a Tetrarch wiped out a village? The truly *terrible* thing about having political power is that you have to preserve the rights of people you hate!" The lump in her throat threatened to choke her. She almost wanted it to. "I can only Probe everyone until I find who threw these poor people off the mountain and dosed the village men with whitesleep—" She froze. Turned. She stared at the group, yards away.

At the large, bearded men in their furs, at the women defiantly meeting her gaze. The answer settled in place, soft as a sigh. *Cursed fucking village.* Blood pounded in her ears. These people never changed.

She stalked back to them. “You can’t be *dosed* with whitesleep, you fuckwits! It has to be rubbed on the eyelids. You searched below ground for someone to blame when you’ve been fucking them! Your women are *sick* of you! So, they made you sick!” And the perpetrators hadn’t cared about who ended up carrying the blame.

She halted before a proud-nosed woman. “Why?” she demanded and went cold when the woman smiled, something horribly blank behind her eyes. Not malice nor glee, but *peace.* Her irises expanded until they grazed the borders of her sclera. Behind Sarai, Méherre inhaled sharply.

“It came to us,” the woman said dreamily. “Like a thought we forgot that we had forgotten.”

“What did?” Sarai whispered.

“The idea that we *could.*”

True, Sarai registered. Marus had turned the color of ash.

Méherre’s throat worked before she undid the knot tethering Caelum and turned to her with grim eyes. Sarai needed no further convincing. Getting into the saddle, she raced down the street and through Arsamea’s gates before dismounting to bow toward the abyss on the right of the winding mountain road back to Sal Flumen.

“May the Elsar cradle your souls,” she whispered to the victims it had claimed.

She stood there until Méherre tapped her shoulder and opened a portal back to Sal Flumen, murmuring that she should rest. Yet, it wasn’t sleep that came in a too-quiet inn but visions of eyes with black sclera, a voice whispering to her that she *could*, and Marus and Silvus reminding her of the same truth.

You have no power.

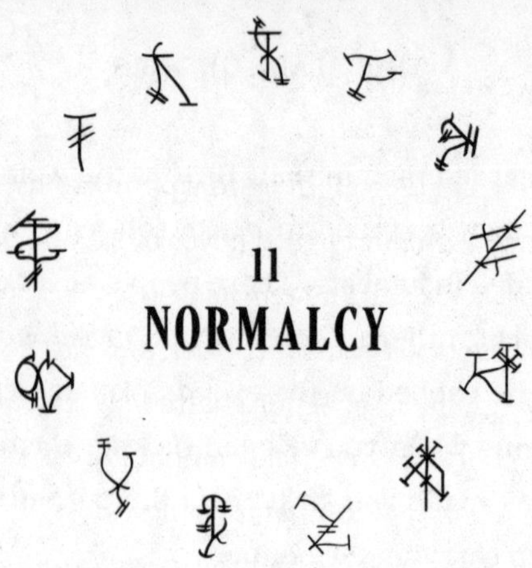

11
NORMALCY

"The Summoning of a god, be it Elsar or Naaduir, isn't a simply religious phenomenon but a violent one. To bring a being of dimensions our minds can never fathom into our three-dimensional world is to warp it. A Summoner tears through time and physical space, and a god emerges from that rift. But the departure of the god does not heal the tear. For centuries, Master Clerics and Inquisitors have secretly documented the odd goings-on that plague the sites of Summonings. Frightening, beautiful, unearthly things extending in a wide circle around the epicenter of the tear. But the allure of the godly persists, and the Elsarian Order remain too eager for a miracle as belief wanes and Summonings fail.

I have little doubt that this knowledge will be lost someday, and that many will attempt Summonings, unknowing of the sliver they make in the fabric of our world and the being they invite to part that veil. And it may well be the case that someone will succeed in Ur Dinyé and so scar a city, a forest, or a mountain with their desperate act.

Ah, but if history could save the future and not merely predict it!"

—excerpt from *A Treatise on All Things Godly* by Magus Hadamann

Sal Flumen wasn't any Urd's first thought of a port town.

It saw too much sleet in midwinter, sported ice-glazed cobblestones that had sent many an unwary tourist skidding toward a broken limb, and the air seemed to eternally taste of salt. Yet, more ships docked here than at the populous southern ports that faced the Meridies Ocean.

Perhaps it was the languorous quiet that permeated the town, chatter kept at a little above a faint hum and peace never more tangible. But she couldn't help thinking that it was Sal Flumen itself—streets paved with hexagonal cobblestones and bordered by stalwart brick and stone homes that the residents refused to call "domii" out of pure hatred for the south's much vaunted, ancient tongue. All achingly preserved remnants of a monarchical past that the town had outlasted and proof that it would continue to thrive here, at the uppermost mouth of Ur Dinyé, whether the world wanted it to or not.

Sarai propped her elbows on the railing of her room's balcony—mercifully only on the second story of the inn—and took in the town's awakening. Wagons trundled along snowy streets toward the docks where they were promptly laden with crates of cold-cured trout, chests of pickling spices—a rarity in Urd cuisine—and clay pots of honey. All from the land of Usten, if she was seeing the flag right.

Beyond the town lay the endless expanse of ice floe–flecked water that formed the Occidens Sea. The air had frothed into a rolling fog that cloaked the divide between sea and land, turning the world into an endless gray shroud. She almost smiled at the brittle wind's caress. Edessa never truly slept, midnight bazaars and taverns allowing for carousing at any hour. But Sal Flumen took its respite seriously, especially these days, as the innkeeper had nervously whispered when she'd requested a room.

"I wouldn't be saying it if you weren't the Magus Supreme's Petitor, but most of us have been driven indoors after work. The town's been in hiding what with so many dying." He had passed her the key to her room with a sigh. "Who'd have thought that Death would hover so closely? Never known of such violence, except in the capital during that last Tetrarch's killings."

She had stopped short. "There's a serial killer here?"

"Elsar's teeth, if only! No, we've a *slew* of murderers. Folk gone utterly mad!" He'd lowered his voice and beamed at a prospective customer—a tall, blond magus from Usten, who promptly walked right out of the inn. The innkeeper slumped. "It's hurting business. Visitors used to dock and stay the night, but they won't hear of it now."

The man had been exceedingly hopeful that she was here to restore some semblance of normalcy to the town. She wished she shared his optimism. Arsamea's wanton cruelty had burned a hole through the little hope she'd had left.

What was normalcy in a land this divided? Should she even be striving for it? Silvus's insistent question the day she had departed Edessa felt prescient now.

Who are you saving?

Her throat thickened. *I don't know.*

A knock sounded on her bedroom door, followed by Méherre's voice. "A moment, Petitor Sarai?"

Sarai bolted the doors leading to the balcony and left her room. She guessed who the man accompanying Méherre was even before he inclined his head graciously.

"Petitor Sarai." Brown-eyed and swathed in furs, Praetor Florus of Sal Flumen had a white shock of curls that he'd bundled into a knot at his neck and a smile so wide that she couldn't help returning it. "It's an honor to have you here."

She managed a few pleasantries, tamping down the urge to slump and bury her face in her hands at the expectant look in his eyes. She had little doubt that he was here to talk about the "slew of murderers" in town.

I don't know if I can help you! The words were broken glass in her mouth. *I couldn't even aid any of the innocents in Arsamea.*

"Breakfast?" Florus suggested.

A smile snapped into place on her face, a reflex borne of long years of feigning normalcy. "Thank you, that would be lovely."

Ignoring the sustained scream in her head, she followed Florus downstairs to a barren table in the inn's dining area. Her vigiles silently trailed her and sat themselves within earshot.

"Word spreads quickly," she remarked. "I've only been here a night."

Florus drew her chair out for her in a surprisingly old-world gesture. "It isn't every day that we meet a Summoner of Lord Death."

Death-Summoner. The fragment of memory that kept trying to resurface twitched in her skull. She managed a weak smile and sat down, surreptitiously sliding a hand into her sleeve for her armilla. Pricking her finger, she felt for *tasum*, the rune for the Fourth Threshold, then *zosta*'s familiar grooves, and pressed blood into both. Small town or not, a politician was a politician.

Gray-tinged sunlight lent a spectral wash to the inn and traced silvery fingers over the hourglass etched on a thick ring on Florus's right hand. She had seen similar rings before. On Clerics.

Catching her gaze, he lifted his hand to give her a better look. "An old life," he admitted. "I was—and remain—a devotee of Lord Time, but I serve him in other ways now." He steepled his fingers. "You must have no affection for the Elsarian Order these days, but I give you my word that I am not among your detractors."

True. "But this is no casual visit," she said with a sigh as the innkeeper set down two bowls of oats before them with a hopeful smile. *No need to ask who informed Florus that I was here.* "I hear Sal Flumen's been suffering from a rash of murders."

Florus grimaced. "I was hoping to bring up bloodshed after you'd had breakfast."

"Edessa has no such qualms. Please speak freely."

The cheerful warmth on his face guttered and died. "The north has always held extremes, Petitor Sarai. Our lowlands border the vicious Xārōmand Desert and taste the whip of both sand and snow, and this mountainous upper north sees a thaw that barely lasts two months. We Praetors of the upper north were foolishly glad that our locales were too cold for the beetle plague to reach us. But Death found a way to balance his scales."

Sarai closed her eyes, a frisson of fear coiling in her gut. "You believe that these murders weren't the work of people? The innkeeper said otherwise."

His spoon cut a wide swathe through his oats as he stirred them listlessly. "What I know, is that, five months ago, dozens in my town and neighboring upper northern locales began falling to whitesleep. At first sight, the deaths seemed to be overdoses. Powder crusted around the eyelids, blue lips. Every healer agreed. The other Praetors and I feared it was a new formulation of the drug–our streets being no stranger to Komis's creations. Until the perpetrators starting confessing." Florus's aged brow pleated in a wince. "I have seen much in both halves of my life, as Cleric and Praetor. But there is little that can prepare you for throngs of placid, *normal* folk offering you the same misty-eyed explanation for why they killed another."

Her spine went taut, alarm thrumming along its length. "Being?"

"That they *could*," he said simply. "That they finally realized that they *could*."

Gooseflesh pebbled her skin at the memory of the womenfolk's blank features the previous night. "I saw the same in Arsamea. The culprits seemed to be in a dreamlike state. Could it not have been the drug?"

He shook his head. "None of the killers–gods help me, what a word for such ordinary people–partook of it. They merely used it to murder. Our regional Petitors verified that for each corpse."

Death, boil beetles, and whitesleep across the country. She thought back to Kadra's most recent finding. Méherre had made brief visits to Edessa over the course of the last sixteen days to update her on his investigations and returned with news that the beetles had entered the city via whitesleep tainted with larvae.

"Were there no beetles involved in this at all?" she ventured hesitantly.

"Not one larva or lesion on any of the culprits or their victims." Florus's genial features whitened with strain. "I'll freely admit that I'm at a loss, Petitor Sarai. I don't think there's any stopping this. I've searched for links between the perpetrators to no avail. They just happened to all live in the upper north and held exceedingly personal motives for the murders."

She set down her spoon appetite gone. "How so?"

"I did some asking around." Méherre broke in, taking the seat at the third side of the table. "Every single one of the killings was a case of retaliation against someone who'd been tormenting the killer for a while. Professional jealousy, harassment, the sort of slow, indirect wounding that the law doesn't entirely punish or is too slow to. Can't blame people for seeing to their own security. I don't see what the crime is."

Sarai's response collapsed into a sharp inhale. "*Innocents* died because of those women in Arsamea."

Méherre's features turned serious. "And they'll be punished for scapegoating the village's poor. But Sal Flumen's folk don't seem to have been as spiteful."

"Therein lies my difficulty." Florus set down his empty bowl, folding his fingers into a tremulous basket, then unweaving them to grip the lip of the table. "The town has but one prison, and it now holds over a hundred. Most have waited months to know if they'll be sent to the mines or suffer a hanging. Other locales have chosen between those mandated punishments, but I like to think that the Corpus Juris Totus isn't entirely devoid of pity."

So, this is an issue of determining judgment. She frowned. Why didn't he seem as interested in finding the cause? "Aren't you worried that these killings will continue? You said it's been five months since—" She quieted as the rest of his explanation finally registered. "*Five months*?"

The Praetor's brow smoothed, worry descending into something that looked awfully like pity. As though he'd been waiting for the reaction and found it unfortunate that she had proven him right. "Since the Month of Radiance," he confirmed.

She stared. "Is there a reason you didn't write to the Tetrarchy?"

He held her eyes steadily. "What would they have done, Petitor Sarai, while your capital was in chaos? Your newest Tetrarch ran off that month, impeached by Aelius's people. What time and resources would the Tetrarchy have spared for us? Even now, you're here because of Edessa's tumult, not our own."

Stung, she curled her hands around her cooling bowl of porridge in a bid for calm. "I also came because a village I *hate* requested my aid. I would have done the same if any Praetor had asked!"

"But would the south have forgiven you for it?" Florus said with a gentleness that held no rebuke. Yet, it dug claws into her anyway. "You would have regretted coming after a few months when their protests and insults worsened. We all understand Edessa well. We've served its needs too long not to." He split his gaze between her and a point past the inn's open doors.

She glanced over her shoulder and winced at the Guild wagon trundling into Sal Flumen's town square. The coat of arms of the Wines and Spirits Guild–a shield with an ornate chalice as its charge–draped the wagon's sides, two Guildsmen casting bored glances at the amassing public from the coachman's seat.

The few puzzle pieces she held melted into a single, dark realization. "It doesn't matter to you if these whitesleep murders continue across the north or south. You want to exonerate the culprits."

Méherre's dark gaze arrowed between them, turning thoughtful as she propped a boot on the table.

Florus's shock of white curls bobbed as he chuckled. "I'd heard you were blunt, Petitor Sarai. Some deaths," he mused, "are judgment from the gods. You saw the eyes of those responsible, I'll warrant." He pulled a satisfied breath at her flinch. "Far be it from me to punish the human hands carrying out their work."

Chilled, she shrank back against her seat at the memory of the Arsamean woman's irises engorging to swamp her sclera, just like Junia's had in Edessa. "The Elsar wouldn't interfere with a land so closely. I'm the last person who'll condemn the use of violence, but the law allowed for remedies for these people. They didn't have to resort to *homicidium*!"

"But the law's remedies forgive too easily. Wasn't this more expedient? The wrongdoer blotted from life without their victims having to watch them meander and fail through supposed rehabilitation." For the horror of his words, Florus's smile held only eager benevolence.

Fear settled beneath her skin like a too-deep splinter. *Has everyone in the north gone mad?* "Don't people deserve the chance to change?"

The pity in his eyes intensified. "I learned much about people as a Cleric and gathered the rest as a Praetor. They don't change." Saying it seemed to deflate him. "Killing the rapacious is no crime. You've done it yourself. It's a shame that you quieted after the Unraveling. You had better options than trying to earn a fickle public's respect."

She stared. "Options that would have likely led to imprisonment for tyranny."

Disappointment snuck into his expression. "A pity then, that the good waste their time fearing that they're evil, and the evil waste no time at all." With a chastening arch of his eyebrows, he bowed and left.

She stared into her bowl of congealed oats for a long moment, conscious of Méherre's silent scrutiny and the vigiles–who'd likely heard everything–muttering awkwardly at their table. Her spoon rose and dipped in. She tasted nothing.

Mass death in Edessa that could have been caused by the boil beetle plague. Larvae had entered the city via tainted whitesleep sacks. But that didn't explain the madness-struck folk and their shared hallucinations.

The plague had originated in the lower, less-cold portions of the north and come out of nowhere.

Murders via whitesleep in the icy, upper-north without any connection to whitesleep but the same black sclera in the culprits as in Edessa's madness-struck.

Death, beetles, whitesleep. All affecting different parts of the country in different ways. All at once. And the puzzle was still incomplete. There was something beyond this, weaving everything together. Or someone?

Didn't you bring this on us, northerner? Our hourglass runs low. A reckoning has followed in your wake. The gods have spoken and call for our end. The sky itself will laugh. Junia and the dying Guildswoman's words repeated in her head until her spoon clattered into an empty bowl. She watched an intricate hourglass of iron sand empty at a corner of the inn. Sal Flumen was too cold for Ur Dinyé's traditional water clocks.

Our hourglass runs low. What would happen at the end?

Wind curled around her ankles, and she realized that she'd wandered outside. A nexus of streets unraveled from the adjacent town square, and she followed one that sloped up in the distance. Something struggled in her chest with every step, a new, bitter bird beating at the bones of its cage. Her thigh burned when she reached the road's abrupt end at a platform overlooking the Kaycakh Mountains.

Thousands of miles away, the mountain range that also served as Ur Dinyé's land border with Errigal seemed startlingly close. Size would do that. Bigger things drowning out all others, like the towns in the Kaycakh Mountains' shadow being invisible from the platform. Or the north's tribulations being invisible from Edessa.

"I did this all wrong," she said to the ice coating the branches of nearby pines like Errigalese glass sculptures.

Florus was right. She had pulled back after the Unraveling and tried to defend and make herself palatable to people who'd never be satisfied. She had merely felled a tree at its trunk. The roots ran too deep to purge, and law, government, and manners had no answer to such quiet, insidious cruelty. She could either dig out the roots, godsdamn the consequences, or fight everyday to keep them from sinking deeper. Florus had chosen to happily accept the former. *I wasted too much time on the latter, didn't I?*

The cage in her chest snapped open at that silent admission. Pain roved free like a hungry beast, gnawing itself without a target.

A crunch of snow before Méherre's gaze speared her profile. "You really aren't what I was expecting."

"Were you hoping for a sly social-climber or a naïve blowhard?"

"Finally. Some spite." A tiny smile ghosted across the Bridger's face. "You're starting to see it. People are foolish. Trying to appease them only makes you join their ranks."

Sarai laughed quietly. "I thought if I proved that the rest of the Tetrarchy had their interests at heart–"

"You could achieve what no politician ever has?" Méherre leaned back against the platform's wooden rails. "National unity is a dream, Sarai."

A flicker of curiosity penetrated Sarai's numbness. Méherre hadn't addressed her or any of the vigiles by name since their journey had begun as though intent on keeping distance between them despite her general frankness.

"Was I foolish for dreaming?"

"Only if you choose not to wake up. You can't convince these people. Take the matter of those scuta. An obvious crime with obvious culprits. There was no real murder mystery after a point, was there? But you still had to go through the tedious process of proof, because the world doesn't ask evil to explain itself, but they will ask *you*. The same holds true here. The south, its people, and its Guilds know what they're doing to the north, and they don't care so long as they can take our metals, oils, ores, and rock."

Méherre tucked a curly forelock back from her brow in a surprisingly graceful gesture before angling to face Sarai. "Let me make this plain. I didn't offer you my aid because I care about the south's woes. Your madness-struck people mean nothing to me. I'm here because I wanted you to aid the north. And now that I know you mean well but lack power, I will aid you too. But understand that there is no saving everyone. Sometimes, the only way to preserve most of the herd is to kill the diseased. And if the gods are doing that for us with these whitesleep murders, I see no reason not to embrace it."

True, zosta uselessly informed Sarai when her mind already knew it. Wind seemed to rattle through the spaces in her ribs. Méherre silently waited as she digested each word, turning them over in the hopes of finding something that she could contest and failing every time.

After a while, the Bridger angled her head toward the Kaycakh Mountains. "Over five centuries ago, they say a demon walked this land. A god, broken and twisted into pure malice, then trapped in a human body."

She recalled Cassandane recounting the same story months ago when she'd learned that the Metals Guild had put out a bounty on her head. Those felt like simpler days now.

"The Scourge."

"And the woman who was mistaken as the Scourgemaster, who would spell his doom. They gave Ur Dinyé a story of love and war that became legend and even influenced our runes. Naiya and Ríukhen, respectively for "heart" and "strength," were their names." She leveled a thoughtful look at Sarai. "You used those runes when Summoning Death."

"I know how the story ended."

"Then, you know that this is cyclic. Gods, love, two people against the world hoping against hope that it'll see reason and allow them to live instead of survive." Pity and something bleaker underpinned Méherre's voice.

Please stop. Kadra's stern but increasingly haggard features flashed to mind. Sarai's throat constricted.

"Love was your salvation. Now, it'll be your ruin." Méherre's voice wasn't cruel, but every word felt like a blow. "As much as you try to put the land first, it's been trapping you using him, hasn't it? And it's been targeting him using you."

Stop. Head bowed, Sarai braced her elbows against the railing. But it was all true, wasn't it?

"You'll always be each other's greatest weaknesses, saving people from their own stupidity while saving each other from their evil. And little things like northern towns and their woes will go forever unnoticed, won't they?"

"*Godsdammit!*" Sarai snarled. "What would you have me do? Kill Aelius's Quarter? The Order?"

Unfazed, Méherre crossed her arms. "I grew up in Komis, where Clan Kader once exerted a reign of terror from the Drust Mountains, and the Tetrarchy did nothing. They had a motto that everyone knew well. *Violentia nervus potesta.* Violence is the sinew of authority." Shards of gravel paved her voice. "Use your authority, and raze those in your way. History won't call you a tyrant when the rest of the land lives in *peace.*"

Sarai's mouth worked in incomprehension. A resonant clanging broke through the town's quiet, coming from the main square. *Another death.* "Do people really not deserve the chance to change?"

"Not at our expense, Sarai." Méherre turned a thoughtful eye to the square. "Even the gods won't allow that anymore."

It was only once the Bridger left that Sarai gave into the urge that had tormented her for weeks. Pressing her head against the platform's railing, she wept.

Long hours later, Sarai wandered back into the town square, quickly finding her worried vigiles and assuring them that she was fine.

Méherre's tall figure was easily visible within a crowd that had gathered around an acting troupe. Sarai made her way toward her, flinching at the accidental brush of a man's shoulder and at the tragic tale the actors were recreating–an apparently well-known part of the town's history. The burning of a heretic from Sal Flumen who had served Time a millennium ago.

Fascinated, she stared as Time granted the priestess Faragathe his favor and began giving her detailed visions of the future in her dreams. This, of course, angered Ur Dinyé's long-dead Seers, who'd prided themselves on meditating for years to receive an out-of-context glimpse that could mean anything. And it had infuriated the Elsarian Order, who hadn't been granted anything at all.

Sounds familiar. Sarai winced as the Order forced Faragathe to a Hearing and demanded that she recant her prophecies, vowing punishment if she dared refuse.

Faragathe's answer had been a single word. "*Audeo.*" Or "I dare," in the ancient tongue.

They had lopped off her limbs and burned her alive that same day.

"The Order's mellowed a great deal, haven't they?" Méherre remarked beside her. Her eyes flickered to Sarai's, then dropped to the ground. She scratched her head. "Look, I shouldn't have said all that–"

"Can you Bridge Kadra here?"

Méherre cleared her throat. "He isn't going to kill me, is he?"

Any lasting awkwardness dissipated like snow. Sarai laughed. "He'll know how to help Florus. No one has a better understanding of the Corpus."

Méherre blinked. Approval glinted in her eyes before she held out a hand. “Welcome to the battlefield, *Petitor* Sarai.”

Sarai clasped it with a wry smile. “I’m not saying that you’re right.”

“Not *yet.*” Méherre’s grin turned her features so elfin that Sarai gaped. Releasing her hand, the Bridger sauntered toward the town’s gates, whistling all the while.

Sarai shook her head. *Anek is doomed if they ever see that.* She resumed watching the troupe bring their tale to a close.

“The Elsarian Order’s records end at the fact that Faragathe died that day,” an actor pronounced. “But one by one, every priest involved in her indictment died afterward of mysterious causes, their bodies contorted like they’d been consumed by fear. Some say Time elevated his protégé to the pantheon of the Naaduir and made her a goddess. Some say she still watches this land and controls our dreams now, as Time did hers. So, if you see her in yours tonight, tell her that there are some in this land who remember. And that there are some in this land who need to.”

Sarai clapped enthusiastically as the actors took a bow. A feathery snow began to fall, peppering the crowd’s faces in a thousand kisses as though in silent thanks.

And perhaps it was. She glanced up at the gray sky above a town where the gods had never seemed closer.

Perhaps it was.

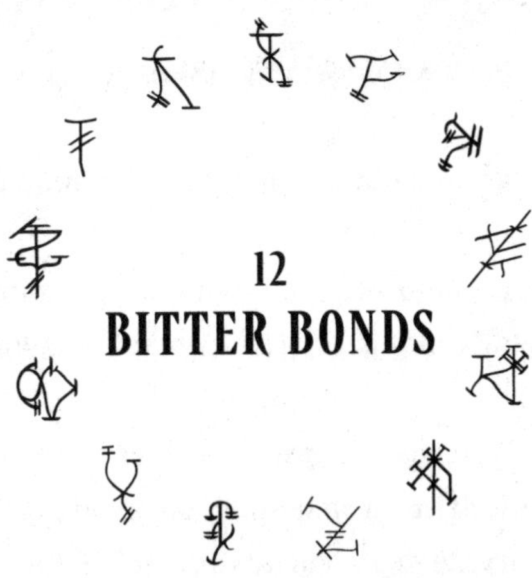

12
BITTER BONDS

Eleven years ago, three weeks before escape

A boot slid against tile, then paused. A ragged breath. The saw of fingernails scraping wooden panels. Another slow step.

Arms folded behind his head, Drenevan lay in bed and listened to his brother's approach down the hallway. He knew better than to open the door and help him in. The only thing Noceo hated more than their father was pity.

Dalvia had come by hours earlier and pressed a jar of salve into his hands. "You need to tell him to stop seeing Parvine." Her timorous voice had held a surprising finality. "He got caught returning today and managed to lie his way out of it, but it won't be long before the Clanlord finds out. I like her. Don't let her die."

She had left before Drenevan had managed to get a word in. The girl could be surprisingly stubborn on occasion.

He considered the salve and decided against passing it on to his brother. Like their father, Noceo tormented Dalvia for her compassion too easily. A pity, when the girl showed immense promise at drug formulation and Illusion magic.

Step. Slide. A sucked inhale. Then, finally, a knock.

Rising, Drenevan pocketed the salve, slunk noiselessly to the door and unbolted it. Noceo staggered inside, avoiding his eyes. Blood streaked his right knee, the telltale newly healed flesh over the kneecap all the explanation Drenevan needed. The bone would undoubtedly still be fragmented.

Clevsin wasn't a religious man, but he placed as much faith in pain as a Cleric did in the gods.

This late at night, Clan Kader's manor slumbered in the Drust Mountains. Only occasionally did its occupants scream. Tonight had been one such night.

Lighting a roll of blazeleaf, he passed it over.

Noceo eased himself into a chair, both battered eyes oozing blood, and took a long draw. "Parvine might run at the sight of me." He let his head loll over the back of the chair, blowing a smoke ring toward the ceiling. "Think I should Coerce her to find the scars dashing?"

"Seems foolish." Drenevan decided not to ask him to curb his worrisome fascination with the baker's daughter. It wouldn't go over well now.

Noceo loosed a long sigh. "I promised that I'd meet her tomorrow."

Drenevan's brows rose at his uncharacteristic melancholia before understanding came. *Ah.* He sat back on the bed, eyeing his brother curiously. An upturned mouth, a glint in his eyes, and a smile despite the red oozing down his face. Was he really in love with the girl?

Mildly concerned, he chose his response carefully. "She'll wait. She's fond of you."

"You think so?" Noceo's blazeleaf roll hung from his mouth. A bashful grin stretched his bruised cheeks.

Drenevan hoped he'd never see that look on him again. "You look ridiculous. She is."

Noceo's grin guttered and died after a few breaths. "How long do you think I have left in this house?"

Drenevan was aware of an uncomfortable desire to say anything but the words on his tongue. Friendship did that, he supposed. Made people want to shield each other from the truth.

"Not long," he said bluntly.

"I figured. My power isn't growing. Not like yours. He had me tested again today." A bitter laugh crawled from his throat. "Seventh-Tier. And I was seeing black spots at the end after draining myself."

"Hmm." His brother may want pity from Parvine, but he didn't want it from him. Uncorking a bottle of wine, Drenevan took a swallow.

Noceo's eyes narrowed. "Back still acting up?"

"Somewhat."

"Clevsin should fix that. Shouldn't damage his powerful, *Tenth-Tier* golden boy too much." Noceo puffed on his blazeleaf roll. "He'll ask you to get rid of me. Same as with our other siblings, only you're old enough to do the deed now. 'Kill him, Drenevan,' he'll say."

It was a passable imitation of their father's tenor. Drenevan didn't laugh. "If it comes to that, I'll kill him," he said matter-of-factly.

His brother's eyes widened. A charged silence, and he spoke, "Can you?"

An icy smile curved Drenevan's lips. "Twelfth-Tier."

Noceo paled. "What?"

He wasn't one for smiling, but it welled within him, and he gave it rein. "Twelfth-Tier," he said and watched Noceo freeze, blazeleaf slipping from his fingers. "I manipulated my test. He doesn't know that I'm more powerful."

His brother's gaze dropped to Drenevan's hands with the sort of hunger he had seen men reserve for lovers before he averted it. "What happens afterward? Do you take his place?"

"No, we let the Clan burn."

Something brilliant flared in Noceo's eyes. Part wonder, part anguish, wholly new. Drenevan tried to place it and failed, but it made his chest tighten, and for a bewildering second, it felt as though they could break the bonds of this prison with a breath.

Red slipped into his brother's mouth, turned his grim words into a vow. "Together then."

13
WEB IN THE ASHES

"Situated in the Drust Mountains, the Am Semni Institute is one of the Clan's lasting achievements. Built after the monarchy's end, the Institute was an attempt by the Clan to hold on to power by moving to a different source: medicine. Within its white-tiled hallways, healers undertook some of Ur Dinyé's boldest experiments, delving deep into the minutiae of tree, root, and herb, in an attempt to better fill the divide between healing magic—only ever capable of mending or tearing—and the irreplicable effects of analgesics, stimulants, depressants, and hallucinogens.

Clan Am Semni might have met great renown had they chosen to share these gifts with every Urd for moderate coin. Instead, they chose to do as the Clans always have—build walls and shutter the Institute to all but the wealthiest.

It's no wonder, then, that their power waned as the south boomed with commerce. No coin-heavy southerner was willing to make the trek to the Institute to pay for the hoarded knowledge of a long-dead monarchical vestige. And few northerners had the coin for it.

Thus, knowledge died a silent death, with no poultice or concoction to save it."

—excerpt from *The Am Semni's: Desert Horsefolk to a Deserted Hall* by former Tetrarch Othus

Homecoming was a bitter thing.

Eleven years ago, he had left the north not yet a man, and yet with more knowledge of that rigid world than others his age could profess. Atop the Drust Mountains and under Clevsin's ruthless hand, he had learned power, control, and cruelty. In Edessa, those tools had raised him above his peers, brought him wealth and acknowledgment. The same past trapped him now.

Cato frowned. "I said, "there's a Bridger outside the tower." She says that Sarai's waiting for you in Sal Flumen."

Kadra's hand clenched around the neck of his wine bottle before he carefully set it down. The port town was a healthy distance from Komis. There was no reason that anyone there should recognize him after over eleven years. Yet, he had the fleeting sensation of a death knell echoing in the back of his mind. He had incurred a debt to the truth for over a decade. He doubted that the past would be merciful about payment. Would Sarai?"

"Praise the Elsar, she must have found something!" Cato threw himself onto one of the couches with a relieved sigh. "Bring this to an end quickly, Drenevan. Over two thousand dead and nearly twice that madness-struck now. *Sixteen days* of no one allowed into or out of the city! You can cut the tension on the streets with a knife. I don't know how long it'll be before they all revolt." An uneasy look crossed his face. "The Order's been suspiciously quiet too. By Truth, any more stress and my heart'll give out..."

The words dulled. A strange cold spread through to the tips of Kadra's fingers, slowing his movements. Dread. It bewildered him even as it sank deep, because he had known this would happen. Had vowed to give Sarai the truth, while knowing that she would likely leave him for it, and had watched her enter the north's icy embrace with the knowledge that it might tell her everything before he could.

"Drenevan?" Cato began to look alarmed. "Are you well?"

Kadra drained his wine bottle in response, spine burning at the too-swift motion. "Stress," he said, more grimly than intended.

Oblivious, Cato sighed. "It's alcoholism, Drenevan. Take better care of yourself. You have Sarai now."

Therein lay the trouble, Kadra reasoned, taking the stairs to his room. He had known from the night he had sat across her in a garden folly that he wouldn't be able to have her for long.

The turn of the hour found him packed and a parting missive slipped under the door to Cassandane's tower, indicating that he would be absent for as long as it took to investigate Sarai's leads and trace the whitesleep manufacturer that had infested the city. She'd undoubtedly be highly displeased but would make full use of the optics of his departure to sell a story of national unity. By his estimation, Edessa would tolerate it for two weeks at most before formally calling for their beheading. He and Sarai were running out of time.

The last of the light dragged its nails over the Academiae's high walls and dappled it crimson as he approached the Aoran Tower Gate where the Bridger waited. She acknowledged him with a wary nod, seeming ill at ease in his company as she offered her summation of the new wounds Arsamea had dealt Sarai and the murders that preoccupied the upper-north.

Unease gathered like stones in his gut. The matter of sentencing those responsible was easily solved, but the connection troubled him. Whitesleep production at this pervasive intensity spoke to distribution far beyond the middling networks, rife with infighting, that he had kept an eye on in the years after leaving Komis. It bore the stamp of the vast, centralized mycelium that his Clan had maintained for centuries prior to Clevsin's end.

Every trail led back to Komis. The cold that had spread questing fingers through him solidified into ice. Over eleven years later, had Noceo and Dalvia finally made their move?

A Bridge split the air before him. Snow and salt blew in from the open portal, rimming his eyes and catching on his air. *Docks*. He had known this mix of salt and wood rot in his youth during frequent trips to the Chaboras River where he and Noceo had loaded crates of illegal blazeleaf and more onto smuggling boats bound for the south.

Preoccupied, he took little notice of the north's aching cold striking at his flesh when he entered. Rivulets of agony ran down his back. They stood upon the port opening to the Occidens Sea. Ice floes groaned at the northern mouth into Ur Dinyé. Water heaved then folded to strike the boats tightly moored beside them. Glazed by moonlight, rowboats packed with overeager adventurers floated further north on the Occidens's sunset-pinkened surface. And something in him knew that he should have returned sooner. Closing the door on his past didn't mean that it had closed the door on him.

Apologies and halting speeches formed in his mind as he walked toward the town square where his Petitor waited. If his suspicions proved true, then he could get ahead of the bitter reveal. He would tell her tonight, he decided, nervous in a way that he hadn't known since before his first taste of Clevsin's beatings with a poker.

Her figure came into view, then the back of her braid, more loosely knotted than usual. Anticipation heated him until she turned. Wan and hollow-eyed, Sarai nevertheless beamed upon seeing him. The same genuine smile she gave him no matter how badly she was hurting. His resolve melted. He couldn't heap more on her.

Inclining his head warmly in greeting, he took his place at her side, stifling the urge to hold her.

"As promised, Praetor Florus, we'll see to your matter of judgment. Will you be able to convene a suitable venue soon?" she asked.

Florus, who rather put Kadra in mind of a better-groomed version of Tullus, rubbed his hands with evident excitement. "Petitor Sarai, the town will be out in minutes when our bell rings." He turned to him and folded forward. "Tetrarch Kadra, you honor us by–" he froze, eyes going from curiosity to startled recognition.

Fuck. Dread moved like an ice cube down Kadra's burning spine even as he nodded to the Praetor. "It is no honor to learn that I have lost my constituents' faith, Florus. Allow me to restore it."

The older man's mouth opened to release a puff of air. He stared between Kadra and a mercifully oblivious Sarai before giving a quick jerk of his head. "Yes," he stammered. "Of course, if you'd follow me to the prison, perhaps you'd like to speak to the guilty parties."

Kadra had the grim feeling that he had now joined that dubious group. He took Sarai's elbow and led her a distance away. "Will you see that everyone assembles in the square?" he asked gently.

"Gods, yes." Her sigh held both exhaustion and relief. "I know what you're doing, Kadra. But I wasn't looking forward to seeing the prisoners' eyes change either. I've had a little too much of unexplained phenomena." She looked up at him expectantly. "You've a way out for them, don't you?"

He slanted a dark glance at her. "Is that doubt I hear?"

A huff of a laugh. "I wanted to hear you say it. You never lie." Some of the anguish faded from her eyes. "You don't know how much of a comfort that is."

An icepick found his heart and cut deep. "They have a way out," he assured her and was rewarded with a brilliant grin before she headed toward Sal Flumen's bell tower, winding up a shoulder in readiness to ring it.

There was a time for the truth, and he was only just realizing that he had missed it.

Kadra's walk to the town's prison with Florus was as excruciating as he had expected. The other man glanced at his profile, then opened his mouth and shut it in a pitiable impression of a trout. An interesting shade of green suffused his lined features before he released a sound, like a goat being strangled mid-bleat.

"*Ask*," Kadra finally ground out.

"Are you–"

"Yes."

Florus's face ran the gamut from white to blue. At this rate, they'd end up at a healer before the prison.

"Does she know?" the Praetor croaked after another moment.

Kadra didn't answer.

They ended the squalid stone building Sal Flumen reserved for its worst, which, until recently, had apparently been the odd drunkard, tourist, or both. Walking past the few vigiles on-duty, he turned the corner to find a long hallway of rusted metal bars and cramped cells. A host of bedraggled people, four to a cell, stared at him from behind the bars, faces torn between fear and awe.

Kadra hissed out a low breath when no less than a quarter of those faces blanched in recognition. *Years* in the south with his own Quarter not knowing him at times, and the north read his father's face in him within seconds.

"What are you?" A wiry man clawed himself upright using the bars. "Have we died or has the Clanlord of Clan Kader come to take us there?"

He was conscious of Florus leaning against the wall, watching him. The next few seconds would determine whether this town chased him out or not. Yet, he had no choice. "Drenevan bu Kadra." He waited for the explosion.

The group didn't disappoint. Those who'd recognized him looked bewildered. Roars of "the Magus Supreme?" mingled with "the fucking Tetrarch?" and his personal favourite, "Who?"

His ego was doing well tonight.

"How the fuck do you sleep knowing you're ruining our lives?"

"I have children, you rich asshole!"

"How does Guild cock taste?"

Kadra's brows rose mildly. "Formerly Drenevan bu Kader."

This set off an even louder storm of garbled yells and accusations about everything from the size of his cock to the state of his mind to claim all these extravagant titles, until a voice croaked above the rest.

"Step up here. Let's see the truth of it."

He went toward the speaker, finding a gray-haired man seated on the floor of his cell. The man stared, the line of his mouth never once relaxing. "I see the Clanlord in him," he said after a moment. "Stronger resemblance than the scion. You're the younger son, aren't you?"

Kadra inclined his head in acknowledgment.

"Thought you died years ago after that fire," another man said. "People stopped seeing you and assumed."

In a manner of speaking, he had. "I went south."

That prompted a chorus of annoyed spitting on the floor, before the older man spoke again. "You're the killer. The one the Clanlord used to butcher folk when he didn't feel like going himself."

"I am."

Silence hung cold and telling. A sardonic smile twisted his lips at the quiet weight of their stares.

"Then, you're the only one of us who deserves to be in here," the gray-haired man finally said. Several bitter voices expressed their accord in epithets. Sarai might do the same.

He smiled humorlessly. "I'm here to release you."

A woman squinted. "Why's that? You want us to owe you?"

"My Petitor wants you free. I happen to agree." He turned to Florus. "Do you have a copy of the Corpus?"

"Every volume." Nervousness seemingly gone now, the Praetor looked curious. "What laws will you be using?"

"Most of them." Weighing the sentences the dead could have received for their quasi-criminal behavior against the time their killers had already served, would shave their sentences down to years of house arrest. "Bring the volumes on sentencing to their trial." Kadra tilted his head toward the imprisoned group.

Florus's eyes cleared. "You'll tout them to anyone who disagrees."

"And you'll keep my past to yourself." He seized their gazes and held them until most of the group flinched back. "That life is gone."

"It'll find you when it's ready," a man spoke in an odd tone, irises widening to cover his sclera. "You should have been ready too."

Ten fucking hells. Kadra surveyed the series of eerie ear-to-ear smiles and dark sclera that slowly bloomed on the inmates' faces. It was no wonder that Sarai hadn't wanted to be here. Behind him, the chorus of fervent pleas to the Elsar told him that Florus's vigiles didn't either.

Only the Praetor seemed to be in awe. "Divine revelation." He reverently made a note of it in the prison's record book.

A howl of laughter cut through Kadra's turbulent mind that sounded suspiciously like Wrath's. The gods, he decided, were a menace.

"Blindfold and gag them when you bring them before the town," he ordered to Florus's squawk of outrage. "Not everyone takes well to revelation. Your heretic priestess should be proof enough."

A second laugh sounded in his head as he left the prison for the town square. It was only much later, midway through eleven dozen cases in front of an irate crowd, that he realized that the laugh had been female. And distinctly bitter.

Long hours later, he stripped off his robes and tunic and slid into bed beside Sarai's sleeping form. She unconsciously curled into him, a habit borne of months in his arms. He wondered whether he would soon live off these memories once she knew the truth.

Her brow creased in sleep, distress twisting her features. Loathe to wake her, he smoothed those troubled lines and painted a row of kisses over her cheeks until relaxation overtook her face. A surge of affection choked him to breathlessness. The gods could offer him every seat in their Bright Realms, yet this was the only one he craved.

"Kadra," she murmured half asleep. "I keep seeing someone else's dreams. These poor boys."

Her last such dream had been eerily similar to his past. He wondered if Petitors could pluck memories out of another's head unconsciously.

He cradled her against his chest. "They'll survive."

His use of the word seemed to rouse her fully. "But isn't that the problem? How many survive without living?" She prodded his chest. "You don't either."

I owe you too great a debt for that. He took her mouth in a languorous kiss, tasting the soft skin of her neck and feeling her toes curl against his feet. "*This*," he lovingly nudged her nose with his, "is living, is it not?"

Gold eyes glowed. "Perhaps," her lips grinned against his. "But so is this."

He reluctantly allowed her to pull him from bed and onto the balcony. Holding her from behind, he wrapped the sheets around their bare bodies.

"Look!" She angled her chin up.

Thousands of stars spilled over night's ink ribbon sky. Even larger masses of rose-streaked gas formed oblong clusters behind them, around them, between them. Nebulae of a thousand striations in hues of sunrise, each larger than the world on which they stood.

Something tightened in his chest. He hadn't seen this in years. Edessa's thousands of oil lamps dimmed the sight.

"That constellation," she pointed at an oblong circlet of stars tilted haphazardly in the east, "is what we in the north call "the Slingshot." See that bright star just outside its reach? That's the—"

Pebble.

"Pebble," Sarai finished. "What do they call them in the south?"

He pinched a lock of her unbraided hair and slid his way down the length of it. "The Crown and its Jewel." He hid a smile against her temples when she scowled.

"They *would* call it that. I suppose it was too much to hope that they'd name it the Pouch and the Coin or the—"

"Noose and the Head?" he supplied helpfully and got elbowed in the ribs for his trouble. He'd barely recovered from the agony when she rose on tiptoe, her breath floating across his ear.

"I want us to live this way too," she whispered.

A bolt of devastation struck him and left him wordless. Her smaller fingers threaded into the ones he had splayed around her waist and interlocked, and it was all he could do to fight the burn in his throat.

"I'll make the world give us that peace." He stilled when the vow came from *her*. "I think I've been entirely too obliging since the Unraveling–oh!"

He hauled her back into their room and tossed her into bed, pressing his lips to her forehead, temple, cheek, drawing a path to her mouth before claiming it hungrily.

Beyond their entwined bodies, he knew that the constellation known as the Slingshot was upside-down. That the Pebble looked poised to tumble down and slam into the town–an ill omen. That he could ruin all of this because he'd simply wanted to wait for one crisis to end before giving her another.

So, when she fell asleep once more against him, he did as he had never done and asked the gods for the only gift they had never given any mortal–time.

He was unsurprised when they didn't answer.

Ensconced in Edessa and consumed by its troubles, he had nevertheless sought to do his duty by the north. Coin, power, legislation, he had used every tool in his considerable arsenal to begin redressing the imbalance between both halves of the nation. He saw now that it hadn't been enough.

Proof that the north was falling apart had taunted him over the past five days of visiting its locales. Poverty, Guild greed, and boil beetles had left a chain of devastation that would take at least a generation to heal.

Most towns had assumed that he and Sarai were there to ensure Guild interests and met them with anger before deflating upon learning the truth. Most of the coalition of northern Praetors had treated him with icy wariness, but their peoples had been more forthcoming. Most admitted that they hadn't wanting to jeopardize their meager allocations from the Guilds but seen little choice in the face of them whittling away at even those quantities.

For all their poverty, the north wasn't devoid of pride and hadn't trusted him or the Tetrarchy with the minutiae of their despair. Much had gone unattended and unreported as a result–the whitesleep murders and the extent of the devastation caused by plague itself.

"Last month, we saw a beetle swarm approaching," the Praetor of a small town had looked close to tears. "A crimson cloud over the horizon, thick as night, venom sacs bloated and yellow. Then, it arrowed into our fields, and we knew it was only a matter of time."

"It's hard enough extracting the *havïd* things from adults, but, gods, the children!" A healer in another town had pressed a hand to her lined forehead. "I swear they dig deeper into them on purpose. I've seen them in brains and intestines." Her voice caught. "I don't understand where they all came from."

He had a guess. Yet, the plague the north described wasn't the same as Edessa's. The corpses Sarai had examined had been attacked by beetle swarms gone carnivorously mad. There was no mention of anything resembling Edessa's madness-struck.

All of which had only left one city that could provide them with clarity and the whitesleep manufacturer who had infected Edessa. *Komis.*

Sarai paced the short stretch of ground between him and the city walls while Méherre argued with the guards and asked for the Praetor to allow them entry.

"On one hand, we've thoroughly confirmed that the north is plagued by boil beetles. On the other, we're no closer to understanding what in *havïd* is happening in Edessa." A pained note to Sarai's voice. "How did we miss so much?"

The south had become the land's cultural epicenter and the Tetrarchy had been too occupied with its foibles to glance up. No, he hadn't done enough for the north at all.

Kadra's gaze followed Komis's city walls to their zenith. His jaw tightened. He had never intended to return, let alone for a task as ironic as investigating a whitesleep manufacturer.

Standing before the crucible where he had been formed, he wondered how much of it Sarai would forgive. Red-eyed and heavily cloaked, she looked impossibly frail against the ancient limestone blocks behind her. They parted with a groan after a few months as the guard waved them inside, muttering that anyone mad enough to want to enter a plague-struck city deserved what they got, Tetrarch or not.

Then, he was suddenly home.

Blood roared in his ears. Memories of flame and a familiar voice's litany of pleas pelted him before he mastered himself and offered a mask of cordiality to the city's Praetor, Ythras.

The thin-faced man loped over to give them an effusive welcome that lasted a quarter hour before he realized that they hadn't come to load his palms with coin and wanted to enter a plague zone for more information. He had since regressed to sulkiness.

Despite being the north's most populous city, Komis was better known as Edessa's darker counterpart. Corruption shimmered below the capital's marble veneer, visible only in political squabbling and in the desolate neighborhoods toward the city's outer rim where poverty ran rampant. Yet, Komis didn't bother with the façade.

Blazeleaf vendors hawked their product at street corners, touting blends of allspice and dried fruit with the potent drug. Pleasure-workers peered out from arches and awnings, artfully parting their thick cloaks to provide him with a glimpse of wares before shuttering them against the windchill. Cardsharps and victims prowled the opposing corners of betting tables outside taverns, denarii and tears leaving the latter in equal measure.

Wind carried the scent of the Chaboras River, where the fishers trawled for a catch while secretly smuggling Clan Kader's drugs across the river for distribution in the south. Where the city hid its bones.

Ythras's men eyed his and Sarai's robes with faint interest. Vigiles in the north tended to be a smaller force, handpicked by their Praetor to assist with crime and emergency efforts. Ythras had amassed himself a sizeable quantity in the hopes of taming Komis to his hand. A fruitless effort.

"So, that's where Clan Kader lived," Sarai whispered with a wide-eyed glance at the Drust Mountains looming above the city. Jagged teeth against a sunset-red sky.

Hearing that name from her lips felt like a blow. Against his will, he followed her gaze to the imposing manor halfway up the centermost mountain. *It's still there.* He'd hoped that the people of Komis would have picked it clean.

"What a home," Sarai murmured.

"Great evil resided there." Méherre looked contemplative.

"But it died out eleven years ago, didn't it?" Sarai murmured. "A lightning strike."

He had never so fully understood what it meant to be between a rock and a hard place.

Méherre's smile guttered right as Ythras let out a bray of laughter. "Nothing dies in the north. It merely takes another shape, ice to water."

That, Kadra mused, was the same bitter conclusion he had reached.

Life hadn't improved for those here, despite the coin he had poured from his coffers into schooling for impoverished youth and improving the structural safety of insulae, apartment blocks, in the city's poorer districts. There was no defeating the underworld, only cutting off its heads. He should have beheaded more.

Ythras led them down streets that steadily grew more dilapidated. Insulae tottered a fraction more with every strike of their mounts' hooves. Snow curdled on the pavement, stained with bodily fluids. The air reeked of desperation.

The Praetor stopped by a wooden barricade erected mid-street around which more vigiles stood guard. "Only a few volunteers in there," one reported before the group transferred their regard to him and stiffened.

"Magus Supreme and the *Elsar-Summoner*," he caught one whisper and glanced at Sarai to see how she enjoyed the title. His brows knit at the flash of pain in her eyes.

"What's wrong?" he murmured.

She rubbed at her temples with a grimace. "I've been getting these odd headaches whenever I hear..." She sighed. "I think I'm just tired. My memory wasn't that stalwart to begin with."

He made a silent note to ensure they rested soon.

"Try not to make a mess when you're there," Ythras grumbled as his vigiles parted portions of the barricade to let them through. "My men have better things to do than clean vomit."

Kadra gave him a cursory glance that doubtless conveyed his familiarity with Death and stepped through the gap in the wood, gratified when Ythras looked ready to swallow his tongue.

Two steps, and he went motionless. Sarai clapped a hand to her mouth.

Death had taken this narrow street. Crimson crusted within grooves in the snow-covered roads. It had frozen as spatters and desperate handprints at strange heights on the walls of surrounding insulae. Diagonal crosses marked boarded-up doors into the apartment blocks. The dried ochre drips leaking out underneath spoke to what had become of the buildings' inhabitants. Bloated bodies formed towers atop thatched wagons, half-open mouths leaking rot. Those bringing out the corpses were equally ashen, bundled against the threat of disease.

His gaze wept over the *other* beings that populated this stretch of road. Fanged arms and coiling tentacles lashing the wagons and prodding at the dead. Entirely disparate from the misty miasma that draped the madness-struck in Edessa. He exchanged a grim glance with Sarai. The north's beetle plague was not the same macabre thing that had swept the capital, yet it was far worse for its curability.

"They boarded up people to die," Sarai whispered.

"A contingent of lightning magi would have saved them all," Méherre grit out, looking close to tears. "No wonder no one's allowed in here."

Ythras scowled. "Once a swarm sets in an area this densely populated, there's little we can do. These people might have had a chance in Edessa, but we're spread thin trying to save the rest of Komis."

Icy fury balled in Kadra's chest at the weak excuse. "These people *had* a chance, Praetor. The coin I sent you should have assured it." Raising a hand when Ythras made to ramble about the economics of disease, Kadra indicated the bodies atop the wagons. "Have any of your dead been found in clusters? Any survivors speaking of laughing skies, eyes, or a reckoning?"

Ythras's sidelong glance bluntly questioned his sanity. "Why would anyone speak of eyes?"

Fair point.

"Where do you treat the victims who have hope of recovery?" Sarai pulled her gaze from an infected child being lowered from a window.

Ythras's ill-concealed scoff said that he didn't think there was such hope. "The Am Semni Institute. Clanlady Dalvia sees to them."

The shock of hearing that name after years froze Kadra's tongue to the roof of his mouth. "She's here?" The words left as a growl that had Sarai glancing at him askance.

Ythras shrugged. "Why wouldn't she be—" he halted, horror turning his jaw slack. His knuckles blanched as he wove his hands in a universal gesture for pleading.

"Because that isn't what you nor any of your predecessors told me in your letters when I asked just that," Kadra finished. Homicidal intent supplanted his fury when the other man rallied. Kadra watched Ythras's mouth move and decided that it would be the first thing he sliced from him.

"She pays well for her privacy. She runs the Institute there." Ythras pointed at the building midway up another of the Drust Mountains. "Twitchy thing though, so I doubt you'll get much sense from her."

"On the contrary," Sarai said pleasantly, "she made a great deal of sense in Edessa."

Shock cleaved through Kadra with such force that his ears rang. He staggered inwardly, then felt his mouth part. Knew he was asking Sarai how and when she had seen Dalvia. Knew he was being unaccountably terse. Yet, he heard nothing beyond the bells tolling in his head to announce that he had been too late, that the reckoning the madness-struck screamed of in Edessa had reached him, and that he had missed more than he ever thought possible.

The tangled skeins that he and Sarai had been attempting to unweave threaded themselves into an ugly tapestry in his mind. The Clan had always been careful to restrict their dominance to the north and the underworld, aware that they wouldn't survive a direct battle with the Tetrarchy. It was why he had allowed himself to believe that Noceo wouldn't risk something this bald-facedly bold.

Most people don't look closely at the world, Clevsin's cool tenor hissed from memory. *To reign forever, you must stay in the shadows. Being a figurehead sets you up to topple.*

Rage moved like an ice floe down his burning spine. *Noceo.*

He had thought he'd understood the extent of Noceo's strengths and ambitions. Had kept careful watch on the institutions where his brother could seek to amass power. Yet, as their last meeting had shown, they hadn't known each other at all.

"Luckily, it's too cold for maggots now," Ythras continued to ramble, "but you should have seen it during the summer months. The Month of Radiance, the entire city *reeked*."

Anger boiled in Sarai's eyes. "This has been happening since the *Month of Radiance*? Over five months, and you couldn't have sent a single letter saying it was this bad?"

"What for?" The Praetor rubbed camphor oil under his thin nose in an effort to block out the stench of death. "Edessa's focus will always be Edessa. The north rallies around its own. It's unfortunate that our troubles have reached you, but you wouldn't be here otherwise."

“We’ve received more than your troubles.” Kadra kept his voice cool with inhuman effort, stepping over a lump of what looked like snow, blood clots, and congealed vomit on the street. “A drug den in Edessa came into possession of a hundred thousand aurei worth of whitesleep rife with beetle larvae. You wouldn’t happen to have heard anything of that, would you?”

Ythras’s eyes twitched. “Of course not!” A void winked to life by the Praetor’s mouth, skeleton hands reaching out. Kadra tilted his head. Lies were interesting things to the gods. Ythras swallowed, unaware of the otherworldly hands scraping off a sliver of his tongue. “I have a close hand in Komis’s affairs, Magus Supreme, but we’re firm on ensuring that no drugs—”

“Every Praetor within Komis has received a hefty share of drug profits since Clan Kader first roosted here. You work with the underworld to supplement your salary, and the only reason I’ve let it stand is that manufacturers would go too far underground if I didn’t.”

Surprise spilled across Sarai’s face. She glanced at Ythras and saw the truth of it in the sweat gleaming on the man’s temples.

The man stuttered, “Even if that were the case, I don’t understand the relevance—”

“Boil beetle venom is the main ingredient in whitesleep.”

Ythras’s mouth closed. Opened. Let out a croak. Méherre had gone perfectly still, eyes unreadable in the dwindling light. And Sarai’s expression altered from bewilderment to startled understanding, as though she were seeing him fully for the first time.

“Will you tell me that it’s a coincidence that the land’s hub of whitesleep production is also its worst affected by beetles?” he asked, tone soft and lethal. “Or shall we be honest with each other, Praetor? Did you look the other way until it was too late?”

As he had. With the north and with the dregs of his family.

Ythras’s scoff was the death rattle of a man clinging to his defenses.

"Whitesleep is a profitable venture, isn't it?" Kadra's steps were soundless as he advanced. Not one vigile stood in his path. "Your tongue can lie, but your ledgers won't."

"You have to understand–"

"Who paid for your silence?" Sparks snapped to life around him. "Who paid for the answers in your letters to me?" His muscles coiled with bloodlust when the man shrank back, mouth widening to deliver an answer that was as much a deathblow.

"You said it too." Ythras's gulp belied the defiance underpinning his voice. "The same people who've owned every Praetor in Komis."

14
HOURGLASS

Sitting opposite Méherre at the inn's breakfast table, Sarai contemplated the empty seat where Kadra should have been and gnawed on her lips some more.

There had been a strange tension to him throughout their northern travels of the past five days. She had initially attributed it to concern that Edessa would be readying to revolt. But his reaction to Ythras's pronouncement yesterday had confirmed it.

Kadra had always known more about this. From the very start of the investigation.

Nothing unusual there. But why didn't he tell me? She drummed her hand against the tabletop. Kadra never did anything without reason, so why hadn't he shared that Komis's Praetors were thick as thieves with their drug manufacturers or that Komis was the country's whitesleep production hub or that boil beetle venom was the main ingredient in whitesleep? Even Ythras had broken down in the face of Kadra's knowledge. Her brow pleated.

How does he know so much about drug production?

Kadra hadn't even pressed Ythras for a name. He had simply whisked her off to Komis's gates and demanded that Méherre take her to an entirely random, *safe*—he had stressed it thrice—inn and keep her there until his return from Edessa.

"You're going home?" Sarai had asked in surprise while the vigiles and Méherre quickly occupied themselves with the sky and portions of dusty soil in an attempt to give them privacy in the open stretch of the Xārōmand Desert outside Komis. "I'll come with you."

"It may not be safe there either." His voice went guttural. "Sarai, I–" She had stilled when he'd cupped her cheek with breathtaking tenderness. In public.

She gripped his elbow. "What's wrong?"

His cavernous eyes traced her with roiling turbulence as though he was trying to absorb her very essence. "You were right. Our culprit's in Edessa," he said grimly. "I would explain and take you with me, Sarai, but I'm out of time." The muscles of his jaw bunched, standing out in stark relief. "If he finds you, even I may not be able to shield you. Give me two days to locate him, and I'll come for you."

She swallowed. "Will *you* be safe?"

He'd threaded her hair through his fingers with a gravity that had chilled her. "I don't know."

"Err…Sarai?" Méherre drew her attention back to the present and to the fact that she had been tapping her spoon into her soup. Chunks of chicken puddled around the bowl.

Shit. Apologizing profusely to the innkeeper and cleaning up after herself, she left in a daze, vaguely conscious of the vigiles following her as per Kadra's–again, thrice repeated–instructions. "I don't understand men," she said after a moment.

As she was referring to both their employer and the land's Magus Supreme, the largely male vigiles exchanged awkward glances and shrugged. Méherre had no such compunction.

"He cut you out of the investigation and relegated you to Clanlady." At her confused squint, Méherre explained, "They never got to fight in the monarchy's wars but were stuck waiting for their Clanlords to return."

The image burned for its accuracy. "He wouldn't have done it without reason."

Méherre's disbelieving brow raise spoke for itself. *But he didn't share it.* When Sarai opened her mouth, she raised both hands in surrender.

"How about this? Yesterday, before your Magus Supreme dragged you from Komis, Ythras told me that they've an infected in custody who swears he saw the location of a nearby beetle swarm. Can't speak–beetles got his tongue–but Komis could use the information. Can you Materialize it from his head?"

"Gods, of course. Anything to prevent more death."

Méherre's shrewd eyes narrowed, something almost pained touching them. "Don't make me like you, Petitor." At Sarai's reciprocal narrow-eyed stare, she laughed. "I'll Bridge you back."

It hurt to see Komis's streets so barren.

Sunset usually brought out a crowd in the north. They sat by fires, gossiping and drinking themselves blind. But the shops here were boarded up, windows shuttered in uninfected insulae. *Not one child throwing snowballs.* Anek would tell her that she cared too much and not to take it all so personally. But she had never known how else to respond upon seeing pain.

Ythras had been ecstatic upon finding that Kadra hadn't come with her, then grown irate once she had made him submit to an Examination to prove that he wasn't leading her into a trap. Despite passing it several questions later, he looked fit to erupt.

Sighing, Sarai quickly asked the vigiles to wait with Méherre by the city walls, assuring them that she'd be well. The worst the Praetor would do was bloviate.

He walked in front of her now, ignoring the wagons heading to the Am Semni Institute for Dalvia to aid the injured.

"Your volunteers are struggling," she noted. "Can't your vigiles help transport the infected?"

The men fencing Ythras blinked, eyebrows rising.

"Seeing to the ill is a woman's job," the Praetor explained slowly, like she was two. "You don't see healers helping the vigiles on their patrols, do you?"

Not for lack of interest. She'd hoped that things would improve in the north after Cassandane became Head Tetrarch, but some biases ran too deep. Women and neutralii still couldn't serve in the vigiles here, and the Tetrarchy couldn't meddle in regional matters.

Her lips thinned. "Having a healer on patrol could be useful if your vigiles come across anyone injured."

Ythras's flat stare told her that he'd rather patrol the streets himself than allow that.

It was twilight by the time she reached Komis's prison. Ythras was red-cheeked with cold when he knocked on the iron double doors.

"Hurry up, godsdammit!" he roared as vigiles fumbled with the locks on the other side. He burst in once it opened. "Is the farmer still sane? Good." He whirled to her. "If he really saw a swarm settle in a field, then we need the location. The pupae molt at night and move into the city."

"I'll have it for you." She noted Ythras's exhausted features and wondered if he had meant for things to go this far when he'd accepted coin from...whoever the culprit was that Kadra knew. A person's morality wasn't easily categorized.

They passed a maze of gray limestone and barred cells, descending to the underground levels of the prison, and stopped before a studded iron door.

"We had to isolate him before he infected anyone else, so don't get indignant," Ythras muttered while officers unbolted the cell. "Even he knows it was for the greater good."

Ducking her head, she entered the squalid room and found a man on a pallet, his frame gone to seed. She held back a flinch at his left eye, pus-soaked and eaten through.

He raised a hand as she approached, opening his mouth to show her the nub of his tongue, then wrote on the slate beside him. He held it up. *I'm infected.*

"That's alright. I'm a Petitor. I'm here to see the swarm you saw that day."

He nodded dully. *Will it hurt?*

"No, I'll just need to touch your head." She crouched beside him and pulled back the sleeves of her robes to display her armilla. "May I?"

At his nod, she withdrew the pin slotted into her armilla and pricked her thumb. *Tasum* for the Fourth Threshold's steady stream of power, and *zosta* for Examination were already alight. She pressed her bleeding thumb into two more runes: *herar* for Probing and *astomand* for Materialization, pulling out memories for public view. Silver flared in the grooves of the runes, a weak light in the cell's gloom.

She gently gripped the farmer's head and closed her eyes. The world faded, Ythras and his men replaced by an unrelenting quiet.

She opened her eyes.

Every mind reflected its owner's temperament. She wondered what the farmer's must have looked like when it had been whole. She stood in a dilapidated barn. A series of stalls extended out on either side. The wood crumbled at a touch, rotted from the inside. Occasional rumbles shook the floor, likely a result of beetles gnawing at the man's brain.

Wrath and Ruin. She went for the closest stalls, gripping and releasing latches upon glimpsing flashes of unrelated memory. A score of doors later, she paused at a vision of a black, seething cloud. *Found you.* She undid the latch and stepped inside.

Sunlight stabbed his eyes as he emerged from the barn. He was going to have to kill the cow. The beetles had stuck in her well and good, and it wasn't like the healers would get them out when they had to prioritize people.

"Fucking gods don't give a shit," he spat. A cloud passed over the sun as he said it. He snorted. "Don't tell me you're actually listening."

He looked up and froze.

A roiling crimson mass swept past, arrowing into the eastern fields with furious determination.

Ruin's damned tits. No! He opened his mouth to yell for help. A buzz and an impact at the back of his throat. The acidic burst of a venom sac. Then, half the cloud descended on his field.

Sarai wrenched herself out of the farmer's head, swallowing hard. "I have it. Give me a moment."

With a deep inhale, she dove back in and prepared to Materialize the memory when a violent bang sounded behind her.

What in havïd? Clutching her pounding heart, she stared at the lone stall door flapping on its hinges yards away. The latch seemed to have burst open. *Perhaps it wasn't a good idea to enter a brain actively being eaten alive.* But she'd been in the heads of dying men before—former Metals Guildmaster Helvus for one—and never seen a mind start acting up on its own.

Hesitantly approaching the swinging door, she reached out, then pulled her hand back in. *Best not to meddle*—the door hit her palm on its way out. Her stomach gave a violent lurch just as the floor dissolved. *Oh shit.*

A riot of color bloomed behind her eyelids. The barn and its stall doors vanished. Sights, sounds, and smells warped in a frenzied scream before her knees suddenly hit cobblestone.

What in all ten hells is this? Standing up, she dusted her palms and jumped when a raeda whizzed by, narrowly avoiding running her over.

"Watch where you're—" the words stuck in her throat as she took in her surroundings, "going."

She stood in the middle of a bustling street, somewhere in Komis. Raedas trundled in both directions on the wide road lined with sellers of every good under the sun—bladesmiths, jewelers, potters. The women behind her were selling roast duck, their weathered faces breaking into identical grins as a customer approached. Crisp morning air whistled between the marketgoers.

It was lovely. And entirely wrong.

Panic wove through her ribs. *This isn't a mind.* Minds were stationary places, receptables for information. Their owners may unconsciously express them as bookshelves or museums or wine casks, but the basic underpinning of storage never changed. *But it isn't exactly a memory either.* To Probe someone was to see their memories from *their* perspective. It was the worst part of the job, having to relive exactly what had gone through a defendant's head as they committed an atrocity. Sarai stared at her crooked quivering fingers and thin scars webbing all over her skin. *Why am I myself?*

She stood on her toes to peer above the crowd and gasped when a figure emerged *through* her. The pedestrian continued walking without concern. She stared at her chest, then at the people passing through parts of her as though she didn't exist. Because she didn't. Not here.

SHIT. Fear banded cold arms around her chest. The air suddenly felt too thick. *Don't panic. Don't you dare.* She coerced in a breath. This was going to be fine. She simply had to understand what *this* was. It felt like the blurry dreams she'd been having since the deaths in Edessa had begun. Glimpses of two abused boys plotting freedom. But this felt infinitely more solid.

She inched down the street and spotted the farmer chatting with a fruit seller. This was his memory then. Why did he seem a stranger to it? Telmar had spoken of similar cases where Petitors had Probed folk who were losing their memory to age. Had the beetles done the same damage here?

The farmer hefted his box of fruit and turned to leave when the blood suddenly drained from his face. She followed his gaze to a familiar woman standing by a Guild wagon. Sarai blinked at the familiar Guild crest burnt into the wood. *Grains Guild.*

"Dalvia Am Semni," the farmer muttered to himself.

Wait, what? Sarai angled for a closer look and gaped upon sighting the pale-haired woman again. Hers was the sort of beauty that historians struggled to put into words. The farmer seemed to believe the same, because he sidled over to the stall behind the Guild wagon and pretended to browse.

"What harm could a few hours of dinner do?" A Guildsman by the wagon grinned up at Dalvia. "I'll give you a discount on anything."

Dalvia took a quick step back. "That's kind of you, but I couldn't."

Cold irritation bloomed in the Guildsman's eyes. "Come now, I don't bite." He seized her wrist with a snakelike lunge when she tried to dart away.

"No–no thank you." Dalvia tried to extricate herself. "I'll pay the full amount."

"But you don't have to," he cajoled loudly. His colleagues guarding the wagon perked up. "She doesn't need to deplete all her coin, no?"

Sarai's nails bit into her palm at the carefully blank gazes of those passing by as the men circled a glassy-eyed Dalvia with easy smiles. Even the farmer whose head she was in seemed fascinated with his feet. *Shit, poor thing.*

"Never had a Clanlady." The first man whistled. "Though I warrant you're better than the Magus Supreme's mountain girl."

Sarai glowered. *Leave me out of it, asshole.*

Dalvia stopped tugging her wrist loose. "You don't like her?" There was an oddly familiar note to her voice. Something sardonic and pained. "They say that she summoned Lord Death himself to save your Magus Supreme."

The Guildsman snorted. "Wasn't there. Didn't see it. He probably wasn't injured that badly, but why not add the Elsar to the tale? Gives the murder of the two Tetrarchs a seal of divine approval. Point is that I can Summon you a bigger monster." He wiggled his eyebrows as the group of magi laughed uproariously.

Rage pulsed in Sarai's chest. Spotting movement at her shoulder, she blinked at the farmer, still standing there. If he'd been pale before, he was white now. *Then, do something, for the gods' sake!*

His jaw slackened, pupils widening in horror. Unnerved, she followed his gaze and found that Dalvia hadn't been alone. A cloaked man came over to her in what Sarai could only describe as a glide. He inclined his head. "Evening."

Sarai went stock-still. His voice was *mesmerizing.* Icy yet alive with warmth, it slid like silk across her senses. She felt the weight of the word down to her toes even though it hadn't been directed at her. *Gods, Kadra has competition.* She tried to get a better look at the man when he turned to the Guildsmen.

"Strike this place with all you have."

The order slammed into her, brought her to her knees despite her having no ability at lightning. Clutching her head, she gasped as the words seemed to slap her, demanding her obedience. Above, the group of men paled, sweat pooling on their hairlines and sliding down. Their eyes turned eerily empty. Then, in a graceful coordinated movement, they pricked their thumbs, set their armillas alight, and raised their hands to the sky.

A breath. A second. A spark in the sky.

Lightning slammed into the marketplace. And the street exploded.

Clapping her hands over her ears, she and the farmer dived for the ground as a fiery orange cloud bloomed around them, spreading fast. Embers rained down from splintered stalls, produce and pottery charred black. Screams rose from the crowd caught in the strike's radius. Others fled the spreading blaze.

Sarai clutched her ringing head. *What in havïd just happened?* Glancing up, she realized that Dalvia and her companion hadn't moved a muscle during the explosion.

"Not very powerful, are they," the hypnotic voice noted. Its owner bent toward the frozen magi. "Now, race out in the pandemonium. You will recall nothing of the past hour. Nothing of me. All you saw was an unfathomable amount of rioting."

The Grains Guildsmen turned and ran like puppets, motions strained and jerky, eyes still blank.

A magus who can mass persuade others. A Coercer. Sarai recalled Telmar's description of the magic with dread. *Who are these people?*

Dalvia quietly examined the red marks the Guildsman had left on her wrist.

"You've outdone yourself with this formula, Dalvia." The cloaked man chucked her under the chin. An edge of amusement underlay his speech. Sardonic. *Familiar.* "And you make excellent bait. If a group of fools can do this much damage, Edessa's best will give us the city itself." He drew back his hood.

Blood rushed in Sarai's ears. She rose slowly, staring at the man's now-uncovered face.

Silver eyes not black. Delicate features unhardened by ruthlessness. But they had the same aquiline nose, the same dark, wavy hair, the perennial glint of amusement as though they'd seen through the world a long time ago and found it a game.

He looked like Kadra.

But that was impossible. Kadra was a former street rat, an orphan like her. And Kadra *never* lied.

Rooted to the ground, she'd forgotten the farmer's existence until he whispered, "Noceo."

Kadra's lookalike—*Noceo*—spared a glance at the floor, silver gaze passing through her to find the farmer. "Now, we can't have that."

The farmer crawled back. "I won't tell anyone. Please spare me!"

"Shhhh." Crouching, Noceo placed a finger over the farmer's forehead. "You're in luck." His voice took on a tender timbre. "I was never here. You never saw me. You don't even know who I am."

Foreboding crawled through her as the farmer blinked. An eerie blankness settled on his face. Taking in his surroundings as though he were waking from a dream, he gaped at the wall of flame. And this too was familiar. Like a book on a hard-to-reach shelf or an overlooked corner that rarely saw a broom, something lurked in the periphery of her mind, screaming in warning. Telling her that there was something she had forgotten. Telling her who that voice in her memory had been.

I'll see you soon, Death-Summoner. Fear bloomed cold at the base of her skull.

"We just killed a few of our own," Dalvia said dully.

"Entirely necessary." Noceo shrugged, and the easy elegance of the motion sent Sarai's heart to her throat for how often she'd seen Kadra do the same. "You've done well."

Tears slid from Dalvia's eyes, all the more eerie for the lack of sobs accompanying them.

"Or not," Noceo mused. "Get us out."

Dalvia stuck the pin from her armilla into her thumb like she wished it was her heart. She pressed the blood into a strange rune, all sharp, curving edges and half circles unlike the angled double lines of Urdish runes. A portal split the air before her. The burning Grains Guild wagon disappeared in favor of a forest of snow-brushed evergreens.

She's a Bridger. Sarai watched them enter with dawning horror.

Noceo caught the farmer's gaze. "And you didn't see this either."

By the time the portal winked out of existence, the farmer was already staring at the blaze as if for the first time again. Seconds later, he was fleeing with the crowd.

I have to get out of here. A thousand questions boiled in Sarai's head. She could barely voice half of them.

It could be a coincidence. What was it Telmar had said about True Illusionists? Magi with Errigalese parentage who could alter their features and mimic everything down to one's voice and mannerisms. Perhaps among them was a man who'd wanted to look like Kadra.

It all rang flat.

Closing her eyes, she focused on the feeling of her perpetually shaking hands pressed against the farmer's head. Flickers of pressure met her palms, and she grit her teeth, controlling her flow of magic to pull free of the memory.

The burning marketplace crumbled, replaced by the barn of the farmer's memories. The swinging door to the altered memory lay stationary now. Both the door and its latch were different from the others lining both sides of the barn. Whatever Noceo had done to this man, it hadn't wiped the truth from his head but blotted it over, the camouflage invisible to the mind but not to a Petitor.

Foreboding and recognition gripped her, a weak signpost in her head telling her to look deeper. She couldn't glance in that direction or bring herself to speak what she had already put together. She needed to sit, to panic. She could do neither in front of Ythras.

Reaching for the memory he had wanted Materialized, she pulled it loose. Reality returned in a slow rush. The cramped cell, officers, Ythras's mouth half open in a tirade over how long she was taking. It fell shut as a translucent landscape bloomed, playing out the farmer's memory through his eyes.

Ythras backed away at the sight of the swarm, eyes growing huge. "Eastern fields!" He roared to his vigiles, who fled upstairs. "Take no chances! Burn them all down!"

She waited for them to depart before speaking. "Did lightning strike a market here some weeks ago?" Was that really her voice? Hoarse and ragged around the edges?

Ythras's face darkened. "Yes, a few Guild magi. They'd escaped before I was informed. Five dead, but those are paltry numbers to the Tetrarchy."

No, they aren't. "Does the name Noceo mean anything to you?" She went motionless when the same fear bloomed on Ythras's features as during Kadra's questions yesterday. Something in her crumpled.

He swallowed. "As I indicated to the Magus Supreme, we only deal with the Clanlord of Clan Kader in one sense."

Clanlord. A high-pitch ringing began in her ears, drowning out his next words. *Clan Kader.* Her pulse throbbed furiously at her temples. *Ruler of the land's underworld and drug maker.* Mysteriously vanished. *Mysteriously.* A lightning strike supposed to have split their manor in two. Whitesleep across the country. Patches of memory she hadn't been able to recall for months.

Goose bumps rippled across her skin. "*We* only deal with Noceo in one sense?" she repeated. "*We?*"

"This is none of your concern," Ythras muttered. "The Tetrarchy's never cared about the north, so we had to consider alternate–"

She stopped halfway up the staircase. "You sit here as the *Tetrarchy's* representative to govern this city. You answer to them, and that means you answer to me."

He wasn't cowed. "Only because you're sleeping with Magus Supreme Kadra."

Sarai stilled. This close to the landing, she caught the silence that fell over the northern vigiles there, could practically see their ears prick in interest. She continued up the stairs, each step slow, purposeful. "Did word reach this city of who killed Aelius?"

She heard a gulp behind her.

"So, you heard." Another step. "Former Magus Supreme of Ur Dinyé, and he died like a stuck pig roasted over flame at my hand. Didn't you wonder why I didn't mind coming *alone* and left my guards behind?" Anger leaked into her voice despite her attempt at nonchalance. "Of the Tetrarchy and its Petitors, I'm the one with the most patience." She reached the top step and turned to face him, still frozen below. "Do you want to keep testing it?"

Ythras's mouth moved faster than a beetle swarm. "I was referring to the coalition of northern Praetors. The Clanlord pays most of us for our cooperation."

Realization and horror crashed through her, twin tidal waves. *We've been played for fools.* The north had silently but fully seceded from the Tetrarchy's grasp.

As a Bridger, Dalvia could send every able-bodied northern vigile outside Edessa's gates in a heartbeat. And Noceo could make every lightning magus on Edessa's city walls raze it to the ground.

Ruin's breath, Kadra. No wonder you sprinted home. Thinking of him brought Noceo to mind. She suppressed a flinch. She couldn't think about what that eerily similar face meant yet.

Chilled to the bone, she allowed herself to be led out to the city walls where the other vigiles and Méherre waited. Wide-lipped braziers perched atop the pavement on either side of the road into Komis, burning as bright as day in an attempt to deter the beetles.

A Coercer, Telmar had said weeks ago. A magus who could make anyone do anything. *That's one mystery solved.* She didn't have to wonder at the blank spots in her mind anymore. Noceo had painted over them. They must have met. Was Edessa's madness-struck tied to him, too?

Then, there was the final mystery. The one that had warned her that everything was about to go wrong. Because Kadra never lied to her. But he'd always kept his secrets close.

Everyone in Edessa and out knew of his story. An extraordinarily powerful street child adopted by Tetrarch Othus. A brilliant student at the Academaie who'd graduated early. Iudex. Tetrarch. And almost five years later, Magus Supreme.

His supporters adored him almost as much as she did, because they knew he understood. That he'd seen the ugliest corners of humanity and fought ruthlessly to blot them out. He'd chosen *her*, a northern street rat-turned-Petitor without formal training and tossed her into the crucible of politics while silently serving as her shield. Given her his life, his body, his heart.

But had he given her the truth?

She barely heard Méherre's worried questions. Forcing out a polite goodnight, she trudged to her room in the inn. And when she slipped into an uneasy sleep, she found fractured memories, screams and fire, and a single devastating question.

When does an omission become a lie?

15
STRINGS IN THE SHADOWS

Night after night, in the years post-Komis, he had kept vigil with a dangerous noose. Oblivion.

He was well-accustomed to the many guises it took. Blazeleaf, blood, whitesleep, wine. For the thousands of times that he had sent people past Death's precipice, there were a few where he had glanced down himself. Those had increased after what he had done to the Sidran Tower Girl, and the realization that he was no different from his family. He had chased oblivion frequently after that. The taste had haunted him for five years until a pair of golden eyes had wrenched him to wakefulness.

Now, another noose dangled before him. Truth. He would hang himself with it tomorrow.

After he hung them first.

Kadra let his gaze rest on those assembled within Delran Tower's ballroom, mildly amused at the array of reactions that provoked. Anger. *As expected.* Fear and grandiosity. *Commonplace.* But the sly derision promised a challenge.

He was in no mood for challenges.

Prying himself from Sarai and the mingled questions and hurt in her eyes had knifed him. His anger had brewed upon returning to Edessa and worsened upon finding that Inquisitor Verentia had forced Cassandane to a meeting with all fifty-eight Guildmasters.

At one end of the lengthy banquet table bisecting Delran Tower's ballroom, Grains Guildmaster Ioratius steepled his fingers and slid a glance at Verentia. She returned an infinitesimal nod.

"Head Tetrarch Cassandane, I'm starting to wonder if you're out to destroy the Guilds. This story that you've spread regarding the spread of this beetle plague has ruined my Guild's reputation and is a *lie.* You've been content to pin this crisis on us and do nothing to aid Edessa."

On the opposite end of the table and to Kadra's left, Cassandane raised her eyebrows. "Guildmaster, the first rash of deaths occurred in your own private horreum. We've since learned that the beetle larvae entered the city in sacks of whitesleep. Your departed Guildspeople were familiar with those sacks either because they brought them in or because they partook of them. The location of their deaths strongly suggests the former," she lied glibly.

Faces shuttered down the table. Hands choked their wineglasses in an attempt to occupy themselves. To Cassandane's right, Harion looked nervous.

How many of them had Noceo gotten to? That this meeting had been called on the night of his return indicated that his brother was dangerously close. Kadra's jaw tightened. This was why he had left Sarai in the north. Even Gaius's loyalty would stand little chance against Noceo's abilities.

"Head Tetrarch," Ioratius tried again, "keeping Edessa closed to entry is an unjustifiable intrusion on our business. You might consider that the culprits are targeting the Guilds and investigate our enemies—"

"That would have been a monumental task even before the plague. It's killed two and a half thousand and left another four thousand as little more than screaming vegetables." The ice in Cassandane's voice could have frozen the Chaboras River.

Guildmaster Etilia of the Wine and Spirits Guild tapped the table. "We're tired of hearing *how* it happened. Give us a solution. Edessa plunges deeper into chaos by the hour. Yet, instead of healing our madness-struck, you disparage our Guilds, humor the north, and even sent a Petitor meant to be serving *us* up there."

An ill mood had him by the throat. It wouldn't do to kill them all, but the idea was growing merit. Kadra trailed a finger down the stem of his glass. Snap it and he could puncture the Guildmaster's eyes. End this fruitless game of words and hunt Noceo down. Yet, they kept talking.

"The Guilds are just as much the lifeblood of Ur Dinyé as the Tetrarchy," snapped Stones Guildmaster Albanus, father to Harion's erstwhile lover and apparently still heartbroken over the vase Sarai had shattered months ago. "If you won't hear us, then we have no choice but to remind you of this fact by ceasing operation. You can posture all you want, but you can't replace us." He shot a glance at Harion, who cleared his throat.

"Perhaps," he avoided Cassandane's irate glare, "we should consider other...options."

Kadra's lips curved. *Still being strung along in the hopes of securing that marriage.*

"Absolutely not," Cassandane grit out. A wave of Guildmasters rose to their feet to roar over her.

Kadra examined Delran Tower's renowned domed glass ceiling. A wave of his hand, and lightning would shatter it. Shards would embed themselves in skulls, frightened eyes, outstretched palms that could shield nothing. A sea of clear scarlet. Every Guildmaster gone. And then, the Guilds would have to start anew. His hands curled around his glass.

"This plague's *source* is the *north*!" Ioratius punctuated every word with a blow against the beleaguered table. "Penalize them!"

"They're victims too!" Cassandane tugged at her collar with enough frustration that the uppermost button fell free. "That's why Petitor Sarai undertook to journey there for *answers*!"

"Or to hide after she began it," Ioratius spat.

The room fell quiet. Cassandane's grip on her glass turned white-knuckled. Harion gnawed at the inside of his cheeks. Behind Cassandane, Anek folded their arms with a glower.

Truly, an entirely predictable night.

"At last, we cut to the heart of the matter. Tell me, Inquisitor." Kadra set down his wine and faced the only person in the room who hadn't yet spoken. "Why are you here?"

Verentia straightened. "Because this land is not safe with you at the helm, Magus Supreme. The Guilds do not feel safe. People are dying and going mad. And at the center of it all are you and a girl who says she Summoned Death."

"You've Examined her. She submitted to your Hearing. No divine strings pull at us from the shadows." He allowed his voice to harden, pleased at the shudder that ran across the table. He had never been as talented as Noceo, but vocal control had come naturally.

Her eyes narrowed to dark slits. "You may not know."

"How would you?"

The burgeoning silence had a weight to it, a texture of seething menace as sharp as a blade. It dragged long and deep over his skin in familiar warning that Verentia was building to a climax.

Her next words were not to him. "Please come in, Clanlady."

Air hissed from him when the door parted warily. She entered as she always had, as though resenting that no one in the room noticed her and fearing that they would. Age and time had tautened her features, but Dalvia Am Semni still couldn't look him in the eye.

"Inquisitor." She inclined her head gracefully as the room exploded into a flurry of questions.

Cassandane rapped a hand on the table until everyone quieted. "Inquisitor, I tolerated your presence at this meeting as a concession to the Guilds, but you have *no* right to bring an outsider to an internal–"

"You won't say that when you hear what she has to say." Malignant glee heated Verentia's voice. "Tell them."

Dalvia walked as a gazelle might into a den of vipers, a tome captured in the crook of her elbow. He tracked her with cold eyes as she set it down and parted its worn pages.

"Clan Am Semni," she began in a voice as timorous as he remembered, "has collected and passed down much history. Older than the Guilds and the Tetrarchy." She avoided glancing at either group. "As the head of the Institute, when plague struck Komis, I began looking for answers." A skeleton hand emerged once from a void by her to gleefully prod at her lying tongue. "If a low-tier magus Summons a god, then there are only two explanations. That the god favored them, or that the magus is more powerful than they seem. In Petitor Sarai's case—" She froze when Kadra began to drum his fingers against the table.

He found her eyes and held them in silent warning. *Besmirch her, and I won't spare you.*

Something desolate burned in her gaze before she tore it away. "Petitor Sarai is no powerful magus. Meaning Death must favor her to have returned your Magus Supreme."

"That theory's borne out by the fact that Death's allowed her to survive in unnatural circumstances *twice* now," Verentia added with spiteful satisfaction. "And here's the best part, Head Tetrarch Cassandane, the book says that where a god favors a mortal, they may simply decide *not to leave*." She beamed. "There is your *answer*. Where it always was. Where *the Order* told you it would be."

A sliver of a second. Then, chaos claimed the room.

Guildmasters vied for who could shout the loudest. Assignation of blame had always been the dominant way to play the game that was politics, and these fools now jousted in earnest.

"You mean to say that his mountain girl's been behind it all?" Ioratius roared.

"Trouble goes where this woman does. Two Guildmasters dead, two Tetrarchs dead, plague sweeps the land. People screaming about fucking eyes and laughing skies! All in under a year. And she's *always* running around, puzzling it all out for us simpletons! What did she trade Lord Death for *his* life?" Etilia jerked her chin at Kadra.

In the face of terror, the north had looked to power. Battling the same, the south looked to religion. Neither understood that both were arrayed against them. Neither understood that they danced on a puppet master's strings. Neither understood that they were wasting his damned time.

He took in the words still being volleyed across the table and raised a hand.

The pressure in the ballroom dropped sharply. A hum throbbed in the air, the foreboding precursor to a lightning strike. A warning and a promise.

Irate roars morphed into panic. The land's wealthiest businesspeople fell to the ground, crawling under the table to join Harion, who had gotten there first. Dalvia shrank back with a scream as sparks hissed around her. Cassandane gave him a wary look.

"Sit." Kadra uncorked a fresh wine bottle. His fingers drummed the table to the tune of the pulsing air as the terrified group scrambled to find their chairs.

Verentia shrank back against the wall. "I *refuse* to obey these coercive—" She paled as a spark scorched her sleeve and sat down immediately.

He considered them all in the silence that followed. "Guildmasters, Inquisitor, let's do away with the playacting. You've been searching for a pretense to supplant my Petitor and I since Aelius's much-deserved end. All tonight has proven is that you're willing to trust an unknown book and an equally unknown woman if they say what you want to hear."

Verentia sputtered incredulously. "Is that your defense? That she's lying?"

Kadra curled his fingers. Filaments of lightning formed and broke around the table. "Sarai submitted to a public Hearing. The least your source can do is submit to an Examination." He angled his head at Anek's grim figure. "It'll only take a moment."

Dalvia's gaze frantically latched onto the door when Verentia turned to her expectantly. His lips curved in sardonic amusement. So, the Inquisitor didn't know that her source was lying.

Cassandane stood. The granite in her eyes said that she had reached the end of her long rope of patience. "If not now, then please do liaise with my Petitor to make the arrangements. And should the Guilds withhold their labor in *any* way," she yelled above the resulting furor, "the Tetrarchy will fill that gap. The north will cross our palms with coin, not yours. We may not have your distribution network. But we aren't without power." She nodded at the suddenly pale faces around the room. "*Tibi gratias ago* for attending tonight. The Tetrarchy has spoken."

The room didn't empty quietly. Dalvia was the first to flee, followed by Verentia, who graced Kadra with a parting look of loathing. The wine in Kadra's bottle sunk lower as Guildmasters raged, attempted to bargain with Cassandane, and finally stormed off with Harion trailing behind them.

This hadn't been the opening onslaught. Far from it. He knew the game, and he knew Noceo. This was too simple an attack for a man who would have been behind the two bounty hunters waiting for Kadra in that whitesleep den *weeks* before he had arrived.

No, Noceo's first direct move would be ugly. Explosive. He might even have Coerced several lightning magi to attack Edessa.

Kadra grimly drained his wine bottle, then went downstairs in time to watch ornate Guild raedae speed away from Delran Tower. Numbness drowned the ever-present line of fire burning up his damaged spine. Old wounds.

Cassandane leaned against the opposite wall. "The Inquisitor, the Guilds, even the skittish Clanlady Dalvia, everyone at that table was hiding something. I can't see a pattern. It's wave upon wave of chaos."

He had thought the same at first, but the strings were clearer now. He was close to seeing the web. He only needed to anticipate where the spider would appear. "Someone's making them all dance."

"You have a guess, don't you?"

"I do. I'm waiting for a move."

Cassandane stared. "And you won't tell me?"

There was no telling if Noceo had gotten to her. "Not yet."

"Is your guess why you've left Sarai in the north?"

He tipped his head to one side and studied her with unflinching intensity, searching for proof that she was fishing for information to relay to Noceo. When her eyes remained clear, he nodded.

She considered the wall beside him. "Do you think things would have gotten this bad if you were Head Tetrarch?"

"No." She was better suited for the mantle. "I'd prefer not to receive even more complaints from irate parents."

Cassandane released a sound that was both laugh and groan. "Gods, I nearly strangled you at the graduation." Her tension eased. "At least you're less bloodthirsty these days because of Sarai. A year ago, you'd have followed at least one Guildmaster home to splatter his guts across the interior."

Kadra wasn't ruling it out just yet. "They know little. Our puppet master has been very careful."

"I once thought we were too."

So had he. Now, he was closer to losing everything than he had ever been.

One more day until he told Sarai everything.

Then, the noose would pull tight.

The blue sliver that was Silun crested behind the wispy clouds over Aoran Tower. Hours bled at a sedate drip until its pale-blue moonlight gilded a slight figure examining the end of the cobblestone path leading to his home. Dalvia pressed her palms against his wards with a sound of frustration and stared at the illusion Cato had crafted of a grassy field as though she would see straight through it to his tower if she looked hard enough.

"Aelius didn't have much luck either," Kadra remarked from his shadowed corner of the pathway to her squeak of surprise. He emerged, raising an inquiring brow when she pressed herself against the barrier shielding his tower. "Did you think that I wouldn't expect you?"

"But you didn't." Dalvia's voice was thin with apprehension. "You didn't see any of this coming, Magus Supreme *Kadra*," she said with a shadow of a smile. "What a name, Drenevan."

Metal hissed in the dark as he drew his sword.

She blanched. "I didn't come to harm you, Drenevan. You know I lack that power."

Empty amusement played on his lips. "You allied with someone who could. Was this the power you wanted? Hiding in Noceo's shadow and doing his bidding?"

"You have no right to pass judgment," she bit out. "You abandoned us. We had little more than the clothes on our backs, and you ran off to play Tetrarch in the south."

"I offered you the chance to come, and you informed Clevsin." Anger roared in him at the memory. "He took me by surprise. I saw a chance to strike and took it. I didn't predict that it would tear through the manor."

She laughed weakly then, a surprisingly bitter thing for all that it was little more than a puff of air. "You still see it as a betrayal, but I *feared* for you! I thought you would fail. And when you didn't..." Her hands fisted. "I had no illusions that the three of us would form a proper family, Drenevan, but I thought better of you than to leave us with nothing."

He studied her tight expression. "Ah, this is about coin. You hoped that I would leave you Clevsin's empire after I killed him."

"Why didn't you?" Her eyes glittered. "Because of you, we inherited all his enemies and none of his strength. That power, that *prestige*, can you understand how desperately we needed it once he was gone? We were fourteen and thirteen when you threw us to the vagaries of the world. Noceo nearly killed himself right after your departure, overextending his magic to make the Praetor his puppet and give us some semblance of strength." She swallowed. "He had no choice but to enter the Order. You could have come back. Put things to rights and set us free.

"You were free. You, of all people, never needed me to escape," he said with cool mockery, approaching her in a glide. There was nowhere she could run. The Academiae's wards prevented Bridgers from opening portals in or out. "You seem to be forgetting that I was thirteen too. You act as though I left without reason."

"I have *never* been free." Her quiet voice held a scream's worth of anguish. An abyss seemed to yawn in her eyes before she shuttered them. Her shoulders sunk. "I shouldn't have come. I thought our shared hell made you care at least a little." Her voice lowered and grew thorns. "If it were your Petitor abandoned to the north, you'd have moved the mountains to give her a better life."

"I would." On that they were in accord. "And yet, she accomplished that on her own."

Dalvia laughed soundlessly. "She's going to start regretting it. Noceo has every intention of breaking her. I thought you should know."

A primal fury that bordered on madness surged in him at the thought of Sarai trapped in her head, screaming as her body followed Noceo's orders. He lunged forward to find Dalvia's pulse with the edge of his blade.

"Are you enjoying this?" he asked softly. "Imagining an innocent being put through what you wanted to be rescued from?"

"No," her voice shook. White-lipped, she finally met his raging eyes and recoiled. Her head struck the barrier of his wards. "I never enjoyed *any* of it. But I don't know what else to do when no one's listening. I have known nothing but the Clan and Noceo, and I am what you all made me." Her chin wobbled. "It's too late for change."

Silence permeated the air. Understanding crystalized. He withdrew the blade. "How long have you been in love with Noceo?"

She winced and took a stuttering breath, pulling the tattered shreds of her pride around her like a cloak against the cold. "I don't think it's love, Drenevan." She inched away from him, dark eyes haunted. "I think I'm just empty."

There was no torturing Noceo's whereabouts from her. His brother would have Coerced her into silence, and her loyalty to him meant that she wouldn't choose to fight it.

"Dalvia," he said quietly when she turned to leave. She halted, her back to him. "I would have returned if I had known that this was not the freedom you'd wanted."

Her shoulders flinched as though he had struck her. Apparently having used up her capacity for conversation, she walked away.

Kadra leaned back against the gates to Aoran Tower with a low exhale. The book of his past opened wide, flipping beyond his revisitations of the night of Sarai's Fall to an equally bitter one, that he had avoided for years. Now, he wondered if he had done the right thing then. Would any of this have come to pass, or would it have been worse?

He was too late in this, too. He could only alter the present.

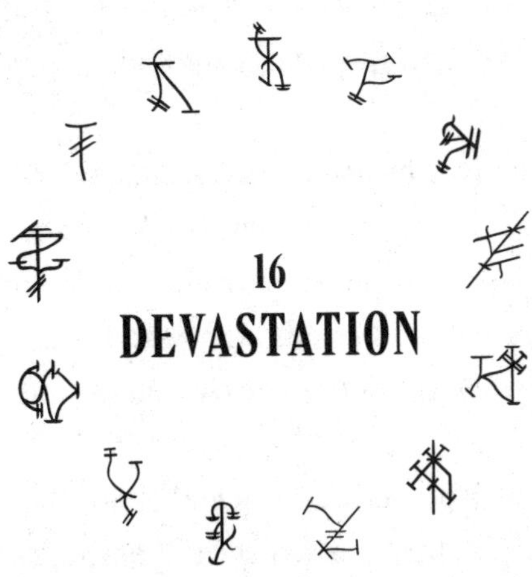

16
DEVASTATION

By the time the sun rose the next morning, she had decided not to think about any of it. *I'm not avoiding anything*, she insisted to her hollow-eyed reflection in the washbasin's mirror. She simply needed more information before she jumped to conclusions.

Kadra had promised to return in one night. She would ask him then. *I won't let doubt creep in.*

Conversing with the vigiles that had accompanied her, she allowed Méherre to distract her with a visit to one of Komis's markets. She Bridged them to the city's western gates—an area barely touched by plague—and the guards waved them in.

Far above them, halfway up the Drust Mountains, the Am Semni Institute shone white over Komis. She recalled Ythras mentioning Dalvia seeing to the aid of boil beetle plague victims and struggled to reconcile it with the woman she'd seen in the farmer's memory.

She didn't want to be there. Still heartsick at the realizations that memory had prompted, she tucked the truth away. She couldn't confront it now.

A mass of color bloomed ahead. At least a hundred stalls clustered in a chaotic jumble. Woven fabrics stretched over the stalls' frames to provide marketgoers respite from the lightly falling snow. She swallowed, disconcerted by the similarities to the market Noceo had decimated. Yet, the people of Komis refused to be cowed. Snow crowned their fur hats as they puttered about with determined focus, blazeleaf rolls smoking between their fingers, like life here would go on at their will and their pace.

A smile lifted her lips. She had never felt at home in Arsamea, but there was something about the north's pragmatic strength that called to her. Funnily enough, it was the same strength she saw in Kadra.

Pulling away from that thought, she was browsing a bladesmith's stall with Méherre when an outraged roar came from the mouth of the marketplace.

Exchanging startled glances, they searched for the source and cursed at the Guild wagons queuing up at a tavern. *Wine and Spirits Guild again.* She didn't have to make out the yelling match between the tavern's proprietor and the Guildsmen to know the source of the conflict.

"This is even less than you brought last time!" the burly tavernkeeper roared across a suddenly silent market. "One hundred amphorae every two weeks. That was our bargain."

"If you paid." The Wines Guildsman driving the first wagon shrugged.

"I *have* paid!"

"Well, price's gone up." The Guildsman raised both hands to forestall further argument. "I don't decide these things. If you want the wine, you pay for it. Or you get less–what the fuck!" He flinched as red spattered across his face.

Sarai groaned as another tomato flew across the street to pulverize itself on his tunic.

"Fuck off, southern trash!" one marketgoer yelled. "Go pray to your gods some more!"

"I got some more scuta for you here!" Sarai muffled a horrified laugh when a stall-owner raised a nasty-looking cudgel.

The Guildsmen in the wagons dismounted, lips pulled back in sneers. "Fucking charity cases think you're something? You'd all starve to death if we cut you off!"

"Do it!" yelled a fruit seller tossing an enormous grapefruit. It hit a wagon and burst. "See how you'll do without our metals, fur, and oil! We could invade you tomorrow!"

Wading into the fruit-slinging would only get her pelted by both sides. She couldn't ask for diplomacy when the north hadn't had a seat at the bargaining table for decades.

"Lively," Méherre noted.

"I hope they'll have some fruit left after all this." Sarai let out a long breath of relief when the Wines Guildsmen retreated behind their wagons, unloading their amphorae with bitter curses while angrily picking fruit off themselves. The crowd returned to their wares and blazeleaf rolls.

Méherre sighed. "The south thinks of us as backward, unsophisticated, crude. There's truth to some of that but they miss the fear." Her voice went taut with a mix of resignation and anger. "We northerners survive, you know that. There's little else we can do."

"You've an advantage," Sarai noted. "As a Bridger, you can go anywhere."

"If only! I have to physically journey to every location before I can Bridge to it, remember?" Méherre stared at her hands. "Are you aware that if Edessa fell tomorrow, Komis would be Ur Dinyé's most powerful city?"

Sarai's neck almost cracked with how quickly she spun to face her. "So, if Clan Kador was still extant, they would have a vested interest in seeing Edessa fall," she mused.

The Bridger watched her for a long moment, looking oddly disconcerted. "You think that's why your Magus Supreme raced off? You think they survived?"

I know they did. Sarai simply nodded.

"Well, they did exist long before the monarchy and Tetrarchy. It stands to reason that they'd hope to outlast the latter too." Still looking perturbed, Méherre rose with a heavy exhale and scowled at the Guildsmen still arguing with the tavern-owner. "I'll go break that up. Last thing we need is a civil war breaking out here."

We're close enough to it already. Sarai considered everything she had heard on Clan Kader while strolling through the stalls. A bladesmith at the far corner of the market cajoled her toward his wares. She had begun seriously considering a dagger when a voice spoke at her shoulder.

"This is unexpected."

She jumped. Behind her, a familiar half-veiled man in blue robes chuckled and stepped away. "Forgive me, I seem to startle you all the time."

Probably because you've the tread of a ghost. "Inquisitor Silvus, how are you here?"

"Someone has to see to the dead. A bitter business, last rites over a mass grave, but that's how the faithful honor them." His eyes were pale as ice. A frisson of disquiet slipped down her spine when she met them.

"Justice seems like a more pertinent way to honor them."

His veiled mouth grinned. "Like I've said, Petitor Sarai, we aren't so different at all. Forest and trees. Your Magus Supreme unfortunately doesn't believe the same. I had the dubious pleasure of speaking to him at the Academaie's graduation, you know? I can't say that I see the appeal. Elsar only know why a man like that wanted to be a Tetrarch of all things. Do you?"

Sarai sighed. "That's because he–" Her mind came up blank.

A strange roaring thundered in her ears. Not the pound of blood, but of dread. *Why did Kadra choose to become a Tetrarch?* A man that brilliant, that powerful, could have been anyone. Why the judiciary, then politics? It couldn't have been for her Fall. That had been nearly five years ago, and he'd become a iudex nine years ago. Why did she know so little about him?

Catching Silvus's expectant gaze, she crossed her arms, grateful for the bracing cold. "I asked this in Edessa, too, but what do you have against Kadra?"

"Men like that have sins deeper than you can fathom. When those sins come calling, they aren't the only ones who pay." Silvus's eyes clouded. "Have you not paid yourself?"

Sarai thought back to the self-hatred she often saw in Kadra's eyes whenever she had a nightmare. "He knows the weight of his sins."

"Yet, he has lost nothing while Edessa sinks into madness, Death-Summoner. At this rate, the city might kill him again for it."

Blood fled her cheeks. Sarai's chest pulled tight. She tried to slow her pulse, but there was no muffling the weight of this realization. It pulsed in her ears, a slip of his tongue, a truth he'd loosed too early, even as he kept talking.

"I'll say it again. I don't want to be your enemy. The Order, the Guilds, and Edessa are arrayed against you. Disengage from the Magus Supreme. Denounce him as the root of all this, and you'll be left unscathed. No one truly wants your head. They're after his, and you're conveniently right in the way, Death-Summoner."

Her vision blurred, like she was looking at the world from the bottom of a stream. "Inquisitor Silvus," she managed a deceptive calm, "why do you keep calling me Death-Summoner?"

Surprise burst in his eyes for a fraction of a second before an insidious light flared in them. And suddenly, she knew *exactly* where she had seen those eyes before.

"Well, that's that then." A gloriously smooth voice replaced the ordinary baritone she'd been conversing with. Silvus—but had that ever been Silvus?—Noceo smiled broadly.

She stumbled back half a step when he spoke again.

"Run and this market dies." He indicated the Guild wagons. A Guildsman unloaded the last of the amphorae and dusted his hands. "Amazing how much damage these Guildspeople can do despite only being Fifth- and Sixth-Tiers. Lightning magic is a marvelous thing. I almost wish I had more of it."

"What do you want?" The wobble in her voice betrayed her.

"A few hours, no more. Then, I'll return you here. You have my word."

Panic flooded her like the tide. If she didn't acquiesce, he would make good on his threat. She either died in this marketplace or died wherever he planned on taking her. This was no choice at all.

"Very well," she whispered.

His gray eyes lit up. "Excellent. Dalvia?" Noceo directed a hand at a patch of space behind him. It wavered, color twisting and re-forming as Dalvia undid the illusion keeping her invisible. The long fall of her hair appeared first, glowing luminous in the sun. The marketgoers were too deep in their haggling and purchasing to notice.

A Bridger and True Illusionist. Sarai cast a final desperate look back at the market for her vigiles or Méherre. But what could they even do against Noceo's voice? More likely that he'd already ordered them out of the way or worse. She swallowed as the air behind her split to reveal a snowy road leading up to an ornate metal gate.

A wintry gust wound around the ground, limiting the audibility of Noceo's words. Yet, they struck her like a knife. "Welcome to Clan Kader's manor, Death-Summoner." Fear curled fingers around her chest when he turned toward the portal. "Shall we?"

She coerced air into her lungs and stepped forward. A gleam lit Noceo's calculating eyes when she hesitated at the edge of the Bridge. "It's perfectly safe. I won't ask Dalvia to close it on you. There are better ways to kill you than a bisection via portal."

She grit her teeth and returned his smile. "Attempt anything you'd like. Death and I are old friends. The consequences will be more yours than mine." Turning from the hint of fear that crawled over his face, she crossed the Bridge. The air warped around them.

And they were gone.

A ferocious mountain wind whipped up the ankles of Sarai's trousers. Intricate iron and steel gates yawned open ahead, the bars parting like jaws. And there stood Clan Kader's compound, richly lit in the approaching twilight.

Unlike the south's penchant for marble, the north favored brick. Clan Kader, it seemed, favored both. A central brick-and-marble domus glowered down at them, crowned with elaborate domed cupolas. Fire had gutted a large swath of the house but the façade still stood.

Twelve pilasters framed the wide entryway, boasting carved approximations of the Elsar, the minor pantheon of the Naaduir, and monarchs past on their capitals and entablatures. More windows than she had fingers and toes shone in the moonlight reflecting off the snow, some long-blackened by soot. To the left rose a tower that looked eerily like Kadra's abode. No, she realized with shock, a replica of it.

Noceo followed her gaze and smiled. "What do you think of the addition?" He traipsed past the front gate, the leisurely walk of a nobleman unlike his brother's elegant prowl.

"Unoriginal."

"Well, we couldn't let Drenevan have all the fun." Noceo indicated the land past the domus. The Clan seemed to have somehow flattened a portion of the broad mountaintop, roads branching like capillaries from the main artery they walked on to direct wagons to warehouses in the distance. "Acres of blazeleaf fields there, so I really wouldn't recommend running. These mountains are ours. Show her around, Dalvia." He sauntered off.

A mass of brilliant snow twitched to Sarai's left. *Gods, I didn't even see her there.*

"Please follow me," Dalvia addressed her feet before slowly, almost hopefully, raising her head. One look at the tightly leashed anger in Sarai's eyes, and she dropped it back down with a blank smile.

Oh. Sarai stilled at the bittersweet familiarity of that motion. How many times had she offered the same smile during the past months of verbal abuse during trials, during her years in Arsamea? Why did Dalvia sport the same look like a second skin?

There was a lifelessness to her that seemed to have burrowed bone-deep a long time ago. Sarai recalled her silent tears in the farmer's memory at the wanton destruction in Komis. And the Am Semni Institute saw to boil beetle plague victims that still had some hope of survival. *Those aren't the actions of a killer.*

Wondering how Dalvia had ended up tethered to her circumstances, Sarai trailed her into the manor's wood-paneled interior, past a dizzying series of once-opulently furnished rooms. Now, they all wore the same patina of ash, mold sprawling across the ceiling. Rotting decadence. Noceo seemed to have left the place as a mausoleum. *But does he hate it, to let it fall so into despair?*

Dalvia silently took her around the mansion. Dead staircases and hallways passed in succession until they reached the base of Noceo's replica of Aoran Tower.

The climb to his study was a long one. Kadra left the upper echelons of his tower to Cato and a vast library of ancient tomes and legal jurisprudence. Noceo apparently insisted on residing at the very top. Her feet ached by the time she was deposited outside an oaken door.

He lounged against it in a gray-green uniform that appeared to be Clan garb, looking strangely paler than she'd seen earlier. He'd removed the veil shielding his face too.

Noceo bu Kader. He didn't look as much like Kadra as she had initially thought. His gray eyes looked silver without the white veil to offset them. His skin held the waxy pallor of someone who rarely saw the sun, which lent his features an almost ethereal fragility. His was the sort of rosy-lipped face that bards spoke of when they described princes in foreign lands and titled gentry. Only his serpentine eyes ruined that illusion. They fixed on her with immense amusement.

"Please, come in." He inclined his head to the chair across his desk. "I apologize for the threats, but you didn't leave me much choice. The next time you notice an enemy make a slip of the tongue, Death-Summoner, do keep it to yourself."

"I'll be sure to," she grit out.

Noceo gave her a reproving look. "We really needn't be enemies." He spread his hands wide, encouraging her to look around.

His high-ceilinged study held all the ornamentation she had expected in her first meeting with Kadra. The furniture, from the oak desk to the cushioned chairs and the bookcases holding strange instruments and vials, was perfect in design and polish. This wasn't the same wealth she saw in the south–loud, desperate for attention. Clan Kader had nothing to prove and only sought to swallow more.

Unlike Kadra's desk and its daily mountains of petitions, Noceo's sported several bound sheaves of parchment written in a precise, exacting hand. Richly embroidered tapestries hung where blank spaces of wall would have shown, detailing the Clan's family tree, and its heraldry–a silver shield with a chalice at the center and a safsher above it, the curved blade dripping blood into the cup. Below it was the Clan's motto in the ancient tongue, *Violentia nervus potestas.*

"Violence is the sinew of authority," she translated.

"Drenevan always did take that seriously," Noceo mused. His eyes brightened when she neared the instruments on his shelves. "I'm sure you've realized by now that we're brothers."

She felt every word like a dagger. Her mouth went drier than the Xārōmand Desert. *Damn it, Kadra.* But perhaps this was what had put that turbulence in his eyes when he'd left her in the north. This might have been the truth he had promised to give her. She didn't want to hear it from Noceo's lips.

"What do you want with me?" she asked, low and careful.

He seemed to digest that as if he wasn't sure. "I *don't* want to harm you. It's a rare woman who wouldn't turn on Drenevan after all the harm he's done. He left you to die post-Fall, nearly got you killed at the Unraveling, persistently hid his past from you, and still gets to use you as he wishes."

She waited for her magic to tell her he was lying. It didn't. "Kadra died out of guilt."

"Does it matter?" Noceo looked curious. "*Death-Summoner.* You could have asked for anything. It's a shame you asked for him. Do you know that a godly incursion on the mortal plane leaves a mark? Summoning used to be forbidden by the Clerics for that reason. It leaves the area where the Summoning occurred vulnerable to other gods. Apparently, they can be a ghastly lot."

She sat across from him. "It wouldn't have changed my decision."

"It seems not," he said ruefully. "But I have you both to thank for everything playing out as it has." He steepled his fingers. "Even before Drenevan's destruction of our home, Clan Kader always operated from the shadows, believing we didn't have the strength to challenge the Tetrarchy. But you came along and got two Tetrarchs killed, practically all by yourself." His shrewd eyes gleamed. "I'd been working my way up the Order for years. Thank you for the impetus to act."

A cold tingle began in her fingertips. "I saw you that day at the Stones Guild, didn't I? Why the subterfuge?"

"I was intrigued," he said with a sheepish smile that could have been charming had something bitter not glimmered in his eyes.

"What happens now?" she asked through gritted teeth. "Will you turn me into a puppet?"

"Drenevan's the one who's always been able to get people to do anything. He's never needed magic. I have to Coerce people." Noceo sighed. "You've seen the results. He's Magus Supreme. I'm not. Which of us do you really think holds power?"

Odd. Her magic registered what he was saying as true, yet it was a soft, numb creature in comparison to the clear gongs of sound that normally rang in her chest. Perhaps Telmar was right, and Noceo's power could be her equal and opposite. Yet, he had wiped the memory of their meetings before.

"Am I here for you to blackmail Kadra?"

"Oh." He looked chagrined again. "No, he's due to fall any day now in Edessa. I don't need to dangle you over his head. No." He stood, leaning over his desk to peer at her. "You're here because I want you here."

An invitation to a tower, and a man who wanted her there for reasons she couldn't fathom. *I've been here before.* With Kadra.

She had a sinking feeling as to what Noceo was going to say but couldn't halt the precipitating question. "Why?"

"Because we want the same thing," he said, as though it were the most obvious thing in the world. At her incredulous snort, he hummed thoughtfully. "It is a difficult thing, Death-Summoner, to see things in others that they don't in themselves. Like the fact that love is not enough for you." He rounded his desk and perched atop it to stare down at her. "Like the fact that you crave power."

The breath in her lungs suddenly burned. "Like *havïd* I do."

"Don't take it as an insult. I wasn't always this powerful either, but there are ways." Something amused formed in the furrow of his eyebrows when she failed to hide her curiosity. He stood and offered her a hand. "Come with me."

She glowered at it. Sighing, he tucked it into his pocket and led her down the never-ending stairs winding out of his tower.

He stopped before a pair of double doors untouched by fire, wards etched into the very doorframe as protection. They parted noiselessly upon unlocking to reveal a hallway that stretched as wide as Aoran Tower. Her steps echoed on the stone-and-marble floor past busts of men with a vague resemblance to Noceo and Kadra and books that looked older than the Aequitas within clear crystal cases.

"Welcome to the Clan's Relic Hall." Noceo looked amused at her dropped jaw. "No one could keep me away from here as a child. There's something powerful about having a people or place or to tie yourself to that you know will go on after you." He glanced back at her. "I hear you're an orphan."

"Are you trying to say that I'm tying myself to Kadra because I haven't known permanence?"

"I think you're rebelling," he said, with a kindliness that set her teeth on edge. "Just like Drenevan is. Do you know why he calls himself 'bu Kadra' instead of 'bu Kader'?" He didn't wait for her response. "It's an obscure Urdish word that means 'no one.'"

Her steps slowed. *Drenevan bu Kadra.* The "bu" was a possessive. He'd gone by "Drenevan of no one."

"Dramatic, don't you think? Orphaning himself like that. But that *is* part of why you went for him. You thought he was like you."

This time, the blow landed. "I don't need someone to mirror me to love them."

"We all do. At the end of the day, we love ourselves most. I hope you can be honest about that."

Glowering, she assessed him as they wove through the Clan's mementos of more powerful days. Like Kadra, he moved with purpose and elegance, body language so contained as to make him impossible to read.

"Why bother with a coup?"

He thought for a moment. "Vengeance. Irritation." He flashed her a grin. "I find the south tiresome on the best of days."

"So, you loosed a plague and turned them madness-struck?"

A frown edged Noceo's lips. "I'll accept every accolade for exacerbating tension, but the rest wasn't me. I don't know why the beetles went rabid either. The north hated the south just fine without me, and I had nothing to do with your madness-struck."

Truth. The words rang clearer than they had so far. Sarai froze. "You had *nothing* to do with the madness-struck in Edessa?"

"Of course not."

True. Everything turned to smoke and snow in her head. *Then, who's behind it?*

Mistaking her terror for thought, Noceo offered her his arm again. An imperceptible shift took place in the line of his shoulders when she stood where she was. "You don't take easy to change, do you? Drenevan's a different beast though. He always adjusted to what Clevsin—our father—demanded so easily. There wasn't an emotion in him that wasn't linked to violence."

Her hands clenched.

He followed the motion with a thoughtful nod. "Yes, his 'love' for you. Every man has their urges, even him. But there is a reason our father was so preoccupied with Drenevan. He's the very best of us. I doubt that there's any child this Clan has raised that has so completely become a monster."

"You set a market aflame *here* to test your strength!"

"Coups don't come cheap," he said wryly. "Targeting a southern city would have brought the Tetrarchy's eyes on me too quickly, but the north never bothers telling you anything, and they blamed the Guilds so quickly." He shrugged. "As they should. I didn't create this conflict. Does it matter that I held the flame to the brazier? Would you rather that they stay impoverished here?"

"There were better ways–"

"Were there?" He closed in, invading the wide breadth of personal space she maintained at all times with men. "Death-Summoner, have you never wanted something so powerful in your hands that the whole world will *finally* sit up and take notice of what you say?"

Her tongue stuck to the roof of her mouth.

Silver eyes pried into hers, a subtle knife unlike the swallowing black of Kadra's gaze. "Are you not tired of screaming into a void, begging a foolish populace to listen? Don't you weary of listening to their infighting and petty prejudices? I can make them behave. Lives were lost, yes, but that's the nature of war. Drenevan would say no different. At least, *I* have been honest with you."

The hand that touched her face held curiosity. Her skin crawled, but Noceo ignored her visible shuddering.

"Tell me that you've never wanted to press a knife to a Guildmaster's throat and shut them up. Tell me that you've never wanted to control their very limbs to force them to do as you bid. Isn't it all because you know you have no power?"

He may as well have skewered her. She was in Arsamea again, seeing Marus loom before her. She was surrounded by the dead in Komis and Edessa. And painfully aware that she could do *nothing.*

"I can make you *more*," he vowed. "I was a Seventh-Tier too, prior to my newfound strength. I'd share it with you. Drenevan can only offer anguish under the guise of independence. He acts like he's supporting you, but really, you're carrying it all alone."

"That isn't true," she said tightly, trying to pull away from his grip.

"Isn't it?" His eyes narrowed to silver slits. "Has this *love* made your life simpler or worse? Has it not subjected you to ridicule? Death-Summoner, have you truly never wanted power?"

The pressure in her veins shot up dangerously. "I don't want *your* power."

His smile held a terrible glee. "Thank you for admitting the converse."

The hand on her shoulder slid down to find her palm. She jerked away, but he locked a hand around her waist and forced her still.

"You crave conquest." He bent to her ear. "I can give that to you every day. I'll show you who Drenevan truly is. I don't need you to profess undying love. I have no use for that. But we could be honest with each other, Death-Summoner. I find that a vastly underrated quality." He eyed the fearful pulse at the base of her neck with amusement. "Now, will you join me?"

There it is. The same question Kadra had asked her eleven months ago. She gave the same answer she had given him then.

She laughed. Long, loud, and with a touch of fury. She laughed until her throat ran hoarse. And his eyes altered.

Fury bled into silver. Goose bumps peaked her flesh as his fingers tightened. A breath, and he let her go with a short laugh, clasping his hands behind his back and walking a few paces away.

He stopped. "Kneel."

Magic slammed into her like a hammer and wrapped invisible vines around her limbs. She staggered.

"You can't breathe," he observed. "You won't unless you kneel."

The air rushed from her lungs. Straining, she fought the compulsion, managing only a thin stream before the world darkened. She fell to her knees. Her lungs suddenly expanded again.

Noceo took a seat and plucked a sheaf of parchment from a nearby table. His voice seemed to come from far away. "Crawl here."

"You fucking–" She grit her teeth as her body tried to comply, biting her lip until it bled.

This is not your will, she reminded her body. *This is not your will.* She repeated it until she realized that she had begun saying it aloud. Strength ebbed from her, muscles cramping with tension. She raked her fingernails over the stone floor, dug them into her palms.

The tightening at Noceo's temples told her that he hadn't seen anyone fight back before, that Telmar had been right about her having some immunity to the magic. But it wasn't absolute.

"*Crawl.*"

Noceo watched the precise moment she broke. Her left hand moved first, then her right hand and knee. She couldn't comprehend what she was doing, moving like an animal. She would have rather he hit her, broke a limb or a cheekbone, but he didn't have to raise a finger as she crawled, silent screams ringing in her ears. His silver-toed boot halted her by pressing against her chin.

Meeting his scathing smile, she spit on his leg. "Your brother never hurt me for laughing at his offer." Kadra had looked delighted at it. "He gave me a fucking key to his tower."

A dangerous glint in Noceo's cold eyes. "I didn't want us to be enemies, Death-Summoner. But here we are." He bent down. "You're worthless. You know this, and you agree with it. You'll say it for me a thousand times."

No. She trapped her tongue between her teeth, but her mouth still shaped the words.

He tsked. "You can't bite your tongue or hold your breath either. Keep saying it."

Blood shrieked in her ears, drowning out the first time she said it. She wasn't as lucky the second time, couldn't take back the horror of hearing the words in her own voice.

Worthless. Worthless. It poured out of her like it was all she'd known. She sat in a corner of her mind watching it leave and screamed and screamed. No one could hear her.

And deep down where even he couldn't touch, something broke.

Blood ran into her mouth from how hard she'd bitten her lips. The pressure in her head was agonizing. *Gods, Kadra, this was why you feared for me.*

The door opened. "Noceo, I—" Dalvia froze at Sarai on all-fours before averting her gaze.

"Just as well, I think she's ready to leave." Noceo's gaze returned to Sarai. "*Stand.*"

She was a puppet, going through the motions as he led her outside the manor. Dalvia bit her lip, looking torn as she opened a Bridge. Sarai could have wept upon spotting the marketplace's familiar, colorful stalls beyond the portal.

"As promised." Quiet rage still suffused Noceo's features. "Walk through."

She complied, a shaky tear tracking down her cheek upon stepping back into the lively space. *Thank the Elsar.*

"You can remember everything now. I might as well give back those memories. Now, *hold still right here*, and *watch* me until I leave." A chilling smile spread Noceo's lips like a blade through flesh. Drawing up the hood of his cloak, he walked to the Guildsmen loitering outside the tavern.

No. Her heartbeat stuttered, froze.

"There you are!" At the corner of her eye, Méherre raced to her. "Gods, I thought your Magus Supreme would have my head!"

Noceo spoke a few words to the Guildsmen. His silver eyes narrowed in amusement.

Time dripped in slow seconds as her eyes shot to Méherre's. "*Run.*" She couldn't move her head. He had ordered her to *watch.*

She screamed to the market, caring nothing for how mad she sounded. "RUN!"

Méherre followed her eyes and paled, gaze hardening to burning coals before she gestured outward. A portal split the air yards away. The market-goers stared at it.

"Run through it! *Please!*" Sarai couldn't. He'd ordered her to hold still.

Eight blank-faced Guildsmen raised their hands to the sky as one. Out of the corner of her eye, she caught a spark flaring overheard.

No.

The air exploded.

And she knew nothing.

17
MANTLE OF MADNESS

How had his brother gone unnoticed?

Kadra downed another glass of wine, splitting his thoughts between dreading Méherre's return to Bridge him back to Sarai, and how he had missed the resurgence of his godsdamned Clan. Footsteps raced through his atrium before the door to his study flew open.

Kadra raised an inquiring brow at Cato's disheveled appearance.

"You've a visitor."

Now for the truth. Kadra set down the wineglass, catching the faint tremble to his fingers. *Fuck.* He rose, mentally going over the halting speech that he'd prepared for Sarai when Cato shook his head.

"It isn't Méherre." Avoiding Kadra's eyes, he stared at the floor, breathing hard. "Come—come outside, Drenevan."

A spark of unease burned a path through him stronger than the persistent ache in his spine. He followed Cato to where Anek stood by Aoran Tower's gates, with red-rimmed eyes and a haunted expression.

Red-rimmed eyes.

Realization flared like lightning before he snuffed it out. *No.* His hands slipped on the gates he had replaced after Wrath's tantrum. He fumbled with the key as he unlocked them. *She's safe.*

"Petitor Anek." He inclined his head, emerging from Aoran Tower's wards.

Their head jerked toward him as pale as Cato. "Magus Supreme Kadra," they said hoarsely, like they had been screaming. "I was calling for you, but your wards—you couldn't hear me."

"I found them outside." Cato's voice was barely a whisper.

The pieces fell into place again before he shattered the picture. "Has something happened to Cassandane?" Kadra asked carefully.

"No." Despite their ramrod straight posture, Anek looked close to tears. "I'm sorry to have to say this, Magus Supreme. But we've received word from Méherre. She didn't have much time, so I came to deliver the news. It seemed that Sarai paid a brief visit to Komis."

Fuck. A bolt of agony burst down his spine when he tensed. "And?" he grit out.

"I don't know how it happened, but there was a lightning strike at a market that tore down the western city walls. The death toll is in the hundreds. Petitor Sarai–" Their voice wavered, and he knew.

Blood rang in his ears, a war drum. His heart cracked like a sheet of ice.

He vaguely registered that he had snarled out a "*speak*" when Anek blurted out the rest. "Méherre says she's unaccounted for, but they're still looking. There's nothing confirming her as…" They shook their head. "Wrath's teeth, I can't say it. She can't be dead."

He couldn't move.

"Méherre said that she saw Wines Guildsmen call down the strike, but that they seemed to be acting under duress. She was by Sarai, and she got out alive. There's a chance–" Anek broke off.

Sarai could be alive. She could be dead. And all because–Anek's words finally penetrated his haze of disbelief and fury. *Duress.* Blood sang to him as strong as grief. *Noceo.*

The rage that swamped him was bone-deep. Tundra currents that would freeze all in his path, their screams still trapped in their throats. "Where's Cassandane?"

Anek flinched at his menace. "Her tower. Look, Sarai could be alive–"

"She *is* alive," he growled, bitterly noting the way Cato and Anek flinched.

Storming back inside, he saddled his horse. When Cato appeared at his shoulder a moment later, he barely listened to the older man's pleas for restraint and set off for Favran Tower.

The ride was a blur of wind. Every hoofbeat a drop on a water clock, a second away from a time when she had been alive. His guilt at her Fall paled in comparison to the fissure that split him now. There was so much he hadn't told her.

He wouldn't allow it. He was Magus Supreme. If she was dead, he would go to that desolate dock facing Death's barge and take her with him. The gods would not have her.

Gaius met him at the base of Favran Tower, features stark with shock. "I heard—" He broke off. "What must I do?"

"Inform me when Méherre returns." Kadra dismounted. "I'm going to Komis."

"Please don't." The doors to Favran creaked open. Cassandane emerged, red dressing gown wrapped around her, features pale but firm.

To Gaius's credit, he didn't waver for a second. "*Certo*, Magus Supreme." He hadn't finished speaking before riding off.

Pain and exhaustion made dark smudges of Cassandane's eyes. "I can't imagine what you're feeling, but you can't leave."

"Don't stop me, Cassandane," he said, voice dangerously soft.

She flinched. "You hold a duty to more than just Sarai. We need you here."

"*She* needs me."

Cassandane's knuckles whitened around the doorframe. "Our people are being mass murdered! We don't know the cause, culprit, or weapon, and the land is teetering upon civil war. No one here has seen true battle or can fathom what it's like. They need leadership, and they will look to whom they believe best capable of quashing this. *It isn't me!*"

"It must be," he said coldly. "I won't abandon her."

"War needs blades not judges! *You* are our strongest. Sarai wouldn't want you abandoning everyone in Ur Dinyé just to run to her!"

His heart cracked. "Don't presume to tell me what she would want when she could be lying in rubble!" he snarled. Cassandane stumbled back, going white as sparks hissed around them.

"I'm sorry, but I've already made the decision. Méherre won't return here until she's found Sarai, alive or dead—" She froze at the knife that materialized in Kadra's hand.

"That was not your choice to make." His voice rose barely above a whisper, but she shrank back.

"*Please*, I'm not doing this without reason. Nearly two thousand fell madness-struck in my Quarter today. Inquisitor Verentia has agreed to submit Clanlady Dalvia for an Examination at the Aequitas tomorrow. If Sarai is alive, can you really have her return to a city that thinks she's Death's handmaiden? Let Méherre find Sarai. We'll set these rumors to rest and ease her path home."

His vision ran red with fury. "Tell me, when did you decide that having the Order as an ally was more useful than finding one of our own?"

"Since I saw that they were our greatest detractors last night." Cassandane swallowed. "If they realize that Clanlady Dalvia's wrong, we appease the people, gain an ally, and keep our seats."

His lips curled contemptuously. "The only *seat* I have ever craved is beside her." The jagged fragments of his heart tore at his chest. "Tell me why I shouldn't kill you now."

Her voice fractured. "I can't presume to know what Sarai would want. But you do. Ask yourself if she would want that."

She wouldn't. His soft-hearted Petitor would never abandon this land no matter how it treated her. His throat thickened.

"This city won't survive without you," she whispered.

"You have ten hours, Cassandane." His voice was a scarred rasp. "I will attend your assembly. And afterward, if I am not Bridged to Komis, this city will not survive *me*."

He couldn't return to Aoran Tower. There was too much of her there; he'd go mad. Returning to Delran Tower's empty ballroom with his saddlebags, he pushed the double doors open into the ballroom in which he had threatened the damned Guilds only last night.

She had been alive then. Not in that liminal space between death and existence where time marked a pendulum between both extremes until it provided an answer.

He slumped against the table, head in his hands. There was so much he had meant to tell her. An entire world he had meant to lay at her feet. His gaze arrowed on one of the balconies overlooking the room. Over nine months prior they had stood there, watching the partygoers at Aelius's convivium weave to music. Yearning had nearly brought him to his knees that night when she had defended him, smiled at him, teased him. How had she done it knowing that he had walked away from her?

He tore his eyes away and entrenched himself deeper in ice, crushing his grief to a dull ache.

A reckoning comes, he had been told. *And it will force your hand between love and country.*

He spoke into the ballroom's desolate quiet. "Wrath."

Red soaked the walls in his next breath. The room undulated and warped into the bleeding maw of an unfathomable beast. Garbled limbs reached from the pooling blood, skeletal mouths agape in suffering. At the center of it all, Wrath flicked away a grasping hand with a sound of disgust. His black robes swallowed all light.

"I did warn you that you would beg." Four rows of fangs glistened when the god grinned.

Kadra didn't contest the statement. They both knew it was true.

"You reek of vengeance and regret, *acolyte.* Was that what changed your mind?"

"A man can save a country. A god can afford to sacrifice it. The Elsar may have brought Sarai to me," Kadra said, his tone soft and lethal, "but you will not take her away."

Worlds crashed, burned, and rose again in the god's eyes. "Regret that you couldn't save her before. Regret that you can't save her now. Regret that you can never return all she has lost. Regret at the entrance to every whitesleep den in this city. Your life, Tetrarch, seems predicated on self-flagellation. You partake in it more than those trapped in the Hell of Whips."

"The gods would do well to try the same."

Wrath's amber eyes gleamed. "We do not repent, because we do not *choose*, Tetrarch. Contrary to mortal belief, the Elsar do not treat you as our puppets. We allow consequence to take its course. Many should be grateful for it."

"Was it consequence that struck Sarai in Komis?" Ice and rage were a bitter chorus in his voice.

"It was." A skull floated to the surface of the blood pooling around them. Wrath stepped on it absently. It cracked. "You'll see it soon. Regret can be a dangerous thing for a mortal. It blinds them to the present while they seek out what they wish had been possible. Too much escapes you while you atone for a past you believe should have been different and force a future you want to exist. So, before I ask, Tetrarch," he drew an unnaturally long sword from a slim scabbard that hissed as it struck the floor of flesh below them, "will you regret this too?"

"No." He would enter any abyss if it restored her to him.

Wrath's blade carved a wide circle arc into the ground, cauterizing the flesh it tore. Tinny screams echoed from the rift. "Then, step inside."

Kadra walked across the pulsing floor to the Elsar. Face-to-face, the god's features were a study in madness. Unnaturally sharp, inhumanely bright, Wrath was all teeth and plunder.

"Draw your sword, mortal. This is your contract. Immense power when alive as one of the Godstouched, and godhood once dead. With both, you will choose who you become. With both, comes the risk of monstrosity. Do you accept?"

The air throbbed, spat blood, burned. "I do." Kadra withdrew the blade he kept on his baldric and, at the god's bidding, thrust it into the center of the fleshy circle. It sank in. The room shuddered.

"*Finally*." Wrath's smile widened, teeth engorging.

Hands burst from the hole gouged by Kadra's sword. He stiffened as they gripped his feet, abnormally long limbs winding up his torso to immobilize him. The cavernous space enclosing them grew infinitely high, Wrath engorging until he stood fifty feet tall, black robes trailing in his path.

Madness. This was why so few survived seeing the Elsar.

"No fear, Tetrarch?" Wrath's enormous form boomed.

"No." Fear was knowing that the woman he loved, to whom he had barely spoken of love, could be dead under the city walls of his former hometown.

"I chose well." The god neared him. A claw the size of an arm tapped his forehead. A previously unknown tightness eased in his chest.

Wrath looked pleased. "Well, Time will tell what this makes of you. They told me that you'd come. A most useful sibling, though this world persists in calling them male." His fangs snapped together with a laugh. "This should be quite interesting. I'll see you soon, Tetrarch."

The cave of flesh receded into Delran Tower's tile and glass.

He stood alone at its center. The floor-to-ceiling windows circling the ballroom told him he hadn't undergone any physical changes. But the Elsar didn't lie. He drew a grindstone from his satchel and sat at the empty banquet table.

Ten hours. He began sharpening his sword, counting down the seconds with each slice of metal against the grindstone. Ten hours, and he would go to her.

And if he found her corpse, if it was too late to pull her from the docks by the river to the afterlife as she had done for him, it wouldn't be Wrath he pledged himself to but Ruin.

18
RUBBLE

She was running out of air.

Sarai stuck her nose through the scant gap between the chunk of the city walls crushing her legs and the right half of her torso. She drew in a shaky breath, blood flooding her throat along with the precious air she drew in. Her lungs couldn't expand to full capacity. *Don't think about that. Don't panic.*

It could have been worse. Another slab of wall had wedged between the ground and the mass pressing on her. It kept most of the weight off, or this would have been a repeat of Sidran Tower. She could hold on. *Someone will find me soon.*

She had clung to that hope for the past ten hours, ignoring the vise of fear and stone suffocating her. The sky wheeled above, pitch-black. Still, she held fast. She had been in a corner of the market when everything went to shit. Rescue would take a while. Screaming would only waste precious air.

Noceo. Between Arsamea, Edessa, and now him, she had learned that being torn apart didn't make one stronger. It warped her reflection of herself until she no longer understood it.

The worst part was that Noceo hadn't been wrong.

She wanted power.

She wanted enough of it to set the corrupt, the hateful, and their acolytes ablaze. To force Noceo to his knees and make him scream as he had her. Her vengeance wouldn't be for the north or south, but for the hapless creature he had proven her to be.

Then, there was Kadra. Her heart felt ravaged. She couldn't think. Could only lie there as her body fulfilled the last of Noceo's commands. Remembering everything.

Memory returned to her, slipping softly into place.

Stones Guildmaster Albanus. She almost smiled as his apoplectic figure bloomed in her head after her infamous destruction of his beloved six-thousand-aurei vase. She'd glanced at the window throughout, noting the eavesdropping Guildspeople passing by in the hope that she wouldn't give in to Albanus's bribes. Then—

Sunlight. Noceo watching her outside.

"Try a different corner."

"Interesting, it didn't take."

"You never saw me today. And you won't notice me again unless I give you permission. I'll see you soon, Death-Summoner."

Noceo trailing behind her one evening at Sidran Tower to ask whether she remembered him. Noceo by the gates of Aoran Tower telling her she had surprised him at her Hearing, asking to be let in, for her to ruin Kadra with him.

He'd been careful not to say much on each occasion, evidently suspecting that she had enough resistance to his magic to remember him as with their longer conversation at the Stones Guild. He hadn't been ready to reveal himself then.

You've outdone yourself with this formula, Dalvia, she recalled his amusement in the farmer's memory. That fucking Bridger wasn't without blame. She had armored him.

A burn in her lungs warned her that air was growing thin.

Shifting closer to the crevice she was breathing through, she hissed as her broken legs screamed at the motion. Moving by fractions of inches, she tilted her head for better access to the opening when a boot passed over it. Voices cursed a blue streak above, their southern accents more pronounced with fury. *Kadra's vigiles.* She closed her eyes upon the burn of tears, relief breaking panic's hold. *Thank Fortune, Noceo didn't get to them.*

"Over here! Underneath!" she rasped loudly, directing them forward, step by laborious step.

A moment later, exclamations filled the air. The rubble over her vibrated and rose to reveal her stalwart vigiles. She could have cried, but blood rushed to her broken legs, swift as agony.

She clenched her jaw with a curse. "*Wrath and Ruin.* No, it's alright," she insisted as they debated on prying her loose. "Help with the rescue efforts. A healer will find me."

A group of them stopped by as she said it. They assessed her grimly. "Just the legs?"

"And right ribs," she wheezed.

"Then you've fared better than most." Soot streaked their skin and their eyes glowed with the reflection of a fire still raging some yards away. "Stay here, we'll assess the rest of this area and return."

"Thank you." She drew a deep breath, trying not to cry once the healers and vigiles left to assist other victims. Trapped in the dark, everything had seemed so inconsequential—her fears that Kadra had lied to her, her foolish insecurities. She had just wanted to get home and sink into his arms.

Smoke stung her eyes. She let them stream, blaming the acrid air when a weary healer came by.

"It was like this during the last strike too," the gray-cloaked woman said as she gripped Sarai's twisted left leg and righted it. Power sped into her palms, mending bone, knotting muscle and skin back together faster than Sarai ever could. "Smoke and screams. You got a pair of lungs on you. Thank you for the warning."

"How many dead?"

"Over a hundred. Could have been worse. Your eyes seem well. Still got your ears?"

"They're ringing," Sarai admitted.

"I'll take a look. The burns and lacerations will have to wait." She indicated the gashes along Sarai's torso from where rubble had cut in. "Too many who need help." She started on Sarai's left leg, pulling strength from some deep reservoir that only those who sought to halt Death's coming possessed.

"Thank you, truly."

The healer nodded brusquely, confirming that all was well with her ears and fixing up her right lung and cracked ribs. "The legs will be shaky for a bit until your rebuilt muscle acclimates to use." She paused a moment. "Don't mean to pry, but that's what you look like?"

Sitting up, Sarai sighed. She'd run out of magic while trapped under the rubble, and her scarring was blatantly visible. "For better or worse," she admitted.

"Here, all we have is worse." The healer patted her arm before racing toward a shrill scream.

Winded, Sarai rested her head in her hands and took a deep breath. The damage was so much worse than she had imagined for the past hours. Sections of Komis's city walls had struck the marketplace like spears, sparing no one in their path. The rubble hid the worst of the bodies, but here and there were patches of peeling flesh, a hand, something that may have been a head. Fire reigned over the market's entrance where the strike had come in.

The blisters on her burned palms popped when she clenched them at the memory of Noceo's amused smile. "*Fuck!*" she screamed, the roar of wind and fire stealing the word as though she'd never spoken. She may as well never have. She had no power.

Forcing herself to stand, she wobbled to the closest support–part of the tavern that the Wines Guildsmen had delivered to. The rest of it had exploded, the amphorae that the tavernkeeper had paid for bleeding through the floorboards. The sight snapped something in her–the same dangerous muscle she had used the day she'd killed Aelius. Today, she had no such available target.

Yet. She raised her eyes to the manor in the Drust Mountains. Then, returning to the rubble, she shifted smaller stones, uncaring of the scrape of rock over her blistered palms. A few northern vigiles approached, and she stiffened, preparing to eviscerate them if she so much as heard a word about what a "woman's job" was. But disaster forced even idiocy to one side. Together, they forced aside the debris, dragging corpses and people alike to the straw mats set outside the market so they could be counted, mourned, or joyfully reunited. The latter occurred far less often than she hoped.

When morning came, the market had been fully excavated, the city wall remnants rolled outside Komis's borders. Those who still had some chance at life were piled onto wagons and sent to the Am Semni Institute despite Sarai's protests that they might fare better with a healer's attention.

"Clanlady Dalvia has a boatload of healers up there," a northern vigile informed her sternly. "The hospital also treats plague victims, but you won't find people here being choosy."

She'd had no choice but to watch the injured being taken away. *They won't believe me.* Komis evidently placed great faith in Dalvia's talents. Sarai simply couldn't reconcile that charity with the woebegone woman she had seen act as an accomplice to Noceo's Coercion. *Is this her idea of atonement?*

"Every vendor is accounted for." Another man sliced a line through the last name on his roll of parchment. "Gods, the Guilds should die for this." He looked Sarai's way as he said it.

For once, it wasn't them. "The Guilds will pay for what crimes they've committed."

"They never do," a woman bitterly scoffed, kneeling by one of the wounded. "The south and the Tetrarchy care nothing for us, why would they vindicate us now?"

Others took up the refrain, spitting questions at her like debris. She let them pelt her and bounce off, knowing their ravaged faces and soot-smudged eyes gleamed with the desperation to hurt. Beside her, Kadra's vigiles tensed in preparation for a fight.

I'm so fucking tired. Why couldn't they see it? Why didn't they even try to look beyond the sphere of their existence to understand the greater forces puppeteering them toward ugliness?

"By the Elsar and Naaduir, I'm not your enemy!" she finally broke in.

"She isn't." An ash-covered Méherre waded into the fray, glowering at those fencing Sarai. "The few seconds of warning you gave us made a difference."

Drawing Sarai aside, she surveyed her wounds with a tight exclamation. "*Fucking* Noceo. Is anything else broken? Are you ready to leave? I have firm instructions to bring you back to Edessa."

"Please."

"There are only a few designated spots within Edessa where Bridgers can bring people in, but Cassandane mentioned that they'd be at the Aequitas, so I'll take you there." Méherre pricked her finger and pressed the blood to the same curving rune Sarai had seen Dalvia use in the farmer's memory. The Bridger closed her eyes, brow creasing in concentration. Power exploded to life by the still-burning entrance to the market, raising the hair on the back of her neck. The air glistened like a heat mirage before splitting to reveal the base of a familiar, unnecessarily large statue.

Inhaling deeply, she and Kadra's vigiles stepped through the portal. The world spun in a blur of color and wind for all of a second. Then, she was on the other side, the north's chill replaced with the milder bite of an Edessan winter. And a clanging in her ears.

Pressing her hands over them, Sarai gaped at the people racing toward the Aequitas over the sunstruck field. Kadra, Cassandane, and Harion's vigiles had visibly abandoned all hope of orderly entrance and shoved people through the main doors. The emergency bells Cassandane had set up across the city jangled cacophonously.

"What's happened?" she yelled to a passerby.

"The Elsarian Order's staging a coup!"

Oh shit.

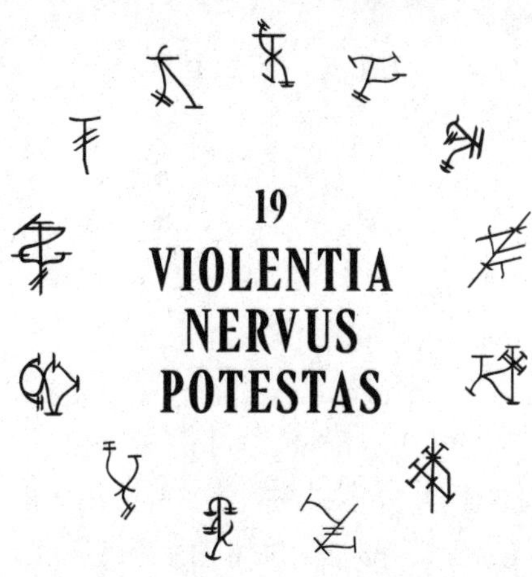

19 VIOLENTIA NERVUS POTESTAS

It was no hard thing to run a country.

Power sparked in the air as he strode through the Tetrarchy's Entrance and into the Aequitas. The low hum announced his arrival even before he took the marble steps to the dais and seated himself.

Fifty-eight Guildmasters swiveled to face him from opulent seating boxes. Blood leeched from their faces. *Wines Guild.* Kadra let his gaze wander along the group until he found its Guildmaster. Etilia stared straight ahead as though avoiding his eyes would save her. A vain hope.

Some of them were undoubtedly Coerced. Others wouldn't have required Coercion. His brother's current ventures must be extremely profitable to allow him to move about the city with impunity.

The Elsarian Order once again marred the Aequitas's stage. Verentia led the pack of indistinguishable priests fanning out behind her. Glee spilled from her like mist. Ioratius and the other Guildmasters seemed mildly perturbed at the sight. He wasn't.

Dalvia's spill of blond hair was noticeably absent from the crowd of blue-robed priests. That, too, didn't surprise him. She wouldn't have volunteered to be Examined before the Aequitas when she knew as well as he did that Anek or Harion would catch her in a lie.

Which meant that the Elsarian Order had sought a gathering for a farce. Cassandane was too eager for allies to see it, but the Order was not here to play her game. And today, he would not be of aid. The game mattered little to him when Sarai waited in a city of death.

His hands contracted into fists. The agony in his spine never worse. Sparks hissed around his seat, leaving scorch marks in their wake.

Halfway through her preliminaries, Cassandane stuttered with a wary glance at him. When she resumed speaking, it was at a significantly faster clip. "This will be a hurried assembly due to recent, distressing news from the north that Petitor Sarai may be...injured. While we still search for a means to end the beetle plague, we can confirm that it spread by means of whitesleep sacks found in a den." She winced when the assembled Guildmasters rose in a wave to blame the north. "Understand that we're still investigating the cause and blaming the north is premature. The Tetrarchy isn't targeting anyone."

On the contrary, he had every intention of doing so. Fissures ran through the arms of his seat with every flex of his fingers. Cassandane had never spoken faster.

"*Why her?*" Gaius had asked, days after Kadra had invited Sarai to live with him. "*Beg your pardon, Tetrarch Kadra, but no one understands it. She hates you, and there are...fairer women*," he had muttered awkwardly.

A faint smile had risen to Kadra's lips. "*Your vision has been better, Gaius. She's the best Petitor Edessa has had in decades. And she sees right through me.*" A note of wonder had seeped into his voice, and understanding had flitted across his right-hand man's face.

Men like him weren't meant to be known or loved. Clevsin had beaten that in early. Everything he had learned of the world since had proven that true. Madman, savior, tyrant, hero. Magus Supreme. Legends people had made of him. They took what they wanted to see and avoided the rest.

Then, she had glanced up at her Robing, known him as a monster, and still defied him. Laid him open, and he had craved more. Knew how little he cared about taking a life and still rested her beating heart over his every night. Only part of her shared his madness, but she had embraced him whole.

"*You've had a night*," she would say wryly when he came to her covered in blood, but would smile up at him, clear-eyed and guileless, and he had waited for another night to tell her that she knew who he was but not who he had been. He would not accept that he was out of time.

"Kadra, I could use some aid," Cassandane hissed under her breath.

The crowd had begun spitting a jumble of familiar accusations and demands. Why the plague persisted, and when Sarai could return with answers.

His mouth curved in a humorless smile. "I would bring her here to tell you myself. Yet, it seems that we're assembling, because the Elsarian Order is convinced that my Petitor is a servant to Death. They forced her to this stage under similar pretenses by citing Ruin. Now, they speak of Death. I wonder how many more of the gods she will have to go through."

Quiet sliced through the amphitheater at the pronouncement. He returned his gaze to the Order, many of whom avoided it. Verentia evidently thought differently. Triumph glinted in her eyes. Bloodlust made his fingers twitch.

"Well?" he asked, smooth and low.

Verentia drew herself to full height. "We, the Inquisitors for the Elsar, and head of Ur Dinyé's chapter for the Elsarian Order, are here to inform you, *Tetrarchy*, that your reign is ended."

Bewilderment settled over the Aequitas. To his right, Cassandane looked winded. "Inquisitor—"

"During our monarchical age, where the king made imprudent choices that led the nation's folk on the path to Ruin, the Clans and the Order would step in to supplant unworthy leadership in favor of clearer minds." Verentia wore a malicious shade of elation and a hunger she couldn't mask as she stared at Cassandane's seat. "Clanlady Dalvia helpfully brought us the text of laws that governed our land prior to the Corpus Juris Totus, as the latter curiously, apparently purposefully, doesn't provide for such an event as impeaching all of you at once." She laughed at Cassandane's pale features. "I would have brought a petition to the land's highest court, but I'm already there."

So, this was your move, Noceo. Kadra smiled coldly. He had warned Cassandane.

A loud, false sound left her throat that could have been a laugh but sounded significantly more pitiful. "This is an unamusing joke, Inquisitor."

Verentia's brows rose. "Your Petitor would have informed you if it was."

Anek, nervously standing behind Cassandane's seat, gripped it for their life. Features tight, they shook their head at Cassandane's terrified glance. Harion seemed torn between crawling into his seat or giving it up altogether. The Aequitas itself was quiet in their utter bewilderment.

Kadra tapped a hand on the edge of his seat and let his gaze roam over the crowd. *Where are you, Noceo?*

After a pleading glance at him, Cassandane gave up. "You've spent several months *swearing* up and down that Magus Supreme Kadra and Petitor Sarai held a coup. Now, here you are, doing the same?"

"Yes." Verentia shrugged. "If she can, then why shouldn't we?"

"That wasn't a godsdamned coup!" Cassandane slammed a fist on the arms of her seat when Verentia opened her mouth. "Sarai's life was at risk, or she wouldn't have fought Aelius. *I was there.* I fought him too, godsdammit!"

"So, now you *defend* Death's handmaiden!" Verentia said incredulously. "You are hereby *stripped* of your position—"

"You have *no* power to do that!" Cassandane rose. Tendrils of crimson lightning sputtered by her. "Stop this or—"

"Are you *threatening* me? Do you see this?" Verentia turned to the crowd, in a poor mimicry of Sarai. Narrowed eyes. A skeletal hand tugging at her tongue to mark her lies with malicious joy. Indignation that went only skin-deep. An absence of genuine concern. A blasphemy of the sincerity with which Sarai walked this stage.

He cared little for Cassandane's whispered pleas for him to intervene, but he wouldn't let Verentia make a mockery of how Sarai played the game.

He waited for her to take a breath and spoke. "No."

Verentia's brows snapped together amid a hiss of fearful whispers from the audience. "Is there something you wish to add, Magus Supreme?" she demanded frostily. "Death goes where your Petitor does, and has now followed her all the way to *Komis* to kill innocents there. I won't give her a chance to feed our souls to the Dark Realms any further. If she's miraculously survived yet again, she will submit to an exorcism."

Ice pricked up his neck and sank in. *A masterstroke, Noceo.* This was his coup. But where was the would-be-conqueror?

Kadra strode down the dais toward her, slow and unhurried. "No."

Bravado fraying, Verentia fled back toward her group of priests. "By the Elsar, stay away from me. Have you gone mad?"

"No. But I'm in danger of growing rather bored, Inquisitor. You've forgotten why I never had a Petitor until *Sarai*." Her name was hoarse in his mouth. "You creatures were always so easy to read."

Verentia gaped. "Creatures," she echoed to the crowd. "*This* is what your Tetrarchy thinks of—"

"Fools," he finished softly, his voice nevertheless rising above the dull thrum of the crowd. "Priests who believe the word of a woman they barely know who tells them exactly what they want to hear. Frauds who espouse ideologies that they don't believe in so as to get a political seat."

Leaving her shaking on the stage, he returned to his marble seat on the dais and tilted his head laconically toward Cassandane's chair. "You must have enjoyed that seat immensely at Sarai's Hearing to go this far for it. Petitor Anek, how much of what she's spouted does she believe in?"

"None of it," a familiar, exhausted voice called.

Every muscle in his body stilled. The ruined nerves along his spine quieted. His heart clawed up his throat as Sarai emerged from the Petitor's entrance. Blood and dirt tarred her skin. An ugly burn ran from the right side of her neck to her shoulder. She had never been more beautiful.

Cassandane slumped in her seat. "Oh, thank the Elsar," she muttered under her breath before speaking formally. "Petitor Sarai, it's good to see you alive."

His throat worked. He would have stood, but for the first time in his life, he wasn't sure if his legs would support him. Unlike him, the Aequitas recovered its voice and pelted her with questions.

Relief lit her golden eyes when she found his gaze, but there were shadows in her smile. She hobbled toward the iron stake where he burned people. Her trousers were shredded below the knee, and her legs had the telltale shine of new skin. They had been broken. His fists tightened.

Patiently bearing the onlookers' queries, she gripped the stake for support. The blood returned to his head the longer he took her in. He wanted to go to her, but the trepidation in her eyes told him that she needed him on this dais.

He learned why upon Cassandane's question. "Do you have answers for Edessa?"

"I do." Grim resignation was a heavy weight on Sarai's slight frame. Pain marred her features for a fraction of a second, and to his surprise, she turned to the crowd. "We do not have a plague."

The Aequitas splintered into a kaleidoscope of disbelief and anger. Cassandane looked dumbstruck. The audience yelled out the growing numbers of dead and the madness-struck, then questioned her sanity, emboldened by the conspiracy a now-laughing Verentia had sown in their heads.

"How did you survive *again?*" some yelled. Many took up the refrain until the Aequitas rung with doubt.

How much do you know, Sarai? Despite her perusal of the crowd and Cassandane, she had yet to turn her eyes back to his. Cold fissured through him.

"Petitor Sarai." He left his voice low, and her eyes flew to his with surprise that he was using the intimate tone that he took with her in private. "What did you find in Komis?" *Do you know who I was?*

Her features took on the same blankness that she used as a shield when she was struggling to hold herself together. And he had his answer. His hands fell from the arms of his seat. The water clock that ticked down the hours to his ruin ran dry. *She knows.*

The tense line of her spine sagged when the crowd didn't quiet. She gave an almost incredulous shake of her head.

"I'm so tired of begging people to listen." Her lips formed the words, but they were lost to the diatribes battering her. Then, in a breath, she squared her shoulders and spoke. "We have *no* plague. We have a tormentor. One who knows that if Edessa and the Tetrarchy fall, then they and Komis will reign. One who gnawed at us from within, while we gave them all the internal strife they craved. One who can make people do anything with a word because he's a godsdamned Coercer." She took a deep breath. "I know you're here, Inquisitor Silvus. But that's also Clanlord Noceo bu Kader, isn't it?"

Kadra went stock-still as everything went to hell around him. Sarai found his eyes then, her blank mask crumbling. A silent plea lay behind it. *Tell me that you don't know him.*

His reckoning was here. *I can't.*

Hurt and anguish warred for dominance on her face before she sagged against the pole. He stood without thought, striding down the dais to her when light rippled on a section of the stage and solidified into Dalvia's pale figure.

She slid a knife against Sarai's throat in a flash of metal. "I wouldn't." Her hand shook.

He stilled on the steps. Voices rose around him in shock and terror. Some wisely fled for the exits, having learned how dangerous it was to be caught in a battle in the Aequitas after the Unraveling. Wind howled over their shrieks. The sun was a brand above. But his only priority was his woman, ignoring the knife to her neck and watching Dalvia with resignation instead of shock.

She knows.

"Let her go." He studied the Bridger with a languid menace and caught the tremble that ran through the arm holding the knife. Dalvia had never been one for blood. "Your quarrel is with me."

"But it isn't," noted a coldly amused voice he hadn't heard in eleven years. "It's with *me*."

A half-veiled man parted from the fleeing group of priests. Verentia paused to stare at him, visibly torn between continued mutiny and self-preservation, before choosing the latter and running out. Blue robes and a veil hit the Aequitas's stage and his brother sauntered across clad in the Clan's gray-green uniform, a specter of the past made flesh.

Silver eyes he had once known as well as his known. An ever-present grin. And a face that had driven a young woman to ruin. Older, harder, but the same.

Kadra's rage morphed into something fractured. Not quite nostalgia and more bitter than grief.

"*Don't leave me! Gods, don't leave me, Drenevan!*" The words burned in his ears, jumbled flickers of memory of that last night arrowing through him. Some part of him had known even then that it wouldn't be their final meeting.

"Noceo." He inclined his head. "It's been some time."

"Over a decade." Hatred burned, then vanished under the sweep of Noceo's lashes as he took Sarai from Dalvia and repositioned the knife to her jugular. "What a reunion."

"It's been all of a day for me," Sarai bit out in granite tones. "I thought you said that you didn't need to dangle me over Kadra's head."

Noceo laughed. "Hush, Death-Summoner. I've already made you crawl."

The hatred that seethed in Sarai's eyes told Kadra everything about what she must have endured. Sparks danced at his fingertips, bloodlust made flame, as he envisioned tearing Noceo's tongue from his throat. "Release her."

"I think I've missed that vicious glint in your eyes." Noceo's lip curled. "But I'm afraid I can't. I made you a promise once." Embers of memory glowed in his eyes. "This is fulfilling it."

"If the gods exist and are fucking fair, you won't know an ounce of peace for this! You will never thrive! You will never succeed!" The words hung between them in the press of his knife at Sarai's neck.

"I made a promise too," Kadra said darkly. *We let the Clan burn.*

He tensed in preparation to lunge when his brother drew the knife tip lightly along Sarai's skin. Rage welled in him along with the drop of blood that ran along the blade.

"Today, we talk." An icy smile formed on Noceo's face. "I have no intention of harming her, not when she's been stubborn enough to survive again. It would be a shame if you force me to, though. Spilling blood isn't my strength. It'll be messy."

A fine lie. Though he seemed to believe it. "*Speak.*"

Descending from the dais, Cassandane prowled to the other end of the stage along with Harion, fencing Noceo in. His brother eyed them with amusement.

"The lovely Cassandane." Noceo bowed. "I should warn you that there isn't much point in this posturing. People are rather pliable in my hands. Petitor Sarai is quite right. They do anything I want."

"You aren't the slightest bit subtle about it either," Sarai noted as though she didn't have a blade to her neck.

Kadra's eyes narrowed at the genuine amusement that broke past his brother's icy mask. "I've no use for subtlety. It keeps no one in line. A hammer does. Edessa has fought you for months, and now there they are, united." He directed a hand toward the remaining stupefied spectators. "It's why Aelius held the land together without major conflict, and you couldn't. People prefer fear." At the immediate insulted yells from the crowd, he sighed. "*Quiet.*"

The order slammed into Kadra's eardrums, sealed his lips, and stuck his tongue to the roof of his mouth in the same breath. Out of the corner of his eye, he saw Cassandane clutch her throat. Others echoed the motion across the Aequitas, eyes huge.

Twelfth-Tier. Noceo's power had been nowhere close to this eleven years ago, at the peak of magical maturity. This command had been effortless, lacking the strained compulsion that he'd seen his brother apply during adolescence.

"Forgive me." Noceo's smile was unrepentant. "I'm a proponent of free will, of course. But you're rather loud. And you'll want to hear me for the next few moments."

Bulging eyes glared at Noceo from every corner of the Aequitas in silent disagreement.

Kadra quietly funneled power into the air. Slender currents of differing temperatures twisted together and sparked. His hands fisted, waiting. Because this was too simple. A hostage. Two opponents. He could take them easily, and Noceo knew it. There was something here that he had missed that would turn the tides.

The answer crystalized when he spotted the lightning magi arrayed throughout the courthouse. Noceo didn't have one hostage. He had thousands. One wrong move and he'd obliterate the Aequitas.

Grim resignation settled over Kadra, a mantle of stillness.

Noceo's silver eyes gleamed. "I'm sure you've all noticed the family resemblance." He pointed between them. "I'll admit, I'm Noceo bu Kader of Clan Kader. That's no secret. But that there, is Drenevan bu Kader, Clanson, killer, and now, Magus Supreme." The barest hint of bitterness laced his voice. "You've done well for yourself, *brother*."

Eyes bulged wider around them. Kadra glanced at Sarai. His heart twisted at her shuttered features. He angled his head toward some of the magi seated on the tiers in silent warning. She paled but tilted her wrist to show him that she had *beshaz* active on her armilla.

A corner of his mouth tugged upward. He poured power into his clenched larynx until the weight on it vanished. "Is this envy?"

Noceo's smile slipped before he slid geniality back on. "I asked you for *silence.*"

Kadra braced himself as the command struck, drawing from the deep reserve of magic Wrath had given him, and pulled his tongue away from the roof of his mouth when it tried to stick there. "You did."

Rage howled in his brother's eyes. "Keep your voice then. It won't help you. I have your priests. I pay your Praetors. And I have your people." He glanced at the onlookers. "Thank you for making it so simple. I emphasized the right stories, and you danced without any Coercion. Murder in the most public of arenas. Blood being touted as justice. A poor decision by a grieving girl to Summon a god. And a man on the throne with no purpose unless he has someone to fight. And you people swallowed it all." He took a step away from the stake, forcing Sarai to do the same or risk being cut. "*This*, people of the south, is a coup, not the Death-Summoner's tired attempts at transparency. Differentiate better next time."

Noceo's voice was a subtle knife, lulling his transfixed audience even as he mocked them. Kadra took in their blank faces and still figures. A magnetism so powerful that it halted all rational thought or they would have fled the Aequitas by now. He had seen Noceo do this to small rooms, but not to tens of thousands. How had he grown so powerful?

Kadra mirrored Noceo's motions when he took another step backward. "Did you come here to impart political theory to my constituents?"

"Partially. I'm here to give them a choice."

Kadra saw the walls of a trap move toward him with slow finality. The high tiers of the Aequitas twisted in the edges of his vision, different scenes playing out at each corner. A flaming battleground scarred with corpses and rubble in one. Screaming faces bleeding from every orifice choking to death on their fluids. And a void so black and deep that it took all life with it. Possibilities and probabilities.

"Being?"

"Life. And death." Noceo addressed his audience. "Kneel to me, Edessa. Disavow your Tetrarchs and accept my rule. Or I'll raze you to the ground."

Cassandane stumbled, eyes huge. Faces boiled red above them. Harion's jaw hung open.

A humorless smile curved Kadra's lips. No one would walk away unscathed today. Noceo wanted to raze the city, and its people would give him a reason to. There wasn't an Urd alive who didn't know that Edessa had always had too much damned pride.

The fear in Cassandane's eyes said she understood the same. "If it's power you want, we've an empty seat in the Tetrarchy. Will you not give us a chance to negotiate?"

Noceo laughed quietly. "That would defeat my goals. No, Head Tetrarch. Let your city vote." He raised his voice. "*Speak.*"

The crowd's forced silence evaporated into furious yells, screams, and northern slurs. Sarai winced at a "fuck off, mountain assholes!"

"Interesting," Noceo said mildly. "I believe the people have spoken."

Cassandane spread her hands. "There is no need for bloodshed. Let us speak and–"

"This won't buy you time. Even my brother knows it. The people have spoken." Black victory laced Noceo's voice. "Now, I get to enact the family motto, don't I, Drenevan?"

Harion pulled himself out of his stupor to scoff. "Come now, be realistic. No Coercer is *that* powerful. So, why don't you walk yourselves to the mines, before we send you to the Elsar?"

Kadra decided that he would kill Harion next when Noceo's eyes glinted.

"Send *me* to the Elsar?" Noceo repeated curiously. "How do you propose to do that when I can make you *kneel.*"

The Aequitas echoed with thousands falling to their knees, spitting their fury all the while. Kadra stood still, noting the way Sarai's knees buckled, but didn't sink. Partially immune.

A smile split Noceo's face when Harion hit the ground and blanched. "Now, I ask again. Edessa, your pride or your city? Give me your final answer."

That answer had been written at the city's conception. Kadra watched every Edessan in the audience swell and unleash a torrent of hatred.

Noceo smiled at the hurled abuse and turned to Kadra. "Well, brother?" Downturned mouth. Pale skin. Sweat at his temples. *Weariness.* Noceo's mask of amusement was near flawless, save for the threads of strain in his eyes. *Whatever he's imbibed, he's nearing his limit.*

Power bunched and ebbed around Kadra's fingertips. "You know my answer."

"That's what makes this so amusing." He tsked at the screaming crowd. "It was all so entirely predictable."

In one breath, he flung out a hand, the knife at Sarai's neck parting ways with his fingers and arrowing into Cassandane's shoulder. In the next, he roared a single word.

"*Begin.*"

It all happened at once. Every magus in the audience froze and raised their hands. Noceo let Sarai go as Dalvia tore open a portal; both ran into it and vanished. Clouds rolled overhead with vicious swiftness. Kadra blanketed Sarai, throwing up layers of latticed lightning shields above the crowd. A winded Cassandane lifted a hand.

And the Aequitas exploded.

Heat burst open the skin on his back. The force of the blast threw him and Sarai off the stage toward the wall. Cupping her head, he absorbed the impact. Something cracked in his spine. His old injuries flared sharp. Within his arms, she turned terrified eyes to him.

"I have you." He gripped her tight. "Hold on."

His shields had been decimated. Orange smog clouded the air and muffled the crowd's screams. He rebuilt the shields around the tiers of the courthouse as those who had remained there now scrambled to freedom. The crimson webs supporting his indicated that Cassandane was alive and doing the same, but Death was already here. The Aequitas had become a weapon.

Slivers of rubble flew through the air like knives and burst upon contacting his shields to drop to the stage. Fiery boulders rained from the balconies, the marble melting to lime. The wall behind them trembled. He hauled them both upright and had taken only a few steps when it ruptured. Something slammed into him, toppling him to the ground. A second, softer impact followed.

"What was—" Sarai peered over his shoulder and paled. "Oh gods, no!"

Shrugging off the heavy weight on his back, he stilled at the quiet thud it made. He rose and turned. A vicious wedge of marble jutted from Gaius's shoulders, half-severing his neck. Limp, he stared at the carnage. Light faded from his eyes.

I seem to have gotten myself a mother hen, he had wryly told Cato only weeks ago. Breath rushed from him and left his chest a hollow cavity. Ice threaded in.

Tears slid down Sarai's face, as frozen in time as he was, before a furious scream tore from her. "Those *fucking*—" She spun to him. "Tell me who to Summon. Wrath? Death?"

"If you call again, they will not come." The words were gravel.

He could call them himself. It would drain him of power and leave the Aequitas to burn. Tens of thousands would die, and the boon he asked of the Elsar wouldn't be to resurrect them but to destroy the Clan and avenge this most undeserving of deaths given to one of the few he called friend. It was an almost acceptable trade.

Wordless, he bent to the other man, staunching the bleeding at his neck for a hopeless second. A pulse jumped beneath his fingers. He stilled. It was a simple choice.

"Sarai, give me your hands."

When she pressed them over Gaius's near-decapitation without question, he brought his over hers and wrenched out the projectile embedded in the man's shoulders. Gaius jerked.

"Do all you can." Kadra flooded her with power, drawing recklessly upon his strength in a way he hadn't in over a decade.

Her irises flared, expanded. Looking dazed, she closed her eyes, vessels healing and tissue closing beneath her fingertips under the surge of magic. It seethed from the unknown spigot Wrath had opened in him and boiled between their hands as he pooled more into her. A tight burn pressed at his fingertips, a scrape and curl of power underneath as though something trapped under his skin sought to free itself. He glanced down and went rigid at the bone-white protuberance forcing its way from his left index finger. A claw that looked like a sharpened fingertip above his own.

Ten fucking hells, Wrath.

Behind them, a pillar crashed down lengthways across the Aequitas's tiers. The smoke had dissipated enough for him to glimpse the wall of flame closing in on the people still stuck there. Withdrawing his left hand from Gaius, he felt for the heat, grasping the wispy tips of flame and redirecting them toward him. The claw seemed to concentrate his power, arrowing it with exacting precision. The conflagration slid over the rails toward the stage. He siphoned away every active source until a fiery wall rose before him, temporarily contained to the width of his arms.

"Done!" Sarai panted, opening her eyes. She flinched at the flames before them.

They had no way of extinguishing the blaze. People piled over each other to flee, trampling those in their path. The Aequitas shuddered, on its last legs. Tiers that had stood for centuries collapsed. He had no choice. He turned to her, but she spoke first.

"I'll find Cassandane and round up everyone stuck here. How much time can you buy us?" Pupils blown wide with fear, she still carried herself like a seasoned soldier. Love stole what air he had left.

"As long as you need." It meant holding up the Aequitas and fencing in the blaze. The shaking fingers she fisted in his robes told him that she knew just how fatally that could stretch him magically.

"I'll see you outside," he vowed, covering her hands with his.

She squeezed them fiercely. "I'm holding you to that." Then, she ran into the chaos.

Releasing a breath, he focused on the supports. Power surged, and lightning twisted to life in his hands, forming a rope that wound around to the crumbling pillars and propped them up. More fiery threads webbed around the Aequitas and netted the structure together. His other hand grappled with the waves of fire trying to spread toward fresh oxygen through the exits. Screams rang in the pandemonium, a song for which Noceo would pay dearly.

Minutes dripped by. Arms outstretched, he shook with strain as magic drained from him, resisting the quiet, distracting horror of the realms reaching clawed limbs into his world of fire.

Vessels erupted behind his eyes; blood filled the back of his throat as he wrenched flame away from those fleeing. His world narrowed to Gaius at his feet and the promise he had made Sarai. The Aequitas quaked. Cracks ran through it like capillaries and burst.

"Kadra!" Cassandane's voice rose over the tumult. "They're all out! No one else in here is alive!"

"Leave!" he roared, waiting for her to run past him before releasing his hold on the fire. It arrowed around the formerly great courthouse in serpentine claim. The air was quiet in Death's wake. All that remained was the crackle and hiss of lightning on a leash, demanding somewhere to go.

Dissipating the lightning supports too soon would bring the Aequitas down on his head. Hoisting Gaius over his shoulder, he let go of a thick rope of lightning holding the northern half of the courtroom together. The Tetrarchy's dais disintegrated in response, shifting the courthouse's weight toward the statue of Aelius. The Aequitas groaned, its last load-bearing walls tilting. Pulling on a god's power, Kadra channeled the remaining lightning ropes into the statue. It shattered.

He dove into the closest exit and sprinted out right as Aelius's marble face landed atop the courthouse amid a cloud of dust.

He had never understood why people hadn't wanted to get rid of it. Tourist attraction or not.

His steps slowed into the field where tens of thousands of voices rose in grief. And for once, he could say nothing. This was his handiwork as much as it was Noceo's. He should never have believed himself safe. The past had demanded blood, and everyone had paid but him.

Kneeling, Kadra gently set down Gaius's comatose body. He shut out grief and drew on rage.

"Rest well, old friend." A door he'd kept locked for eleven years sprung open, ice and madness within. "They'll pay ten times over."

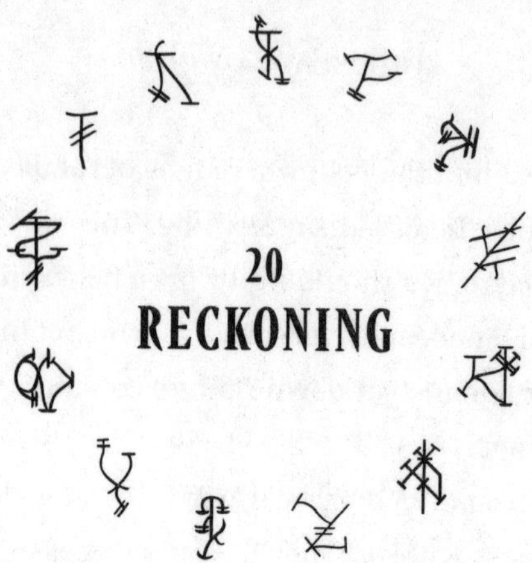

20
RECKONING

This was carnage.

Marble and ash plumed above the sinking wreck of the Aequitas. Shudders groaned through the earth. Thousands veered toward the safety of the Grand Elsarian Temple. Crowned in dust, lacerated, burned, they screamed for the gods. Some held their dead, others wailed at the loss of even that final vestige of their loved ones. Lives snuffed out in an instant.

I don't even know if I saved Gaius. Her healing abilities were rudimentary at best, and his neck—pain choked her at the memory of the cheerful man. The first vigile she had met, the first to treat her with respect, and Kadra's staunchest ally, defending him when even she had believed the very worst. The black ice that had veiled Kadra's gaze upon sighting his body had promised vengeance on a scale that the land hadn't seen since monarchical times. Silently adding her vow to his, she dragged in a breath and stilled when Cassandane staggered out of the Aequitas.

Alone.

Where is he? Her heart hammered in her throat. The ground croaked, a roar building within the Aequitas that spoke to fire. Her nails cut into her palm. *He promised he'd come out.*

"It's breaking apart!" someone yelled.

Lightning exploded out of the courthouse and struck Aelius's statue, splitting it at the neck. A stentorian crack split the air. Everyone ducked for cover as the outstretched, marble figure teetered and came down, rippling the ground with the force of its impact.

No, no, no. She elbowed her way to the front of the crowd and nearly fell to her knees upon spotting the figure darting out of the last remaining exit. Kadra cleared the doorway and ran onward. Seconds later, the Aequitas collapsed. One final victim.

She didn't think. She was already racing to him. Disheveled, covered in soot, and incandescent with rage, he was the most breathtaking sight. He had only just set Gaius down and whispered something to him when he saw her. Some of the grief fell from his eyes in favor of overwhelming relief. Closing the rest of the distance, he fiercely pulled her to him.

"Are you injured?" Smoke had roughened his beautiful voice.

"Nothing serious." Her voice choked. "I'll kill them for this."

A harsh breath against her hair. He drew back to cup her cheek, taking note of her injuries. "Thank you for surviving."

She leaned into his palm, nodding mutely. The world blurred into pinpricks and dull voices as the adrenaline and anger that had propped her up for so long ebbed loose. Kadra held her close while her vision righted, his vigiles coming to take Gaius to a healer.

He looked more haggard than she had ever seen him, features taut with rage and the promise of retribution. She hadn't realized how badly her brush with death in Komis had scared him until she had witnessed the blood visibly returning to his head when she'd entered the Aequitas.

Black eyes caressed her face. "How long has it been since you slept?"

"The night before last, and I'm regretting even that. I should have returned to Edessa right after seeing that farmer's memory and asked you about Noceo—" The rest stuck in her throat when she felt him go still against her. She forced it out. "Drenevan bu Kader," she whispered.

His aquiline features tightened. "Yes." A grim, bleak blow to the chest.

Cracked open, she stared at him, bleeding, robbed of speech. Something almost desperate flared in his eyes the longer their silence strained.

"Sarai, I—"

"Kadra," Cassandane called hoarsely, limping toward them. Raw, healed skin peered through the hole in her robes where Noceo had stabbed her shoulder. "By all the gods and Saints, thank you," she rasped. "I owe you for this."

"No." His voice transformed it to a grim epithet, muscles bunching in his jaw.

Oh. The impasse between them forgotten, Sarai shook her head. "This isn't your fault."

"Agreed." Cassandane's eyes narrowed. "Wisdom knows, the Unraveling is proof that you've an overdeveloped sense of responsibility, but we don't choose our family. No one who bought into talk of omens and fueled the past several months of turmoil has any right to say differently." At his silence, she sighed. "That's a nasty burn, Kadra. See to it."

Frowning, Sarai followed her gaze. Her jaw dropped at the congealed mass of blood and skin across his back. *He took the brunt of the blast.* His arms had banded around her while rock had shattered and burst.

"You need a healer. This is beyond what I can fix." There would be debris embedded within his injuries. She lacked the dexterity to pull out every piece.

He lifted a shoulder in an elegant but weary shrug, telling her that he wasn't keen on it. He only trusted her with his body. Prior to that, he had been content to bandage his injuries without a care for how they healed. *Men.*

"I'll have my healer, Destus, take a look after he works through the dying," Cassandane offered.

Kadra inclined his head. "Thank you."

"Likewise, Magus Supreme. Even Aelius wouldn't have been able to pull that off." She stared sadly at the Aequitas's corpse. "The healers are setting up tents around the Grand Elsarian Temple. Plenty of space for the living and the dead and enough gods to watch over them all." She took in the carnage with muted despair. "Saints and the Wretched, at least he didn't make good on his threat to turn Edessa to rubble."

Sarai's vision blurred. She could see it now. Flames stretching across the horizon, cities pleading for salvation. The fury that gripped her was too much for her exhausted body. Black closed across her eyes. Her newly healed legs gave out.

Kadra scooped her up before she hit the ground.

"Your back!"

"Rest," he ordered.

He was right. Two disasters in as many days. She was at her limit. And yet, they had left so much unsaid that she feared what awaited her upon waking. Kadra watched her for a moment before walking to the tents with her in his arms, ignoring her protests of being able to walk.

"Sleep. I'll be here when you wake." He pressed his stubbled cheek to her forehead in a rare, public caress. "I'll tell you everything, Sarai."

Why didn't you before? She was too groggy to ask. Gray veiled her vision like slow-moving fog, the landscape between wakefulness and dreams parsing out the worst of her fears.

The truth was that she wouldn't have minded as much if it had been anyone else. But among the *many* things that had inexorably drawn her to Kadra was the strange, old-fashioned honor he kept, whereby he spoke nothing but the truth. It was unthinkable as a politician. Gods, how it had baffled her that a man so deeply enmeshed in violence had bound himself to such a strange principle. So, she'd known in Komis that for him to have lied by omission meant that these secrets were cataclysmic.

Wetness rolled down her cheeks. She dimly heard a rough curse before fingers wiped at her eyes.

Then, all was finally, blessedly, quiet.

"...will be with you shortly, Magus Supreme."

A nod against her hair. She blinked. A ceiling of thick, red fabric came into focus. *Cassandane's tent?* It was bare but for a pallet that she and Kadra were sitting on. Groaning as every limb decided to protest being alive, she sleepily turned her face to Kadra's exhausted one above her.

"Good evening." Depthless eyes searched hers. "How do you feel?"

"Much better." She sat up in his lap, wondering why her eyes felt swollen. Her burns seemed to have been healed. "How long has it been?"

"Six hours." There was a bleakness to him that she had only seen at Sidran Tower when he had admitted to walking away from her and at the Unraveling. She flinched in preparation of the blow.

"I'm sorry," he said quietly.

Heart plummeting, she disentangled herself from him and rose. "Would you have told me eventually? Or..." She swallowed, blood pounding in her ears as she voiced the fear. "Was there something I did that made you not wish to tell me?"

"*No,*" he ground out, air sawing from his chest. "You deserved the truth. This isn't your fault."

She released a shuddering breath, pressing the heels of her hands to her eyes against the ache building there. *Of all the things to cry over.* People were dead, and Noceo had all but overthrown the Tetrarchy. She was being foolish.

"Sarai," a flinch ran through Kadra's pale features when he attempted to stand–her only indication of how much pain he was in. He offered his palm. "Please come here."

She took it to ease the lines of strain tightening his face. But her throat felt too thick. On any other day, her hurt might have stayed quiet, until she was able to marshal herself enough to express it without tears. But she'd been scraped raw by too much. The fears she normally fought alone burst free.

"I thought...perhaps you didn't tell me because I was–" Her voice choked. "Cassandane isn't wrong about your overblown sense of responsibility. Sometimes, I wonder if you only ever look at me with guilt. The Aequitas was crumbling, and there I was. Running. Not strong enough to help you. Not strong enough to bear your secrets or your burdens."

Kadra turned to iron. "*Never.*" His voice was a scarred rasp now. "I–" He stilled, emptiness entering his eyes when she released his hand.

"Let me take a breath." Turning away, she spoke past the lump in her throat. "My insecurities are my own. I shouldn't force your secrets from you."

She raked a hand through the tangled mess of her hair. "I'm sorry. Gods, I shouldn't be acting like this at the site of a tragedy–" Kadra's arms closed around her, pulling her hard against his chest, breath rough in her ears.

"You have nothing to apologize for." Voice tight, he pressed a kiss to her temple. "The shame is mine. Eleven years ago–"

"Magus Supreme Kadra, it's an honor to serve you." The curtain to their tent parted. Cassandane's healer, Destus, dashed inside. His jaw dropped. "I can… leave," he finally squeaked.

"It's alright." She squeezed Kadra's hands reassuringly. He released her with palpable reluctance and sat down so that Destus could work, grave eyes watching her all the while.

"Whereabouts is the damage?" the healer looked exhausted.

"My spine."

Destus cast a dubious glance at Kadra's ramrod straight posture that quickly turned aghast upon seeing the wound. Cutting away the torn fabric of Kadra's robes from where they had fused to his back, he placed both hands there and closed his eyes.

It had to burn. She was painfully familiar with a healer's white-hot magic repairing her spine and setting vertebrae back together like salt blocks. But other than deepening his exhales and a furrow creasing his brow, Kadra showed no signs of that agony.

The pain tolerance of a mountain.

Conscious that Destus could still hear them as he worked, she filled Kadra in on what she had seen in the farmer's memory and during the strike he had made her watch.

"I didn't think two people could cause this much harm," she said with a shake of her head. "Dalvia doesn't even seem to want to."

"If matters come to a head, it's because they were boiling for a long time, and no one noticed," Kadra said. "I spent years focused on Aelius and his scuta. I should have done more for the north."

Were you avoiding your brother? "You did everything you could." She recalled their sleepless nights arguing with Guilds over amendments to the Distribution Act and passing mandates that northern mines and quarries could only be owned by collectives where at least fifty percent were northerners.

Why did you work so hard? The question Noceo had asked returned. *Why become a Tetrarch at all?* Her gaze traveled his tired face. Stubble laced his jaw, the stern line of his mouth drawn tight. *There's so much I don't know.*

Destus suddenly paused in his ministrations, then stepped back from Kadra's back with a bewildered expression. "Magus Supreme," he began carefully, "have you noticed any irregularities in your spine prior to this injury?"

Nothing moved in Kadra's depthless eyes, but she felt the air around them grow colder. "Are there any?" he asked pleasantly.

Deflection. A chasm opened at her feet even as she registered the words as true. How many times had he done this? How much had she shrugged off believing that he would expand on his answers at some point?

"I'm seeing signs of several fractures. Whoever your healer was then doesn't seem to have mended them properly. Some of your nerves are pinched between vertebrae." Perplexed, Destus shook his head. "You haven't noticed?"

"It hasn't interfered with my work," Kadra said easily.

Avoidance. But there was something harder beneath his insouciance.

Looking like he wanted to add something, Destus shook his head instead and insisted upon correcting the injuries. "It's a discredit to the profession leaving a spine in this state," he argued when Kadra made to speak. "And you saved so many today."

An hour passed with Destus, Kadra's features growing increasingly strained, both lost to the intricacies of healing. Stretching her legs outside the tent, she walked around the makeshift hospital spread out on the grounds of the Grand Elsarian Temple. Healers ran from tent to tent, pale and wide-eyed. Clerics somberly administered to the dying. People sat on the grass sobbing into each other's arms. The wind ferried blood and death in silent warning to throngs of relatives seeking entry to reunite with their loved ones.

Then, there were the screams.

She sped over to a long cluster of tents after hearing the first. A trio of gray-cloaked healers stood outside, consoling a fourth sobbing one. They straightened at her arrival just as another chorus of caterwauling arose from the tents.

"The people in there, are they…" The question died on her tongue, because of course they were.

"*All those eyes!*" a woman's voice screamed from within the tents. "A reckoning comes for Edessa. The sky itself will *laugh*!"

"Elsar have mercy!" Another shrieked. "No, *no*! Go away! *Please!*"

The healers wordlessly parted the tent flaps. Dread gripped Sarai when she peered in. Two rows of pallets stretched ahead in each tent, the occupants tied onto it with everything the healers had been able to find, including strips of their own tunics. The madness-struck raved, strained at their bonds, veins jumping in their necks as they screamed of eyes and reckonings. She spotted a few too-still faces, lips parted in a scream, skin already taking on the pallor of death.

"I think their bodies can't take it," the healer who had been crying whispered. "Their hearts and brains are practically pulp afterward. It's like they were frightened to death."

Sarai pressed her fingers to her temples, trying not to give in to the pressure building behind her eyes. Nearly a month away from Edessa and she'd been too late. She had nothing in the way of aid for these people. No culprit. No cure.

What was it all for?

She could only thank the healers and ask them to continue their watch. Leaving, she merged into the dazed crowd. Heads turned at her approach, questions struck her like arrows, asking why this had happened.

She fought a wave of anger. She had her own questions too. On why they'd fallen for petty, manufactured squabbles and made her life a hell the past several months. But propriety dictated that she didn't sling arrows back when people were grieving. Propriety was a shackle at times.

"What should I have done?" she finally asked. "Should I have told you all to kneel to Noceo? Should I have abdicated as Petitor? What could I have done to stop him?"

"Nothing," Anek's voice announced crossly. "Get out of my way. I have more to contribute than ill-placed blame." They elbowed to the front of the crowd and took Sarai by the arm, dragging her back toward Destus's tent, visibly trying to gather their words. "We may all need to go into hiding for a bit," they finally said flatly. "I just spotted a contingent of Clerics amassing at the back of the Elsarian Temple with Verentia issuing orders. She seemed surprised at Noceo's appearance, but I wouldn't put it past her to ally with him."

A sustained scream built in Sarai's head, and she almost wished she could shriek to the wind as the madness-struck were doing. "Where do we go?"

"*Fuck.* I don't know." There was no anger in their response. Only a deep, wrung-out hopelessness. "I didn't think we'd see another day like the Unraveling for decades."

"I don't know if the Unraveling ever stopped." Sarai choked down her anger upon sighting a group in white and silver.

Anek's gaze lingered on Aelius's acolytes and dismissed them. "Noceo's our threat. I studied Coercers briefly at the Academiae, and they're extremely rare. His level of power is unheard of. There isn't a recorded Coercer in history that's been more than an Eighth-Tier, and he was easily a Twelfth."

"Not naturally, he isn't. He's using something." She filled Anek in on the formula he had spoken of and thought back to Noceo's quivering fingertips when he had held her hostage earlier. "He pushed himself to his limit to pull this off."

"Which means he could never have made good on his threat to raze Edessa. For once, Harion got it right. Destroying the Aequitas was a ploy.

It'll keep everyone here cowering so they don't challenge the coup when he isn't half as powerful as what your Magus Supreme pulled today."

"Put that way, it sounds hopeful."

"And he's using stimulants," Anek marveled. "Dangerous idea those. They force a body's Thresholds open to draw upon unlimited quantities of power, but risk draining the user's lifeforce too." A frown edged their lips. "He wants this *badly*. And we have Dalvia to contend with too. A Bridger and a True Illusionist. Gods, what a combination. We'll have to be careful that she doesn't turn her face into one of ours."

Sarai couldn't fathom regrouping or wrap her mind around the magnitude of the disaster they faced. The Tetrarchy had just been overthrown. The number of madness-struck might move past the thousands to tens of thousands.

"The entire country's acting *possessed*." She explained the eerie whitesleep murders that had swept the locales there and the odd dreams she'd been having. "I keep wondering if Verentia's calls for me to have an exorcism have some truth to it." She recalled Noceo being strangely concerned for her over that weeks ago and cursed. "I don't understand anything."

"Magic, life, gods, all incomprehensible things. Do you know that our truth-telling abilities originated in the land of Ilohe?" Anek wove through the crowd, ignoring the questions thrown at them. "Over there, they don't even have to Probe. Apparently, the magi only need to ask and their voices force the questionee to spill everything in great detail. They're called Hypnotics. Sound familiar?" At Sarai's start, they nodded. "We aren't that dissimilar from Noceo. He should be very afraid of it."

They were almost back at Cassandane's tent. She halted by the crossed cloth flaps guarding the entrance. "Do you think we can defeat him?"

"Someone will." Anek sounded certain of it. "If Edessa disliked you, think about how badly they must dislike him." They left with a wink before she could so much as stammer a response.

Mouth hanging open, she managed an exhausted laugh. *I suppose there's that.*

The flaps behind her parted. "The Magus Supreme is fully healed," Destus announced proudly, looking inches from fainting.

Relief spread in her chest. "Thank you. Especially for correcting his older injuries. That must have been painstaking work."

"About those." He looked wary. "Petitor Sarai, I reached this position through discretion, so no word of this will pass my lips to even the Head Tetrarch. But there is something you should know about those fractures. They were very old, and there were several."

Foreboding threaded through her at his uneasiness. "How old?"

"Ranging from ten to twenty years back." He gave her a meaningful look. "At least eight breaks."

"He would have been a child."

Destus nodded.

Kadra's distrust of healers. Repeated spinal injuries over a decade, and a tolerance for pain that could rival Wrath's. Shock and understanding pebbled her skin.

"I see," she said numbly. "Thank you for letting me know, Destus."

Nodding somberly, he moved on to his next patient.

Inside the tent, she found Kadra standing, rolling one shoulder back as though he was unused to having it move so smoothly. A faint but *genuine* smile widened his lips. She could have sworn he had gotten a little taller.

"Have you been in pain all this time?" she wondered. "All while I've known you?"

The elation in his eyes turned tender. "I barely felt it around you."

Another secret. Her heart squeezed tight, aching like a bruise. Yet, she smiled back, unwilling to cloud his joy of having a longstanding pain eased. "I should've dragged you to a healer sooner." His gaze altered and turned probing the longer she kept the smile on. "Anek pointed out something useful–Kadra?" She swallowed when he stalked across the tent to grip her shoulders.

"Yell at me," he ordered quietly. "Curse me. Don't pretend that you're well."

The ache spread to her throat. A shiver coasted her neck when he slid a hand across her nape, tilted her chin up, and gravely searched her eyes. "I've hurt you."

Her eyes burned. She nodded, not trusting herself to speak.

"I'm sorry." His face tautened when a tear escaped her. "I was going to tell you–" He swore when Cassandane's raised voice sounded some distance outside the tent. When his eyes turned to hers, they held remorse and determination.

"Kadra–" she squeaked when his mouth covered hers. She wrapped her arms around him with a muffled sob when he pulled her flush against him. He teased the corners of her lips with soft, urgent kisses, sinking in when she parted them.

"I'm sorry." He gripped the back of her neck, drinking deep. "Sarai, I'm so damned sorry."

Heat surged in her. She clung to him, raking her hands through his hair to suck on his lower lip. Nuzzling her neck, he murmured another apology when footsteps penetrated the haze enveloping them. He reluctantly drew from her and wiped her eyes. Seconds later, Cassandane and Anek burst in.

"We need to talk." She searched for something to grip in the tent, and failing that, crossed her arms. "We've had–" She squinted at Kadra. "Were you always that tall? Never mind. Many of the injured from the Aequitas are showing signs of being madness-struck. No boil beetle welts, but they're screaming about eyes and laughing skies." Cassandane pressed her fingers to her temples like she was inches from an aneurysm. "I think we've lost."

Part of Sarai agreed, wanted to sit down and stay there. "We haven't," she said instead. "Whatever the source of his newfound strength, it isn't enough to raze Edessa."

"Does he need to when he's getting half the city to scream about eyes?" Cassandane muttered.

This was the part she had been dreading. "That isn't his doing. We've three separate sets of bloodbaths in the country. Murders via whitesleep in the upper north, though those seem largely handled. The beetle plague in the lower north that reached us. And the madness-struck. I don't think they're related."

"And he denied responsibility for it all?"

"I Examined him," Sarai said somberly. "He wasn't lying."

Cassandane blanched. Giving up all pretense of strength, she wobbled over to the tent's sole pallet and sank onto it. "Then, we have *nothing.* A coup and a second unknown enemy."

"I wouldn't call Verentia unknown, Head Tetrarch." Méherre raced into the tent, eyes still streaming from the smoke. "She's coming."

Beside her, Anek choked. Sarai eyed the other woman curiously. Soot still laced her short hair, a few burns still shining raw on her face, but there was a glow to the Bridger that she hadn't noticed before. She seemed to be in her element.

"Did she always look that way?" Anek whisper-croaked to Sarai.

"You should see her smile," she murmured back.

"If you need a place to hide, I have a home–a small one–in Aelius's Quarter." The Bridger heaved a breath at Sarai's slanted look of surprise. "Land was cheap there after your Unraveling." Méherre's gaze rose to Kadra and dropped just as quickly. "We need to hurry. Those priests are some two hundred strong. Is my offer acceptable?"

Kadra nodded, and Méherre released a breath.

"Alright. The Aequitas's wards are still standing, so I can't open a Bridge here. It'll be the same spot I brought you, Sarai–"

"People of Edessa," Verentia's hard voice boomed across the grounds, amplified. "The gods have spoken once more, and our city reels with new dead and fresh madness. Help me end this. Petitor Sarai must submit to an exorcism before she destroys Edessa. I won't ask again."

Sarai's jaw fell along with those of everyone in the tent. Her feet froze to the ground.

Anek clutched their head. "Wisdom and Wrath, I'd like to help her meet the gods myself. I could flatten her face with—do we still have any of Aelius's scuta?"

"What if we—"

"Give her over, and *I* will raze Edessa to the ground, Cassandane." Murder brewed in Kadra's eyes.

"Gods and Saints, I'm not seriously considering it! I'm panicking! Let me panic—"

"Well, there's our handmaiden to the Dark Elsar herself," Harion drawled, parting the tent flaps to enter. "Ready to be exorcised?"

Sarai stared back. After today, hatred of the north would spike. Noceo had taken their capital, but the south would resist. Was it right for her to go into hiding while people, north *and* south, still struggled for answers? If they lost faith in an absent leadership, they would splinter, even look to Verentia for hope.

"Should I go?" she heard herself ask as if from very far away.

The tent fell silent.

Bloodlust yawned in the black eyes that met hers. A muscle in Kadra's jaw jumped seconds before he took her hand and drew her to the back of the tent. "Sarai," his voice was a gravelly rasp, "the Order isn't like Aelius or Tullus. There is no line they haven't crossed in the name of religion. If this is Noceo's ploy, then know that he's worse. My Clan haven't tied themselves to coin, or the gods, or power. They do what they will, because they can."

Some men might have demanded her not to go, to run from the battleground. But Kadra had always been one to show where the lines were drawn and uphold her decisions. His jaw tensed so hard she feared for his back teeth, but the fingers that brushed her cheeks were as gentle as ever.

"As someone who learned that the hard way, I concur." Cassandane grimly squeezed Sarai's shoulder. "I know I haven't been a half-decent friend of late, but trust me in this."

"Then, we run?" Harion asked, an unusual seriousness in his eyes.

"We run," Cassandane confirmed.

Their exhales formed smoky wreaths circling their faces in the cold.

Outside, Verentia's voice boomed again, repeating her demands.

Sarai placed a hand on the tent flap and took a steadying breath. None of it felt real. Komis crumbling. The Aequitas burning. Now, this.

Fabric slipped open. She stepped outside where a crowd had formed around their tent, held back only by the determination of all three Tetrarch's vigiles. Kadra's people absorbed his terse orders to watch over Gaius's recovery in his absence. Then, they broke rank to allow them all through. Or most of them. Sarai directed a glower at Harion's retreating back.

Kadra's eyes touched on him and tore through. "Some people always find a way to flee."

A touch of emptiness laced his words, discernible only because she was so attuned to him. She glanced at him in surprise, ignoring Harion's inarticulate sounds of indignation that he was still weighing his options. *He wasn't entirely referring to Harion.*

"True. But that's a long story, no?" Their audience parted, and Noceo emerged, silver eyes afire with victory.

Shit. Sarai closed her eyes on a groan as Verentia followed, looking eerily smug. *She seemed like the sanest Inquisitor at my Hearing.* How had it come to this?

Noceo bowed. "You needn't worry, pretty Cassandane, we'll keep you as interim ruler until I finalize my restructuring of the country. Now," he swiveled to Sarai and offered a short bow. "Coming?"

For the world of mockery that question held, Noceo seemed ill-at-ease. Sweat trailed from his hairline, matting what she could see of the shoulder-length hair tied at his nape. The white cast to his features hadn't dulled even over six hours after his orchestration of the Aequitas's ruin. *He's weak.*

She slanted a glance at Kadra and found a similar strain around his temples. *They both are.* This wasn't a battle she could risk now with their audience. She caught Méherre's eye, praying that the other woman could spirit them away quickly, but she had paled, staring at Noceo with pure loathing and something darker, raw.

Had they met before?

Verentia cleared her throat, indicating the sea of blue behind her. "If you don't come willingly–"

"She won't," Kadra's icy voice cut through hers. "If your vaunted gods ordained you to take her from me, then by all means, *try*. Take a step toward her. Test your faith against me."

Power surged from him in a rush that sent the hairs at Sarai's nape to full mast. The air around him seemed to seethe and glow. Verentia muttered a fearful prayer, shrieking of Dark Elsar, but what wholly, utterly stupefied Sarai was the large bone-white claw at the tip of Kadra's left forefinger.

Her chest drew tight. *Kadra, what did you do?*

The soot-streaked faces of the crowd around them lost their tension in favor of awe, but a blue-robed wave pushed past them to advance toward Kadra.

Swords drew. The crowd surged. And she felt it then, a strange twist within the cavern of her chest that told her to make them quiet. To enmesh her hands in their eye sockets and crash their skulls together, break them apart. End this game of greed.

She didn't know where she'd gotten a dagger from, but it was in her hands. She felt herself take a shaky step forward when Harion shoved her to the right.

"What in the Elsar's names are you doing? Run!" he hissed, indicating Méherre's figure by the Aequitas. The air split to reveal a thin road.

"She's getting away!" Verentia shrieked, elbowing her own priests in an effort to reach Sarai.

She ran. Screams, light, bodies. She wanted to tear off her skin, force the world to a stop. Plague, riots, omens. She had nothing. She was saving no one. She was *running.*

Then, someone started laughing.

Long, loud, and full of utter disdain, yet dulcet and so, *so* loud that the peals drowned out the fighting and the crowd. And she got her wish. The world quieted.

Mouths worked like bellows, parting and closing. Bodies went faint. Crimson wormed into the lines of Kadra's hands as he slammed the hilt of his sword into a battling priest's head. The laughter redoubled when a score of priests fell to their knees, scraping their hands over horror-struck faces. Verentia collapsed in a dead faint.

Slowly, as though manipulated by a strength that wasn't her own, she followed their gazes north, past the tents, the Aequitas, up to the sky.

Where a black sun gleamed.

Her mouth parted, tongue frozen like the sludge in her veins. *Not a sun.*

A large black eye blinked over Edessa, the sclera entirely obscured.

And the sky was laughing.

21 THERE IS SOMEONE HERE

Clarity struck him as their warped tangle of evidence and clues sorted into smooth web strands. Thousands dreaming of the same visions and the same doom. A power he had never heard of. *Broad.*

Hemorrhage. Pulverization of the head and brain. A mechanism of action that seemingly didn't require the culprit's presence. *Vague.*

Murders done by whitesleep in the north, by unrepentant victims of pain who had all had the same realization that they could. Beetles gone mad to feed on human flesh. *Unearthly.*

Then, Sarai. Dreaming of the Fall, dreaming of *his* past, eyes glazed even now.

There is someone here who shouldn't be, Wrath had said.

Someone.

The corner of Kadra's lips rose in an icy smile as the sky continued to laugh. Cassandane and Harion yelled their terror to more uncaring eyes blooming dark above them. The answer was so simple as to be absurd. The fools of the Elsarian Order had gotten it right after all.

There was a god in Edessa.

Ahead, Sarai stared blankly at the growing spread of darkness, eyes glazed. Smoke coiled around her and licked at her skin, the nape of her neck, invisible to all but him. Thin wisps prodded at her chest to seek entry. He paused at their familiarity, recalling seeing the same during the Academiae's graduation and within the whitesleep den.

The voice who'd kept trying to crush his skull had a name then.

Sarai's lips parted as she stepped forward. He reached her even before she could whisper his name and caught her elbow. Her face crumpled, irises nearly swallowing her eyes.

"I'm here." He clenched her blindly questing fingers around his arms.

She sucked in a hoarse breath. Her pulse throbbed wildly in her neck. "We need to leave–" Hyperventilating, she struck her sternum when she couldn't draw another breath and simply dragged him toward the portal.

Méherre stared at the sky, awe mingling with terror in her gaze. "Such *power*."

Verentia's shrieks suddenly cut through the air. He glanced over his shoulder to find her clawing at her eyes. Vicious glee bared her mouth in a rictus grin as she reached out, brandishing a knife toward Cassandane.

"You've had it for years," she whispered, stabbing almost blindly as Cassandane darted out of her reach. "Let me sit there too." Her jaw unhinged in another scream, reason seemingly fighting with madness. He knew she fought Death.

Tar oozed from her mouth as she fell to her knees, sanity dwindling to pinpricks in her eyes, which were swallowed by black.

The fragile hold that the god had over Edessa fractured at the sight. People splintered and fled in packs, stampeding all in their path. He drew a web of lightning over their group, parting it as Cassandane and Harion successively entered with numb eyes and slackened faces.

A shudder ran through Sarai. "There's nothing we can do."

"For now," he agreed softly.

One by one, they walked through Méherre's portal and left the Aequitas's carcass to the eyes surveying it. And the god still laughed.

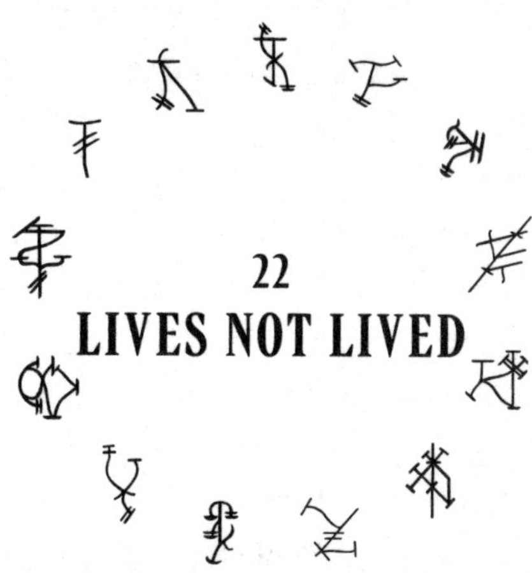

22
LIVES NOT LIVED

Eleven years ago

Noceo's obsession with the Poxtan girl was going to get them both killed.

Drenevan paced outside the baker's shop, watching Noceo lean over the counter to say something to the fourteen-year-old girl working there. Parvine curled an errant strand of hair behind her ears and giggled. He didn't have to hear them to know that his brother was making the same ridiculous sound.

On the other side of the room, Dalvia watched them both with a frown.

"Parvine! Have you seen the flour?" came an annoyed female voice, audible though the windows.

Finaze Poxtan, Parvine's older sister and Noceo's nemesis, emerged from the shop's rear. The corners of her lips tightened. "What the fuck do you think you're doing, Clan scion?" she sneered Noceo's title. "I thought I told you to keep away from her."

Drenevan could see red inching up his brother's ears through the window. Drawing a deep breath, he dared enter the shop. The full weight of Finaze's glare rounded on him. He couldn't deny that it was impressive.

"My brother meant no harm to the young lady," he said gravely. "If we have offended–"

"You bloody well have offended," she hissed. "*No one* comes in to buy anything when you're here. Maybe they do at the bigger shops in the bowels of Komis, but we're upstanding folk here. You're dragging our name into your dirt. Fuck off!!"

"I see." He inclined his head, exchanging a meaningful glance with Noceo.

His brother's eyes widened faintly. "Yes, of course! Please accept my apologies and this." He withdrew a silver denarius and pressed it on the counter. "For the trouble."

Drenevan hid his satisfaction when Finaze suddenly looked torn. He made for the door, shooting a questioning glance at Dalvia when she didn't follow. The Poxtan girls were more inclined to look kindly on her on account of her sex, so they would never ask her to leave. He didn't begrudge her those friendships. She knew the dangers of Clevsin finding out. Stepping outside, he paused when Noceo turned back to Finaze.

"I would never hurt her."

It was Drenevan's turn to go still at that quiet desperation. He had never seen such seriousness in his brother's eyes.

"*Never*," Noceo emphasized, before leaving.

A stunned Drenevan accompanied his brother down the darkening street. Twilight claimed the sky as they wound their way into the heart of Komis where their reputations and Clan were hungered over as much as they were feared. Pleasure-workers winked at them from alleys, gazes fixated on their gray-green uniforms. Cardsharps shot them warning glances to stay away after Noceo had nearly bankrupted a gambling house on his first set of games. This was the world they belonged in. And yet…

"Noceo," he asked, "do you care for the Poxtan girl?"

A stutter in his brother's steps. "Her name is Parvine."

"You're going to get her killed."

"Fuck off!" Noceo roared and veered off into an alley.

Drenevan wondered if he should have been less blunt about it. He sighed, following him in. "Everything has a price. There is no future where you can have her. It's dangerous to expect a chance."

"I said, fuck off! Just because no one will ever want you doesn't mean that it's the same for me."

Drenevan paused, wondering why the blow had landed. It was true. They had discussed it once when Dalvia had asked if he had ever thought of kissing her, and he had truthfully stated that he had once considered removing her tongue after she had pinned one of her failures on him and gotten his spine broken again.

He realized that he had come to a stop in the alley when he heard Noceo yell. This time, it held fear. *Fuck.* Racing to the source of the sound, he stilled at the two men holding his brother down. One had a hand over his mouth, the other searched his pockets for coin. Metal slid into Drenevan's palm on instinct. He darted out of the shadows, blade held aloft when lightning cracked through the air and through the two thieves. They collapsed with a scream. Burns crawled up their faces and into the whites of their eyes, which ruptured. An inelegant death, but a swift one.

Dread settled on Drenevan's shoulders. He turned toward the source of the bolts, expecting Clevsin's fury. He halted.

"Who're you?"

"I think I should be asking that." A gray-haired man in green and gold robes stood at the opposite end of the alley. He eyed their robes as Noceo got up and dusted himself off. "You seem important."

The stranger's robes spoke of a much greater importance, in addition to his power. "Drenevan bu Kader," he introduced himself, ignoring Noceo's dig in the ribs. "This is my brother. Thank you, sir."

"By the looks of it, you had it handled." The man gestured to the knife in Drenevan's palm. "Is that what the Clan's taught you, boy?"

"It's what the world's taught me."

"And do you prefer your Clan or the world, boy?" The stranger eyed him consideringly.

Upturned lips, hawkish features. There was a cunning glint to his eyes that warned of danger, but his finery and the rune-studded armilla on his wrist spoke of opportunity. No man of wealth would venture so boldly into Komis's underbelly unless they knew it couldn't harm them.

"The world," Noceo interjected, voice ragged. "Every fucking day."

Drenevan slanted a quelling look at his brother, but the man looked pleased.

"I'm Tetrarch Othus." He held out a hand, eyes gleaming when they shook it in turn. "I'm sure you've heard much about the Tetrarchy and how awful we all are, but I'm here to make things better. Just like I did earlier." He offered them a genial smile. "Komis is a cruel city. I could do with some eyes and ears here. What do you say? Of course, there will be coin in it for you."

Disappointment settled over him, followed by mild surprise that there was enough optimism left in him to be disappointed. The Tetrarchy was just as mercenary as the Clan.

Beside him, Noceo's jaw tightened. His brother released a long breath, chuckled weakly, then shrugged. "You want all the goings-on in Komis, go ask the fishers on the Chaboras. They'll jump as high as you want for coin."

Othus's eyes narrowed. "I see that I've misstepped."

"You did. Thank you, *Tetrarch*." Anger flushed his brother's pale features when he turned to leave. Anger and something quieter.

And suddenly, Drenevan knew what it was, because it seemed that he had felt it too.

Hope.

There was a sliver of it still within their reach. He seized it.

"We don't want your coin," he informed Othus. Adrenaline brought a rare quiver to his fingers.

"Drenevan, just leave him—"

"I'll give you all the information you need." He didn't have Noceo's talent with Coercion, but he knew how to make his voice silk. "I trust the Tetrarchy a damn sight more than I do the Clan to improve life here." He normally did this with more finesse, but time was of the essence. "We'll be your eyes and ears for six months, Tetrarch Othus." He took a deep breath and turned to catch Noceo's eye. *Do it.* "Then, you'll take us back south with you."

Othus stared at him, then chuckled. "It seems you've vastly—"

"You'll take us with you," Noceo growled behind Drenevan. Compulsion coated each word. "You *will* take us back south with you."

Othus's eyes dulled.

"In six months, after we spy for you and give you every detail you want, you will take us south with you," Noceo spat, the full weight of his power behind his voice. "As sons and heirs."

Drenevan blinked. They didn't need to be heirs.

Sweat slid down Noceo's cheeks as he kept going. "These thoughts are your own. You will forget that we are Clan sons. You know us as street rats. You see greatness in us, and you can't bear to see such potential wasted. And if the Clanlord comes for us, you *will* protect us."

"Of course," Othus murmured. "The soon-to-be Magus Supreme Aelius is an old friend. You don't have to worry on that score."

"You will meet us tomorrow at the docks. Now, leave and remember nothing of being Coerced," Noceo panted. "Your thoughts are your own."

Othus took a few steps back and shuffled out of the alley, eyes glazed. Noceo slumped to the ground, gasping with strain. But his eyes were wild when he looked up.

"You utter fucking madman." He pulled Drenevan down and into a bear hug. "I can't believe you did that."

"You did most of it," Drenevan said dryly. Part of him was stunned that it had worked. "Tetrarchs aren't as powerful as I believed."

"It's not the sort of magic they expect from an Urd." Noceo laughed. "By the Elsar and Naaduir, we're going to be *free*."

"We'll have to leave the Poxt–Parvine," Drenevan added hastily.

Noceo's eyes dimmed before he waved a hand. "She'll wait. I'll tell her I'm coming back for her and to hold on for me."

"Seems inadvisable." But his brother's excitement was contagious. Drenevan sat with him in the odoriferous alleyway and stared at myriad constellations looming over Komis. Soon, they would see what they looked like in the south.

"Everything's going to change, Drenevan." It sounded like a prophecy coming from Noceo's mouth.

Drenevan believed it. "*Everything*."

Shoulder to shoulder, they grinned.

23
UNDERSTANDING

She woke to the realization that she had seen someone else's dream again.

She finally knew whose it was.

Night had fallen outside Méherre's domus. The cozy space lay on the very edge of Aelius's Quarter, surprisingly close to the Grains Guild horreum that had begun the past month of terror. Here, in this strange quiet gifted by snow and seclusion, she could almost pretend that none of it had happened.

Upon arrival, Harion, Cassandane, and Anek had discarded their robes for cloaks and a determination to drink themselves insensate at the closest tavern. She had lain on one of the couches, meaning to join them. *Looks like I fell asleep first.* A thick blanket curled under her shoulders, and she knew who that would have been too. He stood outside, staring at the gloaming, the eyes long since having disappeared from the sky.

No one had wanted to speak of it. She finally understood what might have made Kadra keep the fact that he was Godstouched from her. And the rest of it.

Still covered in soot, she washed her face and pilfered Méherre's well-stocked cupboards to prepare a simple vegetable stew. Despite her dislike of the south, the Bridger seemed to have been planning to move here, given the extensive array of herbs and spices arranged neatly on the shelves.

The front door parted. Kadra's near-soundless steps came through the atrium and halted upon sighting her ladling stew into two bowls.

"I'm a little out of practice," she admitted. "But Arsamea never complained about my cooking."

His throat worked for a moment before he sat across her. The spoon dipped past the stern line of his lips and paused. His brows rose.

"I can see why." His arresting eyes traced her with soft indulgence. "Do you enjoy cooking?"

"More so now when I don't have to do it," she mused. "I wonder if that'll be the same with this job." Unspoken was the question of whether she had one anymore. If the land even had a government now.

"It will be." His gaze grew tender. "And you'd still want to do it."

Heat built behind her eyes. Worry. Fear. Gratitude that they were here together. "When did you first fall in love with me?"

His fingers paused on the spoon. Black eyes found hers. He smiled slowly. "Hmm?"

"Never mind," she muttered, flushing when his eyes traced her like silk, amusement flaring in their depths when she hurriedly stood to search for a mysterious third spoon they didn't need.

"This is unexpected." He prowled after her, lifting her on top of the table when she tried to sidle away. He caged her with his arms, his smile widening. "My stoic Petitor seems to have vanished."

"You'll have her back if you let me off this table," she grumbled, embarrassed. "I don't mean to pry. You don't have to—"

"The day we sheltered under a tree during stormfall," he said in the slow, deep timbre she loved. "You looked up at me, and I craved you. I didn't want you afraid of me." The humor faded from his stern face. "I wanted to shield you from everything, and I knew I couldn't."

Oh. Heat suffused her face as she realized that she was grinning ear-to-ear. He looked fascinated at the sight.

She leaned in. "I loved you first. Since the night you took me to free the Metals Guild debt-slaves."

"Six days." A world of surprise in his voice. He stroked her cheek tenderly. "Even after the Fall, Sarai?"

She leaned against his forehead. “You’re everything I’ve ever yearned for.” His sudden harsh breath against her mouth told her just how much the words had affected him. She found herself crushed against his chest, his mouth moving ardently over hers in a kiss so hungry that she went liquid.

“Dinner, first, yes?” she finally tore her mouth away to whisper.

He reluctantly set her free. They ate in companionable quiet.

“Do you think people will flock to the Elsarian Order and Noceo now that they’ve been proven right?”

His teeth flashed in a rare, genuine grin. “It’s a terrible time to be the Order. The populace will be looking for divine solutions to a divine problem. And the Inquisitors won’t be able to offer so much as a Summoning.”

Sarai nearly choked on her stew with a laugh. “Gods! I shouldn’t gloat, but it serves them right.”

“Let them do as they wish and run amok with religious authoritarianism for the next few days. We’ll find who called this god and why.”

Her spoon clattered against her bowl. “You don’t think I caused it?” she asked quietly.

“*No.*” He reached for her hand with a hesitance that she hadn’t ever seen in him and exhaled heavily when she took it.

“How old are you?” she asked after a moment. “There’s so much I don’t…know.”

His jaw tensed, but his answer was soft. “Almost twenty-five.” A corner of his mouth rose at her doubletake. “Too old?” he asked whimsically.

“It’s just odd to hear you say it aloud. You’ve the gravitas of the Kaycakh Mountains, and it turns out that you’re barely a quarter century? It boggles the mind.”

He traced the back of her hand like she was infinitely precious, absently following a scar’s weave.

“How does one fight a god, Kadra?”

“With another god,” he said, low and quiet. He’d already thought this through.

Anguish boiled in the back of her throat. "You never did say which god claimed you."

The smile faded from his face. "Do you truly want to know?"

She understood what he really meant. "Yes."

His hand stilled on hers. All levity vanished, his features could have been carved from slate. Tension built in his shoulders as they finished their meal, seeping to the lean muscle of his forearms. By the time she had reached the bedroom Méherre had indicated they could use, her perennially trembling fingers shook even worse with nerves.

Inhaling deeply, she turned to Kadra. "We should probably..." The words died in her throat.

He stood before the wardrobes, hands fisted, knuckles straining against the skin as he fought to collect himself. *Well, shit.* One way or another, this would be a reckoning. There was no one to interrupt them. The adrenaline she had tried to contain finally wrested control, turning her limbs into springs of unreleased tension when he turned to her.

"I said I would give you everything." Limned in the wintry glow of twilight, he seemed hewn of ice and granite. Only the sparks hissing the air spoke to his fraying control. "Eleven years—"

"Not out of guilt," she bit out. "I won't have you this way."

The silence between them was thick, fiery. The last time she had seen him like this had been when he had believed her a spy, but tonight, his anger was directed inward.

"How?" The words were too quiet for all their weight. They struck like ice—a gradual slither down her body.

"*Obligated.*" Her throat locked until she almost couldn't speak. "Yes, I want to know. But when you tell me, it'll be because *you* want to. Not because I forced the words before you were ready."

"I hurt you." There was a darkness to his eyes now. "And he did too."

Her throat closed, not ready to think about it yet. "And I'll make him pay. But Noceo doesn't matter to me. *You* do. I think I know why you didn't tell me, and *that's* what burns, Kadra."

It would have mattered little if he weren't ready to speak of his past. She knew all too well what it was like to hold a secret that was hard to utter. But that wasn't why he had kept these.

"We can speak of your reasons." Her heart felt like a thousand boil beetles had torn through it when he stayed quiet. "But do not give me your secrets until you acknowledge that you hid them because you thought that I wasn't strong enough for them."

"*Never.*"

While she struggled to understand that, he flicked a finger at the silent hearth between them, and it roared to life to paint his face in grim swaths of red and umber. Warmth foolishly uncurled in her gut at the familiarity of the sight, at the knowledge that she could make the cruel slash of his mouth tip upward in a smile. He watched her too, something raw and fierce painting his hard face with a flush.

She didn't move when he took a step forward, and cradled her cheek in his palm, holding it featherlight. He gripped her hand and brought it to his pulse. It throbbed beneath her fingertips, sending hunger arcing through her veins.

"I say this, because I *want* you to know." The voice she adored devolved to a scarred rasp. "I have never had anyone to call mine."

Her pulse stuttered against her sternum, memories besieging her of the nights he spent in her, his guttural praise, the desperate, hungry way he took her, and one word. One vow. Every time. *Yours.*

Yours.

He tilted her head up, his hand tightening on her cheek when her breath hitched. "I've been…happy." He said it with the wonderment of a man who was new to the word. "Since the first night you crossed the threshold into Aoran Tower. I didn't want it to end."

She wet her lips with her tongue. His thumb traced the motion. "Why would it end?"

"You'll–"

"Leave? Have you tried and convicted me already?" She fisted a hand in his soot-stained robes to pull him closer. "At least, allow me to plead my case."

His eyes glittered. "You aren't on trial."

"So, you are?" An aching warmth hummed over her body, seeping down to the spaces between her toes. She flattered her grip on his robes to press her palm to his chest. "And have you gone and found yourself guilty? Or did you assume that I would?"

His rough exhale said that her reasoning had struck home. Broad fingers slid over the ones she had splayed over him, nudging her grip wider so he could interlock their hands. Every bone in her body begged her to draw closer.

Letting go, she stepped back. "I'm yours," she whispered. "Let me know when you decide to believe it."

Fighting tears, she pushed open the door to the adjoining bathing room, and stripped off her blood-and-dust-covered clothes to sink into the granite bathtub. She loved him. She craved him. But it wasn't enough for her to have his heart if he doubted that he had hers.

"Noceo and I aren't too different."

She stilled in the act of washing her face.

"Eleven years ago, Clan Kader's manor was my home." Kadra paced the bedroom. "I preferred being by the servants' quarters. The others were determined not to fraternize with them, so I had all the quiet I wanted."

"Others?"

Kadra's gaze was distant as if he were staring all the way to the farthest corner of the world. "My siblings. At the time, Clevsin was as powerful a lightning magus as the Magus Supreme before Aelius. But he was risk-averse. He preferred the underworld to ruling above ground. He enjoyed creating a dynasty to rule from the shadows. He had little trouble finding the women."

Understanding dawned. "Noceo's your half brother."

He nodded, unbuttoning his robes. "The oldest now. There were others, older and younger, but Clevsin was a harsh taskmaster. Not everyone survived."

Heat licked behind her eyes, and she drew a choked breath. "You and Noceo did."

"I inherited Clevsin's power and then some. Noceo had no ability with lightning, but his voice reached Seventh-Tier even as a child. It takes a great deal to fight Coercion. That made him extremely useful for the Clan's dealings. Drug distribution–blazeleaf at first. Women for Clevsin."

She was scrubbing herself raw, she dimly realized. "Were those your dealings too?" she whispered.

His fingers paused on his buttons. "An aptitude for bloodshed and limited remorse afterward marked me as better suited to enforcing." The dark look he leveled on her left her in no doubt as to what that was.

Torture and elimination of the Clan's enemies. His last contact with them had been eleven years ago. *He would have been thirteen.*

"I caused the strike on the manor eleven years ago. Dalvia informed Clevsin of my plans for escape, and he cornered me. I reacted. He, the manor, and its spoils, burned."

She swallowed. "Why didn't you take Noceo or Dalvia with you?"

"I had reason." The dark intensity edging into Kadra's gaze said that the tale was an ugly one. "I expected for him to seek vengeance, but after eleven years, I grew complacent."

"Anyone would," she murmured. "Why is Dalvia a part of this? She doesn't seem to want any bloodshed, and so far, she's acted like a strong wind would scare her."

"She believes that, in killing Clevsin, I left her and Noceo powerless in a city of predators." His voice was hard.

"But what good would it have done her to cling to a power that ugly and which wasn't hers?"

"Because she felt safest with it."

As she reeled under that simple, bitter truth, Kadra shrugged off his robes, the ripple of his muscular frame sending her pulse into a gallop. There had always been an innate elegance to his movements, not a whit of wasted motion. Her throat burned. *He's former nobility.* Their pasts had nothing in common after all.

She realized she had said it aloud when his eyes darted to her, starkness penetrating the ice in their depths. He leaned over the washbasin with a jerk of his head, almost blindly going through the motions, and she saw it then. Saw what it was like to see him afraid.

Oh.

When she left the tub, he barely looked at her, seemingly girding himself for war by the vicious set of his features. While he got clean, she wrapped herself in one of the bathrobes in the closet, still reeling. She had let her insecurities get in the way of seeing the truth. *He really thought I'd leave.*

His was an ugly past, but no more than she had guessed during her short stay in Komis, and she had long known that Kadra's hands were bloodstained. *This* wasn't what he had kept from her. There was more. Something that had made him avoid broaching the topic from the start. She saw it in the tension coiling his muscled back as he emerged from the bath and drew on a robe. He seated himself in an armchair by the bed with unconscious grace, dark hair spilling over his forehead. She wondered what he would have looked like back then.

"I think my younger self would've found you quite handsome at thirteen," she mused.

Kadra's fingers fell from the stern line of his lips. He blinked when she strode over to him, and knelt, dropping her cheek on the velvety fabric over his lap.

Face turned up to his, she smiled sadly. "You were little more than a child, Kadra. An intelligent one, no doubt, but a child forced to make adult decisions."

He exhaled roughly, a calloused palm settling on her hair to stroke it with breathtaking tenderness and a strange finality before letting her go. As though his next words would alter them irrevocably. Dread wove through her ribs when his lips parted.

"Eleven years ago, I created whitesleep."

True.

Her mouth opened. Closed. She raised her head, the threads comprising the past eight months unraveling and weaving themselves into a different tapestry. His knowledge of the ingredients. His strange tension during raids of whitesleep dens. The coin he allotted toward healers treating addiction.

Wood creaked on either side of her as he gripped the arms of his chair. "Clevsin needed a new product." All emotion had fled his eyes. "I dried beetle venom to powder and concentrated it."

"Did you distribute it too?" Her tongue felt like a ship's anchor.

He lifted a shoulder in an elegant shrug. "An irrelevant distinction. I would have, if escape had failed."

"Whitesleep has saved as many as it has destroyed. A bladesmith can't be faulted for how the wielders used their swords."

That winded him. She saw it in the slackening of his grip on the chair.

She rested her chin on his knee. He didn't seem to notice. "Anything else?"

"I started killing at nine. Clevsin enjoyed his games, and I showed talent at them. Few of my victims deserved it."

"I know," she said. "But will you now tell me why you trusted me enough to try and crown me as Tetrarch last year, but didn't mention this?"

His face was utterly remote. "You'd leave." He said it as if it was only right that she did.

Her heart squeezed. "*Never*," she returned his declaration. "I'm familiar with what people do for survival even if I was lucky enough to avoid the worst of it. You wouldn't have escaped that manor if you had enjoyed what happened there." She closed her eyes on a shaky sigh. "Do you doubt my judgment?"

"*No.*"

"Then, trust me when I say it." Rearing back on her knees when he reached for her, she said it starkly, hungrily, and with all the faith she'd always had in him, "I love you, Kadra."

Registering the stunned shattering of the void in his gaze, she stood and leaned over his seated form. "I would have loved you then, if I had known you."

A rush of air left him. Disbelief. Relief.

Reaching between them, she undid the tie of his robe, letting hers slip down one shoulder. "And I'll love you even if you fear to give me your burdens."

She let her robe part and pool to the ground, baring herself to him. Longing and hunger drummed through her, echoed in the hungry flush sweeping his cheekbones. It deepened when she knelt between his muscular thighs. "Now, call me yours."

Lips parted, pupils blown, he was a man undone. Tar-black eyes caressed her, painting her with gooseflesh. She moved an inch forward, gripping the thick stalk of his cock, her breath frozen at its zenith in pure anticipation. Breathing hard, they stared at each other.

"Mine." His voice was low and deliberate, sinking into her bloodstream. Love and hunger, wine and lightning.

Her throat drew tight. "Now, don't stop saying it." She drew him into her mouth, glorying in his harsh groan, in the way his hips thrust to meet her mouth halfway. His fingers tangled almost desperately in her hair, pulling her in and down his length. She gripped his thighs, eagerly taking him deep to the music of his rough sounds of pleasure.

He slid and withdrew, murmuring hoarse words of affection, letting her lave him with her tongue. She burned with need, transfixed at his eyes, the broad expanse of his hair-dusted chest, the rich timbre of his voice. *As potent as a god.* She worshipped at his feet, hollowing her cheeks and relishing his filthy praise.

"Fuck, my beauty. Take a little more," he ordered, his jaw like iron.

Senseless with arousal, she obeyed until he pried her loose with a groan, parting her swollen lips with his thumb. Locking an arm around her waist, he snatched her off the ground and settled her onto his lap.

They moved as one, her thighs involuntarily straddling him, their bodies slipping against each other with need. His mouth cut off her gasp of pleasure.

Hands buried in her hair, he dragged her lips against his own, pupils bleeding into the black of his eyes. He took her roughly most days, knowing that she loved it, but tonight, he was near feral, palming her breasts, her ass, rocking her over his cock and leaving them both slick.

Her skin was fever hot as he pushed two fingers into her mouth and went heavy-lidded when she sucked on them. He kept them inside, drawing her breasts into his mouth as she needily tasted his skin. Hunger gripped her, drilled through her core when he removed his fingers and replaced them with his tongue. She writhed against him, returning his open-mouthed kisses, biting his neck, grazing her teeth over his chin, pushing down the shoulders of his robes. His teeth clenched, abs rippling when she drew her nails down them, curling them into his chest hair.

Lust-inked eyes trailed over her nude body. She moaned when he slid a finger inside her. "Ten fucking hells, you're soaked."

Another bitten-off epithet, and her head hit the bed. His tongue trailed down her abdomen, then parted her to lick deep, growling his approval when she gripped his hair and shamelessly used his mouth. He pressed her hips down, voracious, lost. She could see herself in the vanity, mouth swollen, eyes glazed with pleasure, praising him, desperate for him. Throughout it all, he watched her with such love, this fearsome man of hers.

Her pulse clamored through her veins, desperate for more. His mouth never stopped devouring, stubble scraping along her inner thighs with every flex of his jaw. All thought vanished as ecstasy boiled up in her core. Tremors sizzled down her legs, meeting in the middle, and she flew, screaming his name, while he nuzzled her through the aftershocks.

At least, until he flipped her onto her stomach, drew her knees in and made her sit on his face. Minutes and orgasms blurred until she slumped face-first onto the bed, begging for him. He withdrew to push her to all-fours. His cock strained against his stomach. Biting off a curse, he stroked himself hard, teeth gritted.

She met his gaze over her shoulders. His eyes held a brazier's heat. "Give me everything."

His muscles bunched, shuddered. Then, everything left of his control vanished. Blanketing her with a curse, he fit his cock to her entrance and drove in, muffling her scream. He found the tender skin between her neck and shoulder and pulled it between his teeth, marking her as he drove ferociously, desperately.

A dark hum against her skin when she clenched around his girth. He interlocked their hands, shuttling further into her. She tossed her head back against his muscular shoulder, surrendering to the onslaught with pleas and whimpers, adoring his low groans of pleasure.

"Beautiful woman, letting me take you this hard." Turning her head to face him, he took a drag of her mouth, his teeth clinging to her bottom lip, pressing her upper half down into the bed and giving her his weight. "You love this. *Fuck*, so do I."

She couldn't speak beyond moans, sensation holding her captive, so she simply arched her back. He sucked another mark into her shoulder, one hand coming under her stomach to stroke her as he thrust, thick and demanding. A cataclysmic claiming.

She half sobbed into the mattress at the repeated fullness, the slap of his body against hers, the desperate praise in her ears, the way he kept vowing that he belonged to her. His drives came at a vicious, hungry pace.

She was burning up, relishing his harsh grunts, the possession in his gaze. He moved in a frenzy, like a man fighting for sanity. "*Fuck, fuck.* I adore you." Half declaration, half plea, the words left as a visceral, seething hiss. The dazed love in his eyes, the utter loss of control on his cruely hewn features, it was too much. She screamed his name, her body trembling, clenching around his until she was gasping for air, insensate. Her orgasm came on in fiery waves.

He hunched forward, wrapping his arms around her to thrust through her ecstasy. A slurred stream of filth and adoration left him as he stiffened. "*FUCK*," he spat. "Sarai–" Her name ended in a clenched groan as his body shuddered behind hers, flesh jerking between her legs. He pressed her into the bed for a few deep, *deep* thrusts, flooding her with come.

Breathing fast, he cradled her as they gasped through the aftershocks.

"Too much?" he murmured into her neck.

She hummed in contentment. "I think you've killed me," she mumbled and felt his smile against her hair.

He squeezed her against the protective warmth of his chest for a long moment before reluctantly withdrawing to wipe her clean.

When he returned and gathered her close, it was with lingering incredulity and a certainty of possession that she hadn't felt in him before. "Thank you."

She trailed a finger down the long blade of his nose. "Are you burden-free now?"

"One more," he said gravely.

She propped herself up on her elbows, eyes widening as he recounted the nature of what he'd begun seeing after returning from the dead and the bargain he'd made with Wrath. Fire crackled in the hearth, night claiming the sky by the time he finished.

"And you feel well?" she fretted. "Telmar said something about recipients of Wrath's strength going mad. You looked quite ill after your bout at the Aequitas."

"I feel no different." He slanted her a droll look. "The madness might take a moment to discern."

He wouldn't joke if he was feeling poorly. "I always did see you as one of the Wretched," she admitted, laughing when he dryly raised an eyebrow.

His lips ghosted down the column of her neck, eliciting a shiver from her sensitized skin. "I have given you everything. The rest is all detail."

She traced the length of his spine. "Like how your father repeatedly broke your back. Was it healed poorly on purpose?"

"No child of the Clan should fear pain. We got to know it intimately."

What an unfathomable level of cruelty. "How does your back feel now?"

"Like I can do more." His eyes made a meaningful sweep of her flushed body. "Seductress."

She turned red. "Well, I couldn't have you keep believing that I'd leave!"

He traced her chin with a rough finger, dulcet voice going guttural. "I adore you. Language itself is inadequate. I'm no wordsmith before *this*, my Sarai." He brought her hand to his still-rapid pulse, stern features raw and undone.

"I'd say you are." She nuzzled his stubbled cheek. She'd thought him deeply private and perhaps too jaded to speak of love, but he was simply unused to it. He had never known it growing up and was still learning to utter it, let alone believe himself a recipient.

"I believe I was born around midwinter," he murmured after a moment. "Clevsin didn't place value in birthdates. There was nothing I was particularly good at or enjoyed as much as bloodshed. I became a Tetrarch to prevent the rise of those like the Clan. It was a practical application of my talents. Fully-fledged criminality never interested me."

He said it with utter detachment, as though guilt had played no part in the decision when this was the same man who had tried to end his life for leaving her the night of the Fall. *How much have you buried without knowing it?*

"I think I've been seeing portions of your life." She blinked when he looked unsurprised. "You knew?"

He smiled. "I guessed."

"It's the god looming over the country, isn't it?" She sighed. "Like northerners killing with whitesleep and my having the urge to slit everyone's throat at the Aequitas earlier. Whoever this is, they aren't benign."

"Hmm." He brushed a kiss against her jaw.

She loved seeing him so languorous, menace quieted, tanned skin backlit by fire. A predator at rest. “I’m dreading leaving this room.” And thinking of coups and gods and men who used their voices for ill.

Kadra drew his knuckles down her throat. “The land may fall, but I will lift you above it. Ruin and Death will lay no claim on you while my hold persists. I may become a most exacting member of the Wretched upon death, and you will still be *mine*.” Strength pulsed off him in waves. “Do you understand?”

Mesmerized, she nodded.

“Keep looking at me like that, and I’ll take you again,” he murmured.

“Really?” she asked hopefully.

“A Tetrarch lives to serve.” He rolled her on top of him, a wicked gleam in his eyes. His cruel-edged smile turned tight. “The gods enjoy their games. We’ll have to play them if we’re to learn this one’s identity.”

Her haze of contentment crumbled. “Swear to me that you won’t do anything reckless. Bad enough that Noceo wants you dead without you taunting a god.”

“I won’t.” He soothed the goose bumps rippling over her flesh. “Noceo won’t kill me either. We’re too evenly matched, and he’d find my death unacceptably boring.”

Thank the Elsar for strange cruelties. She dropped her head to his chest. “How do we plot against a being who can hear our every word?”

For all the tenderness in his eyes, his voice was decidedly grim. “We wait for them to slip.”

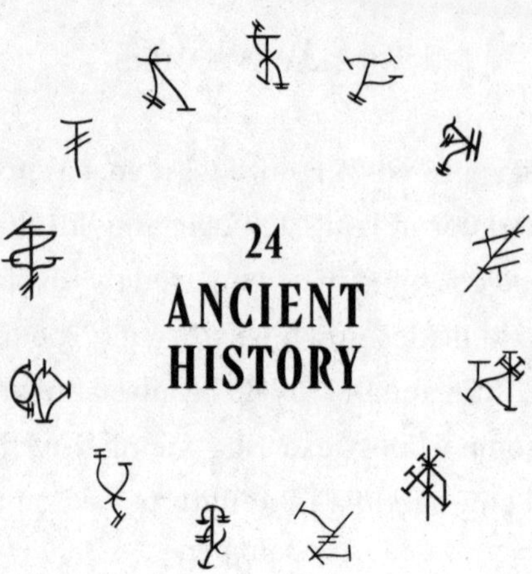

24
ANCIENT HISTORY

Night was quick to draw over the sky in the Month of Breath.

Smoke clouded the horizon from the direction of the Aequitas, the courthouse still burning itself to death.

It was a decidedly grim group that convened outside Méherre's domus. The brisk scent of crushed pine soaked into the muddied air as Méherre related what news she had gathered within Edessa.

Noceo apparently hadn't needed much time to acclimate himself to sitting at the top of a country.

He'd dragged every available priest and vigile he could bribe or Coerce to watch Cassandane's tower and Kadra's. He had also spent the better part of a day attempting to brute-force his way into Aoran Tower with little luck in the face of Cato's wards.

He wondered what it was about his home that inspired such devotion.

"Edessa will lead him on a merry dance, *certo*, but how do we fight a god? We don't even know which one it is!" Cassandane finally whispered. "Six and a half thousand dead and nine thousand madness-struck now. Perhaps we should face it. Noceo's one thing, but this is all far, *far* beyond our reach. We're…" She waved her hand in search of words that weren't coming.

A green-faced Harion bemoaned his existence, trying to determine which of the Dark Reaches he might be condemned to.

Anek looked grimly resolute. “We research. Gods have their foibles. We aren’t without recourse. *You*,” she snapped at Harion’s moaning figure, “we’re going to the Hall of Records.”

“I’m heading to the horreum again.” Sarai crossed her arms. They had decided on that course of action last night. “That was our first bloodbath. It might be able to tell us something.”

“Kadra?” Cassandane glanced at him.

“I’ll tie up a few loose ends and join her.”

Cassandane’s brow pinched. “One of us could theoretically perform a Summoning ourselves and ask one of the Elsar to aid us.”

Kadra had considered it. A Summoning created an obligation on the part of the god. He had the power to call one forth and demand aid. Taxing, but it would end the greater battle here. Cassandane’s narrow-eyed glance at him said that she was hoping he would do it.

“Summonings are dangerous,” Méherre broke in quietly. “I know the south popularized them during your former Head Tetrarch’s reign, but there are dangerous caveats that could invite the wrong attention.”

Sarai winced. “Noceo said the same. Something about how anything can slip through the cracks.”

Cassandane’s brows hit her hairline. “Alright. No Summonings.”

They parted at the artery of a main road to make for their respective leanings. He caught the smile Sarai sent his way and tucked it close as he veiled himself in shadow. The pines lining either side of the mountain road breathed with him and shielded him from the worst of the snow. Wind wove the snap and spice of conifer needles into harmless eddies. No one was out tonight. A darkness like this was an invitation to hunt. Prey grew braver when they couldn’t see. They lauded themselves for being among the few to stalk the night and mistook their adrenaline for strength.

Desperate men amused Kadra greatly.

The old tunnel from the city into Sidran Tower remained well functional. He emerged from the trapdoor within Sidran Tower’s broom closet to the dulcet sounds of Noceo roaring at least a mile away in an effort to cajole Cato into undoing his own wards and let him into Aoran Tower. *Interesting approach.*

His brother was no fool, but the god's appearance seemed to have thrown him from meticulous to desperate. Kadra stalked toward Aoran Tower, staying off the cobblestone path and watching his brother storm away after more screaming.

Padding toward the gates, Kadra took in Noceo's guard standing watch, back facing him. Kadra yanked the man back and clapped a hand over his mouth before he could loose a scream. The furious epithets meeting his palm were proof that the man wasn't Coerced. Bribed then. No loss.

Kadra slid the man's dagger from him and slipped it through his throat. It sank in with ease. A well-maintained blade. Drawing it loose, he waited for the man's dying gurgles to end, then rolled him onto the path.

Moments later, he caught steps nearing the gate. It swung open. "I wouldn't recommend leaving, Cato."

"Why not–*gods.*" A sconce parted the dark and vanished just as quickly as Cato hurriedly retreated from the corpse. He wiped his sweating forehead as Kadra entered Aoran Tower. "Who's that?"

"Your jailor apparently."

Cato nodded. Downturned lips, misty eyes. *Sadness.* "I've heard a great deal."

Ah. This had been a long time coming. "I apologize for how long it took for me to say it," Kadra said gravely.

"What stopped you?"

Kadra leaned against the tower's exterior, crossing one leg at his ankles. "I considered it until the Fall. Nothing mattered after that."

"Can I hear it now?"

A reasonable expectation.

The outraged roars beyond the Aoran Tower's gates spoke to Noceo having found the guard's body. Behind Cato's wards, Kadra told the man who had been the closest thing to a father of who he had been and how he had come into Othus's life.

Cold and sorrow lined Cato's weathered features by the end. "Othus could never explain why he brought you with him. What did you tell him when Noceo failed to show?"

"That he had died while gathering the information Othus wanted."

Cato winced. "You used guilt."

"I did."

The older man watched him sadly. "But things didn't get better, Drenevan."

"Hmm." It hadn't taken long for Othus to put together the sort of monster he was. His attempts to force the evil from him hadn't been successful. Beatings and public disdain simply hadn't been effective on Kadra when he had known worse.

Cato blew out the sconce against a wall and heaved a long breath. "From one abusive home into another. Othus was wrong for it. I'm sorry, Drenevan. I didn't try hard enough to stop him."

"It was nothing compared to the Clan," Kadra reflected. He had his regrets but consequence had brought him here. "I held no ill will. Think nothing of it."

Cato cleared his throat and gripped Kadra's shoulder for a few quiet seconds. Side by side, they watched Noceo return, howl some more, and cart off the body.

"Don't leave the tower for the time being," Kadra added after a moment.

"I won't." The old man smiled. "Thank you for coming, son."

Kadra stared, nodded, and left with the same smile on his face.

The moons were thin crescents on his way back to Sidran Tower, an indicator that a moondark night approached. The stars had their time on those nights when both moons were new moons. The Order preached of them being an ill omen. Kadra wondered if they had it right.

He slowed his steps when two familiar shapes entered the corner of his vision.

Noceo and Dalvia appeared lost in conversation, unaware of his presence. Kadra slipped into the tree line ten paces away. His boots slid quietly into the powder-soft snow, masking his footsteps as he tracked them.

"You wanted power." Noceo's voice was low and tight, pale eyes boring into Dalvia.

She held them for a moment then looked away. "To *change* things. Not bring wanton death."

"The two go hand-in-hand. Don't tell me that after everything we've done, *this* is where you balk," he said mockingly.

"I'm trying not to be a hypocrite."

"No chance of that."

Dalvia's throat worked for a moment before she smiled. Something squeezed too tight in Kadra's chest at that look. Sarai had given him the same only yesterday. Glassy eyes, a pinched brow, and upturned lips. Hurt, resignation. He suddenly had the urge to return to his Petitor and apologize a hundred times over.

"You're deviating from what we planned for Sarai," she finally murmured. "Weren't you going to turn her against him? Why did you torture her that day in Komis?"

Kadra's blood went from ice-floe cold to the temperature of lightning, his mind already plotting vengeance.

"If reason doesn't work, then it'll have to be fear," Noceo grit out.

"Do you—" Dalvia took a deep breath. "You seem intrigued."

Noceo gave her a cold once-over. "Jealous?"

That resigned look again. "There was a time when I might have been."

The abrupt widening of his brother's eyes was Kadra's only sign that he had been thrown off.

Noceo drew his cloak tighter around him, walking faster than her. "You swore that you'd obey me. Do it. I didn't ask for your thoughts on strategy."

Dalvia slowed her paces, staring at the sky. It took Noceo several yards to realize that she wasn't dogging his steps. He turned to her, exasperatedly roughing his hair with both hands.

He took a loud, drained breath. "I didn't mean that I wasn't grateful for your help." The words seemed to be pried from him with a blade. "Your formula gave me more power than I thought possible. Three months of research and Bridging back and forth every night. None of this would have been possible without you."

Kadra's eyes narrowed at Dalvia's near-soundless laugh.

"Sometimes, I wish it hadn't been." Her whisper hung in the air, too quiet for Noceo's ears but close enough for Kadra's. He watched her leave, brow furrowed.

Could I have saved her from this?

Sarai would tell him that he had been thirteen, that he had given Dalvia a choice, and that she had chosen to betray him to Clevsin. All true. But the question lingered as he returned to the city, using the white claw Wrath had gifted him to see in the tunnel's darkness, and then through a maze of alleys he was intimately familiar with for how often he had butchered people therein.

The god's gifts were dangerously useful. He could understand why men had gone mad.

"It's rather aggravating having that thrown in my face all the time," a cold voice mused beside him in the next breath. Black robes swept his as Wrath materialized, long hair knotted atop his head. "Good evening, Tetrarch."

"I haven't asked for help," Kadra reminded him.

"You aren't getting it. I try not to fight with my colleagues." He stroked his chin. "Do I need to have an occasion to visit my acolyte?"

"Preferably."

Voids and stars burned in the god's robes. Kadra grew faintly nauseous, watching suns crash into each other and die.

The alley they stood in bulged. Long gouges tore through the walls. Hands of striated muscle reached from them, whether for mercy or to deliver condemnation, he couldn't say. Blood dripped from the invisible wounds to pool around his feet, lapping at his boots. To act was to leave a mark upon the world. There was no changing what he had done here.

"Life and death, blood and time." Wrath examined the tears in the rock. "Echoes of what you've done, what you could do, and things that happened a long time ago that could happen again. You saw those very futures at the Aequitas, did you not? Death or obliteration."

"Do you want gratitude for providing me with a third choice?" Kadra followed the god's slow glide across his cell. "And the claw?"

"A nice touch, wasn't it? I didn't think a fang would suit." Wrath prodded at one of the hands reaching from a gouge in the wall and set it ablaze. "But the worst would have come to pass had you not chosen my power. Which you only did because your woman was injured in Komis. Which, in turn, wouldn't have occurred if your brother wasn't seeking vengeance for what happened eleven years ago. *That* is the nature of a god. Consequence."

You will see it soon, Wrath had said at their last meeting. He understood now.

"The process should still have more in the way of safeguards if I'm in the running," Kadra dryly noted.

Wrath's fangs flashed in the dim light of the cell. "You amuse me, Tetrarch. And you understand consequence better than most. So, when you dwell on the past and wonder what you could have altered, ask yourself what you would have lost in the present. Everything has a price. Even regret."

Everything has a price. He had warned Noceo of that once, pointed out what his obsession with Parvine Poxtan could cost her. It had cost them both.

Wrath's fiery eyes narrowed knowingly. "Stay alive, acolyte. Contrary to the opinion of the masses, I don't enjoy losing those I mark." He was gone in the next breath, the alley's brick rearranging itself in an impossible snarl behind him.

The gods, Kadra reflected, were a headache to understand.

But he was starting to think that he did.

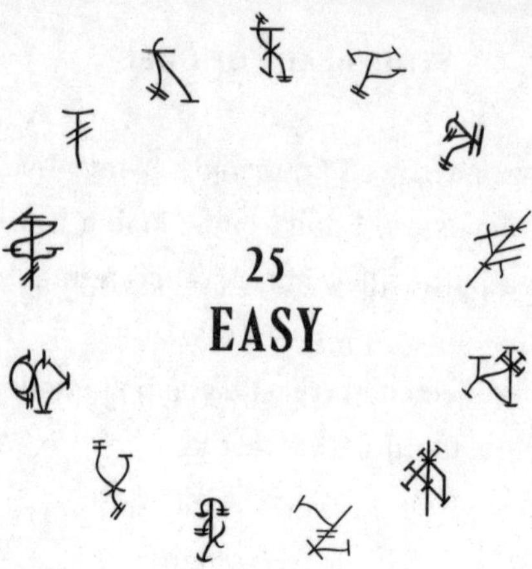

25
EASY

Sarai stared at the sky, lost in thought as they rode to the Grains Guild's horreum.

Having never been there, Méherre had only been able to open a Bridge as far as Aelius's vigile station, where they had stolen two horses and ridden like the wind. She stared at the familiar wooden gates crawling close on the horizon. By all the gods, to what purpose was a god tormenting their city?

"You're quiet." Méherre nudged her mount to trot beside hers.

"I'm lost," Sarai admitted. "I wish I had more in the way of power to halt Noceo and this god. But I can barely get people to take me seriously let alone the divine."

Méherre shot her a look that she wasn't used to receiving. Kind but also implying that she wasn't very bright. "Noceo and the Order came for you," she said slowly. They could have ignored you when you positioned yourself as a target, but they drove you straight to a Hearing instead." Méherre spread her hands wide at Sarai's bewildered shrug. "You really don't see it? They only sought to take away your social capital because you *had* some. Ever thought that you might be focusing too much on the few who dislike you and not the multitude who couldn't care less either way?"

Sarai nearly lost her grip on the reins.

Méherre raised her brows meaningfully. "That's why Noceo keeps offering you power, so he can take advantage of your name beside his. Yesterday's display earned him more fear than it did respect. Your allegiance would place a thumb on the scale in his favor."

Something stuck in the back of Sarai's mind. She opened her mouth when Méherre spoke again.

"Freedom without power is a curse for people like us." She examined the sleet-covered farmhouses on either side of the road. Icicles hung from the eaves, dripping. "I saw you recognize it too in Komis after the strike."

"People like us?"

"People who want to set the world right," Méherre clarified. "You care a great deal. A dangerous thing for a woman with power. You ran yourself ragged around Edessa."

Sarai's brow furrowed. "Méherre, how do know so much about–"

"Anything you'd like me to examine with Cassandane? She's the only one of us wandering in a daze about what to do, so I thought I'd help her after leaving you here."

Sarai lost her train of thought. "Perhaps a search of the Hall of Records too? Anek may as well be on their own there with Harion."

Méherre snorted. "Nothing between his ears, and he does get so touchy about it."

Sarai studied the deep downturn to her lips, the weariness lining her face. "Thank you, truly. You must have imagined there would be more to the capital than a couple of tired Tetrarchs, Petitors, and several hundred vigiles trying to hold the country together."

"Not precisely. But you needn't worry." Méherre's smile was that of a woman who had known too much compromise and now took no quarter. "I've only ever wanted to see this through."

Sarai registered the ring of truth in the words as they drew up before the gates into the horreum and bid Méherre farewell.

The cold howled around her, striking invisible knives through her thick birrus to penetrate skin as she circled the horreum. Her footsteps plunged deep into fresh flurries, sinking to the ankle as her mind turned to the unique question of Dalvia.

To Kadra's knowledge, Dalvia had been an only child, and after the death of her parents, she'd been left to depend on the mercy of Kadra's

Clan. But try as she did, Sarai couldn't fathom why the woman hadn't left Noceo if she abhorred what he was doing.

Her feet sank into a footprint. A frisson of warning ran down her spine upon sighting a second trail in the snow. *Shit*. Who else was here?

Holding her breath, she eased backward, stepping in her own footprints until she had come back the way she'd entered. Turning, she froze at Noceo standing before her.

Hands behind his back, he stared at her in equal shock, then surveyed her scarred skin with the arrogance of a man who believed his judgment crucial to the existence of most. "You could pass for the Xārōmand Desert. Cracked earth."

A few words and he reduced her to so little. *Worthless*. She ground her teeth at the memory. "About to imbibe more stimulants and fight a god?"

Noceo scowled. "Where's Drenevan?"

"Not here." She was suddenly heartily thankful that he had stopped by Aoran Tower first. "Where's Dalvia?"

"Who knows? Still upset at your defeat?"

Sarai watched him as one would a blackstripe bear. Her breath fogged out in the cold. "I don't know where you get the idea that you're doing any good, but nothing will change with you around. At least there's hope with the Tetrarchy, flawed as it is."

"Hope. Illusion." Noceo kicked at a tuft of snow. "You haven't seen enough to know the difference."

An exhausted laugh escaped her, tinged with a bitterness that took a moment to ebb off. "I have. Enough to know the difference between the illusion of power and hope of it." She performed a pointed once-over of his quaking hand. "Drugs wearing off?"

He ignored her. "The south needed a lesson after the all the north has suffered."

"Please, you wanted to stick it to Kadra." The replica of Aoran Tower, the assumption of Kadra's position. This had always been revenge. "Anyone who gave a *havïd* about the country would have held every piece of the

Aequitas together as people escaped. What can your voice do beyond force *others* to do what you can't?"

He stilled.

"It isn't that you didn't want war." She watched the pallor of his face worsen, letting her tongue run untrammeled. "You can't control it. That's why you vanished after triggering the lightning strike on the Aequitas. Why should I tie my lot in with a man who can't so much as shield himself from a single bolt without ordering someone else to protect him—" He slapped her hard enough to whip her head to one side.

Pain burst white-hot through her skull. Winded, she wordlessly touched her bleeding lips, exhaling through the ringing in her ears. When she turned to meet his eyes, he had never looked paler.

He might have drawn her blood, but the blow was hers.

He stared at his hands for a moment as though still comprehending that he had struck her. "His life should have been mine," he whispered. "I'm taking it back. You're the one clinging to a monster."

Furious denial sprung to her lips. He laughed it off before it left.

"He didn't single you out?" That unearthly voice wove around her like a vise. "Didn't make you feel bared to your soul and entirely known? Didn't praise you as beyond compare or give you what he vowed he gave no other? And then, you felt called to him despite what you saw of his evil until common sense vanished and all that was left was a desperation to *please*," he hissed with bitter vehemence.

"Not for the reasons you *think*!"

"Really? As children, Drenevan and I were ordered to lure people into working for the Clan." He stared at the horreum's gates, weak of moonlight spilling over his delicate features. "Our targets were fellow children, though the difference in mental acuity was so wide as to be unfair. We'd encourage them to join our blazeleaf production warehouse for coin, and then lock them in with the rest of the workers. Once their families came crying and begging, Clevsin would force them all into servitude. We had a thriving workforce. But how did we get children to turn their skin to leather while curing and drying blazeleaf?" He turned back to her. "The same tricks. Lure them in. Make them feel seen. Promise them that you and only you can help with their struggles. Prove it with little things, and when they're well and hooked, reel them in. No one was immune to Drenevan. Not you. Not Tetrarch Othus."

She winced at the memory, staring at the sweat lining the grooves of his palm, and the pale, almost-ill waxy sheen of his skin. "Two things can be true. Taking away Othus's free will was wrong, and you were desperate and didn't have anyone to turn to." Her heartbeat was a staccato of pity and anger. "You act like your motives are efficient, and Kadra's were evil, but so many are dead. Because of envy."

Noceo dropped his hand. "He got *everything*, while I remained stuck in Komis with *nothing*, always slaving away, always afr—" He cut himself off with a shake of his head and a laugh.

Afraid? "You're mad if you expect me to believe that Kadra heartlessly abandoned you. That man carries more guilt than the Chaboras River has water!"

"You barely know him. He *left* eleven years ago without a backward glance," he snarled.

"Gods, there isn't a chance in any of the ten hells that it's true, but it was up to *you* to build a life of your own!" she said incredulously. Dalvia was one thing, but this silver-eyed snake could have made his home in the Xārōmand Desert if he so chose.

"You don't see it." Noceo pricked his thumb and pressed it to the runes for Coercion on his armilla. Power roared to life, the seething press of magic a tangible weight over them. His skin turned a shade paler. "I could have forced you to join me at any point. But it has to be real. You have to see it as I have or I become the villain of the piece."

She was inches from slapping him. "All I *see* is a pathetic piece of former nobility who's spent eleven years wallowing over his life being hell when you had it easier than I ever did."

"That's what you believe?" His silver eyes glittered, something almost mad in their depths. "Then, *look*!" He seized her wrists, twisting them ruthlessly when she tried to escape. "Tell me that I didn't suffer." He wiped some of the blood from her bleeding mouth wound onto her armilla and pressed it into *herar*, the rune for "Probing." "Let's see how long that high horse of yours stands."

He touched her fingertips to his head. The world dissolved in a familiar rush.

She opened her eyes to a well-organized library, still able to feel the grip of his hands around hers. She had no hope of leaving his head until he let her go.

Cursing roundly, she took in the library. After months on the job, she'd learned that they were the most common unconscious structure that people chose for their memories. Endless oak shelves labeled by letter and topic stretched out ahead. Noceo had lived quite a life. Perusing the stacks of books, she walked toward a series of shelves of topics beginning with the letter *W* "*Whitesleep*."

She opened the first volume.

Her surroundings reshaped and re-formed into a cramped but well-furnished bedroom. She was outside Noceo's perspective in the memory just as she had been with the farmer. Whoever this god was, they seemed to affect the unconscious realms immensely, down to warping her abilities.

A large, austerely built bed of mahogany, pristine but for the carving of a wolf on one of the posts, occupied much of the space. Gray sunlight streamed through barred windows and spread fingers over an ebony writing desk, washbasin, and a wardrobe stocked with silver robes that would have fit an adolescent. Fire crackled in the hearth. Despite the decidedly grim stamp of the room's layout and the cut of its furniture, everything was of the finest quality. Several pieces sported the geometric patterns that had been ubiquitous during the monarchy's time.

A smile broke over her face at the adolescent boy hunched over a mortar and pestle, grinding the distinctive yellow venom sacs of boil beetles to dust. A series of vials and powders littered his desk. Behind Kadra, Noceo lounged on the bed and made notations on his scroll, spilling ink onto Kadra's sheets. The scene was so wholly comfortable that it hurt.

"It won't work," Noceo insisted as Kadra continued to mash the beetles, adding small quantities of leaves to the mortar.

"Hmm," was Kadra's only response. Like his half brother, he hadn't yet grown into his features. The strong nose and stern mouth that would harden as he matured gave him the look of a very serious hawk at this younger age.

His fingers slipped on the pestle. It clattered to the ground. He gave it a look of consternation before turning to the blazeleaf roll he'd left smoking on a nearby plate. Her jaw dropped when he took several deep draws, blowing a ring at the ceiling. *So, it was blazeleaf before you turned to alcohol.*

Noceo leaned over the edge of the bed and picked up the pestle. "Overdid it?"

"A little," Kadra admitted.

His half brother cautiously sniffed the pestle. "What kind of drug is it for to you to pound away at it for so long? Hallucinogen?"

"Analgesic." Kadra took a puff of blazeleaf. "Thought it might help with my back but it isn't strong enough yet."

She stilled. *That's why you made it?* He had been in pain.

"So, you're concentrating it?" Noceo swung his legs over the bed and peered over Kadra's shoulder. "That'll take hours."

The tight lines around Kadra's mouth said he was aware and didn't give a damn. She watched him in dawning understanding. She had always thought that he drank to numb himself from the weight of what he did, but it had been to numb his *body* as much as his mind. Recalling how often he'd reached for a glass after they'd made love, she resolved to swat him at her next available opportunity. *His spine must have been in agony.*

"I'll never understand Father's preoccupation with drugs," Noceo muttered. "What good is an empire from the shadows? I need a better weapon, Drenevan. Something that'll bring the world to its knees."

"Your voice already does that."

"But it's so fucking limited!" Noceo flopped back against the bed. His jaw tightened. "I can barely take on a crowd, and even then, I'm drained after a one-word command. Not all of us can weave lightning." He stretched his hands in front of him and splayed his fingers. "I wish I were a Twelfth-Tier too. Parvine might like that. I could aim a word into a crowd and watch it dance."

Kadra blinked. "Don't aim one at me," he said with a strange seriousness, before he began grinding away again.

Sarai caught a flash of resentment in Noceo's eyes. Had he thought that Kadra was looking down on him?

"I'd make the world mine." He scowled. "Maybe then, Clevsin'll finally be pleased. I'm sick of getting my legs broken."

A fissure of sadness tunneled through her chest as everything clicked.

Broken legs in one son. A broken back in another. Kadra had left his spine in agony as penitence for what he had done, because pain was all he understood. Noceo's agony had steered him into megalomania. How bitter it was that he had grown to subject others to the same hell that he had lived through. Seeing him young and hurt and *scared* felt like looking in a mirror. *No wonder he saw through me.*

"You'd be starting a war," Kadra noted.

"Life is war." Noceo propped himself up on an elbow. "Take you. That's what you were molded for. You'd be lost without a knife in your hand. You'll never be normal."

An ache spread behind her eyes when Kadra considered that gravely. "True," he said without inflection.

True. The crack in her chest grew. The crucible that had formed him had burnt off too much of his morality for that. Clevsin had boiled him in blood and violence until he had conquered both and gained an enjoyment for their simplicity and familiarity.

The world Kadra lived in was a world at war. He was one of the rare few who could see the battlelines that people had queued up at before the fighting began. It was part of what made him such a brilliant politician, because the games of one-upmanship he had learned young had easily translated to politics. She had always wondered which parts of him had been innate and which ones had been a byproduct of experience. It was a miracle he'd turned out as honorable as he had when he'd traded one abusive home with Clevsin for another one with Othus.

No wonder he had hidden so much. How did anyone explain such a childhood?

The memory devolved to Kadra walking in on Clevsin bringing a poker on Noceo's legs. Noceo had given Kadra such a desolate look that she had choked.

The jerk of her body outside his memories told her that he had pulled her hands away from his head. The world reemerged in flashes of light and sound.

"Well?" His voice was dim. "I had it easy, did I?"

Her lips parted on a soundless exhalation before she found the words. "I'm sorry. You didn't."

Every muscle in his pallid face stilled. He let her hands go. "Will you join me then?"

She looked at him then. Truly looked at his too-pale features and the imprint his clammy hands had left on hers. "The baker's girl you cared for, how did Parvine Poxtan die?"

Noceo's eyes darkened. "She's none of your concern."

On the contrary, she's in every one of your memories. "You were fond of her. If you want me to understand you, then—"

"I never asked for *understanding*, Death-Summoner."

"Why else would you show me your mind?" she asked quietly.

His features went bloodless. The subsequent silence was a knife between them. Jaw tight, he took a sharp breath when a portal split the air outside the horreum. Dalvia emerged and started at the sight of her.

Noceo composed his features into an admirable blank mask and took a step forward. “You shouldn’t have been wandering about alone, Death-Summoner.”

“Is she?” Kadra stepped out of the night behind her.

This should be good.

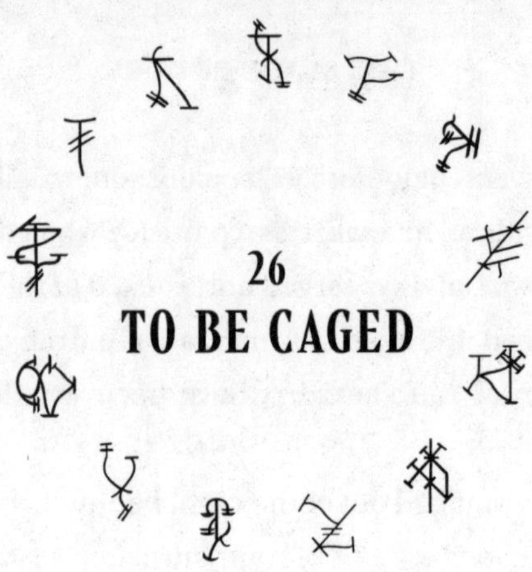

26
TO BE CAGED

Lightning was easier to summon in Edessa's wet cold, the thick humidity wafting off the lower floor of the horreum especially conducive to building a charge. It sizzled around Noceo in a sinuous web. He showed no signs of pain; they had both known it too well.

"Let's manage this without the theatrics, this time." Kadra examined Sarai's features, wiping the blood from her lips to pin his brother with a homicidal smile.

Cool amusement filled Noceo's eyes. "By all means. You—"

Kadra flicked a finger. The lightning cage shrunk to seize his brother in brutal coils. Noceo screamed as tendrils sizzled up his torso. Once, there had been a time when he had done everything to protect his brother from this fate at Clevsin's hands. Yet, it had come to this. Dalvia froze like a trapped animal, breath coming fast.

"Did you really think that you were my equal?" Kadra wondered conversationally. "You needed hostages to keep us on an even footing at the Aequitas."

"Ever the show-off!" Fury and fear seeped from Noceo in waves, voice flooding with power. "*Stop this. Now!*"

The world warped around Kadra, the command trapping his head in a vise much stronger than that at the Aequitas. Blood vessels burst behind his eyes, flooding his vision with crimson. *Damn.*

"You threw us all away," Noceo croaked, skin peeling from the burns on his neck as he stumbled toward Dalvia. "Now you play the martyr."

Is that how you've chosen to remember that night? Eleven years and a few spare months separated them from the past. A chasm had broken open in his chest when he had forged a path down the mountains, evergreens standing in silent nighttime vigil to witness the end of the only friendship he had known since childhood.

"*I* threw nothing away," he bit out, surprised at the hoarseness that coated his voice. "Did you forget that so easily?"

Noceo's bitter snarl morphed to faint bewilderment. As if he'd stepped into one of the worlds Kadra saw at the edge of his vision, and could neither make heads nor tails of it. A sickly flush darkened his cheeks. "But you..." he tottered.

Movement flashed. Dalvia planted herself in front of his brother as a shield, supporting his sagging weight. "Don't," she said quietly. "Please just let him go. You know as well as I do that you've a greater threat at hand."

Kadra considered her, trading a resigned glance with Sarai. "Your choices are your own. But I'll ask you again. Do you wish to leave?"

Anguish and something older, pained, coagulated in her eyes. Too loud for indecision but too muffled to be a choice. A scream that didn't know its way out. "Let us go."

A bitter thing, sentiment. He nodded. The air immediately split. Snow blew in to catch on his hair. He glimpsed the manor beyond where Noceo would undoubtedly lick his wounds. Dalvia looped an arm around the suddenly mute man's shoulders and drew him in, stopping when he disengaged from her and staggered onward. She paused at the mouth of the portal, a dark silhouette veiled in flurries, hands at her sides. Komis, its harsh mountains, and fierce ice couldn't touch her. She was pieces to the wind and would never put herself back together. The past and this manor had caged her, and she believed in nothing outside those bars.

He waited by the portal for a breath. A final question, because Wrath did have him right, and the past fettered him. He would never know how much of this he could have changed.

She walked on. The portal closed behind her.

He entered the horreum with Sarai. There was no speaking of doom to those who sought it. His woman, his people waited.

He would avert theirs.

27
RANCOR

Despite her exhaustion and anguish, all thoughts of Noceo fled her mind as she stepped foot in the warehouse again, parting with Kadra at the same fork she had during their first foray here, over a month ago under the dead of night.

There were places, the Elsarian priests said, that were tainted by the dead. Lands, homes, woods, and streams once unblighted, but now, forever altered by the brutality of the acts that had occurred within them. Death took all who came to him, but some weren't so eager to leave. They sat, festered, demanded until the place of their end took on a fearful new life, and through it they lived and lived and ate all that crossed their path.

Perhaps it had happened here too. An odd lethargy took her as she strode into the warehouse. Her feet seemed to know the way as though she had walked it a thousand times since. Sconces flared to life as she walked. She didn't question the light.

A left, another turn, and the hallway where she had found the dead stood bare, pristine but for the odd fleck of blood on the wall.

Closing her eyes, she sank into her memory. When she resurfaced, it was to blood pooling on the ground past the tiled step running across the hallway. *Strange. Why a step in the middle of an otherwise flat hallway?* She had been too preoccupied with the dead and the Guildswoman split in two to pay it much heed. Now, she crossed it and crouched.

Around seven inches tall and practically invisible without the blood lapping at it. A precautionary measure, perhaps? Or something to trip up anyone who entered this portion of the horreum, to make them stumble, drop whatever they were carrying. *A trap, an obstacle, a marker.* Regardless of the step's purpose, its presence indicated only one thing. A secret.

She tapped against the tile, pressing this way and that before relinquishing it to stride further down the hallway. The dead had been arrayed here, frozen in flight.

In fright.

In her mind's eye, she saw their gaping mouths anew, bulging eyes weeping blood.

"Like they died of fear," she whispered aloud, and something seemed to whisper in the back of her mind. *A laugh?* Her trembling hands vibrated faster.

They were running down the hallway. She followed it to the end, where it widened into an unremarkable dead end. Four tiled steps led up to a storage room, piled high with sacks of assorted grains. She stared. *That doesn't make sense.* The room was too small to have fit all those Guildspeople which meant…

A hidden room. And if it wasn't here, and wasn't an offshoot of the hallway, then that left… *below.* She examined the four steps into the room, kneeling to take a better look at the tile. A handle in the bottommost step gave it away. She tugged and all four steps came up and away from the floor. A blood-smeared staircase led down into the horreum's depths, the nose of each step stained like the teeth of a serrated knife. Down, down, all the way at the bottom, she could make out a hand, reaching for help that had never come.

She stared at that gaping maw. This had been the true scene of the crime.

"*And they deserved it,*" a voice noted in her head with a trace of laughter. "*You all might.*"

Sarai stilled, aware that she was sucking air in at frenetic speeds. When had her breathing grown so harsh?

Something creaked from within the staircase's bowels. She peered over the edge and froze as the hand at the bottom *moved.* It clawed an inch forward, then another. The beginnings of a matted head emerged at the base of the staircase. Half the head, then the entire thing. Her breath came faster. Hoarse. The neck tilted up, slow and fluid, and pinned her with its—half a head. A nose and teeth smiled. Terror made her its quivering instrument, drumming at her throat.

A hand clamped over her eyes, another drawing her up—when had she gone halfway down the stairs?—and back into the hallway. Citrus met her senses, and she sagged. *Kadra.*

He steadied her back against his chest. "Breathe," he murmured against her ear. "That's it, Sarai. Let it out. I have you." He made her take a few more shuddering breaths before removing his hand from her eyes. "There's no one here but us. Remember that when you look down."

Heart in her throat, she dared blink. Her vision cleared, and she found a bloodstained staircase before her. There was nothing at the bottom.

"I saw…" She stepped back, suddenly chilled to the bone. "This god is really starting to irk me."

Tamping down her nerves, she strode downstairs before she could halt herself. Her pulse thudded with every step.

Death had long come and left this place. The miasma of rot hung heavy and putrid in the air. A spark from Kadra's free hand lit the sconces bracketing the walls. She flinched.

A small lake of now-dried blood swamped the stone tile floor, embedded in the crevices between divans, the odd sack of whitesleep, and crates of *ibez.*

"This is no cellar," she whispered.

"An *ibez* den." Kadra withdrew an amphora from an open crate with mild amusement. "Where does the Grains Guild find the time?"

Ur Dinyé had banned the dangerously potent mix of fruit, spices, and wheat years ago for its near-hallucinogenic strength. *Looks like the Grains Guild were secretly distributing it.* And imbibing it.

The dead here perched upon sofas, bottles smashed beside them, jaws agape in the same screams their compatriots had made on their way to the afterlife. Rot oozed from their decaying flesh, dripping black onto the ground. She steeled her spine against a shudder.

"It began here." Kadra's piercing gaze raked over the dead with disinterest.

Fear raked long fingers across the back of her neck. "They were drinking their way through a crate. A few were rubbing on whitesleep. Then, someone started raving. They would have chalked it up to intoxication at first."

"Until fear took hold."

"Then, they ran, like they thought that what was causing the madness was infectious."

"In their eyes, it would have been. The more their compatriots fell to it, the more they must have believed it to be a disease or contaminated drink." Kadra moved toward a corpse at the corner of the room, examining the *ibez* bottle beside him.

"But that doesn't match what happened at the Aequitas." Sarai's boots scraped over a thick layer of dried blood. "All the madness-struck there weren't imbibing *ibez* or whitesleep."

"Hmm." He leaned against a crate and studied the tableau. An imperceptible shift took place in the line of his shoulders.

She followed his probing stare to a body frozen half out of its chair. "What do you see?"

"A devouring." His face darkened. "This god enjoys carnage."

Ibez-drinkers, whitesleep users, the spectators at that marketplace, the crowd at the Aequitas, what did these groups have in common for the god to choose to take them?

By the time they returned to Méherre's home, she was weary to the bone. A glance at Kadra's tight jaw told her that it was little more than bloodlust still keeping him upright.

She ran a bath and was struck by how similar the tile here was to that in Clan Kader's Hall of Relics. She had crawled across it, acknowledged how worthless she was. She had put herself back together in the rubble because she had had no choice. But the pieces she had found hadn't fit quite right. They were missing corners and had too many teeth. She had wedged them back inside anyway.

"Sarai?"

She realized that she had been standing in the doorway of the bathing room, staring at the tile for several minutes. "Oh." She stepped away. The metal handle was ice against her clammy skin. "It's been a long–" *No.* That wasn't what she'd wanted to say. She let it out before she could think: "He had me say that I was worthless."

A pause. She heard Kadra's steps behind her. He turned her to face him. Ice and fury twisted in his eyes. "How," he asked evenly, "would you like him to die?"

"That's just it," she whispered. "I don't want him to. Even though the asshole had me–" she broke off before she could admit that she had crawled.

Kadra drew her against his chest, holding her like a fortress. "I've seen powerful men turn catatonic after an hour of what he did to you. This shame isn't yours." Scooping her into his arms, he strode into the bathroom and deposited her in Méherre's stone bathtub. Black eyes held hers. "I'm proud of you."

When her hands moved to the buttons of her tunic, he took them in his. "Let me take care of you, yes?"

She let him gently undress her and join her under the water. Taking the scrub cloth on the ledge of the tub, he ran it over her skin. She leaned into his touch, absorbing the feeling of him trying to put her back together. Had anyone done the same for him?

He dried her off and enveloped her in a robe.

Looking at those black eyes that terrified most people, she saw the quiet adolescent he had been–powerful and resigned, dangerous and lonely. "Thank you for choosing me." His heart was all the greater a gift after what she knew of his past.

"You chose me too." He rose from the tub, magnificently nude, cupping her face to kiss her. She parted her lips and clung to him in a surge of affection, peppering his cheeks and jaw with more kisses, and relishing the leonine way he nuzzled her.

Lifting her easily, he dropped her onto the bed and joined her. She cuddled close, wanting more but conscious of his exhaustion after battling Noceo. Several burst blood vessels still reddened his eyes. The lines in his brow deepened, and she could see him turning the past over in his head in search of a pivot point where he could have changed everything.

"This isn't your fault." She followed the path of a stray water droplet slaloming through his chest hair. "You're much too used to manipulating the world, Kadra, but some things are outside your control."

"Hmm."

Swatting him, she straddled his waist. "Not. Your. Fault," she repeated.

His eyes softened. "I'll try to believe it," he said dryly, tangling a hand in her wet hair. "As should you."

She sighed. "Noceo wasn't wrong about me though. I do crave power."

"You crave security." Strong fingers massaged her scalp. She melted into his chest. "Noceo sees the means not the end."

She stilled as the simple truth struck her. Suddenly, the world felt infinitely more hopeful. Sitting up on her elbows, she pressed her fingertips to his strained temples, soothing what she could.

"Today was a fatal blow to Noceo's ego. Nursing it will keep him occupied." Bloodlust bloomed in his eyes. "Tomorrow, we prowl Edessa's hospitals for answers."

She nodded, raking a hand through his hair. He pressed into the caress like an affectionate northern wolf.

"Should I call you Drenevan?" she wondered.

A wry smile curved his lips. "Noceo told you what *Kadra* means, hmm? Call me anything that pleases you."

She propped herself up on an elbow. "My Tetrarch," she tried. "No, everyone uses that. My love? My dear?" She paused when he didn't join in the fun. His eyes were the rarest, softest black, glowing with contentment. It struck her then that this wasn't a bit of banter to him, but something he'd craved for a long time.

Leaning down, she touched her nose to his. "Perhaps I'll try all of them."

His cock stiffened against her legs. "Perhaps you should."

She lost her battle with desire.

His gaze narrowed when she slid down his body. "You're demanding to be sore tomorrow."

"Well, I'm certain that the Magus Supreme can soothe me."

A predatory gleam lit his eyes. "I'll do a damn lot more than that."

She yielded to him, relinquishing all fears and cares for a few hours while he sank into her and drove them to bliss.

But when she fell asleep, it was to stormfall and blood. And each time she tumbled from Sidran Tower, the god's eyes found her.

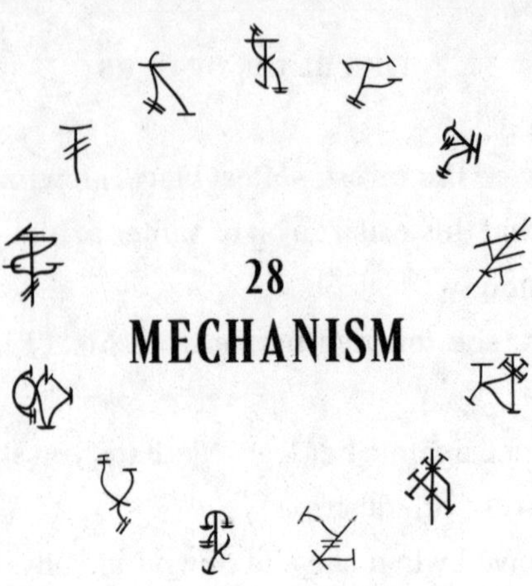

28
MECHANISM

Above, Silun and Praefa slid behind a cloud. She mirrored Kadra's footsteps, one with the shadows as they glided from street to street, sans mounts—their routine of the past two nights. They'd gone through most of the hospitals in his Quarter, finding sparse tiled hallways and rooms of pallets and screams. Narrowing down a god's identity while an angry populace kept Noceo occupied.

Who called forth a god this vicious? And why?

She squinted at the smaller hospital at the edge of his Quarter where they'd planned to meet Cassandane and the others. A dying brazier crackled weakly by unguarded main doors. She pulled up her sleeve, confirming that *beshaz* was active on her armilla before following Kadra across the road. Snow masked their approach, giving way softly under their boots. A lone owl called to the sky.

The hospital doors swung open noiselessly under Kadra's grip, sending forth a draft that blew out the brazier. Smoke and ash wreathed the air. He took a step into the tiled atrium. Quiet seethed around them, interrupted only by the creak of the door falling shut. Moonlight snaked past the curtains to dapple the steps of the twin staircases that led up to the patients.

Kadra moved with languid grace, broad shoulders loose and eyes alight at what he saw waiting in the dark. They had reached the landing when a blur of quiet steps launched at them.

Three men. Holding back a flinch, she gripped one's wrist before they neared Kadra, closed her eyes and sliced. Tendons snapped beneath his skin. The knife fell from his suddenly nerveless fingers.

"What the *fuck*?" He snarled as a wretched gurgle came from his companion. Kadra's sword emerged through his gut with a glide of crimson. She took advantage of the man's brief distraction to grip his throat and limit blood flow through both carotid arteries. He slumped with a strangled moan. A thud behind her said that the third man had met his end.

"Bounty hunters." Kadra indicated the bronze hunters' pins on the bodies. "Noceo."

"Anyone else?" She peered into the dark hallway ahead.

"No."

A dull languor washed over her as he wiped his sword and sheathed it. The stretch of tile ahead seemed to grow wider. Something shifted in her chest the longer she stared, telling her to walk onward, that answers waited for her within the black.

Come closer and you'll see it.

She stepped forward when a hoarse gasp sounded to her right. Flinching, she stared at the bounty hunter she'd just downed. His face contorted in the dim light, sweat droplets bulging at his temples.

"No," he whispered. "No, no. There's so many. *Stay away!*" He jackknifed upright with a scream. "All these *eyes! STOP!*"

Chilled, she shrank back as he screamed.

Cold curiosity flared in Kadra's eyes, something otherworldly turning them luminous. "Smoke veils him."

Her heart thudded so hard that blood rang in her ears. "As it did me when that eye appeared above the Aequitas?"

He raised his head. "As it does now, Sarai."

Realization struck with the force of a lightning bolt. She almost sank to her knees as it registered.

Kadra smiled darkly. "You see it too."

Mouth dry, she swallowed. "*Ibez*, whitesleep, catastrophe, the only thread they have in common is unconsciousness. The moment anyone falls comatose—"

"This madness takes them," Kadra's piercing gaze ignored the bodies at his feet to find the dark ahead and look far beyond. "I may be killing them too quickly," he mused. "Maiming seems the better course."

She gave him a reproving look. Leaving the raving man to his torment, they moved down the hallway and into the wide hall where patients were kept. Their shrieks reached them first. Bound to their beds, they ranted in hoarse voices, pupils narrowed to pinpricks with fear.

She wondered if Dalvia saw a similar sight in Komis at the Am Semni Institute. Granted, her patients were lucid and would have some hope, so long as the boil beetles could be displaced from their bodies before they tunneled too deep into their organs. But there was nothing easy about seeing people in pain.

"Why *the fuck* are there bodies on the godsdamned floor?" Harion's roar came from the landing.

Sarai sighed. "He's awful enough that I'm glad he's on our side. But he's *loud*."

Steps came down the hallway before Cassandane entered, mouth flattening into a grim line. "Your brother's apparently making an announcement in three days on the dissolution of the Tetrarchy."

Stunned, Sarai tottered against the desk. *He's actually doing it.*

She turned to Kadra and paused to find him looking amused. "He'll regret that soon."

Anek whistled, Méherre and Harion behind them. "I'll say. Word at the Academiae is that no one has any idea what to do with him seeing as he's of no use during stormfall."

Harion snorted. "People won't abide a useless leader."

Méherre gave him a speaking look.

"Very funny," Harion said sardonically. "But this is all terrible for everyone's bottom line. The Guilds are excellent for business, but your idiot brother isn't. If I'm going to suck any toes, they had better be on powerful feet."

Anek's brows rose in unison with everyone else's. "I'll leave you to that fetish. Why don't we target that Bridger of his? Clanlady Dalvia. Jumps at her own shadow."

Cassandane's gaze slitted. "Women like that sicken me. She's a Bridger and True Illusionist. She could have melted into a crowd, altered her face, and found freedom. Instead, she plays the trembling victim to Noceo's usurper."

Sarai thought back to the way the men in Aelius's Quarter had spoken of Dalvia and Kadra's comments that she cared for Noceo. "Some cages aren't so simple. And she's done much good at the Am Semni Institute."

Méherre looked faintly startled. "She's flawed, of course," the Bridger said slowly. "But freedom probably seems less tolerable for her in a country constantly at odds with itself. It could be that she wanted the power to reshape it so that everyone was truly free."

Cassandane sank into a visitors' chair, pouring herself a glass of water. "That doesn't excuse her complicity."

"Everyone in this room has blood on their hands." Méherre shrugged. "To have power is to lose the moral high ground. There will always be someone to argue that you could have used it better."

The lines in Kadra's brow deepened. "The north would be right to say so."

Sarai squeezed his hand at the tinge of guilt in those words. He absently kissed her knuckles, prompting Anek to gape and accidentally bring her foot on Cassandane's instep at the uncharacteristically affectionate gesture.

A barrage of stifled curses later, Cassandane massaged her smarting foot. "Still, by the gods, it isn't as though we didn't try to curtail the Guilds' abuses. We–"

A fleeting sense of familiarity struck Sarai, like she'd stumbled upon a fragment of a grander whole just within reach. She gripped it, stared, and stilled when its meaning coalesced. "I think I have it!" She cut off a startled Cassandane. "Power. Morality. Abuse."

"Are we composing poems?" Harion muttered.

"There's a pattern here after all! If we look at this from north to south, Sal Flumen to Edessa, then…" She widened her eyes meaningfully. Anek looked bemused.

A broad smile broke the firm line of Kadra's mouth, the same dark knowledge dawning in his eyes. "Well done."

Beaming, Sarai rapidly detailed their discovery that unconsciousness was a prerequisite for being madness-struck. "So, I think–"

"Let's see if I have this right. It doesn't matter *how* they fall unconscious, but once they're there, they go mad." Harion scowled. "Does this god hate drugs?"

"No." Kadra pulled in a satisfied breath. "They hate people."

Every head swiveled toward him. Midway through her water, Cassandane choked. "What?"

Anek blinked. "I never thought I'd have something in common with our tormentor."

Méherre stared thoughtfully at Kadra. "Why do you say that?"

"The whitesleep murders centered around abuse." Kadra propped a booted foot against the wall, reclining into the shadows. "The boil beetle plague asked for the south to behave morally toward the north."

"And the first set of madness-struck victims were members of a powerful Guild, operating a secret *ibez* den," Sarai finished. "I'm willing to bet that we'd find more than a few unsavory deeds if we investigated our madness-struck victims. This god hates a very specific kind of asshole."

Anek crossed their arms. "A strong sense of justice in a god?"

"And a mechanism of unconsciousness and hallucination. What could go wrong?" Harion sourly muttered.

"Will it be enough to narrow them down?" Méherre wondered.

The gleam in Kadra's black gaze said that he thought it would be. Brimming with excitement, Sarai spared only a brief look down the hallway as the others chatted excitedly of cornering a god. A dark tendril seemed to reach out from the floor, lengthening a neighboring shadow. Gripping Kadra's hand, she ignored it and let the darkness seethe behind her.

Soon, a voice whispered in her head. *Soon.*

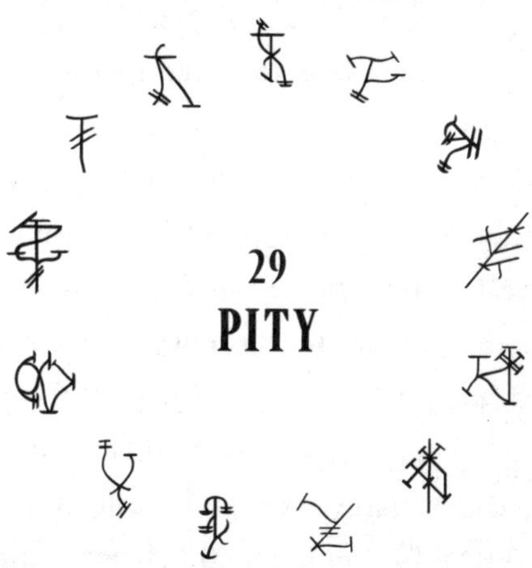

29 PITY

"Why do the Elsar elevate some humans to godhood? Priests and sceptics alike have posited hundreds of theories as to the purpose of the Naaduir's existence. Many among the Elsarian Order only revere the major pantheon, pointing to the Saints and the Wretched as little more than national heroes that were formalized into religious significance. There is truth to this, certo. But it also remains that the gods created the minor pantheon of the Naaduir and would have done so for a purpose. Was it to show humanity the rewards they could reap by obedience? Or do even the gods, in all their might, require assistance managing our foibles?

The latter theory is further compounded by the fact that living in service of one of the Elsar can result in formalization as a Naaduir. On the other hand, living in service of a Naaduir will, at most, result in dwelling in that minor god's realm upon death. The better option, then, is to predominantly worship the Elsar as the Clerics do, but leave space in your hearts and altars for the minor gods. Who knows? Some Naaduir are even said to have consorts. If you can't become a minor god, marrying one is an option!"

—excerpt from *So You Want to Become One of the Naaduir*, author unknown

There were eighty-three manuscripts in the Codices that formed the canon purported to be the word of the Elsar according to the Elsarian Order. This land was doomed if they were going to have to read through all of them.

Hiding in a corner of the Hall of Records' Archive of Elsarian Texts, Sarai flipped another page, eyes blurry with reading about another battle between Wrath and Ruin. The six High Elsar—seven if Wrath counted—and three ambiguous Elsar aside, there were tens of Naaduir that could induce visions and had strong senses of justice. Saints and Wretched of such domains as rot, song, literal darkness, hunting, pacts, knowledge, and even the supposed Naaduir of dreams, Faragathe, herself.

The hours bled by into evening as they tried to narrow it down, with Sarai hiding a smile as Anek flirted outrageously with Méherre.

"So, you can only Bridge people to places you've already been to?" Anek rested their head on their elbow.

Méherre's gaze caught theirs before the beginnings of a smile came to her lips. "I picture it in my head. Then, I imagine the sounds, smells, the gravel under my feet. It's like I leave a bit of myself in each place I go to, and I pull myself back to it when I open a portal there."

"*Fascinating.*"

Grinning, Sarai turned the page when Harion groaned.

"Where a Summoner asks a god to curse a person or place, the only way to end it is to kill the Summoner and relieve the god of the obligation to fulfill it," he read aloud from a volume and tossed it aside, looking green. "We're all going to die."

Méherre eyed him with mild irritation. "Has anyone ever told you that you're loud?"

Beside her, Anek let out a besotted wheeze.

He glowered. "There's also the fact that the more the god tightens their hold over a mortal realm, the easier they can swallow it."

Méherre's brows drew together. "A vanished city. History is littered with them."

"We've seven thousand dead and ten and a half thousand madness-struck now," Anek sucked in a breath. "Evil folk or not, those deaths mean we're well on our way to becoming history. Could this be someone in the Elsarian Order, trying to prove a point?"

Méherre snorted. "If those fools were capable of Summoning anything more than a swollen head, they wouldn't have forced Sarai to a Hearing, like she was Faragathe herself."

Wisdom's breath, she really can't stand the Order. Sarai made a mental note to ask the other woman why when a hubbub rose in the distance, loud enough to penetrate the insular grouping of buildings forming the Hall of Records.

Anek wearily rubbed their eyes. "What now?"

"Sounds like it's coming from the public square down the street." Sarai rose, trying to discern whether the yells were cheers or protests.

"Let's take a look." Méherre shelved the tome in her hands. "I'll pull you both out if it gets dangerous."

They raced out of the Archive of Elsarian Texts and past the Hall of Records' three-faced statue of Time. The air parted easily under Méherre's hands, leading into the square. They shrank back upon entry as a mob rushed past them to join an even larger crowd snarling at a figure standing in the center.

Sarai stood on tiptoe and went motionless. Fenced by a group of northern vigiles, Noceo, unfortunately well-healed from their last meeting, eyed the Edessans spitting hatred his way with cold fury.

Gray-green banners draped the square in Clan Kader's heraldry, the eerie image of blood dripping from a safsher into a chalice glowering down at every corner. Silver abounded in color and metalwork, glinting off the elaborate braziers ringing the square at strategic intervals against the wind. The columns of the colonnade circling the square had been painted gold.

Gilding a throne. After destroying the Aequitas, he'd had no other choice. This was the largest public square in the city.

"For the last *godsdamned* time, I have nothing to do with the so-called madness-struck in your city," he spoke sharply over his roaring audience.

Her jaw tightened at the memories his voice evoked. *You have to see it as I have or I become the villain of the piece.* How did he believe himself in the right?

"Gods, he's decorated this even more garishly than the Am Semni Institute," Méherre muttered. "And that's saying something."

"What does it look like?" Anek smirked when the crowd resumed its verbal attacks.

"Opulent," the Bridger said wryly.

Sarai watched Noceo's features pale further when he began barking orders at the spectators to cease obstructing his path. That people felt free to roar at him now was proof that they had smelled weakness. He was visibly sweating, features as strained as Kadra's had been when he had overexerted himself at the Aequitas. The two were remarkably similar in that sense, pushing past their limits.

Noceo's men lit the braziers around the square. Fire danced gold and red under the light of the twin moons, spreading long arms to the sky in silent devouring and nuzzling into the wood to sear everything within. She'd give anything for a fraction of that destructive strength.

"*You crave security*," Kadra had said. Why was power the only way to ensure it?

"Whatever conversation you're having with yourself, please do let us join in," Anek remarked to Sarai's right.

Sarai grunted. "I hate him."

"So do I."

"And I pity him."

Méherre's brows jumped high along with Anek's. "Why bother? He's done much harm."

"He wanted me to understand him." Sarai cursed silently at the memory of what she'd seen in his head. "I did."

The Bridger went quiet. "That feels unfair," she said after a moment. "Ahead, we have a man who's robbed people of free will and murdered them without care, and you're quick to *understand* him when *you* didn't get half as much compassion from him or from Edessa's population."

"I second that," Anek said with a wince. "Pity's best reserved for those who can change, Sarai. I'm not interested in finding out if he will." They slung an arm around her shoulder. "Let's leave him to receive a lovely Edessan chewing out, hmm? Once this all blows over, they'll be back to swearing up and down that the Tetrarchy is evil incarnate."

Sarai managed a smile, mulling over their arguments throughout the brief journey back to Méherre's home. *They aren't wrong.* Yet, it was hard to shake off the sense that she had seen more of him that day than he had intended.

Perhaps that was why she walked toward Dalvia's blond hair upon spotting her.

The other woman drew up her hood before entering a tavern and sat there, staring out of the window for a long moment. Pulling up her own hood, Sarai entered and spoke to the barmaid there. A few moments later, she plunked two bowls of soup before Dalvia and took the seat across from her.

"Dinner." She smiled. "It isn't drugged. Would you like to eat with me?"

Dalvia's empty gaze seemed to look through her before slowly moving to the soup. Something perturbed and resigned crossed her face before she picked up her spoon.

Sarai had never known anyone so utterly broken down. How bitter it was that people could emerge from the same crucible so differently.

They ate in silence, though Sarai noticed that Dalvia was careful not to make too much sound as she gingerly sipped from her soup, as though she feared drawing attention to her existence. Surprisingly, she spoke first.

"If you're looking for me to betray Noceo, I'm afraid I'll disappoint you."

"In truth, I wasn't. I just–" Sarai sighed. "I wanted to understand you."

Dalvia raised her head at that, dark eyes inscrutable. "Why bother? I've done much harm."

"You've also been seeing to the care of Komis's injured. I saw how many people struck by plague were being carted by the wagon to the Am Semni Institute for recovery."

Dalvia looked away with a click of teeth and a hard swallow. "I do nothing. My Clan built that hospital centuries ago. It only made sense to use it once the plague rose."

Sarai scrutinized the other woman's almost ethereal frailty. "Have you never wanted to leave?"

Dalvia set down her spoon. "That possibility vanished early on."

A shudder made a cozy home in Sarai's already shaking hands at the empty way she said it. "But you've had the best chance at escape of all of them. A portal could take you anywhere."

"Bridgers can only open portals to places they've already visited."

"Was there nowhere that felt safe to you?"

"Freedom, meaning, hope. There isn't a square mile in this country that can provide me with all three." Dalvia's eyes were dead. "I don't have the privilege of considering my safety. That has always had to be the least of my concerns."

"I'm sorry. I shouldn't have assumed that leaving would be simple."

"No, you shouldn't have." Dalvia stared outside the window. "Have you ever felt as though your life was fruitless, Sarai? That nothing you do has meaning and even screaming that you're in pain will only earn you ridicule?"

Sarai stiffened in recognition, nearly choking on her memories of Arsamea, of her time at the Hearing, even in the Aequitas before Noceo brought it down. "I have."

"So have I, and forgive me if this sounds cruel, but I would take your scars to mine. Noceo's father was a monster."

Sarai stilled when she grasped Dalvia's meaning. "Did—"

Resignation and a strange glimmer of relief flickered on the other woman's face. "I was too young at first for Clevsin's tastes." She stared absently at the table. "Not that the risk wasn't there. Noceo and Drenevan suffered at his hands too, but I always had to be careful. I wasn't blood-related to him and completely at his mercy after my Clan died out. There was every chance that I'd be a target once I was grown. And once I was, Noceo saw to it that I'd be kept safe."

No wonder she's loyal to him. "I'm sorry." The same part of Sarai that had killed Aelius curled lovingly around the idea of going back in time and murdering Clevsin. "Truly, I am."

"I know." Dalvia's voice held a wondering note. "I didn't realize it then, but I think Noceo and Drenevan were too. Drenevan offered me the choice of coming with them. I betrayed his confidence and paid for it. I wonder how much would have been different if I hadn't."

Sarai shivered at the slump of the other woman's shoulders, the dull pain in her eyes that spoke to being tossed about on the waves of much greater forces. It felt like looking into a mirror of where she had been a year ago. Forcing herself forward. Surviving, not living.

Turning, Dalvia surprisingly held her gaze. "You asked why I didn't leave. There comes a time when you realize that fighting changes nothing, Sarai. I think you've already started to see it in these games of politics. I simply found another way to rattle my fetters because power like yours doesn't have freedom. And freedom like mine, didn't have power."

There was no arguing with that. They spoke little until their meal had ended.

Dalvia rose first. "Thank you. It was good to do this as I am and not as I want to be."

Sarai's smile tilted over to a perplexed frown. "What do you–"

"Name your favor. This chat wasn't only to gauge me, was it? Ask. I don't like being in debt."

Sarai released a sigh. *This could be a terrible idea.* But she had to know. "Can I meet with Noceo tomorrow night? In Kadra's morgue." She raised her hands defensively at Dalvia's rising eyebrows.

"Will you harm him?"

"No," Sarai whispered. "Not until he tries to harm me."

A sad smile found Dalvia's lips. "Very well then."

Sarai watched her depart and wondered why her heart hurt worse than ever.

Returning to Méherre's home, she found Kadra poring over a volume of the Codices with bloodstained fingers. Frost bloomed like lichen across the thick glass, more flurries piling high beyond the door.

She gave him a reproving look. "Is someone dead?"

"Soon." His smile glinted like a blade in the moonlight before he relented and explained. "I've been attempting a few Summoning runes in the event that we may have to scar the mortal plane after all in order to disperse this god." Fathomless eyes slid over her profile before he reached for her hands. "What troubles you?"

She pressed a kiss to his knuckles. "You'll think I'm mad, but I want to meet with Noceo."

He blinked and waited.

"Something keeps troubling me about how he's gone about his vengeance and what he wants of it. He was entirely reasonable as Inquisitor Silvus until your name came up. He's *convinced* that you abandoned him. Utterly set on taking the life he believes you stole. With anyone else, I'd say that they had seized upon any excuse to call themselves a victim, but Noceo truly believes he has cause."

"He may." Limned in soft moonlight, Kadra's profile held the quiet strength of a mountain. "I left him behind."

"That's your overblown sense of guilt speaking," she said with a squeeze of his broad shoulders. He still hadn't spoken of what happened that night eleven years ago, and she was loathe to pry at the seam of that wound. "What I know is that you arrived here from Komis and closed yourself off to everything and everyone. No lovers and almost no one in your life that you trusted. I thought to blame your father for it at first, and he undoubtedly played a part, but he didn't have the power to emotionally wound you. I think Noceo did."

His lips lifted faintly. "You have a stout heart, my Sarai. But he may not see reason."

"I know. Anek and Méherre think the same. And by all the Elsar, I hate him for what he Coerced me to do, but we're missing something." She rubbed the back of her neck with a sigh. "When the dust settles across the capital, I want to be able to say that I was fair, even if I won't be lauded for it."

A soft drip on the water clock, and he drew her close, sliding an arm under her knees to lift her onto his lap. He exhaled like a man who'd come home.

"When?"

She held him tight. "Tomorrow night."

30
TANGLED REGRET

Kadra surveyed the exterior of his morgue where he and Sarai were to meet Noceo that night. The building had a singular entrance and exit, sans balconies or ledges. The ice room was too small for him to call down a bolt if things went awry, but Noceo would be in excellent distance of his blade, and Sarai's rather ruthless hands.

Satisfied, he walked onward, crossing the street toward his mount when a shock of pale hair materialized at his shoulder. He slanted a narrow-eyed glance at the Bridger.

Dalvia flinched and gripped the post to which he had tied his mount's reins as a shield between them. "He'll come. He thinks Sarai wants to join him."

Pained eyes, pale cheeks, throat flexing and swallowing. *Regret.* It bit him too, locking jaws around the cavity of his chest as he wondered what this woman could have been.

"I never thought I'd say this." She seemed to wrestle with the words. "But I might have gotten a great deal wrong. I'm glad one of us survived properly."

"I believe I failed to give you the chance to change," he said somberly. "If it were Sarai, she wouldn't have accepted your refusal. She would have dragged you out of that manor by the hair even if you'd betrayed her to Clevsin."

A startled laugh erupted from Dalvia. "She would, but I don't think it matters." This time her smile was genuine. "I was loathe to extend others the chance to change, so this probably serves me right. I craved true freedom too dearly."

"True freedom doesn't exist." He dryly indicated the black birrus and mask shielding his face despite him being Magus Supreme. "I tried to impress this on Noceo once, but there is more to power than might. My right-hand man," he smiled faintly and corrected himself, "my closest friend, Gaius, doesn't have any power to his name. But when the day comes, he will have the finest grave Edessa has seen. One that will bewilder future generations for how ordinary they will judge him. Yet, he will have been a powerful man. Not because he saved my life and Sarai's at the Aequitas, but because when I was a fifteen-year-old iudex straight from the Academiae, he carried himself with honor and wanted nothing to do with corruption. Unlike my name, his is unimpeachable. That is also power."

Dalvia swallowed. "I'm sorry that I nearly made you lose him."

"I know." He couldn't summon anger. She would pay for her crimes. "Noceo won't succeed. He'll crumble and take you with him."

"I know." Upturned mouth. Downturned eyes still avoiding his. *Grief.* "I guessed as much from the start when he insisted that a coup was possible. Yet, I had to hope. Or nothing would have meaning."

Love and resentment. Hope and fear. It wasn't merely salvation that she had sought but understanding and a power that could finally give her peace.

Wind blew down the streets of Edessa to part the air between them. "The offer to leave remains. Sarai cares."

"A dangerous thing for a woman in power," Dalvia said half to herself. "But my course is set. I'll see you, Drenevan."

He inclined his head as she walked past him. A portal split the air several yards away. He spared a fleeting look for the past. Then, he walked across the street.

31
TRUTH

Midnight found her in Kadra's morgue. The Lugens' examining tables were quiet at this hour, few willing to work into the night or with the dead these days.

She soundlessly went down the flight of stairs at the back toward the door at the end of the hall where Kadra placed the victims of cold cases in his Quarter on ice to preserve their corpses until he could ascertain a culprit. It scraped open, loosing a frigid blast. Moonlight rolled in like fog from square windows by the ceiling. An unmoving patch of shadow at the back of the room was all that spoke to Kadra's presence.

Hands locked behind her, Sarai leaned against the opposite wall, trying to quell her roiling stomach when she caught footsteps on the landing. Soft taps approached the door. It parted, and Noceo emerged.

Anger and whispers of remembered fear sank teeth into her bones, pumping her full of venom. For the last few hours, she had wondered if her hate would override her pity when she saw him again. Apparently, she held both in equal quantity.

"If this is a trap, I would advise against it, Death-Summoner." Dark hair coiffed back, gray-green robes immaculate, he looked like a Naaduir of winter and ice.

"I never had your flair for it," she said into the quiet.

He jerked before turning unerringly in the direction of her voice. Silver eyes found hers and gleamed. "Well?" he murmured smoothly. "Are you finally here to ask me for power?"

She laughed, emerging from the shadows. "I don't think yours would serve me well. Edessa hates you."

"They'll grow used to me once they realize that I'm not going anywhere."

"From drugmaker to ruler." An empty smile bled across her face. "Would you have chosen the same if life had taken a different turn?"

Noceo cast her a surprised look that he quickly veiled with insouciance. "Why do you ask? Trying to see if things would have been different had Drenevan kept his word?"

"Perhaps." *I need to know what happened the night of their escape.* Only that would tell her if there was any hope for this man.

Noceo was silent a moment. "A iudex would have been boring," he finally said. "I have no patience for fools making poor decisions and asking me for clemency. I probably would have formed a Guild for weaponry."

Weapons again. "Does life need to be war, Noceo?"

This time, shock openly blanketed his face. She had used his name for the first time on purpose. "It *is* war." His gaze didn't waver. "The powerful win."

And that's all you've ever wanted to be. "What happens now? You take the throne and sit there until death?"

"I'll have won. He'll have nothing. And there'll be no one above me." He looked at her like he was saddened that she hadn't understood. "A complete unfettering."

Of you, she realized sadly.

A brow went up at her silence. Noceo's mouth formed a dazzling grin. She hated him. She pitied him. She was so fucking tired. Perhaps Méherre was right, and people didn't deserve the chance to change. Yet, she wanted to try a last time here.

"You sought me out." A brilliant, *genuine* gleam of elation lit his eyes. "You've made your decision."

"I have." She approached him hiding *beshaz*'s bright flare. Her placid mask, the shield that had kept her sane for so many years, kept her serene, armored as she faced him.

Noceo's lips twitched before a deep laugh left him. "I wish I could see the look on Drenevan's face when he realizes that I've stripped him of everything."

"You can."

She struck while his eyes were still narrowing. Gripping his hands, she sent magic beneath his skin to shred every major tendon. He staggered with a gasp of pain, lips parting to issue a Coercive order, when she pulled a blindfold from her pocket and gagged him swiftly.

Knocking him unconscious would only turn him madness-struck. She tripped him to the ground and pinned him, *herar* already active on her armilla.

"I'm truly sorry for this," she eked out between labored breaths. At the end of the day, Probing was a punishment. But it was time to have the truth out in the open.

She gripped his head. The world turned black and morphed into the library of Noceo's mind.

Alright. She strode quickly through the incorporeal shelves of his memories, trailing her hands over them until she reached the *E*'s. A cobweb-covered book titled *Escape* was the first book there. She frowned at the dog-eared one beside it. *Poxtan.*

Shelved out of order and beside Escape. She recalled Noceo's infatuation with Parvine. It must have all gone wrong eleven years ago then. Foreboding moved like an ice cube down her throat. She flipped the book open. And opened her eyes to horror.

She only took one look before spinning around, hands over her mouth. Tears involuntarily sprung to her eyes, a choked sob of disbelief wedging in her throat. She dared turn around again and struggled to hold down her bile.

Parvine's body lay on the rocky shore of the Chaboras River. Waves roared around her, splattering her with vicious spray. She would never feel it.

Sarai had only seen Parvine once in Noceo's first memory of meeting Othus. A glossy-haired vivacious girl with friendly eyes. The mutilated body at Clevsin's feet sitting in a puddle of blood and entrails looked almost nothing like her. Almost.

Kadra's kills had been emotionless pieces of work designed to satisfy his father and inspire terror with a few knife strokes. This had been personal. The girl was missing her nose. And she was naked.

Clevsin nonchalantly kicked a tooth as one would a pebble. "Did you think I wouldn't find out?"

A sob several feet away. Sarai turned to find Noceo on his knees, strangled cries tearing from his chest. His face was ravaged, streaked with tears and blood. Clevsin strode to him, a crimson-drenched dagger in hand, and struck the hilt against his son's head.

"You really thought I wouldn't know you were trying to fuck some no-name whore?" He hit him again when Noceo sobbed like his heart had broken.

Sarai's teeth cut into her tongue.

"She wasn't going to hurt anyone," Noceo wept. "We just went for a walk. Why would you come and—" He dissolved into a series of curses and screaming.

Clevsin snorted. "Well, she was a terrible fuck. On your feet. Get rid of the body."

"Die!" Noceo screamed. "*DIE! DIE!*"

She winced at the brittle roar of power in his voice. It wasn't enough. Clevsin shrugged it off and raised the dagger again.

She pulled out of the memory, shaking with silent tears.

No wonder he craves power. Enough to indulge in stimulant use. He hadn't been able to protect Parvine, and no one had protected him. Had it been her in his place, wouldn't she have gone mad too? She dared flip to the last few pages of the book and took a glimpse.

Noceo's haunted features came to life in front of her. He sat beside Kadra in the same stretch of shore where Parvine's body had been, staring at the waves lapping the shoreline. Foam flew into the air and settled again and again.

"I can't ever face her family," he said after a long silence. "I said that I would never hurt her. And I threw her body in the Chaboras."

"I spoke to them. Got there before Clevsin could plant a story." The ice in Kadra's eyes was so deep, she wondered how it had ever thawed for him to have become the man he did. "Lied that she committed suicide after you rejected her."

The emptiness bled from Noceo's face. He swiveled to face Kadra with sudden fury. "She would *never*!" he snarled, seizing his brother's tunic. "You couldn't come up with a better fucking story?"

"Exactly." Kadra didn't move. "She would never. No one will believe it. Any story Clevsin spins afterward will not take. Her memory is safe."

Withdrawing, Sarai shoved the book back in the shelf with shaking hands. This was so much worse than she'd imagined. And there was one more. The incident that had changed everything and set these men down different paths.

She gripped the volume titled *Escape* and wiped her eyes. *Alright.* She inhaled sharply and dove in. This time, when her mind detached herself from Noceo's perspective, she moved back in.

Finaze Poxtan was here.

Noceo blankly stared at the girl screaming for answers in the snow, prostate at his feet. The road down the Drust Mountains wound down behind her. Why did it have to be tonight? Drenevan was due any moment. They had to leave.

"Please just tell me why," Finaze pleaded. "You came around for months to flirt with her. You seemed to *like* her, so why don't you care?"

Noceo glanced around. What if Drenevan had failed at subduing Clevsin? He had snuck out to unlock the manor's gates once the two had started fighting. But if Drenevan lost, then Clevsin would know that they had been working together. And this fucking girl kept *screaming*.

"Why did you abandon Parvine?" Finaze wailed.

FUCK. She had never liked him. Never wanted him around Parvine. Beneath the anguish in her eyes was hatred. His adrenaline surged to the beat of his pulse. She was right. Gods, she was right. But he couldn't have her ruin everything. She had chosen to come here despite knowing the consequences. This was her fault. Didn't she understand how hard he had fought for Parvine? *Everything* Clevsin had done to him while he tried to protect her that last night?

Sweat slicked his palms. "You're right," he finally said quietly, pitching his voice low and wrapping it around her. Her brow smoothed, blankness entering her face. "But I can't say much out here. Come inside and I'll explain."

A hint of fear surfaced on her face. She was fighting it.

"Don't worry." He bent to her, forcing a smile that felt like a rictus grin. "I'll keep you safe. As your friend, I owe you an explanation."

Finaze nodded, eyes glazed.

Moonlight glinted off the metal gates, transforming them to spears as he led her through. They shut behind her. The flashes of lightning within the manor told him that Drenevan and Clevsin were still battling. Finaze's limbs jerked in front of him.

"Keep going and don't talk." His hands shook. He had to do this. He had no choice. He couldn't stay here anymore.

Finaze's feet dug into the snow carpeting the gardens as she fought his compulsion. Her neck turned back to face him in a slow, terrifying fashion. "What…are—" She choked on the words.

"Look ahead." He embedded a boulder's worth of power in the words, and her neck snapped back around. "Keep walking."

He drew her to the back of the house. His right hand dropped to the dagger Clevsin made them all carry. Silver with Clan Kader's crimson insignia engraved over the hilt. He had never used it. That had always been Drenevan's task. He had kept his hands clean and used his voice.

Finaze stopped again. How was she so strong? Why didn't he have power over anyone?

"You...killed...her." Her eyes spat hatred at him.

"I did," he whispered. "I should have known better and stayed away, but I thought he would never know. He got her because of me."

Her features altered into startled understanding, then hatred. "Then... you...die too!" Her hand whipped up, a knife in her grip. She sliced into his arm before he could blink.

He reared back, unsheathing his blade with age-old instinct. His vision went white.

She was a few years older, but he was stronger. His first strike was ugly. He had never killed with his hands before. Drenevan had always done it for him. The second was easier, the flesh more malleable now. Wet. And then, he couldn't stop. It poured out under the silent moons, blood upon snow. Silver and red. He stabbed her until she was a mass of flesh, then dropped the blade and rose.

Drenevan stood at the end of the path. Silent.

There was no judgment in his gaze, yet Noceo felt bared to the core. Not that his brother had any right. Even he knew he was the Clan's monster.

"I had to." The words came out ragged. His lips tasted of blood. He hadn't realized how it could arc. "She was screaming and demanding answers. She would have told Clevsin after we left."

His brother blinked. Nodded. "You had to," he repeated tonelessly. Snow fell softly, carpeting his dark hair. "Did you see to the gates?"

"I did." Noceo drew back from the body and realized that Drenevan's own dagger was dripping blood. "Did you make him suffer?"

"Just enough." An eerie smile broke across his brother's lips.

Noceo stilled at its ugly familiarity. Moonlight illuminated the vicious glint in his brother's eyes, the severe planes of his face, hardened despite its youth. He looked just like Clevsin. *A monster.* And Noceo was about to unleash him in the south.

"Let's go," he mumbled, leaving Finaze's corpse in the snow. He felt Drenevan's black gaze on him for a long moment before his brother followed.

Was this right? Noceo walked past the gates and into the deep furrows wagons had made in the mountain road. Jubilation escaped him. His first real taste of freedom sat sour on his tongue while the second most dangerous man he knew walked beside him. Drenevan wasn't Clevsin through and through. He had never so much as looked at a woman to Noceo's knowledge. But he was a Twelfth-Tier Urd whose power had surpassed Clevsin's if today's battle was any indication. And his brother had never lied about his enjoyment of murder.

He stopped walking, feigning a smile when Drenevan turned to him with an inquiring look.

"I almost forgot." Noceo jerked a thumb to the right, letting the barest tendril of magic infuse his voice. Enough to suggest or convince, not to compel. "Father was anticipating a meeting with the Praetor tonight. Can't risk him and his retinue seeing us down the road. We'll have to take the forest. The snow should cover us."

Not a change in Drenevan's hard mask. "Very well."

They slipped into the coniferous woods. Pine needles littered the crisp blanket of snow. They crunched under their feet as he walked down the slope, letting his brother take the lead. Clouds hid the moons from their eyes and illuminated Drenevan's back. An easy target. His fight with Clevsin would already have weakened him.

Yards away, a series of boulders littered the ground. Landmark stones, he had called them, back when he and Drenevan would take this shortcut down the mountain.

He didn't want to do this.

Darkness pressed on them from all sides. The air grew oddly damp for winter, bringing with it the crisp scent of pine and Komis's smoke.

"It'll rain soon," his brother muttered.

Noceo couldn't stop staring at the boulders. *Shove him into them, then slam one over his head before he can recover.* The plan kept repeating in his head. One more life, and he would be done. If anyone deserved to leave this shithole, it was him. Drenevan was another monster in the making. Clevsin was a scourge, but his brother at adulthood would be one of the Dark Elsar themselves, if there was a god for blood.

He swallowed at the image of red spraying through the air again. Of his brother's head caved in, a vessel for worms. He didn't want to do this.

The gray stones loomed ahead. *Only one more death.* They were a yard away, and then a hair's breadth away. Noceo's resolve hardened.

In a swift move, he shoved him down the slope. Caught off guard, Drenevan rolled into the boulder with a sickening crack and went limp. *One last death.* Noceo seized a rock and lifted it over his head in a smooth sweep. He had no choice.

"I'm sorry, Drenevan." He brought it down on the prone form on the ground.

And it moved.

He only caught a glimpse of black, feral eyes before his brother rolled to the side, just barely missing the impact. The rock crashed against boulder and shattered.

Noceo's breath heaved as Drenevan rose, one arm hanging uselessly at his side. *Broken. Good.*

Rage roiled in his brother's eyes. "Why." A bare statement.

It hurt. He hadn't wanted to do this. "You're too much like him. I can't allow you out."

Something that looked almost like pain flashed in Drenevan's eyes. His arm must be worse than he was letting on. Noceo was willing to bet that there were a few cracked ribs in there too.

"Don't fight me." He lifted another rock with ease. "Just accept it and die before you turn into Father."

Emotion seethed in his brother's eyes like he had never seen before. Drenevan's icy mask was gone, violence behind it. *I made the right decision.*

"*I'm* like Clevsin?" Drenevan ground out. "When you just killed a girl for no reason?"

"For *every* reason!" Noceo roared. "She would have taken my freedom. Told the world about her sister and hunted me for the rest of my life. While she's alive, the past will *always* follow me." He advanced forward, relishing the way his brother stumbled back. "I don't kill without cause. But you? Clevsin barely had to instruct you. You will walk away from innocent bodies. You will leave them to fester, because you have his soul. You've always been—"

A thunderclap rent the sky accompanied by a male roar of pure fury. Startled, he nearly dropped his weapon. Madness swirled in his brother's eyes as he raised his good hand. The pine needles still clinging to the trees quivered. Steel-gray clouds seethed above, limned by moonlight.

"I warned you that it would rain." Drenevan brought down his hand.

Noceo froze.

Lightning arrowed to the earth in thin, terrifying streams, warping into a cage around him. Drenevan bared his teeth, straining as he shaped it.

The blood rushed from Noceo's head. This was beyond Clevsin's power. This was beyond anything he had ever seen. The bars crept so close that he screamed at the heat.

"You won't." He threw every ounce of power he possessed into the command as the cage closed around him. "You *won't* hurt me."

"There's nothing I won't do." The quiet, murderous boy he had known was gone. In his place was a commanding madman with lightning at his fingertips. The cage sealed shut around Noceo. It was too late. He had gambled and lost everything.

Drenevan had won.

His brother stepped back.

No. "Drenevan, don't do this," Noceo whispered. "I was wrong. Don't do this, *please*."

Silence. Then, another step away.

"Don't you *dare*!" Noceo snarled. "Or you'll pay for this all on your own. You can't hide what you are, and the world will see it." He scoured his depleted reserves of magic for some vestige of power. "If the gods exist and are fucking fair, you won't know an *ounce* of peace for this! You will never thrive! You will never succeed!"

His brother turned and walked away. To a future Noceo would never see. *No. Please.*

"*Don't leave me! Gods, don't leave me, Drenevan!*" Noceo threw the last of his strength into it. His last arrow. One final compulsion.

Drenevan's figure vanished into the night.

Alone among the pines, Noceo wept.

It was hours later when Dalvia found him and Bridged him out of the lightning cage. He had time to weave his story then. About how Drenevan had threatened him, dragged him from the manor and intended to use his voice to complete his escape. He'd crafted better lies than this, but his mind had kept veering toward the same horrific conclusion over the hours he had stood in that forest. He couldn't examine it. It couldn't be true.

He didn't know how he returned to his half-burned room, but he was sitting on his bed so it must have happened. The door creaked open. Dalvia's pale shock of hair floated past the jamb.

"Go the fuck away, *traitor*," he hissed. "I've already lost everything."

She watched him solemnly. "You lied."

"*Leave.*"

She stumbled back into the doorway but gripped it tight. "You betrayed him," she noted with uncanny insight. "You could have been free if it weren't for that."

Furious, he seized her hands. "He *left* me, but you won't, will you?" he bit out. "You'll stay. You *won't* leave."

"Noceo, stop!" She paled, wriggling in his grasp, and he ordered her again and again until her eyes glazed and she burst into tears. Then, he let her flee the room.

He raked a hand through his hair. This wasn't his fault. It couldn't be. Insensate with pain, he staggered to his feet and faced the mirror. "None of this was your fault," he whispered to his reflection. "Drenevan abandoned you. He *stole* what should have been yours. You never attacked that girl or him. You did nothing wrong. *You* were the victim."

The anguish in his chest eased, so he said it again. Then, again. Memory and torment softened with every repetition until his eyes lost their raw, glassy sheen.

Then, he began to plot his vengeance.

Sarai wrenched herself from the memory, winded by the breadth of agony she had witnessed. Ice, horror, and sheer rage melded in her chest. She allowed them reign. Pulling herself out of Noceo's head, she gripped him by the collar.

"You absolute fucking *coward*!"

Metal slid out with a snick. She darted back an instant before he slashed wildly at her, tottering as his ruined hand floundered.

"So be it. You can die." His eyes glittered. Blood seeped through a head wound he must have gotten when she had tripped him.

She darted a glance to where Kadra lurked in the shadows and discreetly shook her head when he shifted. *I can handle this.* She twisted out of his brother's reach with a hard kick to his chest. He doubled over with gritted teeth.

"You Coerced yourself, you stupid fuck!" she snapped. "This story you've told yourself isn't true!" *Gods, poor Dalvia.* No wonder she hadn't been able to leave.

The breath seemed to rush out of him even as his body kept fighting. And she knew this too. The feeling of having one's legs cut out from under them and reduced to little more than mindless fighting instinct. He had made her drink deep from that sour well.

"You're hopeless! You'll never understand."

She dodged the next slice of his blade. "But I do, and you know it. That's why you've tried so hard to convince me to join you. Noceo bu Kader, you thought we were alike!"

She had realized it upon seeing Parvine's death. Noceo would have drawn parallels after hearing of Kadra's demise. "*Death-Summoner*," he had kept calling her. Because she had done what he hadn't been capable of. She had made everything right again. And perhaps that was all he had wanted.

Desperation and anger battled on his face. He lunged at her, cutting into her arm. Sarai felt a hot wash of blood drip down it and refused to give him the pleasure of acknowledging the wound. When he sprung toward her with a roar, she absorbed the blow and gripped his throat.

"Move and I'll destroy your vocal cords," she hissed.

Clammy and flushed, he dropped his knife, and she kicked it away.

"You said that I had to see it as you did, or you'd be the villain of the piece." She wiped the blood from her arm over *astomand*, the rune for "Materialization." "Well, I did, and you look no different."

She reached into his head a final time and pulled the truth out in the open. Noceo spat a barrage of curses as younger versions of himself and Kadra bloomed in the cramped morgue but quieted at the sight of Finaze, memory and fear turning his pale skin colorless. The quiet tragedy played out among ice blocks. By the end of it, Noceo had shrunken into himself, trembling like an aspen.

"You're lying," he whispered.

She fisted the material of his robes. "Truth is my only task," she repeated what she'd told him over a month ago in the Academiae's chapel, then echoed his own words. "Did you want it sugarcoated?"

"It can't be true." He stared at a blank point over her shoulder, and she realized that he hadn't been speaking to her. He withdrew from her grasp as though he was barely cognizant of her existence. "It has to be a lie, because if it isn't, then—"

All of this was over nothing. She didn't say it, simply watched as he stumbled toward the door like his legs wouldn't hold him up anymore. He turned to her, lips parting, then stilled, his gaze unerringly finding Kadra in the shadows.

Something crumbled in his silver eyes.

He turned.

He ran.

32
ELEVEN YEARS IN THE MAKING

The day of Noceo's announcement on the Tetrarchy's fate dawned to grim skies and an absentee usurper.

Kadra eyed the angry, curious throngs circling the public square that Noceo had gilded in the vein of a convivium. A group of confused northern vigiles occupied it now and cast nervous looks at each other. Many seemed to have realized they had been abandoned.

He waited until evening came, and the crowd dispersed with grumbles about idiot northerners wasting their time. Damp hung in the air. A storm was brewing in more ways than one.

"Head inside," he murmured into Sarai's ear.

Nodding, she darted inside the closest tavern. Moments later, lightning lashed the swathe of black above. The gargantuan, long-fingered hand of smoke that controlled stormfall sent pale streaks arcing over the heavens and down. He anticipated and let the lightning approach before redirecting it back up with a flick of his wrists. Wrath's strength had made the task significantly easier.

Sleet and rain struck him and hardened at his feet as he worked. He, along with the thousands of magi around Edessa, calmed the skies. Red streaked his armilla when the rain petered to a drizzle, a testament to the volume of power he had used. Fog rolled in to blanket the square.

He readied to retrieve his Petitor when a bedraggled figure stalked through the mist. Kadra's brows rose. Haggard, pale as smoke, sweating, and sopping wet, his brother looked as though he had gone several rounds at a tavern and lost. Blood still matted his forehead from the wound Sarai had dealt him the previous night. He evidently hadn't slept.

Kadra leaned against one of the pillars comprising the colonnade. "Power's treating you poorly."

"Not a *word* out of you." His brother snapped, eyes wild. "I was supposed to have your life."

"You've enjoyed it for a little," Kadra noted.

"It isn't *real*! No one in this damn city respects me without threats or coin." He raked a hand through the hair plastered to his head. "I've been better than Clevsin, do you understand? The Guild magi I Coerced? They *wanted* to do it. Your people *chose* to target you and Sarai. I only amplified what already existed here and across the country. These idiots kneel to everything! The Guilds, the Order, coin! But I make it explicit, and *I'm* the villain."

"That isn't what you're here to say."

Noceo took in the soaked banners emblazoned with the Clan's heraldry and swallowed hard. "You apparently see it all, don't you? Then, why didn't you come back? I was grieving that night. You knew I wasn't thinking clearly." He rounded on Kadra. "Why didn't you come back?!"

Flashes of remembered betrayal tautened his spine. "You weren't the only one who grieved."

Noceo looked away. His hands fisted. "Back then, you seemed capable of anything, *Twelfth-Tier*." A bitter snarl. "I may have struck the first blow, but you still left me with nothing while you climbed up the judiciary. Did you never wonder whether I was surviving?"

"I knew you would," Kadra said tersely. "I searched, but I didn't want to know what you became."

Noceo flinched like he'd been struck. Scrubbing his face with a hoarse laugh, he slumped against a pillar opposite Kadra and slid to the ground.

Rain drizzled between them and iced over within grooves in the cobblestone. Sunset set the sky ablaze, turning the fog a heady scarlet. It was a rare moondark night, both silver Praefa and blue Silun presenting their dark side to the world. Kadra glanced at the tavern where Sarai waited.

"You don't have the time to be doing this," Noceo said after a moment. "The madness plaguing your city is spreading. The Order wants to tear your woman for being Godstouched." He knocked his head back against the pillar. "She hasn't even realized that she's doing it, Drenevan. I tried to tell her that Summonings leave a mark of–"

"Incursion, yes."

Noceo scowled. "Then, you know. The god we all saw must have latched onto her." He gestured absently at the surrounding streets. "Go to your woman. Fight your remaining battles."

Kadra regarded his brother grimly. One hand fell to the hilt of his sword. "Is this one over?"

If it wasn't then, he would end it tonight. He had little doubt that his blade would taste blood. His brother was weakened by more than guilt and revelation. Purpose had been stripped from him. An easy path to madness.

"Eleven years waiting for revenge." Noceo lifted his head, features ravaged. "Against who?" What could have been rain slid down his face. Kadra knew otherwise.

He released his hilt. "Sarai isn't Godstouched." Drawing away from the pillar, he stalked to one beside his brother. "I am."

Noceo stilled. A humorless laugh broke from his chest. "Isn't that just the most ironic thing? You already have power, and the gods give you more–" He broke off and started to his feet. "And you let the Order tear her apart for *months* before at that Hearing!"

Kadra released a slow breath. It fogged out in the damp wet. "She doesn't want my strength."

"Or mine," his brother muttered. "Too damned proud."

He pinned him with a hard glare. "The city's opinions were worming into her head even before you took a cudgel to her." Months of watching her struggle and forge onward flashed behind his eyes. He'd worked night and day to try and take that strain from her.

"For the Elsar's sakes, she isn't *helpless*! That bit of torture was just to make her join–"

"I can accomplish in an instant what she tries to do on her own for months. Few respect her unless I step in. What is she to feel if not helplessness when she comes up against brick walls that I don't? Can you imagine being treated that way your entire life?" he bit out and watched the blow land.

Noceo shoved his hands into his pockets. He said nothing.

"She wants to fight her own battles," Kadra said dryly. "That's harder than fighting them for her."

Noceo closed his eyes on a sigh. "She wasn't tempted to join me at all, was she?"

"More so to borrow the stimulant that's giving you all that power." Sarai stalked into the square, looking relieved to see Kadra unharmed.

Noceo deflated. "Then, I'll show it to you," he said hoarsely. At their raised eyebrows, he scowled and indicated *zosta*'s glow on Sarai's armilla. "You'd know if this was a trap. If you want what amplified my strength, it's yours. I have little use for it now."

Kadra's gaze swept his cowed frame. Eleven years had turned him brittle and fragmented. In the Drust Mountains high above Komis, he had festered along with his wounds and become one with his turmoil. He looked lost without it to inflate him.

But he was no longer a danger.

"Favran Tower then." Kadra angled an amused glance at Sarai, who grinned.

"We're going to give Cassandane a heart attack."

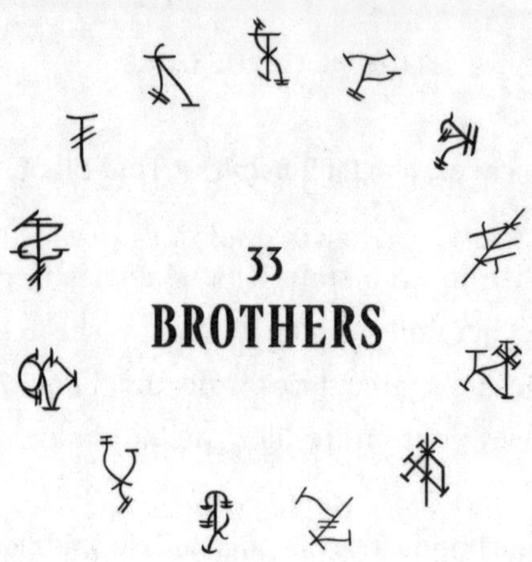

33
BROTHERS

"If the odd Illusionist is born in Ur Dinyé, it is for one reason alone: Errigalese blood in the family tree. For all our infamous wars with our neighbor across the Kaycakh Mountains, Errigalese-Urd intermarriage remains the most common sort in the country. But the manifestation of that power can take multitudinous forms.

There'll be the odd Illusionist magus, certo. Like me. We're powerful enough to perform moderate illusions and complex wards. The two go hand-in-hand. Illusions temporarily alter physical appearance, and wards shield physical locations from unwanted entry.

Then, there are the True Illusionists. Capable of remaking themselves into anyone for a duration. There is only one use for that talent. Espionage. The Tetrarchy is careful with these magi, usually assigning them to government positions laden with coin so that they don't turn traitor. It stops most True Illusionists. As for the rest, well, it's impossible to figure out who they've altered themselves to be, let alone what they've done."

–excerpt from a lecture given on Illusionists by former Magus Cato at the Academaie

"You've what?" Cassandane asked calmly within Favran Tower's bronze and crimson atrium.

"Given up. Keep your seat, the Tetrarchy." Noceo waved a hand to encompass everything. "I want none of it."

The Head Tetrarch took a deep breath and turned to a wide-eyed Anek who nodded, then turned to a bewildered Harion who also nodded.

Sarai nodded in turn. “He isn’t lying.”

“Hundreds dead,” Cassandane said in that same too-even tone. “Thousands injured. And you want none of it.” She smiled.

“Shit.” Anek shuddered beside Sarai. “He’s better off walking into a public square without his guard. That’s the scariest smile I’ve seen in my life. I wouldn’t put defenestration past her.”

Noceo turned a dull red. “I was mistaken.”

“Were you?” Cassandane’s teeth gleamed. Sarai was suddenly heartily glad that she had never really had to face the Head Tetrarch as an enemy. “Was there a reason you couldn’t *talk* to your brother before going on a murderous rampage?”

For all that he was the older of the two Kaders, Noceo decidedly looked like a woebegone child. He shrugged, splaying his hands uselessly. “I tried Coercing the Death-Summoner into letting me into his tower, but she kept recognizing me. I could only wipe her memory so many times.”

Kadra’s stern face suddenly took on the same murderous cast as Cassandane’s.

Unaware of the small war brewing in the atrium, Harion strode in briskly. “I hear we’re all going to take stimulants and fight a god.” He seized Noceo by the shoulder. “Where are they?”

Noceo blanched. “We *all* are?”

Kadra cleared his throat, and Noceo immediately nodded. Head bowed, he spoke quietly into the atrium, a far cry from the cold-eyed snake who had ruined so many lives. Sarai cast a worried glance at Méherre, seated in a corner, eerily quiet. *This’ll be bad.*

Anek caught her eye and grimaced. “It feels wrong to ask her to work with him when she seems to despises him.” They scowled at the pallid man. “But this is one temporary alliance we need. Narrowing down our unknown god is taking too long. Power like Noceo’s will go a long way when battling them.”

"That makes him palatable, does it?" They both jumped at Méherre's sudden question. Disappointment marred the other woman's eyes.

"He isn't receiving a pardon, Méherre. He knows he'll face a reckoning after this, and I think he'll welcome it." Anek jerked a thumb to Noceo's almost catatonic state.

Méherre's smile was bitter. "You may be right. A reckoning approaches." She raised her voice. "*You.* Where's this mysterious source of your strength?"

"The Am Semni Institute." Noceo's melodious voice was a ragged whisper now. "Five months ago, Dalvia concocted it to help me. I'll go find her. She's been vanishing of late but—"

"Leave her alone." Kadra's tone brooked no disobedience. "We have a Bridger."

"I've been there before," Méherre said without emotion. "When do we leave?"

"As eager as I am to turn almighty, I don't know if that's the wisest choice at present." Harion raised a hand for pause, flipping through a tome to present them with a paragraph in the ancient tongue. "The more who fall to a Summoned god's curse, the more they tighten their control over that realm. At thresholds of a quarter of the area's population under the god's spell, the god will come and swallow the rest," he translated aloud. "With over seven thousand dead and nearly twelve thousand madness-struck, we're too close to our god making an appearance to risk going north, no matter how temporarily. Wouldn't be a surprise if one showed up now. *And* it's a moondark night. Both moons in their new moon phase. We'll be stumbling."

Sarai had a horrifying vision of an enormous claw descending upon Edessa to pluck it from the map of Ur Dinyé and shuddered.

Cassandane looked equally staggered. "Do we have any names?" she turned to Anek. "Any idea of who this god could be?"

"If our god is a Naaduir, then Dorcone, Wretched Ruler of Rot, Hwiliath, Wretched Master of Manipulation, and Faragathe, Wretched

Seer of Sleep are suspects. Faragathe, especially, has been associated with nightmares for a millennium." Anek checked them off their fingers. "The few paragraphs that I found spoke to them being rather," they winced, "unpleasant."

"We'll have to divide ourselves then." Cassandane hovered a hand between her eyes, portioning the room in two. "Méherre, Anek, Sarai, Kadra, and *you*." She glowered at Noceo. "Go to the Institute. I'll stay here with Harion, and round up Cato and Telmar. The god aside, our Summoner will also be powerful. It wouldn't hurt to dose every magus in the Academaie with your stimulant."

A flurry of activity ensued. Withdrawn, Noceo watched everyone bustle around him. Sarai pitied him all the more when he shuffled after them out of Favran Tower and onto the road that led to the Tower Gates. Mingled with that pity was anger. She couldn't separate the two, unable to reconcile why he'd forced her to her knees despite knowing how bitter it was to crawl. Perhaps hopelessness twisted a person into a feral thing determined to burn the world for a sliver of joy. Vengeance against a world that had let them hurt.

Have you ever felt as though your life was fruitless, Petitor Sarai? Dalvia's question returned to her. *That nothing you do has meaning and even screaming that you're in pain will only earn you ridicule?*

Resolving to find her afterward, Sarai trekked to the Favran Tower Gate. The city spread out below them, hundreds of hearths and braziers twinkling in the gloaming. The center of a veritable snake pit of a country that she still cared for. She wouldn't see it ruined.

"This should be far enough." One foot propped on a rock overlooking a broad swathe of Edessa, Méherre closed her eyes and concentrated.

A portal carved through the air. Beyond it, the Am Semni Institute's gray walls perched by a cliff's edge midway through Komis's Drust Mountains. Centuries old, there was a grimly resolute air to the building as though it had weathered a thousand wars and would continue to do so. The few northern vigiles stalking the gargantuan walls around the perimeter had the same mien. They warily scuttled away upon a pointed glance from Noceo.

A surprisingly ill-kept dirt road led to the main gates. Anek wisely spent the walk staring at Méherre. The Bridger seemed more interested in her feet.

Past the wooden double doors though, the Institute took on a haughty opulence. Less a place for the ill and more a showpiece of Clan Am Semni's power. Heraldry featuring a desert horse hung from the walls, a testament to their equestrian roots, staircases wound through three floors by Sarai's estimation, and the white tile–a daring choice for a hospital–was unstained, albeit dusty.

Anek whistled. "You weren't joking about it being opulent here."

But for all its beauty, the hospital was devoid of healers. No one greeted them from the healers' offices. A few servants puttered about, cleaning the banisters and scrubbing the floors, but the place was almost deathly silent. *Odd.*

"Up here." Paler than ever, Noceo led them up a staircase and down a hallway, knocking on a door at the end. He twisted the handle down when no one answered. "I thought she'd be here. Elsar only know why she vanishes these days."

Likely because she has more of a conscience than you do. What he'd done to her had been horrific.

Dalvia's office was surprisingly messy, vials, glass and metal implements heaped together in piles across several surfaces. What looked like a dried and dissected boil beetle had been pinned to one of the tables, yellow venom sacs empty. Anek hovered over it with trepidation.

"Here it is." Noceo retrieved a vial of yellowish liquid and a bewilderingly thin, hollow needle next to it. "Cauterize the tip for me?" He held it out to Kadra who raised a finger. A spark singed the needle.

Sarai's heart squeezed at the guarded but familiar way they interacted. *What a mess.*

"You insert it like this." Noceo struck one end of the needle through the vial's wax seal, then rolled up his sleeves.

Wrath and Ruin. Anek's swift intake of breath mirrored hers at the mottled holes in Noceo's arms. They looked as though someone had snuffed out several blazeleaf rolls down his arms and then dug their fingers into the boils.

Noceo flipped the vial upside-down and plunged the other end of the needle into a vein. The yellowish fluid within drained into his body. A faint flush of color returned to his cheeks.

"Power comes easy after that," he said dully.

And this is the cost. She looked away. With *beshaz*, she could tear tendons and capillaries, but this drug would have her killing with a touch. She'd be as powerful as Kadra. Her fingers clutched her elbows, suddenly unwilling to inject the liquid into herself. *I'd never want to stop.*

She peered down the hallway as Noceo bundled more vials and needles into a satchel. Dalvia was more skilled than she had ever expected, to have concocted something of this magnitude. At least Komis's patients were in good hands—she paused in sudden confusion.

"Where are all the plague infectees?" She stuck her head back into the room.

Noceo's brow wrinkled. "I told you. I had no part in that."

"But Dalvia's been treating the victims." Sarai strode down the hallway, opening the rest of the doors on either side. They parted easily, revealing empty pallets, smothered in a heavy layer of dust. "Praetor Ythras said so. Many were carted here after that godsdamned lightning strike of yours too. I *saw* them leave." She reached the end of the hallway, an insidious fear clawing at her gut. "Where are they?"

"I don't know." Noceo looked hounded when everyone's eyes flew to him. "I never took an interest in what she did."

What if... She caught Kadra's cavernous eyes, gooseflesh pebbling her skin. His gaze altered and grew sharp. *We never considered her as a possibility.*

His jaw tautened. “Spread out and search the hospital for them.” He pinned Noceo with a knife-sharp stare. “Come with me.”

Méherre hastily took the cellars, while Sarai and Anek prowled the upper floors.

“It’s been over a month.” They raked a sweaty, reddish curl behind their ears as they ran, slamming doors without a care. “What if she healed them all and sent them home?”

“These beds haven’t been used for months.” Sarai grimly ran two fingers through the dust atop a mattress. “There isn’t so much as a bloodstain on the tiles either.”

Anek exhaled through their teeth. “We could be jumping to conclusions too quickly. She’s a weak sort. All those gods I mentioned, Dorcone, Hwiliath, and Faragathe, are powerful and *dangerous*. As difficult to Summon as the Elsar and twice as cruel because they have no obligation to listen to mortals. You were mad with grief, but it’s impossible for a lower-Tier magus to pull that off in cold blood.”

Sarai’s gut clenched, fear raking it with vicious swipes. “I don’t think it was coldblooded. *Gods!* I was so focused on Noceo! I didn’t think–” She stiffened at a scream from below.

Méherre. She moved without thought, Anek racing downstairs with her. Kadra and Noceo joined them from the uppermost floor. They congregated in the now-empty atrium. The Bridger was gone.

“There’s no one upstairs,” Noceo panted.

“Then, they’re down there.” Anek jerked a thumb toward the open door to the cellars where Méherre’s scream had come from. “I’m going.” They darted in before anyone could stop them.

Sarai followed them down a narrow flight of stairs, gripping Kadra’s hand as a hallway loomed at the bottom. “Are you thinking the same thing?”

“Yes.” His austere features had never looked more forbidding.

Shit. Kadra had shades of homicidal looks. Bored but murderous. Amused but murderous. Disgusted and murderous. A predator playing with its food, aloof and uncaring. But she knew this look, had once provoked it herself months ago when he had discovered her wearing an illusion rune in his fiercely guarded tower. It was the face of a man who'd learned that someone had slipped past his guard and would do anything to avenge it.

It was all there. Dalvia's apathy, her hatred that Noceo had forcibly bound her to him, while still caring for the man.

"Power like yours doesn't have freedom. And freedom like mine, didn't have power," she had said when they'd had dinner.

I spent so much time battling Noceo that I didn't see it.

"You can't really believe that she'd be behind this," the same asshole said incredulously. "Drenevan, we grew up with her. She's only ever tried to please—"

"You don't understand what that does to someone," Sarai bit out. Ahead, Anek's footsteps had halted as they entered the hallway. "Breaking yourself over and over again for others because you've no other choice. All you're left with are pieces."

Sometimes, people rearrange them in the wrong way.

She hit the landing right as the door to the cellars slammed shut behind them. Turning in surprise, she jumped at Anek's terrified gasp. They stood in front of her, blocking her view as they backed away slowly.

"I think I found her patients," they whispered.

All breath left Noceo in a strained moan. Sarai peered past Anek and froze at the endless line of barred cells lacing both sides of the hallway. Crimson, gleaming wings buzzed inside the cages, tunneling into groaning human flesh, yellowish sacs overblown with venom. The people inside twitched, some bearing the waxy bloat of the dead, others long decomposed. Few alive.

Bile rose in Sarai's throat. She cast a terrified look at the now-shut door through which they'd come. She had little doubt that it was locked. Likely by someone loyal to Dalvia.

Wrath and Ruin. We're trapped.

34
UNTETHERED CONSEQUENCE

There was an inherent violence to the process of Death, no matter now benign. A stoppering of a heart, an expulsion of life through a breath. The sight before him lacked that elegance. It was turmoil, hatred, and glee, enacted without conscience.

Young and old, most lay half rotted in their cells, eyes and portions of their nostrils missing. They may not have been beyond hope before this place, but they were now. Those with eyes had begun slowly swiveling to them, taking in the newcomers with the hungry interest of the delirious. Invisible to everyone else was the gaping maw at the end of the hallway. Arms with teeth rising from the floor to tear into all in their path.

Ten fucking hells. I should have seen it.

Dalvia had learned the same lessons at the same knee that he and Noceo had. She had watched them deceive and butcher throughout their childhood and been taunted for her inability to do the same. Yet, he had hoped that one of them had emerged sane from Clan Kader's manor. Instead, she had used his guilt and thoroughly insulated herself from suspicion.

"She was never helping these people." Sarai vibrated with rage beside him. "She brought them here as cattle."

The beetles stirred at the timbre of her voice, and she clapped a hand over her mouth as a small cloud rose in the air in search of prey. Their yellow venom sacs quivered eagerly. He strode in front of her and Anek and placed a finger to his lips just as one of the infected spotted him. The man opened his mouth. A stream of nonsense came from his throat that other prisoners echoed, shoving at their cell doors.

Kadra closed his eyes on a curse when they clanged open. Anek mumbled a horrified plea to the Elsar as a group of infected tottered out of their cells.

"She didn't lock the doors." Noceo sounded as though he were in shock. "By the gods—"

"Help me break down the door," Sarai bit out as more infectees began racing forward with surprising speed. "We don't have time for fatalism." She gripped his sleeve. "Kadra—"

"I'll hold them off." His hand covered hers. She squeezed it, terror flaring in her golden eyes for a second before she steeled herself and ran upstairs with Noceo and Anek, slamming her weight into the door.

This would be unpleasant.

A wave of infectees neared. Delirious and half dead, they ran at inhuman speeds.

He raised a hand, fingers swiping the air. Pressure dropped like an anvil within the hallway. A net of lightning stretched over the doorway, dividing him, the beetles, and the infected from Sarai, Anek, and his brother. He sank into the familiar liminal calm of anticipation before a fight.

A man approached, eyes unseeing. Kadra moved.

He kicked out at the closest one and sent him into another, gliding behind them to snap their necks in seconds. With the crook of a finger, lightning flared in his cramped quarters and arrowed through their corpses with precision, reaching ghostly, white-hot fingers for the others just beyond.

Fiery tendrils sank into each one, twisted through their skin and up to their screaming mouths. At least ten dropped to the ground within. Thick, branching burns bloomed red under their skin before their eyes rolled back in their heads and went unmoving.

That seemed to enrage the rest. Feet thudded toward him. Avoiding the teeth-laced arms on the ground, he incinerated a swarm of beetles with a lazy flick of his wrist, dispatching another group in a flash of heat and burning flesh. Behind him came the desperate smack of boots, elbows, and bodies against wood.

"Stay back you both. I might have it," Anek yelled.

Waves of pressure coiled and uncoiled in the cellar as he razed everything that approached. Shrieks tore into the air, skin slid from flesh, smoke stung the air. Blood ran down the divots of the tiles. And a crack snapped through his focus. The door was down.

"Kadra!" Sarai yelled.

He dissipated the shield over the doorway in one breath, sprinted through it in the next, then re-erected it. Bodies howled as they struck the lightning barrier. He could do nothing else. They were too far gone down Death's road to pull back.

He ran up two steps at a time and found Sarai and the others bruised from their exertions but otherwise unharmed. The doors into the Institute parted and Méherre stumbled in, blood dripping from a deep head wound. She frenetically pulled them shut behind her.

"Wisdom's breath!" Anek ran to her. "What happened?"

"The Elsar only know. Someone knocked me over the head and the next thing I knew, I was outside." She thrust a shaking hand at the doors. "We can't leave. Beetle swarms *everywhere*."

"Dalvia." Dread tautened Sarai's voice. "What do you want to bet that Edessa's under siege by a god right now?"

Convenient. Dalvia had always been a step ahead. She had known they were coming to the Institute.

"Ready a portal to Komis, Méherre." He pushed the hospital doors open against the Bridger's exclamations and welcomed the rush of winter air. Light from nearby braziers mirrored off snow and into his eyes, providing rich contrast to the thick crimson swarms undulating like waves between the evergreens, venom sacs bulging. Some had already swallowed a few fleeing northern vigiles.

"Ruin's tits, we're fucked." Anek skidded to a halt behind him, rucking up snow. "There must be thousands! Tens of thousands?"

Given the speed of their approach, they had all scented the blood Kadra had just spilled in the cellar. *No matter.*

His jaw clenched as he channeled more power into his palms and balled them into fists. Roving air currents warped to his command. The pressure dropped dangerously low. Sarai pressed her hands against her ears in discomfort when her eardrums popped. As the first wave of beetles neared, he brought both hands down into the snow.

Shield upon golden lightning shield flared around them like fishing nets, radiating cruel barbs outward. The insects sizzled and fell, unable to penetrate the weave. Venom sacs burst yellow onto the snow. Veins corded in Kadra's temples as he kept up the barriers through assaults from every angle. A sea of red grew beyond their circumference. Then, long moments later, came quiet.

Kadra carefully dissipated the shields. The ground before them looked like scarlet, iridescent snow, rife with beetle carcasses. He turned to the dumbfounded group behind him. Noceo and Méherre had gone white.

"I'm *never* living in the north," Anek whispered.

Sarai inclined her head with quiet awe. "Magus Supreme." Her smile faded when Méherre made a frustrated sound.

"I can't Bridge you into the city." Lines bunched on her forehead as she strained. "*Shit.* It'll have to be the city walls."

It had begun then. Kadra lifted the edge of his sleeve and examined the crimson runes on his armilla. Sarai followed his gaze and paled.

"You fought a storm only hours ago too. And now this." Red threaded her eyes. She'd lost weight over weeks of exhaustion. "I didn't see it," she confessed tautly. "I overlooked her entirely."

Kadra sighed at the knowledge that he had been no different in his preoccupation with remorse.

Wrath had said as much, weeks ago. "*Regret can be a dangerous thing for a mortal. It blinds them to the present in favor of what they wish had been possible. Too much escapes you while you atone for a past you believe should have been different and force a future you believe should have existed.*"

As Sarai was so fond of saying…

"I may have an overblown sense of guilt," he mused.

"*Finally*, you see it."

"Stop blaming yourselves and leave some self-hatred for the rest of us!" Anek yelled. "I felt sorry for her too!"

Méherre cried out in pain. A portal slit the air, a thin sliver taking too long to widen.

Sarai eyed it with dread and pressed her and Kadra's clasped hands to her chest. "If the worst happens," she whispered, "it has been the greatest of honors."

He tipped her chin up and caressed the underside. "Every day meant *everything*," he said softly.

Her eyes grew wet. "Be careful."

Noceo lifted a few vials from his satchel. "Anyone want these first?"

"Fuck no, I'm not touching anything she's made." Anek flinched at the sound of screaming from within the portal. It broadened enough for them to enter. "Elsar preserve me," they muttered to the sky with heavy irony before walking in.

Face tight, his brother followed.

Kadra entered with Sarai's hand in his. A black wind swallowed them. Their feet left the ground. Gold eyes found his before black closed around them and spun, hurtling them into the center of a whirlwind.

He dimly heard Sarai's scream. Her hand tore from his grasp, his roar of her name lost to the howl of air and flashes of color. Other faces whipped around them, hapless within the same fury. Sight and sound blurred in a tumultuous shriek until his feet hit the road.

His sight cleared.

And he knew where he was.

Rain struck cobblestone with bitter fury and pelted the body at the base of Sidran Tower. She twitched, mangled fingers inching forward in an attempt to hoist herself upright before realizing that it was fruitless.

Kadra knew pain. Its corners and tunnels had ceased being a mystery to him in childhood. But in this, he, who had borne the pain of a cracked spine for a decade without complaint, was rendered in agony.

He approached her as he had then and knelt, brushing a waterlogged strand of hair from her face. A harsh breath sawed from him. As the years passed, the memory of Sarai's original face had faded long before he'd met her again. Now, he would never forget.

Half of her was pulp. The rest quietly pleaded with him for mercy. Brown eyes, hollow cheeks. "Please," half her mouth slurred, the rest broken against cobblestone.

He cupped her cheek with a hand that shook. His heart choked in his chest when she leaned into the touch. She felt solid, broken. Fury sharpened his bloodlust. This god knew his weakness well.

An unnaturally large shadow loomed over them and blotted out the scant moonlight.

He didn't turn around. "Is this real?"

"In life, I was Time's acolyte," a melodious voice spoke behind him. "I can make it real."

Anguish threaded through the cracks in his heart.

A dark blue-green foot touched the ground in front of him. He raised his head to the goddess standing beside Sarai. Her black hair floated in defiance of the rain. Bone-white horns gleamed like blades, and eighteen eyes surveyed him with cold amusement, twelve pupilless orbs scattered across her shoulders and clavicles, four on her cheekbones, and two human ones.

He had an idea of who she was now. "Faragathe, Wretched Seer of Sleep. The one who's been trying to crush my skull."

"You've a hard head. And you owe her," she said with a hard glance at Sarai's body. "So much pain could have been avoided this night, if you'd placed her life above your petty gains."

"What will undoing it cost me?"

"*Everything.*" Her teeth gleamed as sharp as Wrath's. "You and your city for her future. We should understand each other better than most, *Gods-touched*. The objects of this world do not matter. Cities rise, fall, and burn. It's all a day in the life of a god. Let this one go, and I will spare your woman. She will have the life she should have had. You have my word."

"Will that life be real?" he asked, voice clipped and hard.

She laughed. "You of all people should understand how very variable reality is. But she will be happy. Tragedy will not find her."

And neither will I. He understood the cost.

Thunder roared around them. Sarai's mouth worked under his hand. "Please don't go," she croaked.

Heat built behind his eyes in a way he hadn't known since childhood. He wiped a trail of blood from her chin. Wrath had been right. *Everything has a price. Even regret.*

His guilt had allowed Dalvia and this goddess to rake their claws into Edessa.

"You owe her, acolyte of Wrath." the goddess said.

"I do." Everything he was and all he had become. Bending, he pressed a chaste kiss to Sarai's forehead. His hand fell from her face. It took everything he had to stand. The storm seemed to stutter as he did. Sarai's body briefly vanished before returning. *She has me in a dream.*

Faragathe's human eyes hardened. "Will you walk away from her again?"

"I'm walking to her."

"How?" she asked curiously. "You're in my realm."

A menacing smile parted his lips. "Not yet."

Her eyes flared. She opened her mouth, jaw unhinging to reveal a swallowing darkness. He sent a burst of power to his left hand. The claw Wrath had gifted him burst from the tip of his index finger. *The bastard knew.*

When Faragathe lunged, he cut through the dream imprisoning him with a slash of his hand. Reality bled from the rift, two worlds superimposing. A snarl of pain, then the goddess and Sarai's body vanished.

Stormfall still roared around him, that nameless eerie hand of smoke manipulating the sky with delight. He stood on the Academiae's grounds outside Sidran Tower amid hundreds of people shrieking. Drenched, they rocked back and forth on the ground, trapped in Faragathe's nightmares.

A familiar roar caught his attention. Cassandane strode across the Academiae's grounds, directing people to drag as many as they could indoors. Sighting Kadra, she groaned in relief.

"I would thank the gods, but I'm a little furious at them right now," she yelled above the rain. "Did that teal goddess try to cut you a deal too?"

"She did."

Cassandane glanced at him standing under Sidran Tower and winced in understanding. "I see. Where are Sarai and Anek?"

"I have a guess." Kadra grabbed a screaming magus by the collar and shoved them into the tower. "Can you hold the Academiae?"

She wordlessly pointed at Cato, Telmar, and to Kadra's surprise, Harion, who were dragging insensate people inside as the storm raged. With a grim nod, Kadra sprinted inside Sidran Tower, almost slamming into Noceo on the stairs.

His brother looked inches from collapse. "I figured she would be—"

"Upstairs." Kadra took the steps at a run up to the fifth floor where Aelius had held many a convivium until Sarai's fall. He tore the portrait of a former Magus Supreme from its nail and pressed the depression beneath it. The wall parted and revealed a black hall, dusty with disuse, and a staircase to the upper level from which Sarai had fallen. Breathing hard, he ran up the final set of steps, Noceo behind him.

And there she was.

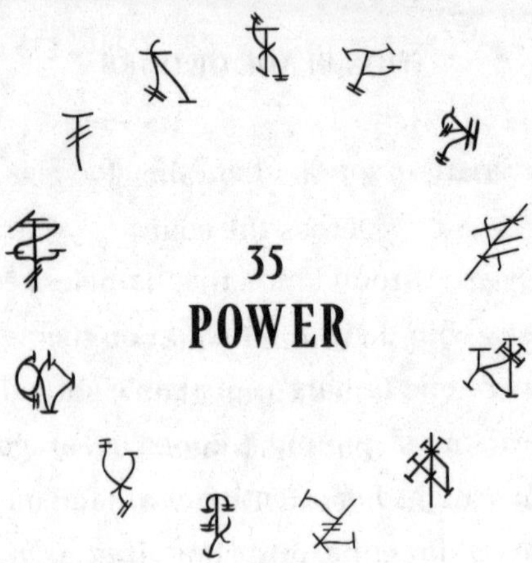

35
POWER

Her knees struck the ground with bruising force.

Winded, she clutched her head until the world stopped spinning and slowly stood. The tile at her feet gave away where she was before the snarl of thunder outside. *Oh, for the Elsar's sake!*

"This is getting tiring!" she roared, gripping the railing of the balcony atop Sidran Tower. "What's next? Will Aelius rise up from the dead to shove me off once more?"

A throaty laugh boomed in the air. The view past the balcony darkened until it seemed as though she and the tower were suspended in a black void.

A face emerged from it. All eyes, *eighteen* eyes—black to the reaches of her sclera, all swallowing any semblance of light. She understood now who the madness-struck saw. The goddess hovered midair, ribbons of what could have been night sky wrapping around her lithe frame.

Understanding lanced through Sarai. "Faragathe," she whispered, recalling the play in Sal Flumen.

Of course. Burned alive for supposed heresy by greedy, apathetic folk who'd called themselves devout. And then, she'd ascended to incredible power. Dalvia would have seen a kinship.

"Most people react differently." The goddess laughed. Her voice made Noceo's sound like rocks cracking against each other. "I show the evil their fears, and they scream *so* loudly."

You showed me mine a few times too many. Sarai took a shaky step forward. "Why hold massacres across the country? Could you never forgive the land for hurting you?"

"I massacred your evil to remind your people that they *could*. Many still chose not to." Horns crowned Faragathe's void-black hair.

"You won't convince me that everyone who died was evil."

"I took my share of innocents. This world didn't deserve them. The goddess's smile had too many teeth. "But you need not join them. Give me this city, and you'll never lack for power again. Not the vials that the scion of Clan Kader swears by, but true power." Faragathe watched her unblinkingly. "I can rearrange the very essence of your being to make you a Twelfth-Tier lightning magus. You could surpass your Magus Supreme in a heartbeat."

Blood rang in Sarai's ears. The country would deign her the same respect that Kadra enjoyed. A week ago, in the rubble, her answer might even have looked different.

"It doesn't need to change." Reading her mind, Faragathe angled her head in the way of a curious owl.

It has to. It was one thing to crave power. But her goal wasn't power for power's sake but to feel secure, unthreatened. *I won't earn that at the cost of the lives of everyone in Edessa.*

"Dull," Faragathe pronounced, nearing her. There was a quiet horror to seeing the goddess up-close, all eyes and horns. Unfathomable power leaked from her in waves to lick at Sarai's skin. She flinched back. Any hell she presided over would be monstrous indeed.

Faragathe grinned. "Everyone's in a hell of their own, child. I just make it real."

She closed in right as footsteps sounded on the staircase up to the ballroom.

A bloodied Anek emerged, clutching what appeared to be a broken elbow. They flinched at the sight of the goddess. "Wrath's blade, you again.

Does it strike you that this entire business will really besmirch your name going forward?"

Faragathe glided past Sarai and into the ballroom to give them a pitying look. "I'm inevitable. And now this land will remember that when they sleep, I rule the roost of their mind." She smiled. "Good devotees are so hard to find."

Sarai shuddered. *Gods, no wonder they're called the Wretched.* The general theological consensus was that devotees of the High Elsar became Saints. Those of the Dark Elsar became the Wretched. How cruel had this former Seer been that *Time* himself hadn't been able to push her into Sainthood.

"I could kill you for that thought alone," Faragathe mused, examining her claws.

"And you wonder why I had it," Sarai said, voice hard.

More footsteps struck the stairs. Black and gold swept in before he did. Sarai relaxed at the fierce glitter in Kadra's eyes. Noceo looked no less cowed by the goddess.

"My, we're getting a crowd." Faragathe didn't sound irritated but oddly thoughtful when Méherre came up the stairs as well, sweating from the exertion. Anek rushed to the Bridger. "I'll ask you again. Power and your friends' lives in return for this city."

Sarai stiffened at the addendum. "My friends' *lives*?"

Lightning flared to life and encased the small group and Sarai to separate them from Faragathe.

"That won't happen." Kadra's voice was dangerously quiet.

The goddess perched atop the balcony's railing and grinned. "Why did you think that the threat would come from *me*?"

A loud, startled wheeze sounded behind her. Sarai whirled around to find Méherre gripping Anek's throat, fingers pressing hard around their windpipe. Her eyes weren't glazed. Kadra halted Noceo when he stepped forward. Realization hardened his severe features.

"Well," there was an eerily familiar blankness to the Bridger's voice now, "this has probably gone on long enough."

Her short hair lengthened in a smooth rush, lightening until it reached an ephemeral brightness that went beyond white. Her features sharpened, turned graceful. Dalvia's nails bit into Anek's skin and forced them down. Wordless and pale, they sank to the ground, kneeling.

A True Illusionist. It had been an easy thing to overlook in the chaos of fighting battles at multiple fronts. *Especially when I ruled you out as a suspect from the start.*

Pieces fell into place with devastating rapidity. Méherre's convenient appearance at the start of Edessa's woes. How she had seemed to always know so much about her. How much she had known about gods and Summonings. For all the rarity of Bridgers in the country, Sarai hadn't questioned meeting two in short order.

"You seem surprised." Dalvia spoke to Sarai. She didn't release Anek. "I'd actually hoped you'd put it together."

"We'd have to know you for that." Anek vibrated with rage, uncaring of the threat to their life. "You acted righteous among us but you treated the *injured* of your own city as cattle!"

"There was no saving them." Dalvia considered them with a perturbed frown. "The goddess told me which ones were worth saving and which ones weren't. Most really weren't, and it worked well for him." She leveled an assessing glance at Noceo. "Farmed him more power."

Sarai stilled at the memory of the yellowish liquid in the vials Noceo had retrieved from the Institute. And the boil beetles' yellow venom sacs.

A raw sound left Noceo. He seemed to be seeing her for the first time. "Is that what I've been injecting into myself for five months? *Venom?*" Fury built in his silver eyes.

"You wanted power." Something turbulent roiled in her eyes. "I provided it. You never asked why or how so long as you had it, and I was only useful to you so long as I kept you supplied." Another empty smile. "Why act angry about the cost now?"

"I would *never* have agreed—"

"Wouldn't you?" She hadn't tightened her grip, but Anek was starting to turn puce. "You killed hundreds at the Aequitas. You killed an innocent, grieving woman eleven years ago and forced yourself to believe that you hadn't done it. You forced me to *stay*." A crack in her blank mask. "Don't play the Saint."

Noceo crumpled against the banister, mouth working uselessly.

Sarai's throat ached. "You resented the world for allowing all of it."

The fracture widened. Dalvia's fingers twitched, letting color back into Anek's skin. "I resent everyone." Wildness flushed her delicate features. "I resent the *foolish* things you all do to appease yourselves while others suffer. The capital has always craved attention. They've hoarded yours for years with their tantrums. Now, they get all the eyes they want on them."

"I'm sorry for what you've endured," she whispered, moving slowly forward. "But what will hurting them," she indicated Anek, "accomplish?"

"I got you out of this city!" Dalvia snapped. "You should have stayed in the Institute. I wasn't trying to hurt you until you wanted to stop this. Let Edessa go. Sometimes, in order to heal a land, you must first break it."

The words struck a bitter pang of understanding, hitching Sarai's breath. "And what happens to you afterward?"

Dalvia blinked, something faintly confused appearing then vanishing from her gaze. "Anything. Because now, when you reign, you'll know that it's all the smoother because of me."

Sarai took another step and caught Kadra's eye. He inclined his head in silent understanding of what she was attempting to do. The grave set of his face told her that he would take no pleasure in this kill.

"Why the subterfuge?" Anek asked through gritted teeth. "Was playing the weakling not enough?"

"I wasn't playacting," Dalvia said tonelessly. "Méherre could say things that Dalvia couldn't. She was the honest one, outspoken. She'd save me from harm in a heartbeat. The guise took on a life of their own after a while. It was nice not being me."

Sarai's gut churned. "You're a fool."

Tears rolled down Anek's cheeks. "I really liked you. You could have built a life of your own. You bought a *havïd* house here!"

For the first time, warmth blossomed on Dalvia's face. "That's the strange thing. I liked you all too. I thought about stopping all this, but it was too late. I had already promised my goddess this city, and without her, I faced the same fate I had with Noceo—freedom without true power. No," she shook her head sadly, "there's no life waiting for me."

Another step, and Sarai stood before her. She gently gripped the wrist that was holding Anek prisoner. "Won't you at least try?"

Dalvia studied her. "Wanting something to be true isn't the same as reality, Sarai." She dropped her arm. Anek scrambled away, gasping for air. "I just wanted to snap my fingers and fix it all," she said dully. "It all just never made sense."

A lump choked Sarai's throat. "I'm so sorry." She stepped back. "I wish this could all have been different."

Dalvia blinked right as multiple cages of lightning domed around her and atop each other, hissing across the ballroom floor. She examined the bars of lightning with mild curiosity and no surprise.

Kadra's jaw was granite. "Call your goddess away. You've convinced yourself that you have no hope of survival here, but there may be a future for you yet."

"A future where these cages will disappear, and a more permanent one will take me." Dalvia turned to Kadra and smiled. "I meant everything I said that day. I did get some of this wrong. But not all of it." She glanced at Noceo, and every mask slid from her face in a silent relinquishing of self. Hatred and yearning suffused her gaze. "I would have stayed every day if you hadn't forced me," she whispered.

The man looked like he'd been struck by lightning.

Dalvia considered the bars of her cage once more, and Sarai had the horrible feeling that she knew what was going to happen. She wanted to beg the other woman not to do it. But who was she to demand that a woman who had been trapped in a cage for so long return to a different one?

The same realization coalesced in Kadra's face. "This is what you want," he said in the heavy timbre of a man who had seen too much and would now bear one more stain on his soul.

"I knew it was coming from the moment Sarai tried to resolve things with Noceo." She glanced at Kadra. "I'm tired." She exhaled. "I'm ready."

Sarai swallowed. "If it's death you want, let me do it instead." She stalked to the other side of the cage to face Dalvia. "This will hurt him," she said fiercely.

"It'll hurt you too." Dalvia's mouth tilted up. "That's nice to know. That's a good way to be remembered." Before Sarai could speak, she turned to Faragathe, who had been watching them intently all the while. "It seems that I can't give you a city, my goddess."

Sadness crossed Faragathe's inhuman features for a fleeting moment. "I knew."

"Oh," Dalvia breathed.

Hot tears washed down Sarai's cheeks. She clutched her arms to steady herself.

Noceo finally unlocked his knees and stepped forward. "*Stop*," he ordered with full Coercive force. "We still have much to discuss, you and I. You can't do…whatever it is that you're—"

"What will my punishment be?" Dalvia angled a slim hand through the bars of her cages toward Faragathe. Sparks caught portions of her skin, but she didn't so much as flinch.

"Quiet." The goddess took her wrist with a brief glance at Kadra. He returned it and dropped the cages around Dalvia. "For many, many centuries until the gods send you down to the mortal plane again."

Dalvia smiled. "I think I'll like that." She stepped forward. Anek made an anguished sound.

Noceo screamed her name right as Faragathe faced them with a glower. All eighteen eyes pinned them with quiet fury before goddess and girl vanished.

And the screaming in the courtyard suddenly stopped.

Numb, Sarai trailed one hand along the wall, walking until she found Kadra's solid frame and leaned against him.

"She was–" she swallowed, "she was right about a great deal."

Kadra's arm came around her shoulders. Grief burned in his eyes. "She was wrong about just as much."

"The worst of it," Anek sucked in a breath between sobbing, "is that I can't fault her for it or forgive her for it."

Steps bounded up the stairs. "I think it's over! Everyone's waking up!" Harion's voice arrived before he did. "Gods, I *never* want–" He and Cassandane stared at the dismal tableau in the ballroom.

The Head Tetrarch glanced each of them swiftly. "Casualties among us?"

"None," Kadra confirmed.

"Then, why the long fucking faces?" Harion squinted at a still-crying Anek and reared back in shock.

Sometimes, you can see who someone is and who they wanted to become. And they do too. And the dissonance between the two eats at you both.

"And where is Dalvia?" Harion cracked his knuckles menacingly. "That bitch deserves a public beheading."

"She's free," Sarai said quietly, glancing at the moonless sky and knowing that Dalvia had passed far beyond it. "She's finally free."

36
RECOMPENSE

Twenty-fifth day of the Month of Breath

Two days after Faragathe's descent upon Edessa, Sarai strode down the Am Semni Institute's hallways. Most of the dead had been cleared in the morning, but she didn't want a reason to have to come back here after today. *Komis'll be a wound for some time.*

She paused at the door on the end of the first-floor hallway and went in. Dalvia's study looked just as it had during their last visit. Everything had changed since then, so Sarai had strangely expected the study to have done so as well.

The madness-struck in Edessa had woken in droves, terrified and requiring immense healing of brain and heart damage, but otherwise whole. The psychological trauma done to them would likely take decades to heal, though.

Noceo sat in a cell in Kadra's vigile station in Komis being readied for trial. Kadra had already recused himself to ensure impartiality. Whatever the punishment, it would pale in comparison to what the man now inflicted on himself. She had briefly visited him the day before and found a shell who had offered a firm apology and then returned to contemplating the walls.

What if? The worst of questions.

She trailed a hand along one of Dalvia's desks. Vials and jars had been stuffed haphazardly into crates. Boxes of animal secretions, roots, leaves, and powders lay by the door. She felt the first tear slip free. *This was a tragedy.*

Footsteps sounded behind her before Kadra's rough finger took the tear from her cheek. She turned into him, fighting tears. "She wasn't wrong."

Kadra rested his forehead against hers, and she felt his silent accord. Something fluttered on the desk, a sheaf of parchment covered in Dalvia's writing. She stilled at the realization of what it was.

He followed her gaze and something quiet and contemplative lit his face. "Her formula for Noceo's stimulant."

She was already moving, drawn to it like a moth to flame. "It wasn't entirely beetle venom." She leafed through the pages. "No one else knows how to make it."

"Yet," Kadra said dryly.

She half laughed. "True. Someone will discover it again. People are too enterprising not to."

"Immense power." He simply watched her. "In two pages."

Gods, the temptation. It would destroy her arms if she injected it, but it remained a powerful advantage. "We could change the face of this land without an angry goddess. Reshape it properly. Make every Guildmaster and Praetor grovel."

Kadra's mouth curved. "An appealing prospect."

He leaned against the doorjamb with lazy elegance. Only the dark intensity in his eyes showed that he knew how much this meant to her. That she still wanted a power of her own that would never be belittled or dismissed as coming from him. He wouldn't stop her from taking this, no matter the consequences. Within both their hearts lived a wounded despot, eager to press its stamp on the world to prevent others from suffering the same pain they had.

But an emotionally scarred tyrant was still a tyrant. Dalvia's wounds had made her take ugly, thorny roads that had stained her hands with grief and blood, and resulted in unintended consequences like the dead in Arsamea.

Right now, hurting innocents seemed anathema to Sarai's nature. But within the grasp of unfettered power, she could see the downward slope of decisions that would lead her there. They wouldn't be simple ones, borne out of a desire to avenge and protect, but over time they would snowball and come a little easier and easier until she would look in the mirror like Noceo and Dalvia and no longer recognize what she had become—tearing the world to pieces to heal their wounds, long having lost sight of those in it.

I can't.

For all her powerlessness, she valued who she was now too much to do that. She loved Kadra more than life to condemn him to that. Taking a deep breath, she crumpled the parchment and stalked toward the fireplace.

Heat stung her eyes. She raised a trembling hand over the hearth and dropped the first wadded ball of parchment in. Her breath caught as it erupted in flame.

She drew a deep gulp of air and unclenched her fist. The parchment clung to her palm at first, held in place by sweat and blood, before gravity tugged it free. It fell in slow seconds, glowing golden as it neared the firelight then a brilliant fiery yellow as it struck the fire in a shower of sparks. For a second, the writing on it deepened. One last showing, one final temptation of the power contained within those lines, as it hovered on the precipice between existence and obliteration. Then flame swallowed it whole.

Lightness expanded in her chest as she watched it burn to ash. She turned and raced right into a worried-looking Kadra's arms and hugged him tight.

"I'm well," she whispered into his neck. "I'm well, Kadra."

Lifting her against him, he kissed her for a soft, adoring second. His eyes held a world of pride.

She sighed against him, completely boneless. "Gods, a boot just lifted off my neck."

His eyes narrowed. "Whose?"

"Mine," she said ruefully. "Still, it was a nice dream, wasn't it? You and I terrorizing them all?"

He cupped her face. "I will always wage war with you. If you had kept her notes, I would have set fire to the world if it came for you." His voice was fierce. "I have belonged to you from the moment I saw you."

Heart in her eyes, she stared up at him.

"But this crisis is at an end, and I must ask before a new threat finds us." The voice she loved so dearly was ragged. He made to step back, but she wouldn't allow him to kneel, clutching him to her as he palmed her cheek. "Let me bind my years to yours. I can't give you a quiet life, and I may never be a good man. But I will give you all I am and everything I will be."

She took in his stern, beloved face and recalled it through their many first meetings. Fourteen. Eighteen. A market. A tower and a garden folly. An ice-cold god and a fierce lover. Some might call theirs too short a courtship, but she had known him even when she hadn't had his secrets. There was no answer but this. "*Yes.*" The air that she had only just regained caught in her throat at the way his gaze changed, burned with hope and joy and yearning. At the warm spill of happiness that crinkled the corners of his eyes in the most stunning, genuine smile.

He circled her waist and lifted her off the ground. She laughed in delight and found his lips first, sealing their vow softly, a sigh bridging them when he stroked her nape and kissed her with increasing ardor.

A horrified sound from the doorway startled them apart. Anek walked straight out of the room.

"No, thank you. *Tibi gratias ago.* That's enough existence for me today," they called loudly as they strode off. "Come outside when you're done with *whatever* I absolutely did not see and will wipe from memory immediately."

Huffing out a laugh, Kadra only kissed her again.

By the time they were all assembled in the compound's courtyard, Sarai had had to rebraid her hair, and Anek looked traumatized. They had taken "Méherre's" death hard, but life went on, they had told Sarai shortly afterward. They would too.

Cassandane folded her arms, casting a wary eye toward central Komis in evident dread of the upcoming trial they were holding there. "Did either of you happen to find Dalvia's formula for Noceo's stimulant?"

Sarai smiled brightly. "It was better left lost." She tilted her head toward the hospital. "Imagine all the boil beetle venom we'd have to farm to produce it."

"And I doubt people would be circumspect with its usage." Cassandane's shrewd gaze found hers. "Yes, it's better left lost. Ready for our trial?"

"Fuck me," Harion said gloomily, staring down into Komis like he could already see the five Guildmasters trussed up there for judgment—ones that he himself had indicted for exacerbating resource shortages in the north, leading to sedition. Retribution hadn't been as enjoyable as he had hoped when the other Guilds had promptly turned their back on him. "The other Guilds will have me assassinated at this rate."

"It won't be *that* bad," Anek mused. "To think that one of the criminals is Albanus himself? I thought he was going to be your future father-in-law?"

"Happy to be associated with their money. Not happy to be associated with their crimes," Sarai said. "The Guilds really are *so* displeased about this, aren't they?"

"Stop enjoying this! I haven't even made a will." He radiated dismay.

Ah, divine retribution. Sarai grinned. "You can start on the wagon ride into town."

The public square in Komis barely held a finger's width of space for anyone else to squeeze in. This trial was less a determination of guilt than it was a public show of support and interest in the north and their suffering.

"Bring in the accused," Kadra ordered smoothly.

The northern crowd quieted. Just as many were there to see him as they were for the trial. Cassandane had brought together every Bridger in the country to send up lightning magi to scorch extant boil beetle swarms, which had pulled some goodwill from many a northerner. And the prospect of the north getting to claim the south's most infamous Tetrarch and Magus Supreme as the only decent member of Clan Kader? Pure gold.

Vigiles dragged in the five Guildmasters and tossed them on their knees by the stake in the ground. Ioratius of the Grains Guild, Etilia of the Wine and Spirits Guild, Albanus of the Stones Guild, whose glower said that he still hadn't forgiven her for the loss of his six-thousand-aurei vase, Septimus of the Clay Guild, and the new Metals Guildmaster she hadn't met. They glowered, eyes like burning coals, their previous finery reduced to stained tunics and stringy hair. Cheers rose from the crowd.

Kadra addressed their ringleader. "Guildmaster Ioratius and company, you stand accused of sedition." He passed Cassandane the scroll on which to write her judgment. "How do you plead?"

Struggling with his manacles, Ioratius gave him an incredulous look. "Not guilty," he spat, along with the rest. "Good business is no crime."

A dangerous gleam flared in Kadra's eyes, and Sarai leaned back in her seat, watching him quietly eviscerate every one of them for worsening the north's food and resource shortages. The swell of the crowd had never been louder by the time he was through.

"Well, I don't think your 'not guilty' plea will change much here." Cassandane's reed-pen arrowed across the parchment as she wrote. She set it down, looking tired. "We heard your voices time and time again in Delran Tower to no effect. We weren't listening to *them*, and they paid for it." She pointed at the crowd. "The Guildmasters are hereby found guilty. They're sentenced to whichever one of the Dark Elsar's hells the Magus Supreme decides to deliver them to, which truly I wouldn't wish on my worst enemies." She turned to him. "Kadra?"

He caught Sarai's eye and turned to the audience. An unholy bloodlust glittered in his eyes as he rose from his seat. "They're yours."

Oh dear.

Horror dawned in the Guildmasters' eyes as the vigiles unbound the group and kicked through the group into the crowd. Not one to disdain a show of blood, Kadra's lips quirked.

Furious hundreds advanced on the Guildmasters like a swarm of boil beetles. Blood sprayed high in the air as the first limb was ripped off. Feet met their faces. The russet earth grew stained and stank of iron and bodily fluids as agonized pleas filled the air and ended.

Kadra's furrowed brow said that he thought their justice was too swift.

But then again, she thought, watching the northerners turn some of Ur Dinyé's most prominent businessfolk to meat. *They waited a long time for it.*

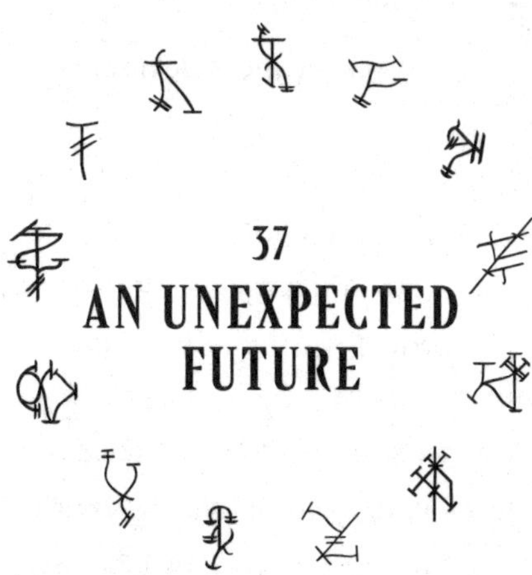

37
AN UNEXPECTED FUTURE

He was no stranger to rebuilding.

Kadra strode down the stairs into the holding cells below his vigile station. The next couple of days had seen a flurry of activity as he and the Tetrarchy capitalized on their newfound goodwill to anchor their position in the north and south. Visits were made to northern towns, apologies offered, and ties strengthened. Cassandane had made arrangements for the Aequitas's rebuilding.

People believed what they believed.

Some whispered that they had known a god. Others called it a disease or mass hallucination. Telmar and Cato tirelessly worked to educate the latter. Those who avoided the truth were far too susceptible to manipulation.

Gaius ran into him on the way up. "Tetrarch Kadra, I just checked on him. Do you know, he apologized for the Aequitas and getting me injured?" He looked bewildered. "Gods, the faces people possess."

Indeed. Thanking him, Kadra proceeded. His feet hit the bottommost step. Cells passed him in succession before he found the one he sought, far from the other arraigned prisoners awaiting the mines. His brother had requested it.

He approached the bars. Noceo lifted his head and nodded. "You came."

"Hmm." Kadra withdrew a brass key and unlocked the cell to sit beside the other man.

Noceo's mouth twisted bitterly. "My trial is that soon, is it?"

"Yes."

"When?"

"A week. Cassandane expedited it under guise of public interest, but I think she's eager to send you off to the mines." Kadra considered Noceo's drawn features. "I won't be there."

"To prevent accusations of bias." Noceo laughed weakly. "Though it sounds like that's already happened. My crimes merit execution under the Corpus, don't they?"

"Death is simple. Living is the trial."

Noceo was quiet for a moment, tracing patterns on his scarred, mottled arms. "I don't know how to live."

Kadra nodded thoughtfully. "I felt the same at first upon arriving here with Othus, then again, after Sarai's fall. But there are always paths. We found some hope even as children. There may be some where you're going."

Noceo exhaled. "You'll be the last of the Clan then. The last of all five former Urd Clans." He nudged him. "*Clanlord.*"

"No." Kadra gave him a speaking look. "You are. I have enough in the way of titles without claiming that."

"Claim some of it." His brother folded his arms. "It is no small thing to have a history. To look back and know that there were others worse than you and that you can do better. I think the Death-Summoner would like that. She enjoyed the Hall of Relics."

Kadra smiled faintly. "There's a historian in her."

"Any children you have would carry on the name too."

It was Kadra's turn to blow out a breath, thinking of Sarai and a family waiting for him in Aoran Tower. *More than I dared dream.* He smiled faintly.

"You look ridiculous." Noceo let out a watery chuckle and caught Kadra's gaze, reminding him of the last time Kadra had said that, when the world had seemed too far and yet, at their feet.

Kadra gripped his brother's arm firmly and let go. "Probably."

There was nothing more to say. He rose and locked the door behind him.

"The mines…will you know where I am?" His brother's voice cracked at the end of the question.

"I will." Black eyes found silver and held them. "Farewell for *now*, Noceo."

This time, when he walked away, the air was quiet behind him. Steady with regret and the simple acknowledgment of who they'd been and who they could be. It was no simple feat, learning to live. But Noceo would learn. Just as he had.

Kadra's chest twinged with every step away from the cell. He smiled ruefully and kept walking.

Sunset cast the sky in crimson when he passed the statue of Wrath on his way back to Aoran Tower. His eyes narrowed. Pausing beside it for a breath, he exhaled in relief when the god didn't show and walked onward. The gate to Aoran Tower was midway to swinging shut behind him when a muscled, armored arm shoved past with a clank.

Kadra sighed. Things had been too quiet.

Blood bubbled from the ground to form a wide pool around Wrath. He was clad for battle today, a skull welded to one shoulder, jaws still moving in a never-ending scream.

Kadra arched an eyebrow. "Yes?"

Wrath grinned, fangs brushing his jaw. "You've passed."

Something about that sounded vaguely ominous to Kadra. He stared.

"You weren't wrong, mortal." Wrath gripped a bony hand trying to claw its way up his leg and snapped it cursorily. "Of course, there's a vetting process for the Naaduir. You just went through it. And passed."

Kadra leaned against the gaze. "Explain."

"As touching as it has been to hear your gratitude for the 'powers' and 'strength' I gave you, I didn't." Wrath raised his index finger and tapped it to his forehead in a mimicry of what he had done to Kadra that night in Delran Tower. "I simply removed every Threshold from you. You drew from your own power with complete abandon. It's why most people go mad, you know?" He indicated the screaming skull on his shoulder. "They get a taste of power and feast."

Understanding penetrated, and Kadra pinned the god with a hard stare.

"You tricked me," he said in a voice that promised retribution. Though the god had never denied the existence of a vetting process. He sighed when Wrath laughed.

"Mortals only believe that gods speak to them in riddles, because they can never understand what we see." Fire roared in his unearthly eyes. "But you do now, don't you?"

Kadra's lips curved. "Consequence is necessary for man but is the making of a god."

"We become the gods we choose." Wrath looked lost in thought for a moment. "Faragathe screamed that years ago as she burned alive. She chose her road, but I believe that you'll preside over something vastly more interesting than murder and mutilation, acolyte. Perhaps Judgment."

"It sounds like I'll be working even in death," Kadra said dryly.

"The Naaduir are allowed their consorts. You'll enjoy it." Wrath's smile was knowing.

"Will this be our last meeting?"

The god shrugged, sending another screaming skull tumbling within his black hair into the pool of blood. "I don't get much conversation. You'll do." His heavy, clawed hand struck Kadra's shoulder in brief parting before the god winked out of existence.

Kadra warily surveyed the gate to his tower and exhaled to find it in one piece. Smiling, he entered his home, Wrath's chuckle still ringing in his ears.

EPILOGUE
KADRA

Fifth day of the Month of Moons, Spring Equinox

Rebuilding a country could be a thankless endeavor at times, Kadra mused after a second round of Guild elections.

The past week had seen an exacting inquiry into Guild practices and accounting. Several Guildmasters had subsequently been forced to step down for assorted crimes. The subsequent intra-Guild elections were a logistical nightmare given the Tetrarchy's final mandates that Guilds supplying a resource that was primarily sourced from the north had to be comprised of a majority of northerners. He wasn't fond of supervising them, but north-south relations weren't yet improved to the point where he could let the parties negotiate on their own. Some would see that they had more in common than they didn't. Some wouldn't. Life went on.

The Tetrarchy hadn't.

He dismounted outside Aoran Tower, pace quickening as he unlocked the gates, knowing that she was home.

"Good evening, Councilor Kadra," a student passing by squeaked.

He inclined his head. "Good evening."

The two girls exchanged startled glances for a fraction of a second and scurried off.

"He's scary!" he heard them whisper when they thought they were out of earshot.

He was still fearsome, it seemed.

"Scary," Sarai repeated with amusement when he entered. "Quite the reputation, Councilor Kadra."

He pulled the gates shut behind him and lifted her into his arms. "Good evening, love."

She kissed him sweetly. "Long day?"

"The Guilds are imploding," he said dryly. "How was Noceo's trial?"

There would have been voices on the new Council of Ur Dinyé to see that justice was done.

Cassandane's final act as Head Tetrarch had been to dissolve the Tetrarchy in favor of a council that represented north and south interests. What had followed had been the fastest election period Kadra had witnessed. The people had known who they had wanted. Bridgers had facilitated easy access to ballots, and Harion had nearly given himself an aneurysm by campaigning in every town and village across Ur Dinyé. He had been elected, to Kadra's immense displeasure, which had firmed his resolve to improve wide-scale electoral education. The people simply shouldn't be electing fools.

Kadra had retained his former seat, as had Cassandane as Head Councilor of the South. Florus was a welcome addition as Head Councilor of the North in addition to a Praetor and a military Tribune. And the northern vigiles were finally allowing women and neutralii in like their southern counterparts.

"The Council was unanimous on the mines being the best course," Sarai said as they entered his study.

He nodded. "Duration?"

"The Council agreed that it'll take a great deal to blot out all the harm he's done." A sad smile bloomed on Sarai's face. "Twenty-five years."

A fair ending. "He has a long road ahead."

"So do we."

He raised an inquiring brow, shrugging off his robes.

"I have plans," she informed him.

"Is that right?" He stalked toward her.

"We have to travel, Kadra. It's simply nonnegotiable." She perched atop his desk, grinning when he caged her. "We're both far too entrenched in work. It isn't sustainable, and–"

"Yes," he said firmly, nuzzling her jaw. "To all of it."

She grinned. "I hope you don't regret that when I drag you to Errigal or try to import your Clan's Hall of Relics here. Telmar's already salivating," she confided.

He watched her speak, smile growing wider before he brought his mouth to her ear. "I love you." He never tired of the stars in her eyes when he said it.

Flushing in surprise, she kissed his jaw. "And I'm getting better with a blade, so I can at least attempt to be your equal there."

"You'll surpass me in a month," he murmured. "I'll be relegated to wiping dishes."

She winked. "I can think of more useful tasks."

"*That*, my dear, is never a task." His mouth found hers, and there were no words spoken for long moments.

A sharp rap on his tablinum door had him raising his head, dazed with hunger.

"I'm not coming in, because I fancy keeping my eyes *in* their sockets," Anek yelled from the other side. "But you're late!"

He had almost forgotten. A rarity for him, but he would forget most things with Sarai in his arms. Putting her to rights, they left Aoran Tower where Anek gave them a narrow-eyed glance before riding with them to a tavern.

Not content with retirement, Cato had opened a tavern by the Hall of Records. At the end of every week, they would all gather here and enjoy a meal. Friends–he took in Gaius's delight at being included, Anek, and Cassandane. Allies–Florus, who drank almost as much as Kadra once had. Nuisances–Harion opening his mouth to argue that the wine could be stronger and shutting it when Anek threatened to pour it over his head.

Family—Cato and the woman beside him, who had forever altered his life the day she had asked him for directions into the Academiae at fourteen.

His heart was full.

The days would pass like this. Some longer, some bloodier, some more beautiful than he had believed he would see, until their names passed from life and history. But here and now, she was Sarai of Arsamea, Petitor, strategist, and beloved. And he, who held a country in the palm of his hand, knew she was his land and his home, and he was hers.

Taking his hand, she tilted her head toward Cato, who was listening to Telmar with rapt attention as though he were telling him the secrets of the Elsar and not about his new position as an archivist at the Hall of Records. Kadra's brows rose, and Sarai beamed up at him with a distinct "I told you so" in her eyes. Her expression altered upon Harion saying something about the date, then turned incredulous.

"It's the spring equinox," she said with wonder. "Kadra, it's been a year since my Robing!" She laughed. "Gods, I was *furious* with you back then."

"I recall," he said dryly. "The Petitor and the monster."

"No." She took his face between her shaky fingers. "Two sides of the same blade."

Wordless, he traced her face when Anek waved a hand.

"Alright, enough of that you two. There are children here!" they pointed at an irate Harion, who choked on his wine trying to sputter out a retort.

Kadra took it all in, the ribbing, the laughter, the love in Sarai's eyes when she looked up at him.

It was enough. It would always be enough.

And the most beloved judge in Ur Dinyé smiled back.

THE END

ACKNOWLEDGMENTS

Three years ago, I wrote two decisive words in the manuscript for *This Monster of Mine*—The End—thinking there wasn't more to Sarai and Kadra's story. Time has since proved me wrong.

There are books that leave my fingers struggling to keep pace with the deluge of words. Then, there are books that have me reconsidering my career choices, whether I have any talent, and why I exist. This book was the latter. And now it really, truly, is the end. But let me start at the beginning.

In August 2021, I made three decisions that would change my life. I watched Ji Sung in a Korean drama called *The Devil Judge* and followed it with Ben Barnes in Netflix's *Shadow and Bone*. I wrote a book after falling in love with both lead characters. And I dared hope that book might become something great. So many people have ensured that it has:

My eternal thanks to my incredible agents, Molly Jamieson and Ginger Clark, for seeing merit in my work and championing me through thick and thin. Your enthusiasm and wisdom genuinely eases the perennial tightness in my chest, and I couldn't ask for better advocates in this industry.

A thousand editing Emmys to my extraordinary editors, Mahalaleel M. Clinton, Delayna Spencer, and Calah Singleton, who saw this book at its worst and pried the best parts free from the chaos. Thank you for encouraging me throughout the difficult process of rewriting this endlessly and for doing *so much* to support a terrified debut author. I'm endlessly grateful.

I remain indebted to the brilliant publishing teams at Union Square & Co. and Hodderscape. It's a dream to be a part of your roster of authors (and I hope you'll keep having me!). A huge thanks to Hachette Book Group and to Alison Skrabek, Jared Oriel, Patrick Sullivan, Lisa Forde, and Sandy Noman and to everyone at Hodderscape who worked on TBOO. To my copyeditors for scouring my messy draft for errors, to TBOO's fantastic cover illustrators for nailing what was a very difficult book to conceptualize, and to Rachael Ward of Cartographybird Maps for creating the incredible maps in this book–I appreciate you a ton!

All my love to Iris Huang (@atelier.iri) who brought all sixteen (!!) gods to life so beautifully, creating detail and mythos from my barebones creepy ideas, Avendell (@avendellart) for taking on Sarai and Kadra once more and being so wonderful as to post them, and Bella (@bergoltsbella) for gamely creating such stunning portraits of TBOO's key players!

A million hugs to the incredible bookish folk who gave *This Monster of Mine* so much time in the sun. Marina Dominguez-Salgado for pushing TMOM *everywhere.* Nabeela (@nabzrealbooktalk) and Lochi (@lochislibrary) for being TMOM's *first* reviewers and the greatest friends. Dear Georgie (@readinginthepeaks), who shouts about it every day; I emphasized his slutty robes for you! Salima (@salimateez), who's championed TMOM since day 1 and commissioned the most *stunning* art and special edition of it, I adore you. My edge queens: Alexandra (@the.book.serpent), Elisa (@erii.bookish), and Victoria (@victoria.foxdenreads), who created *incredible* sprayed edge editions for TMOM. I'm still crying. The impeccable Joshua Strank (@joshua_.strank), Flavia (@atheina_vismark) for being the loveliest, Ahana (@tohearts_content) here's to late-night chats!, Jessica (@_spiritbound_) for tagging me in the best posts, Carthi (@raconteur.recs) edit genius and fellow ZB1 fan!, Sidrah (@sidthesffkid) moderator extraordinaire with the best story highlights, Erin (@erinsreadingroom) for being the first to preorder this book, and Athena Freya aka Kadra's wineglass (@thenafreyag). And to the people who never stopped talking about TMOM: Dione (@rickevescrolls), Sumbal (@kanejscorner), Jamie (@afloodofbooks), Emmy (@whatemmyreadss), Farah (@lighttanddarkkbooks), Lilly (@fantasyandfern), Allison Chiang (@galactine.reads.), Lucie (@roman tasyreads), Katie (@thestarlessdragon), Alice (@alicereadsromantasy), Ana (@reads.by.anaid), Clara (@bookish_clara), Irene (@dbookishprincess), and so many more! I could fill up a thousand pages with how grateful I am!

A lifetime subscription to anti-writer's block for the authors whose work, kindness, and marketing skill inspires me daily, Alex Kennington (I can't *wait* for book 2!), my beloved Isabella Ford (who deserves everything), agent sib Jackson P. Brown (you're brilliant!), the *incredible* Markus Redmond (I'm so privileged to call you friend), Brittney Arena (angel and uplifting queen), Imani Erriu (I remain in awe of you), C.J. Hamilton (your talent!), Rachel Phan (I love you, sis), Liann Zhang (genius, mastermind), M. K. Lobb (I will never be normal about us being colleagues now), Maithree Wijesekara (look at us SL girls go!), Sarah Mughal Rana (inject all your books into me), Taylor Grothe (icon, queen, I look up to you), and Rachel Kitch (so excited for you!).

As always, my eternal devotion to Tolkien and every creative involved in bringing his Middle Earth to life for providing a defeated teenager with solace and instilling the urge to create in me even when I wasn't sure it would go anywhere. *Annon allen, mellyn nin.* My everlasting gratitude to Ji Sung, whose work has genuinely saved my life, thank you remains inadequate. 늘 감사하고응원합니다!

A million paid days off to my family, to my patient partner, Demille, who continues to calmly drag me from every new well of self-doubt I find and sighs at my fascination with hot Sauron, I love you loads. To my sister, Andrea, who takes the best author photos and sends me a steady stream of cat videos, and my brother-in-law and fellow rabid gamer J.C., who's driven me to a thousand signings, I'd hug you both if you wouldn't panic at why I'm being mushy. To my hardworking mom, who continues to partially fund this career and tells me not to give up every time I panic over longevity, I write some strange things, don't I? I owe you so much for never making me feel guilty about what we've given up.

And to God, here we are on round 2! I couldn't have done it without you. I'll keep holding on.

RUNES IN URDISH

ASTOMAND: An Urdish rune meaning "Materialization." This rune can be used only by Petitors to pull out memories for public view from the minds of those they are Probing. Attempts by magi who do not possess this magic won't work. *Astomand*, *herar*, and *zosta* are colloquially known as the "Petitor's Trio."

BESHAZ: An Urdish rune meaning "Heal." This rune can be used only by healers to reach into another's body and perform muscle-deep repairs, a talent that requires great precision. Contrary to the rune's literal meaning, it can also be used by healers to perform destruction to the body, shredding muscles and bone from within.

FRAZAM: The Urdish rune for "End." Used to cease or destroy something by a magus with the appropriate bloodline. Powerful Urdish magi use it to dissipate lightning. Those of other countries can use it for halting mudslides or even quelling tornadoes.

GORHOLYN: An Ilohessen rune meaning "Demand." Combined with *seniwyn*, the two runes can be used by Coercers to force people into obeying their instruction. Attempts by magi who do not possess this magic will not work.

HAST: The Urdish rune for the Eight Threshold. Those who can sustain the flow of power it provides for long periods of time are considered Eighth-Tier magi.

HERAR: An Urdish rune meaning "Probe." This rune can be used only by Petitors to reach into another's mind and view the archive of their memories. Attempts by magi who do not possess this magic won't work. *Astomand*, *herar*, and *zosta* are colloquially known as the "Petitor's Trio."

KHON: The Urdish rune for "Blood." Any invocation of this rune does not bode well. Across lands and cultures, it has traditionally been used for sacrifice and dark rituals.

LAYK: The Urdish rune for "Unity." Largely used when combining elements or runes into a greater whole.

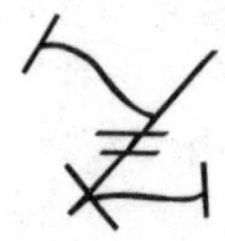

MODRAI: An Urdish rune meaning "Death" and the very last rune used in every sequence of Summoning runes. Ur Dinyé's draconian laws require a Summoning as punishment for certain crimes, which has given the rune a reputation as a criminal's mark.

NAIYA: The Urdish rune for "Heart." The rune's original name faded into obscurity some eight centuries ago after people colloquially began referring to it as the "Naiya" rune after the former Kashyalin debt-slave. Now, the latter term reigns.

NIBAS: The Urdish rune for "Sleep." Largely a Summoning rune, knowledge of the sort of magus who might have once been able to use such a power has been lost to time.

NIHUMB: The Urdish rune for "Concealment." A minor illusion used by Sarai to hide her scars.

RIUKHEN: The Urdish rune for “Strength.” As with *naiya*, the rune’s original name was lost to time in favor of being titled after Naiya’s powerful husband.

SAFSHER: An Urdish rune meaning “Sword.” The rune has little practical use for Urds, but is useful in the southern land of Ysāññe, whose populace can manipulate metal as the Urds do lightning.

SAYAG: The Urdish rune for “Shadow.” Largely a Summoning rune, knowledge of the sort of magus who might have once been able to use such a power has been lost to time, though it is rumored that the people of a now-sunken land north of Ur Dinyé wielded such magic.

SENIYWN: The Ilohessen rune meaning “Sound.” Used at the start of every bit of Ilohessen magic, as the country’s magic is sound-based.

TASUM: The Urdish rune for the Fourth Threshold. Those who can sustain the flow of power it provides for long periods of time are considered Fourth-Tier magi.

TUHIG: The Urdish rune for “Void.” Purely a Summoning rune, as no known magi can call forth a void.

ZEFIS: The Urdish rune for “Weave.” A rune frequently used by lightning magi when weaving lightning into a shield or barrier.

ZOSTA: A rune meaning "Examination." This rune can be used only by Petitors to read when someone is lying. Attempts by magi who do not possess this magic won't work. *Astomand*, *herar*, and *zosta* are colloquially known as the "Petitor's Trio."

ZUVRAI: The rune for "Time." Rarely used save by Seers or in Summonings. A Tenth-Tier rune.

GLOSSARY

GODS

DORCONE: A Naaduir. The Wretched Ruler of Rot, patron of decay and those who seek it.

THE ELSAR: The pantheon of gods worshipped in the Elsarian religion. Divided into High Elsar, Dark Elsar, and ambiguous Elsar, the gods are considered benevolent, malignant, and mercurial, depending on who is asked.

ELSARIANS: Those who worship the Elsar. Elsarianism is also Ur Dinyé's most dominant religion.

FARAGATHE: A Naaduir. The Wretched Seer of Sleep, patron of fear and nightmares, the fearful and the nightmarish.

THE GENERALLY ACCEPTED PANTHEON OF THE DARK ELSAR: Avarice, Deceit, Discord, Famine, Indolence, Pestilence, Ruin.

THE GENERALLY ACCEPTED PANTHEON OF THE HIGH ELSAR: Charity, Harvest, Radiance, Temperance, Truth, Wisdom.

HELL OF WHIPS: One of the Ten Hells in the Elsarian religion. Those sentenced to it are whipped endlessly for their crimes or self-flagellate.

THE HIGHLY DEBATED, AMBIGUOUS ELSAR: Death, Time, Wrath.

HWILIATH: A Naaduir. The Wretched Master of Manipulation, patron to Coercers and narcissists.

THE NAADUIR: The minor pantheon of gods, comprised of humans who achieved deification through devotion to the Elsar. The Naaduir are divided into Saints and the Wretched, who are presumed to respectively serve the High Elsar and the Dark Elsar, though this remains a point of contention between sects. Some Elsarians see the Naaduir as aspirational figures; others cast doubt on the existence of certain figures at all.

PERFIDIA: A Naaduir. The Wretched Countess of Conspiracy, patron to schemers.

WRATH: The ambiguous god of violence and vengeance.

EXPRESSIONS/ANIMALS/OBJECTS

ANCIENT TONGUE: The language of Ur Dinyé's long-dead monarchs and scribes that persists in use across academia and the upper class.

ARMILLA: A bracelet of a metal of choice, carved with runes used most often by the wearer. A quick way to perform magic without having to draw runes in blood. Instead, a drop of blood pressed into a rune is enough to activate it. Repeating the process will turn the rune dark.

ASSARIUS (*pl*: ASSARII): A bronze coin of Ur Dinyé. The head of the coin is engraved with approximations of the many Saints or their emblems. The tail sports the seal of the Metals Guild, verifying the coin to be authentic.

AUREUS (*pl*: AUREI): A gold coin of Ur Dinyé. The head of the coin is engraved with approximations of the seven Elsar or their emblems. The tail sports the seal of the Metals Guild, verifying the coin to be authentic. An aureus is equivalent to ten denarii or a hundred assarii.

BIRRUS: A woolen half-cloak of sorts worn over the head and shoulders.

BISECTION: The accidental or purposeful closing of a Bridger's portal while a person is still entering it. So named for slicing the person in two.

BRIGHT REALMS: The joyful afterlife where the High Elsar are rumored to reside.

CAESTII: Battle gloves composed of leather strips that wrap around the fist and lower arm. These are sometimes accentuated with metal tacks for maximum damage.

***CERTO*:** "Of course," "yes," or "certainly" in the ancient tongue of Ur Dinyé.

THE CODICES: The eighty-three manuscripts depicting and detailing the workings of the six High Elsar, seven Dark Elsar, and three ambiguous Elsar. A collection of firsthand and secondhand events, the Codices are sacred to Elsarians.

COMMON TONGUE: A near-universal language adopted by all twelve countries for trading purposes.

CONVIVIUM: The ancient term for a party held by the upper classes.

CORPUS JURIS TOTUS: The collated volumes of Ur Dinyé's body of law and legal procedure.

***DAMNATIO AD METALLA*:** A phrase meaning "damned to the mines" in the ancient tongue. The severity of the punishment depends on the mine and its Minewarden.

DENARIUS (*pl*: DENARII): A silver coin of Ur Dinyé. The head of the coin is engraved with approximations of the seven Elsar or their emblems. The tail sports the seal of the Metals Guild, verifying the coin to be authentic. A denarius is equivalent to ten assarii.

DISTRIBUTION ACT: A centuries old contract between the north and south stipulating that resources mined, harvested, or collected in both regions must be shared with the other as per the percentages in the Act. The wealthy Guilds used their superior bargaining power to set lower percentages for the north. As a result, northerners mine and harvest but see little of the yield. Centuries later, the results remained catastrophic. Every locale north of Isbuk sees almost none of their own resources. The people there are used by the Guilds as little more than indentured labor.

FULGUR SCUTUM (*pl*: FULGUR SCUTA; COLLOQUIAL: SCUTUM, SCUTA): "Lightning shield" in the ancient tongue of Ur Dinyé. A fabrication by former Head Tetrarch Aelius, scuta were metal rods that supposedly protected the stormfall-plagued southern half of Ur Dinyé from their homes being struck by lightning. The rods were inscribed with runes for protection that tied the strength of the shield to how devoutly the homeowner believed in the Elsar. If lightning struck, their faith must not have been strong enough. The south swore by the invention for four years, ignoring all signs that it was a fraudulent enterprise until Petitor Sarai exposed Aelius and his cronies, Tullus and Metals Guildmaster Helvus, for the liars and murderers they were.

FURTUM: The ancient tongue's term for the crime of theft. Used largely in judgments and the Corpus Juris Totus.

THE GREAT UNRAVELING: A term used by the people of Ur Dinyé to refer to the day in the Aequitas when Tetrarch Aelius's scuta scheme was unveiled to the public and the resulting battle that followed where Tetrarch Kadra was killed and Petitor Sarai Summoned Death to bring him back and dispatched Aelius for good measure.

***HAVÏD*:** "Shit" in the Urdish language.

HOMICIDIUM: The ancient tongue's term for the crime of murder. Used largely in judgments and the Corpus Juris Totus.

***HORREUM*:** A warehouse for storage of all manner of dry good.

***IBEZ*:** A potent, highly illegal wine made of fruit, spices, and wheat. Banned for its near-hallucinogenic strength, the drink used to be a staple centuries ago, during times of warfare. In present-day Ur Dinyé, it is the fodder of those seeking escape for a few hours, though with *ibez*, there is no saying how long that escape will last.

INIURIA: The ancient tongue's term for the crime of assault. Used largely in judgments and the Corpus Juris Totus.

INQUISITORIAL HEARING: A hearing convened by Inquisitors of the Elsarian Order to interrogate a target on theological heresy or determine the truth of an event supposedly involving the gods.

KADRA: An obscure Urdish word meaning "no one."

MAGUS SUPREME: An office earned by the most powerful magic-user in Ur Dinyé. Currently held by Drenevan bu Kadra, formerly held by Caeso Aelius. The Magus Supreme heads the Academiae and oversees magical education across various disciplines.

MOONDARK NIGHT: A rare occasion when both moons, Praefa and Silun, are in the new moon phase and therefore not visible.

THE PEBBLE: The star located a distance from the very tip of the Slingshot. It looks as though it's been launched forward.

POWDERHOLE: A slang term for a whitesleep den. See *whitesleep* on page 414.

PRAEFA: One of the planet's two moons, white in color. Nights where Praefa is full and Silun is in its new moon phase are known as full moon nights.

RAEDA (*pl*: RAEDAE): A four-wheel carriage owned primarily by wealthy families, Guildsmasters, or Tetrarchs.

SILUN: The planet's second moon, a pale blue in color. Nights where Silun is full and Praefa is in its new moon phase are known as blue moon nights.

THE SLINGSHOT: A constellation in the east that looks like a circlet of stars.

TABLINUM: The ancient term for a study.

TEN HELLS: The halls of eternal damnation where the Dark Elsar supposedly scheme.

***TIBI GRATIAS AGO*:** "Thank you" in the ancient tongue of Ur Dinyé.

URDISH: The language of the people of Ur Dinyé and that of its runes, now replaced by the common tongue. It is rarely in use in the capital, where the ancient tongue or common tongue is preferred, but isolated pockets in the north still write and speak in the language.

WARDS: A series of protections and traps laid by a warder magus across a plot of land that serves to defend it from intrusion or even sight, as in the case of Cato's wards over Aoran Tower. All wards will seal off Bridger entry.

PEOPLE

AELIUS: Former Head Tetrarch of Ur Dinyé. Killed by Sarai.

ALBANUS: The Stones Guildmaster of Ur Dinyé.

ANEK: A neutralis with a strong sense of justice and a healthy dose of diplomacy. Petitor to Cassandane.

BOUNTY HUNTERS: Ur Dinyé's bounty hunters are an eclectic sort. Once a thriving profession from which anyone with sword skill could make a living, the job is now largely confined to the north and the shadows. Hunters rank from Crimson to Bronze Grade and wear a crest pin that indicates their status.

CASSANDANE: The only female Tetrarch and current Head Tetrarch. Shrewd but careful.

CISURÉ: Sarai's former friend of ten years. Now working in a military outpost in Kirtule.

CLAN AM SEMNI AND CLAN KADER: Once one of the five all-powerful Clans serving the Qās, only they and Clan Am Semni survived the abolishment of the monarchy by retreating to the north, where they were still able to find some deference. Clan Am Semni died out after a lack of male heirs and was swallowed up by Clan Kader, who rebuilt itself into the rulers of the north's underworld, partaking in every form of trafficking.

CLANLORD: The title used for the head of a Clan.

THE CLAY GUILD: The Guild that oversees and manages the extraction and distribution of clay in Ur Dinyé. Headed by Septimus.

CLEVSIN BU KADER: Clanlord of Clan Kader.

DALVIA AM SEMNI: Last Clan daughter of Clan Am Semni. A true Illusionist.

DESTUS: Cassandane's personal healer and Lugen.

DRENEVAN BU KADRA: Tetrarch, Magus Supreme, murderer, and madman. Devoted to Sarai.

ETHRA: Arsamea's healer and Marus's bit on the side.

ETILIA: The current Wine and Spirits Guildmaster of Ur Dinyé.

FINAZE POXTAN: A baker in Komis. Sister to Parvine.

GAIUS: Kadra's right-hand man and the head of his vigiles.

THE GRAINS GUILD: The Guild that oversees and manages the growth, production, and distribution of all grains across Ur Dinyé. Headed by Ioratius.

HARION: Former Petitor to Tetrarch Tullus and current Tetrarch of Ur Dinyé. A notorious gossip, Harion lives to prod at others' lives to camouflage the massive chip on his shoulder.

HELVUS: The former Metals Guildmaster of Ur Dinyé with a terrible sense of fashion. Killed by Admia.

INQUISITORS BLASIUS, SILVUS, AND VERENTIA: Inquisitors to the Elsarian Order, they rank above Master and Grandmaster Clerics and are considered the foremost word on the gods, their dealings, and interpretations of the Codices.

IORATIUS: The current Grains Guildmaster of Ur Dinyé.

IUDEX (*pl*: IUDICES): An Urd judge.

JUNIA: A plaintiff whose case brings to light that the boil beetle plague has reached Edessa. (See: Lucanus)

LUCANUS: The defendant in the boil beetle case that brings to light that it has reached Edessa. (See: Junia)

MARUS: Arsamea's pompous chieftain and Cisuré's abusive father. Dislikes Sarai intensely for daring to aspire above her station and blames her for supposedly ruining his daughter's life.

MÉHERRE ROSTAG: A Bridger from the northern city of Komis.

THE METALS GUILD: The Guild that oversees and manages all metal craftsmanship in Ur Dinyé.

NEUTRALIS: An individual whose gender identity and/or gender expression expands outside the traditional gender binary. The term encompasses a variety of genders, as the elevated circles in which the ancient tongue developed didn't concern themselves with language for gender-nonconforming people. As a result, more detailed terms were only built into the Urdish language.

NOCEO BU KADER: Clanlord of Clan Kader and a mysteriously powerful Coercer.

PARVINE POXTAN: The daughter of a baker in Komis, in love with Noceo.

PRAETOR FLORUS: Cleric-turned-Praetor of Sal Flumen.

PRAETOR YTHRAS: Praetor of Komis.

SARAI: A former northern barmaid-turned-Petitor to Magus Supreme Kadra. Devoted to him.

SEPTIMUS: Clay Guildmaster to Ur Dinyé, whose son is betrothed to Albanus's daughter.

THE STONES GUILD: The Guild that oversees and manages all marble, limestone, and other necessary stone in Ur Dinyé. Headed by Albanus.

THE TETRARCHY: The four elected judges that rule the country.

TULLUS: Formerly Ur Dinyé's longest-running Tetrarch of fifteen years. Killed by Kadra.

URD: A citizen of Ur Dinyé, person of Urdish descent.

VIGILES: Soldiers who serve a particular Tetrarch and act as that Quarter's nightwatch, storm brigade, and investigative force.

THE WINE AND SPIRITS GUILD: The Guild that oversees and manages the production and distribution of all alcoholic beverages across Ur Dinyé. Also called the Wines Guild. Headed by Etilia.

YTHRAS: Praetor of Komis.

PLACES

ACADEMIAE: Ur Dinyé's most prestigious school. Highly guarded and situated on a citadel at the center of Edessa. The Tetrarchs occupy four of its eight towers.

AMPHITHEATRUM AEQUITAS: Ur Dinyé's highest court and the largest in size, easily seating twenty thousand.

AORAN TOWER: The Academaie's west tower and Tetrarch Kadra's residence.

ARSAMEA: Ur Dinyé's most remote town, located high in the mountains.

CHADORAS RIVER: Ur Dinyé's main internal water body, a winding river that stretches from Isbuk all the way down to Dídtan. The river is kept dammed at each end and holds water reserves for much of the southern Urd cities.

DELRAN TOWER: The Academiae's southeast tower and the glitzy location of many a convivium. The Tetrarchy use it for meetings of domestic and international importance.

DÍDTAN: A military port town in Ur Dinyé's southwest. Harion's birthplace.

DRUST MOUNTAINS: Ur Dinyé's shortest mountain range at two peaks, located in Komis.

EDESSA: The capital city of Ur Dinyé, divided into four Quarters, each named and ruled by a Tetrarch.

FAVRAN TOWER: The Academiae's south tower and Tetrarch Cassandane's residence.

GRAND ELSARIAN TEMPLE: Ur Dinyé's largest house of worship to the Elsar.

HALL OF RECORDS: The repository in which the country's records are filed and maintained. Access is extremely restricted.

ILOHE: A land to the south of Ur Dinyé across the Meridies Ocean, where the populace's magic comes from sound. Its people are known as the Ilohessen.

INSULA: (*pl*: INSULAE) Apartment-style buildings occupied by lower-income Urds.

ISBUK: The former capital of Ur Dinyé during its monarchical era, now a port town situated in the west.

KASHYAL: A land to the south of Ur Dinyé, infamously and brutally colonized by it some five and a half centuries ago. The land continues to suffer the aftereffects of its colonization and has never forgiven Ur Dinyé for it.

KAYCAKH MOUNTAINS: The mountain range marking Ur Dinyé's border with the neighboring land of Errigal.

KOMIS: Northern Ur Dinyé's most prominent town, often referred to as the "northern capital" due to its reputation for corruption, drug manufacturing, and being a hub for tradespeople.

MERIDIES OCEAN: An ocean to the south of Ur Dinyé, between it and Kashyal.

OCCIDENS SEA: A sea to the west and north of Ur Dinyé.

ORITI: A land far to the east of Ur Dinyé where the populace has fire magic.

QUARTERS: The four segments into which Edessa is divided, each overseen by a Tetrarch. The rest of the country is ruled jointly.

SAL FLUMEN: A port town at the base of the mountains housing Arsamea.

SIDRAN TOWER: The Academiae's north tower, and the one at the heart of Sarai's fall.

UR DINYÉ: A land to the northeast in the world of Severance. Half-frozen in the north, the southern cities are plagued with lightning strikes. The land is resource-scarce and suffers from a lack of freshwater during summer, owing to its crackled soil, deadly storms, and long stretches of desert between cities. Agriculture and lightning magic are prized fields of study for magi for this reason.

USTEN: A land far to the east of Ur Dinyé where the populace has ice magic.

VIGILE STATION: The central compound to which a Tetrarch's vigiles report.

XANN: Inns of disrepute, often run by brothel madams, but can be a safe haven for women traveling on their own.

XĀRŌMAND DESERT: The broad swathe of desert that parts much of the north and south and extends all the way east to the Kaycakh Mountains.

PLANTS AND ANIMALS

BLACKSTRIPE BEAR: A species of Arsamean bear with off-white fur, sporting a black stripe running down its spine and into its tail. A single strike from an adult is enough to gut a man. However, the cubs are clawless and toothless for a year and, thus, hunted for meat and fur. To down an adult blackstripe bear is a dream for most Arsamean men.

BEMIZAN: A plant with flavorless, neutral-tasting leaves that blazeleaf is rolled in for smoking.

BLAZELEAF: The cured and dried leaves of the dazidan plant that provide a pleasant buzz of languor when smoked. Can be highly addictive.

BOIL BEETLES: Fingertip-sized pests with bright-yellow venom sacs that nest within heavily forested areas and live off animal flesh. Upon biting their targets, their venom loosens the top layers of skin so that they can gnaw at the meat underneath. Boil beetle venom is a key ingredient in whitesleep.

BUSHASP: Named after the Urdish word meaning "to sleep" or "to dream." The main ingredient in whitesleep.

CAELUM: Sarai's trusty horse.

SNOWGRAPE: A particularly small type of grape found in the north that grows near-frozen on the vine but yields an incredibly sweet wine.

WHITESLEEP: A street drug that arose eleven years ago and is rubbed on the eyelids. When diluted, the drug allows most to lead largely normal lives, but the pure version of the drug is highly addictive. One rub on the eyelids provides relaxation. Two gives relief from all aches and pains for a day. Three for euphoria. Five for respiratory distress. Once a user is hooked, it's difficult to wean them off the high.

MAGICS AND RITUALS

BRIDGER: The term for a magus with Kashyalin heritage capable of opening portals across vast distances between locations to which the Bridger has already been. A valued asset of the land of Kashyal, Bridgers can be incredibly useful bodyguards, and conversely, dangerous assassins. The other twelve lands ward their most secure locations against Bridger penetration. Bridgers who attempt to open a portal within the boundaries of these wards suffer often horrific deaths.

COERCER: A magus, usually of mixed-Ilohessen and Urd ethnicity, who can use their voice to compel people into performing what the magus wishes. The compulsions can include any number of physical or biological actions that the person may not have been able to do under normal circumstances. When rooted deeply, the compulsions are extremely difficult to fight off, though it can be done. Death of the Coercer will end all compulsions they set.

FORMALIZATION: The process of recognizing a new Naaduir, be they a Saint or one of the Wretched.

ILLUSIONIST: A magus, usually of Errigalese ethnicity or heritage, who can cast illusions to alter and camouflage their features. True Illusionists are rare and monitored by the Tetrarchy. Touch will usually reveal the presence of an illusion, though true Illusionists can mimic skin texture to realistic effect.

LIGHTNING MAGUS: A magus of Urd descent who can create, manipulate, and fight with lightning.

MATERIALIZATION: The process of a Petitor pulling out a memory for public view using *astomand*.

PETITOR: A magus, usually of mixed-Ilohessen, Urdish, and Kashyalin ethnicity, who can determine when people are lying, look into their minds and memories, and extract the latter for public view. They are highly sought after in Ur Dinyé as the right-hand to government officials and judges.

SUMMONING: The act of calling one of the Elsar, High or Dark, to the material plane. The process is incredibly taxing, and most die, drained of magic in the attempt. The few who succeed are granted a wish from the gods, but the reason for the reward remains unknown.

WARDER MAGI: Magi who set wards around a property or area to prevent unwanted outside entry. Every country has their own form of warding magic. Different countries may be susceptible to other lands' warder magi.

ABOUT THE AUTHOR

SHALINI ABEYSEKARA is the #1 international bestselling author of *This Monster of Mine*. As a former corporate lawyer, she enjoys using fantasy to interrogate reality, explore monstrosity—perceived and real—and center on neurodivergent women of color reckoning with themselves and their place in a world that tells them they're too much and not enough. She is passionate about demystifying traditional publishing for all writers. When not writing, she games her life away and tries to make the perfect entremets. Most days, though, she can't believe she's an adult and hopes you don't either.

RAISING READERS

Books Build Bright Futures

Thank you for reading this book and for being a reader of books in general. We are so grateful to share being part of a community of readers with you, and we hope you will join us in passing our love of books on to the next generation of readers.

Did you know that reading for enjoyment is the single biggest predictor of a child's future happiness and success?

More than family circumstances, parents' educational background, or income, reading impacts a child's future academic performance, emotional well-being, communication skills, economic security, ambition, and happiness.

Studies show that kids reading for enjoyment in the US is in rapid decline:

- In 2012, 53% of 9-year-olds read almost every day. Just 10 years later, in 2022, the number had fallen to 39%.
- In 2012, 27% of 13-year-olds read for fun daily. By 2023, that number was just 14%.

Together, we can commit to **Raising Readers** and change this trend. How?

- Read to children in your life daily.
- Model reading as a fun activity.
- Reduce screen time.
- Start a family, school, or community book club.
- Visit bookstores and libraries regularly.
- Listen to audiobooks.
- Read the book before you see the movie.
- Encourage your child to read aloud to a pet or stuffed animal.
- Give books as gifts.
- Donate books to families and communities in need.

BOB1217

Books build bright futures, and **Raising Readers** is our shared responsibility.

For more information, visit **JoinRaisingReaders.com**

Sources: National Endowment for the Arts, National Assessment of Educational Progress, WorldBookDay.com, Nielsen BookData's 2023 "Understanding the Children's Book Consumer"